SHARPE'S SIEGE

Bernard Cornwell was born in London and raised in Essex, and now lives mainly in the USA, with his wife. He has sold over five million copies of his books and is translated in nine languages. As well as the Sharpe series he is author of the bestselling Warlord trilogy about King Arthur and the King Alfred series. Bernard Cornwell was awarded an OBE in 2006.

For more information visit
www.bernardcornwell.net

D1169246

See page 322 for more titles by Bernard Cornwell

BERNARD CORNWELL

Sharpe's Siege

Richard Sharpe and
the Winter Campaign, 1814

HARPER

Harper
An imprint of HarperCollins*Publishers*
77–85 Fulham Palace Road,
Hammersmith, London w6 8jb

www.harpercollins.co.uk

This paperback edition 2008
30

Previously published in paperback by Fontana 1988
Reprinted five times

Copyright © Rifleman Productions Ltd. 1987

Bernard Cornwell asserts the moral right to
be identified as the author of this work

A catalogue record for this book is
available from the British Library

ISBN: 978 0 00 729860 0

Set in Baskerville

Printed and bound in Great Britain by Clays Ltd, St Ives plc

Mixed Sources
Product group from well-managed
forests and other controlled sources
www.fsc.org Cert no. SW-COC-1806
© 1996 Forest Stewardship Council

FSC is a non-profit international organisation established
to promote the responsible management of the world's forests.
Products carrying the FSC label are independently certified
to assure consumers that they come from forests that are managed
to meet the social, economic and ecological needs
of present and future generations.

Find out more about HarperCollins and the environment at
www.harpercollins.co.uk/green

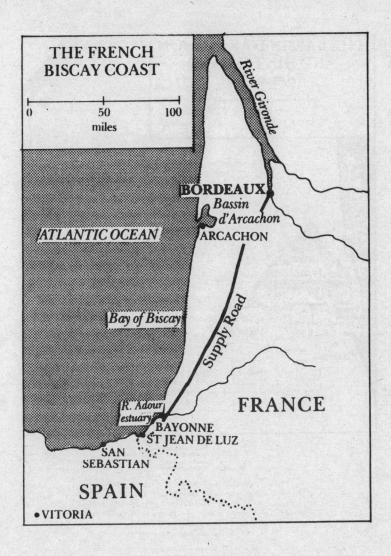

THE FRENCH
BISCAY COAST

0   50   100
        miles

River Gironde

ATLANTIC OCEAN

BORDEAUX
Bassin d'Arcachon
ARCACHON

Bay of Biscay

Supply Road

R. Adour estuary
BAYONNE
ST JEAN DE LUZ

SAN SEBASTIAN

FRANCE

SPAIN

• VITORIA

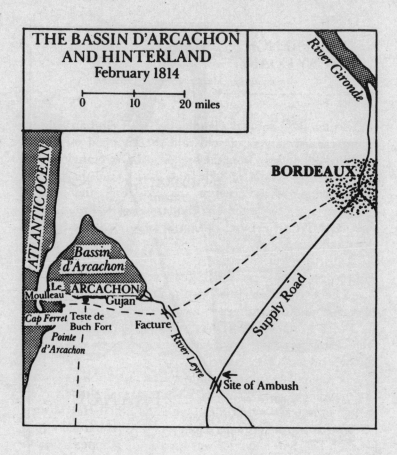

THE BASSIN D'ARCACHON
AND HINTERLAND
February 1814

0   10   20 miles

River Gironde

ATLANTIC OCEAN

BORDEAUX

Bassin
d'Arcachon

Le
Moulleau   ARCACHON
              Gujan

Cap Ferret   Teste de
             Buch Fort   Facture
Pointe
d'Arcachon

River Leyre

Supply Road

Site of Ambush

CHAPTER 1

It was ten days short of Candlemas, 1814, and an Atlantic wind carried shivers of cold rain that slapped on narrow cobbled alleys, spilt from the broken gutters of tangled roofs, and pitted the water of St Jean de Luz's inner harbour. It was a winter wind, cruel as a bared sabre, that whirled chimney smoke into the low January clouds shrouding the corner of south-western France where the British Army had its small lodgement.

A British soldier, his horse tired and mud-stained, rode down a cobbled street in St Jean de Luz. He ducked his head beneath a baker's wooden sign, edged his mare past a fish-cart, and dismounted at a corner where an iron bollard provided a tethering post for the horse. He patted the horse, then slung its saddle-bags over his shoulder. It was evident he had ridden a long way.

He walked into a narrow alley, searching for a house that he only knew by description; a house with a blue door and a line of cracked green tiles above the lintel. He shivered. At his left hip there hung a long, metal-scabbarded sword, and on his right shoulder was a rifle. He stepped aside for a woman, black-dressed and squat, who carried a basket of lobsters. She, grateful that this enemy soldier had shown her a small courtesy, smiled her thanks, but afterwards, when she was safely past him, she crossed herself. The soldier's face had been bleak and scarred; darkly handsome, but still a killer's face. She blessed her patron saint that her own son would not have to face such a man in battle, but had a secure, safe job in the French Customs service instead.

9

The soldier, oblivious of the effect his face had, found the blue door beneath the green tiles. The door, even though it was a cold day, stood ajar and, without knocking, he pushed his way into the front room. There he dropped his pack, rifle, and saddle-bags on to a threadbare carpet and found himself staring into the testy face of a British Army surgeon. 'I know you,' the Army surgeon, his shirt-cuffs thick with dried blood, said.

'Sharpe, sir, Prince of Wales's Own . . .'

'I said I knew you,' the surgeon interrupted. 'I took a musket-ball out of you after Fuentes d'Onoro. Had to truffle around for it, I remember.'

'Indeed, sir.' Sharpe could hardly forget. The surgeon had been half drunk, cursing, and digging into Sharpe's flesh by the light of a guttering candle. Now the two men had met in the outer room of Lieutenant Colonel Michael Hogan's lodgings.

'You can't go in there.' The surgeon's clothes were drenched in prophylactic vinegar, filling the small room with its acrid scent. 'Unless you want to die.'

'But . . .'

'Not that I care.' The surgeon wiped his bleeding-cup on the tail of his shirt then tossed it into his bag. 'If you want the fever, Major, go inside.' He spat on his wide-bladed scarifying gouge, smeared the blood from it, and shrugged as Sharpe opened the inner door.

Hogan's room was heated by a huge fire that hissed where its flames met the rain coming down the chimney. Hogan himself was in a bed heaped with blankets. He shivered and sweated at the same time. His face was greyish, his skin slick with sweat, his eyes red-rimmed, and he was muttering about being purged with hyssop.

'His topsails are gone to the wind,' the surgeon spoke from behind Sharpe. 'Feverish, you see. Did you have business with him?'

Sharpe stared at the sick man. 'He's my particular friend.' He turned to look at the surgeon. 'I've been on the Nive for the last month, I knew he was ill, but . . .' He ran out of words.

'Ah,' the surgeon seemed to soften somewhat. 'I wish I could offer some hope, Major.'

'You can't?'

'He might last two days. He might last a week.' The surgeon pulled on his jacket that he had shed before opening one of Hogan's veins. 'He's wrapped in red flannel, bled regular, and we're feeding him gunpowder and brandy. Can't do more, Major, except pray for the Lord's tender mercies.'

The sickroom stank of vomit. The heat of the huge fire pricked sweat on Sharpe's face and steamed rain-water from his soaking uniform as he stepped closer to the bed, but it was obvious Hogan could not recognize him. The middle-aged Irishman, who was Wellington's Chief of Intelligence, shivered and sweated and shook and muttered nonsenses in a voice that had so often amused Sharpe with its dry wit.

'It's possible,' the surgeon spoke grudgingly from the outer room, 'that the next convoy might bring some Jesuit's bark.'

'Jesuit's bark?' Sharpe turned towards the doorway.

'A South American tree-bark, Major, sometimes called quinine. Infuse it well and it can perform miracles. But it's a rare substance, Major, and cruelly expensive!'

Sharpe went closer to the bed. 'Michael? Michael?'

Hogan said something in Gaelic. His eyes flickered past Sharpe, closed, then opened again.

'Michael?'

'Ducos,' the sick man said distinctly, 'Ducos.'

'He'll not make sense,' the surgeon said.

'He just did.' Sharpe had heard a name, a French name, the name of an enemy, but in what feverish context and from what secret compartment of Hogan's clever mind the name had come, Sharpe could not tell.

'The Field Marshal sent me,' the surgeon seemed eager

to explain himself, 'but I can't work miracles, Major. Only the Almighty's providence can do that.'

'Or Jesuit's bark.'

'Which I haven't seen in six months.' The surgeon still stood at the door. 'Might I insist you leave, Major? God spare us a contagion.'

'Yes.' Sharpe knew he would never forgive himself if he did not give Hogan some gesture of friendship, however useless, so he stooped and took the sick man's hand and gave it a gentle squeeze.

'*Maquereau*,' Hogan said quite distinctly.

'*Maquereau?*'

'Major!'

Sharpe obeyed the surgeon's voice. 'Does *maquereau* mean anything to you?'

'It's a fish. The mackerel. It's also French slang for pimp, Major. I told you, his wits are wandering.' The surgeon closed the door on the sickroom. 'And one other piece of advice, Major.'

'Yes?'

'If you want your wife to live, then tell her she must stop visiting Colonel Hogan.'

Sharpe paused by his damp luggage. 'Jane visits him?'

'A Mrs Sharpe visits daily,' the doctor said, 'but I have not the intimacy of her first name. Good day to you, Major.'

It was winter in France.

The floor was a polished expanse of boxwood, the walls were cliffs of shining marble, and the ceiling a riot of ornate plasterwork and paint. In the very centre of the floor, beneath the dark, cobweb encrusted chandelier and dwarfed by the huge proportions of the vast room, was a malachite table. Six candles, their light too feeble to reach into the corners of the great room, illuminated maps spread on the green stone table.

A man walked from the table to a fire that burned in an

intricately carved hearth. He stared at the flames and, when at last he spoke, the marble walls made his voice seem hollow with despair. 'There are no reserves.'

'Calvet's demi-brigade . . .'

'Is ordered south without delay.' The man turned from the fire to look at the table where the candle-glow illuminated two pale faces above dark uniforms. 'The Emperor will not take it kindly if we . . .'

'The Emperor,' the smallest man at the table interrupted in a voice of surprising harshness, 'rewards success.'

January rain spattered the tall, east-facing windows. The velvet curtains of this room had been pulled down twenty-one years before, trophies to a revolutionary mob that had stormed triumphant through the streets of Bordeaux, and there had never been the money nor the will to hang new curtains. The consequence, in winters like this, was a draught of malevolent force. The fire scarcely warmed the hearth, let alone the whole huge room, and the general standing before the feeble flames shivered. 'East or north.'

It was a simple enough problem. The British had invaded a small corner of southern France, nothing but a toehold between the southern rivers and the Bay of Biscay, and these men expected the British to attack again. But would Field Marshal the Lord Wellington go east or north?

'We know it's north,' the smallest man said. 'Why else are they collecting boats?'

'In that case, my dear Ducos,' the general paced back towards the table, 'is it to be a bridge, or a landing?'

The third man, a colonel, dropped a smoked cigar on to the floor and ground it beneath his toe. 'Perhaps the American can tell us?'

'The American,' Pierre Ducos said scathingly, 'is a flea on the rump of a lion. An adventurer. I use him because no Frenchman can do the task, but I expect small help of him.'

'Then who can tell us?' The general came into the aureole of light made by the candles. 'Isn't that your job, Ducos?'

It was rare for Major Pierre Ducos' competency to be so

challenged, yet France was assailed and Ducos was almost helpless. When, with the rest of the French Army, he had been ejected from Spain, Ducos had lost his best agents. Now, peering into his enemy's mind, Ducos saw only a fog. 'There is one man,' he spoke softly.

'Well?'

Ducos' round, thick spectacle lenses flashed candlelight as he stared at the map. He would have to send a message through the enemy lines, and he risked losing his last agent in British uniform, but perhaps the risk was justified if it brought the French the news they so desperately needed. East, north, a bridge, or a landing? Pierre Ducos nodded. 'I shall try.'

Which was why, three days later, a French lieutenant stepped gingerly across a frosted plank bridge that spanned a tributary of the Nive. He shouted cheerfully to warn the enemy sentries that he approached.

Two British redcoats, faces swathed in rags against the bitter cold, called for their own officer. The French lieutenant, seeing he was safe, grinned at the picquet. 'Cold, yes?'

'Bloody cold.'

'For you.' The French lieutenant gave the redcoats a cloth-wrapped bundle that contained a loaf of bread and a length of sausage, the usual gesture on occasions such as this, then greeted his British counterpart with a happy familiarity. 'I've brought the calico for Captain Salmon.' The Frenchman unbuckled his pack. 'But I can't find red silk in Bayonne. Can the colonel's wife wait?'

'She'll have to.' The British lieutenant paid silver for the calico and added a plug of dark tobacco as a reward for the Frenchman. 'Can you buy coffee?'

'There's plenty. An American schooner slipped through your blockade.' The Frenchman opened his cartouche. 'I also have three letters.' As usual the letters were unsealed as a token that they could be read. More than a few officers in the British Army had acquaintances, friends or relatives in the enemy ranks, and the opposing picquets had always acted as an unofficial postal system between the armies. The Frenchman refused a mug of British tea and promised to bring a four-pound sack of coffee, purchased in the market at Bayonne, the next day. 'That's if you're still here tomorrow?'

'We'll be here.'

And thus, in a manner that was entirely normal and quite above suspicion, Pierre Ducos' message was safely delivered.

'Why ever shouldn't I visit Michael? It's eminently proper. After all, no one can expect a sick man to be ill-behaved.'

Sharpe entirely missed Jane's pun. 'I don't want you catching the fever. Give the food to his servant.'

'I've visited Michael every day,' Jane said, 'and I'm in the most excellent health. Besides, you went to see him.'

'I should imagine,' Sharpe said, 'that my constitution is more robust than yours.'

'It's certainly uglier,' Jane said.

'And I must insist,' Sharpe said with ponderous dignity, 'that you avoid contagion.'

'I have every intention of avoiding it.' Jane sat quite still as her new French maid put combs into her hair. 'But Michael is our friend and I won't see him neglected.' She paused, as if to let her husband counter her argument, but Sharpe was quickly learning that in the great skirmish of marriage, happiness was bought by frequent retreats. Jane smiled. 'And if I can endure this weather, then I must be quite as robust as any Rifleman.' The sea-wind, howling off Biscay, rattled the casements of her lodgings. Across the roofs Sharpe could see the thicket of masts and spars made by the shipping crammed into the inner harbour. One of those ships had brought the new uniforms that were being issued to his men.

It was not before time. The veterans of the South Essex, that Sharpe now had to call the Prince of Wales's Own Volunteers, had not been issued with new uniforms in three years. Their coats were ragged, faded, and patched, but now those old jackets, that had fought across Spain, were being discarded for new, bright cloth. Some French Battalion, seeing those new coats, would think of them as belonging to a fresh, unblooded unit and would doubtless pay dear for the mistake.

The orders to refit had given Sharpe this chance to be with his new wife, as it had given all the married men of the Battalion a chance to be with their wives. The Battalion had been stationed on the line of the River Nive, close to French patrols, and Sharpe had ordered the wives to stay in St Jean de Luz. These few days were thus made precious to Sharpe, days snatched from the frost-hard river-line, days to be with Jane, and days spoilt only by the illness that threatened Hogan's life.

'I take him food from the Club,' Jane said.

'The Club?'

'Where we're lunching, Richard.' She turned from the mirror with the expression of a woman well pleased with her own reflection. 'Your good jacket, I think.'

In every town that the British occupied, and in which they spent more than a few days, one building became a club for officers. The building was never officially chosen, nor designated as such, but by some strange process and within a day of two of the Army's arrival, one particular house was generally agreed to be the place where elegant gentlemen could retire to read the London papers, drink mulled wine before a decently tended fire, or play a few hands of whist of an evening. In St Jean de Luz the chosen house faced the outer harbour.

Major Richard Sharpe, born in a common lodging-house and risen from the gutter-bred ranks of Britain's Army, had never used such temporary gentlemen's clubs before, but new and beautiful wives must be humoured. 'I didn't suppose,' he spoke unhappily to Jane, 'that women were allowed in gentlemens' clubs?' He was reluctantly buttoning his new green uniform jacket.

'They are here,' Jane said, 'and they're serving an oyster

pie for luncheon.' Which clinched the matter. Major and Mrs Richard Sharpe would dine out, and Major Sharpe had to dress in the stiff, uncomfortable uniform that he had bought for a royal reception in London and hated to wear. He reflected, as he climbed the wide stairs of the Officers' Club with Jane on his arm, that there was much wisdom in the old advice that an officer should never take a well-bred wife to an ill-bred war.

Yet the frisson of irritation passed as he entered the crowded dining-room. Instead he felt the pang of pride that he always felt when he took Jane into a public place. She was undeniably beautiful, and her beauty was informed by a vivacity that gave her face character. She had eloped with him just months before, fleeing her uncle's house on the drab Essex marshes to come to the war. She drew admiring glances from men at every table, while other officers' wives, enduring the inconveniences of campaigning for the sake of love, looked enviously at Jane Sharpe's easy beauty. Some, too, envied her the tall, black-haired and grimly scarred man who seemed so uncomfortable in the lavishness of the club's indulgent comforts. Sharpe's name was whispered from table to table; the name of the man who had taken an enemy standard, captured one of Badajoz's foul breaches, and who, or so rumour said, had made himself rich from the blood-spattered plunder of Vitoria.

A white-gloved steward abandoned a table of senior officers to hasten to Jane's side. 'The cap'n wanted to sit 'ere, ma'am,' the steward was unnecessarily brushing the seat of a chair close to one of the wide windows, 'but I said as how it was being kept for someone special.'

Jane gave the steward a smile that would have enslaved a misogynist. 'How very kind of you, Smithers.'

'So he's over there.' Smithers nodded disparagingly towards a table by the fire where two naval officers sat in warm discomfort. The junior officer was a lieutenant, while one of the other man's two epaulettes was bright and new, denoting a recent promotion to the rank of a full post captain.

Smithers looked devotedly back to Jane. 'I've reserved a bottle or two of that claret you liked.'

Sharpe, who had been ignored by the steward, pronounced the wine good and hoped he was right. The oyster pie was certainly good. Jane said she would deliver a portion to Hogan's lodgings that same afternoon and Sharpe again insisted that she should not actually enter the sickroom, and he saw a flicker of annoyance cross Jane's face. Her irritation was not caused by Sharpe's words, but by the sudden proximity of the naval captain who had rudely come to stand immediately behind Sharpe's chair in a place where he could overhear the conversation of Major and Mrs Sharpe's reunion.

The naval officer had not come to eavesdrop, but rather to stare through the rain-smeared window. His interest was in a small flotilla of boats that had appeared around the northern headland. The boats were squat and small, none more than fifty feet long, but each had a vast press of sail that drove the score of craft in a fast gaggle towards the harbour entrance. They were escorted by a naval brig that, in the absence of enemies, had its gunports closed.

'They're *chasse-marées*,' Jane said to her husband.

'Chasse-marrys?'

'Coastal luggers, Richard. They carry forty tons of cargo each.' She smiled, pleased with her display of knowledge. 'You forget I was raised on the coast. The smugglers in Dunkirk used *chasse-marées*. The Navy,' Jane said loudly enough for the intrusive naval captain to hear, 'could never catch them.'

But the naval captain was oblivious to Mrs Sharpe's goad. He stared at the straggling fleet of *chasse-marées* that, emerging from a brief rain-squall, seemed to crab sideways to avoid a sand-bar that was marked by a broken line of dirty foam. 'Ford! Ford!'

The naval lieutenant dabbed his lips with a napkin, snatched a swallow of wine, then hastened to his captain's side. 'Sir?'

The captain took a small spyglass from the tail pocket of his coat. 'There's a lively one there, Ford. Mark her!'

Sharpe wondered why naval officers should be so interested in French coastal craft, but Jane said the Navy had been collecting the *chasse-marées* for days. She had heard that the boats, with their French crews, were being hired with English coin, but for what purpose no one could tell.

The small fleet had come to within a quarter mile of the harbour, and, to facilitate their entry into the crowded inner roads, each ship was lowering its topsail. The naval brig had hove-to, sails shivering, but one of the French coasters, larger than the rest of its fellows, was still under the full set of its five sails. The water broke white at its stem and slid in bubbling, greying foam down the hull that was sleeker than those of the other, smaller vessels.

'He thinks it's a race, sir,' the lieutenant said with happy vacuity above Sharpe's shoulder.

'A handy craft,' the captain said grudgingly. 'Too good for the Army. I think we might take her on to our strength.'

'Aye aye, sir.'

The faster, larger lugger had broken clear of the pack. Its sails were a dirty grey, the colour of the winter sky, and its low hull was painted a dull pitch-black. Its flush deck, like all the *chasse-marées*' decks, was an open sweep broken only by the three masts and the tiller by which two men stood. Fishing gear was heaped in ugly, lumpen disarray upon the deck's planking.

The naval brig, seeing the large lugger race ahead, unleashed a string of bright flags. The captain snorted. 'Bloody Frogs won't understand that!'

Sharpe, offended by the naval officers' unwanted proximity, had been seeking a cause to quarrel, and now found it in the captain's swearing in front of Jane. He stood up. 'Sir.'

The naval captain, with a deliberate slowness, turned pale, glaucous eyes on to the Army major. The captain was young, plump, and confident that he outranked Sharpe.

They stared into each other's eyes, and Sharpe felt a sudden certainty that he would hate this man. There was no reason for it, no justification, merely a physical distaste for the privileged, amused face that seemed so full of disdain for the black-haired Rifleman.

'Well?' The naval captain's voice betrayed a gleeful anticipation of the imminent argument.

Jane defused the confrontation. 'My husband, Captain, is sensitive to the language of fighting men.'

The captain, not certain whether he was being complimented or mocked, chose to accept the words as a tribute to his gallantry. He glanced at Sharpe, looking from the Rifleman's face to the new, unfaded cloth of the green jacket. The newness of the uniform evidently suggested that Sharpe, despite the scar on his face, was fresh to the war. The captain smiled superciliously. 'Doubtless, Major, your delicacy will be sore tested by French bullets.'

Jane, delighted at the opening, smiled very sweetly. 'I'm sure Major Sharpe is grateful for your opinion, sir.'

That brought a satisfying reaction; a shudder of astonishment and fear on the annoying, plump face of the young naval officer. He took an involuntary step backwards, then, remembering the cause of the near quarrel, bowed to Jane. 'My apologies, Mrs Sharpe, if I caused offence.'

'No offence, Captain . . .?' Jane inflected the last word into a question.

The captain bowed again. 'Bampfylde, ma'am. Captain Horace Bampfylde. And allow me to name my lieutenant, Ford.'

The introductions were accepted gracefully, as tokens of peace, and Sharpe, outflanked by effusive politeness, sat. 'The man's got no bloody manners,' he growled loudly enough to be overheard by the two naval officers.

'Perhaps he didn't have your advantages in life?' Jane suggested sweetly, but again the scene beyond the window distracted the naval men from the barbed comments.

'Christ!' Captain Bampfylde, careless of the risk of offending a dozen ladies in the dining-room, shouted the word. The outraged anger in his voice brought an immediate hush and fixed the attention of everyone in the room on the small, impertinent drama that was unfolding on the winter-cold sea.

The black-hulled lugger, instead of obeying the brig's command to lower sails and proceed tamely into the harbour of St Jean de Luz, had changed her course. She had been sailing south, but now reached west to cut across the counter of the brig. Even Sharpe, no sailor, could see that the *chasse-marée*'s fore and aft rig made the boat into a handy, quick sailor.

It was not the course change that had provoked Bampfylde's astonishment, but that the deck of the black-hulled lugger had suddenly sprouted men like dragon's teeth maturing into warriors, and that, from the mizzen mast, a flag had been unfurled.

The flag was not the blue ensign of the Navy, nor the tricolour of France, nor even the white banner of the exiled French monarchy. They were the colours of Britain's newest enemy; the Stars and Stripes of the United States of America.

'A Jonathon!' a voice said with disgust.

'Fire, man!' Bampfylde roared the order in the confines of the dining-room as though the brig's skipper might hear him. Yet the brig, head to wind, was helpless. Men ran on its deck, and gunports lifted, but the American lugger was seething past the brig's unarmed counter and Sharpe saw the dirty white blossom of gunsmoke as the small broadside was poured, at pistol-shot length, into the British ship.

Lieutenant Ford groaned. David was taking on Goliath and winning.

The sound of the American gunfire came over the wind-broken water like a growl of thunder, then the lugger was spinning about, sails rippling as the American skipper let his speed carry him through the wind's eye, until, taut on the opposite tack, he headed back past the brig's counter towards the fleet of *chasse-marées*.

The brig, foresails at last catching the wind to lever her hull around, received a second mocking broadside. The American carried five guns on each flank, small guns, but their shot punctured the brig's Bermudan cedar to spread death down the packed deck.

Two of the brig's guns punched smoke into the cold wind, but the American had judged his action well and the brig dared fire no more for fear of hitting the *chasse-marées* into which, like a wolf let rip into a flock, the American sailed.

The hired coasters were unarmed. Each sea-worn boat, sails frayed, was crewed by four men who did not expect, beneath the protection of their enemy's Navy, to face the gunfire of an ally.

The French civilian crews leaped into the cold water as the Americans, serving their guns with an efficiency that Sharpe could only admire even if he could not applaud, put ball after ball into the luggers' hulls. The gunners aimed low, intending to shatter, sink, and panic.

Ships collided. One *chasse-marée's* mainmast, its shrouds cut, splintered down to the water in a tangle of tarred cables and tumbling spars. One boat was settling in the churning sea, another, its rudder shot away, turned broadside to receive the numbing shock of another's bow in its gunwales.

'Fire!' Captain Bampfylde roared again, this time not as an order, but in alarm. Flames were visible on a French boat, then another, and Sharpe guessed the Americans were using shells as grenades. Rigging flared like a lit fuse, two more boats collided, tangled, and the flames flickered across the gap. Then a merciful rain-squall swept out of Biscay to help douse the flames even as it helped hide the American boat.

'They'll not catch her,' Lieutenant Ford said indignantly.

'Damn his eyes!' Bampfylde said.

The American had got clear away. She could outsail her square-rigged pursuers, and she did. The last Sharpe saw of the black-hulled ship was the flicker of her grey sails in the grey squall and the bright flash of her gaudy flag.

'That's Killick!' The naval captain spoke with a fury made worse by impotence. 'I'll wager that's Killick!'

The spectators, appalled by what they had seen, watched the chaos in the harbour approach. Two luggers were sinking, three were burning, and another four were inextricably tangled together. Of the remaining ten boats no less than half had grounded themselves on the harbour bar and were being pushed inexorably higher by the force of the wind-driven, flowing tide. A damned American, in a cockle boat, had danced scornful rings around the Royal Navy and, even worse, had done it within sight of the Army.

Captain Horace Bampfylde closed his spyglass and dropped it into his pocket. He looked down at Sharpe. 'Mark that well,' the captain said, 'mark it very well! I shall look to you for retribution.'

'Me?' Sharpe said in astonishment.

But there was no answer, for the two naval officers had strode away leaving a puzzled Sharpe and a tangle of scorched wreckage that heaved on the sea's grey surface and bobbed towards the land where an Army, on the verge of its enemy's country, gathered itself for its next advance, but whether to north or east, or by bridge or by boat, no one in France yet knew.

CHAPTER 2

He had a cutwater of a face; sharp, lined, savagely tanned; a dangerously handsome face framed by a tangled shock of gold-dark hair. It was battered, beaten by winds and seas and scarred by blades and scorched by powder-blasts, but still a handsome face; enough to make the girls look twice. It was just the kind of face to annoy Major Pierre Ducos who disliked such tall, confident, and handsome men.

'Anything you can tell me,' Ducos said with forced politeness, 'would be of the utmost use.'

'I can tell you,' Cornelius Killick said, 'that a British brig is burying its dead and that the bastards have got close to forty *chasse-marées* in the harbour.'

'Close to?' Ducos asked.

'It's difficult to make an accurate count when you're firing cannon, Major.' The American, careless of Ducos' sinister power, leaned over the malachite table and lit a cigar from a candle's flame. 'Aren't you going to thank me?'

Ducos' voice was sour with undisguised irony. 'The Empire is most grateful to you, Captain Killick.'

'Grateful enough to fetch me some copper sheeting?' Killick's French was excellent. 'That was our agreement.'

'I shall order some sent to you. Your ship is at Gujan, correct?'

'Correct.'

Ducos had no intention of ordering copper sheeting sent to the Bassin d'Arcachon, but the American had to be humoured. The presence of the privateer captain had been most fortuitous for Ducos, but what happened to the American now was of no importance to an embattled France.

24

Cornelius Killick was the master of the *Thuella*, a New England schooner of sleek, fast lines. She had been built for one purpose alone; to evade the British blockade and, under Killick's captaincy, the *Thuella* had become a thorn in the Royal Navy's self-esteem. Whether as a cargo ship that evaded British patrols, or as a privateer that snapped up stragglers from British convoys, the schooner had led a charmed life until, at the beginning of January, as the *Thuella* stole from the mouth of the Gironde in a dawn mist, a British frigate had come from the silvered north and its bow-chasers had thumped nine-pounder balls into the *Thuella*'s transom.

The schooner, carrying a cargo of French twelve-pounder guns for the American Army, turned south. Her armament was no match for a frigate, nor could her speed save her in the light, mist-haunted airs. For three hours she was pounded. Shot after shot crashed into the stern and Killick knew that the British gunners were firing low to spring his planks and sink his beloved ship. But the *Thuella* had not sunk, and the mist was stirred by catspaws of wind, and the wind became a breeze and, even though damaged, the schooner had outrun her pursuer and taken refuge in the vast Bassin d'Arcachon. There, safe behind the guns of the Teste de Buch fort, the *Thuella* was beached for repairs.

The wounded *Thuella* needed copper, oak, and pitch. Day followed day and the supplies were promised, but never came. The American consul in Bordeaux pleaded on Cornelius Killick's behalf, and the only answer had been the strange request, from Major Pierre Ducos, that the American take a *chasse-marée* south and investigate why the British collected such craft in St Jean de Luz. There was no French Navy to make the reconnaissance, and no French civilian crew, lured by British gold, could be trusted with the task, and so Killick had gone. Now, as he had promised, he had come to this lavish room in Bordeaux to give his report.

'Would you have any opinion,' Ducos now asked the tall American, 'why the British are hiring *chasse-marées*?'

'Perhaps they want a regatta?' Killick laughed, saw that

this Frenchman had no sense of humour at all, and sighed instead. 'They plan to land on your coast, presumably.'

'Or build a bridge?'

'Where to? America? They're filling the damned harbour with boats.' Killick drew on his cigar. 'And if they were going to make a bridge, Major, wouldn't they take down the masts? Besides, where could they build it?'

Ducos unrolled a map and tapped the estuary of the Adour. 'There?'

Cornelius Killick hid his impatience, remembering that the French had never understood the sea, which was why the British fleets now sailed with such impunity. 'That estuary,' the American said mildly, 'has a tidefall of over fifteen feet, with currents as foul as rat-puke. If the British build a bridge there, Major, they'll drown an army.'

Ducos supposed the American was right, but the Frenchman disliked being lectured by a ruffian from the New World. Major Ducos would have preferred confirmation from his own sources, but no reply had come to the letter that had been smuggled across the lines to the agent who served France in a British uniform. Ducos feared for that man's safety, but the Frenchman's pinched, scholarly face betrayed none of his worries as he interrogated the handsome American. 'How many men,' Ducos asked, 'could a *chasse-marée* carry?'

'A hundred. Perhaps more if the seas were calm.'

'And they have forty. Enough for four thousand men.' Ducos stared at the map on his table. 'So where will they come, Captain?'

The American leaned over the table. Rain tapped on the window and a draught lifted a corner of the map that Killick weighted down with a candlestick. 'The Adour, Arcachon, or the Gironde.' He tapped each place as he spoke its name.

The map showed the Biscay coast of France. That coast was a sheer sweep, almost ruler straight, suggesting long beaches of wicked, tumbling surf. Yet the coast was broken

26

by two river mouths and by the vast, almost landlocked Bassin d'Arcachon. And from Arcachon to Bordeaux, Ducos saw, it was a short march, and if the British could take Bordeaux they would cut off Marshal Soult's army in the south. It was a bold idea, a risky idea, but on a map, in an office in winter, it seemed to Ducos a very feasible one. He moved the candle away and rolled the map into a tight tube. 'You would be well advised, Captain Killick, to be many leagues from Arcachon if the British do make a landing there.'

'Then send me some copper.'

'It will be dispatched in the morning,' Ducos said. 'Good day to you, Captain, and my thanks.'

When the American was gone Ducos unrolled the map again. The questions still nagged at him. Was the display in St Jean de Luz's harbour merely a charade to draw attention away from the east? Ducos cursed the man who had not replied to his letter, and wondered how much credence could be put on the words of an American adventurer. North or east, bridge or boats? Ducos was tempted to believe the American, but knowing an invasion was planned was useless unless the landing place was known. Yet one man might still tell him, and to know the answer would bring a victory, and France, in this bitter, wet winter of 1814, was in need of a victory.

'Looking for us, sir?' A midshipman in a tarred jacket stood at the top of weed-slimed watersteps on St Jean de Luz's quay.

'Are you the *Vengeance*?' Sharpe looked apprehensively at the tiny boat, frail on the filth-littered water, that was to carry him to the *Vengeance*. Sharpe had received a sudden order, peremptory and harsh, that offered no explanations but merely demanded his immediate presence on the quay where a boat from His Majesty's ship *Vengeance* would be waiting.

27

Four grinning oarsmen, doubtless hoping to see the Rifle officer slip on the steep stone stairs, waited in the gig. 'The captain would have sent his barge, sir,' the midshipman said in unconvincing apology, 'but it's being used for the other gentlemen.'

Sharpe stepped into the rocking gig. 'What other gentlemen?'

'No one confides in me, sir.' The midshipman could scarce have been more than fourteen, but he gave his orders with a jaunty confidence as Major Sharpe crouched on the stern thwart and wondered which of the ships moored in the outer harbour was the *Vengeance*.

It seemed to be none of them, for the midshipman took his tiny craft out through the harbour entrance to buck and thump its bows in the tide-race over the sandbar. Ahead now, in the outer roads, a flotilla of naval craft was anchored. Amongst them, and towering over the other vessels like a behemoth, was a ship of the line. 'Is that the *Vengeance*?' Sharpe asked.

'It is, sir. A 74, and as sweet a sailor as ever was.'

The midshipman's enthusiasm seemed misplaced to Sharpe. Nothing about the *Vengeance* suggested sweetness; instead, moored in the long swell of the grey ocean, she seemed like a brutal mass of timber, rope and iron; one of the slab-sided killers of Britain's deep-water fleet. Her chequered sides were like cliffs, and the ponderous hull, as Sharpe's gig neared the vast craft, gave off the rotten stench of tar, unwashed bodies and ordure; the normal odour of a battleship becalmed.

The midshipman shouted orders, oars backed, the tiller was thrown across, and somehow the gig was laid alongside with scarce a bump of timber. Above Sharpe now, water dripping from its lower rungs, was a tumblehome ladder leading to the maindeck. 'You'd like a sling lowered, sir?' the midshipman asked solicitously.

'I'll manage.' Sharpe waited as a wave lifted the gig, then jumped for the rain-slicked ladder. He clawed at it, held on, then scrambled ignominiously up to the greeting of a bosun's whistle.

'Major Sharpe! Welcome aboard.'

Sharpe saw an eager, ingratiating lieutenant who clearly expected to be recognized. Sharpe frowned. 'You were with . . .'

'With Captain Bampfylde, indeed, sir. I'm Ford.'

The elegantly clothed Ford made inconsequential conversation as he steered Sharpe towards the stern cabins. It was an honour, he said, to have such a distinguished soldier aboard, and was it possible that Sharpe was related to Sir Roderick Sharpe of Northamptonshire?

'No,' Sharpe was remembering Captain Bampfylde's parting words in the Officer's Club. Were those the reason for his summons here?

'One of the Wiltshire Sharpes, perhaps?' Ford seemed eager to place the Rifleman in a comforting social context.

'Middlesex,' Sharpe said.

'Do mind your head,' Ford smiled as he waved Sharpe under the break of the poopdeck. 'I can't quite place the Middlesex Sharpes.'

'My mother was a whore, I was born in a common lodging-house, and I joined the Army as a private. Does that make it easier?'

Ford's smile did not falter. 'Captain Bampfylde's waiting for you, sir. Please go in.'

Sharpe ducked under the lintel of the opened doorway to find himself in a lavishly furnished cabin that extended the width of the *Vengeance*'s wide stern. A dozen officers, their wine glasses catching the light from the galleried windows, sat around a polished dining table.

'Major! We meet in happier circumstances.' Captain Horace Bampfylde greeted Sharpe with effusive and false pleasure. 'No damned American to spoil our conversation, eh? Come and meet the company.'

Seeing Bampfylde in his ship made Sharpe realize how very young the naval captain was. Bampfylde must still lack two years of thirty, yet the naval captain possessed an ebullient confidence and a natural authority to compensate for his lack of years. He had a fleshy face, quick eyes, and an impatient manner that he tried to disguise as he made the introductions.

Most of the men about the table were naval officers whose names meant nothing to Sharpe, but there were also two Army officers, one of whom Sharpe recognized. 'Colonel Elphinstone?'

Elphinstone, a big, burly Engineer whose hands were calloused and scarred, beamed a welcome. 'You haven't met my brother-in-arms, Sharpe; Colonel Wigram.'

Wigram was a grey-faced, dour, bloodless creature who acknowledged the ironic introduction with a curt nod. 'If you could seat yourself, Major Sharpe, we might at last begin.' He managed to convey that Sharpe had delayed this meeting.

Sharpe sat beside Elphinstone in a chair close to the windows that looked on to the big, grey Atlantic swells that scarcely moved the *Vengeance*'s ponderous hull. He sensed an awkwardness in the cabin, and he judged that there was disagreement between Wigram and Elphinstone, a judgment that was confirmed when the tall Engineer leaned towards him. 'It's all bloody madness, Sharpe. Marines have got the pox so they want you instead.'

The comment, ostensibly made in a confiding voice, had easily carried to the far end of the table where Bampfylde sat. The naval captain frowned. 'Our Marines have a contagious fever, Elphinstone; not the pox.'

Elphinstone snorted derision, while Colonel Wigram, on Sharpe's left, opened a leather-bound notebook. The middle-aged Wigram had the manner of a man whose life had been spent in an office; as though all his impetuosity and enjoyment had been drained by dusty, dry files. His voice was precise and fussy.

Yet even Wigram's desiccated voice could not drain the excitement from the proposals he brought to this council of war. One hundred miles to the north, and far behind enemy lines, was a fortress called the Teste de Buch. The fortress guarded the entrance to a natural harbour, the Bassin d'Arcachon, which was just twenty-five miles from the city of Bordeaux.

Elphinstone, at the mention of Bordeaux, gave a scornful grunt that was ignored by the rest of the cabin.

The fortress of Teste de Buch, Wigram continued, was to be captured by a combined naval and Army force. The expedition's naval commander would be Captain Bampfylde, while the senior Army officer would be Major Sharpe. Sharpe, understanding that the chill, pedantic Wigram would not be travelling north, felt a pang of relief.

Wigram gave Sharpe a cold, pale glance. 'Once the fortress is secured, Major, you will march inland to ambush the high road of France. A successful ambush will alarm Marshal Soult, and might even detach French troops to guard against further such attacks.' Wigram paused. It seemed to Sharpe, listening to the slap of water at the *Vengeance*'s stern, that there was an unnatural strain in the cabin, as though Wigram approached a subject that had been discussed and argued before Sharpe arrived.

'It is to be hoped,' Wigram turned a page of his notebook, 'that any prisoners you take in the ambush will provide confirmation of reports reaching us from the city of Bordeaux.'

'Balderdash,' Elphinstone said loudly.

'Your dissent is already noted,' Wigram said dismissively.

'Reports!' Elphinstone sneered the word. 'Children's tales, rumours, balderdash!'

Sharpe, uncomfortably trapped between the two men, kept his voice very mild. 'Reports, sir?'

Captain Bampfylde, evidently Wigram's ally in the disagreement, chose to reply. 'We hear, Sharpe, that the city of Bordeaux is ready to rebel against the Emperor. If it's true, and we profoundly hope that it is, then we believe the city might rise in spontaneous revolt when they hear that

His Majesty's forces are merely a day's march away.'

'And if they do rise,' Colonel Wigram took up the thread, 'then we shall ship troops north to Arcachon and invade the city, thus cutting France in two.'

'You note, Sharpe,' Elphinstone was relishing this chance to stir more trouble, 'that you, a mere major, are chosen to make the reconnaissance. Thus, if anything goes wrong, you will carry the blame.'

'Major Sharpe will make his own decisions,' Wigram said blandly, 'after interrogating his prisoners.'

'Meaning you won't go to Bordeaux,' Elphinstone said confidingly to Sharpe.

'But you have been chosen, Major,' Wigram's pale eyes looked at Sharpe, 'not because of your lowly rank, as Colonel Elphinstone believes, but because you are known as a gallant officer unafraid of bold decisions.'

'In short,' Elphinstone continued the war across the table, 'because you will make an ideal scapegoat.'

The naval officers seemed embarrassed by the contretemps, all but for Bampfylde who had evidently relished the clash of colonels. Now the naval captain smiled. 'You merely have to understand, Major, that your first task is to escalade the fortress. Perhaps, before we explore the subsequent operations, Colonel Wigram might care to tell us about the Teste de Buch's defences?'

Wigram turned pages in his notebook. 'Our latest intelligence demonstrates that the garrison can scarcely man four guns. The rest of its men have been marched north to bolster the Emperor's Army. I doubt whether Major Sharpe will be much troubled by such a flimsy force.'

'But four fortress guns,' Elphinstone said harshly, 'could slice a Battalion to mincemeat. I've seen it!' Implying, evidently truthfully, that Wigram had not.

'If we imagine disaster,' Bampfylde said smoothly, 'then we shall allow timidity to convince us into inaction.' The comment implied cowardice to Elphinstone, but Bampfylde seemed oblivious of the offence he had given. Instead he unrolled a chart on to the table. 'Weight the end of that, Sharpe! Now! There seems to me just one sensible way to proceed.'

He outlined his plan which was, indeed, the only sensible way to proceed. The naval flotilla, under Bampfylde's command, would sail northwards and land troops on the coast south of the Point d'Arcachon. That land force, commanded by Sharpe, would proceed towards the fortress, a journey of some six hours, and make an escalade while the defenders were distracted by the incursion of a frigate into the mouth of the Arcachon channel. 'The frigate's bound to take some punishment,' Bampfylde said equably, 'but I'm sure Major Sharpe will overcome the gunners swiftly.'

The chart showed the great Basin of Arcachon with its narrow entrance channel, and marked the fortress of Teste de Buch on the eastern bank of that channel. A profile of the fort, as a landmark for mariners, was sketched on the chart, but the profile told Sharpe little about the stronghold's defences. He looked at Elphinstone. 'What do we know about the fort, sir?'

Elphinstone had been piqued by Bampfylde's discourteous treatment and thus chose to use the technical language of his trade, doubtless hoping thereby to annoy the bumptious naval captain. 'It's an old fortification, Sharpe, a square-trace. You'll face a glacis rising to ten feet, with an eight counterscarp into the outer ditch. A width of twenty and a scarp of ten. That's revetted with granite, by the way, like the rest of the damned place. Climb the scarp and you're on a counterguard. They'll be peppering you by now and you've got a forty foot dash to the next counterscarp.' The colonel was speaking with a grim relish, as if seeing the figures running and dropping through the enemy's plunging fire. 'That's twelve feet, it's flooded, and the enceinte height is twenty.'

'The width of that last ditch?' Sharpe was making notes.

'Sixteen, near enough.' Elphinstone shrugged. 'We don't think it's flooded more than a foot or two.' Even if the naval

33

officers did not understand Elphinstone's language, they could understand the import of what he was saying. The Teste de Buch might be an old fort, but it was a bastard; a killer.

'Weapons, sir?' Sharpe asked.

Elphinstone had no need to consult his notes. 'They've got six thirty-six pounders in a semi-circular bastion that butts into the channel. The other guns are twenty-fours, wall mounted.'

Captain Horace Bampfylde had listened to the technical language and understood that a small point was being scored against him. Now he smiled. 'We should be grateful it's not a tenaille trace.'

Elphinstone frowned, realizing that Bampfylde had understood all that had been said. 'Indeed.'

'No lunettes?' Bampfylde's expression was seraphic. 'Caponiers?'

Elphinstone's frown deepened. 'Citadels at the corners, but hardly more than guerites.'

Bampfylde looked to Sharpe. 'Surprise and speed, Major! They can't defend the complete enceinte, and the frigate will distract them!' So much, it seemed, for the problems of capturing a fortress. The talk moved on to the proposed naval operations inside the Bassin d'Arcachon, where more *chasse-marées* awaited capture, but Sharpe, uninterested in that part of the discussion, let his thoughts drift.

He did not see Bampfylde's plush, shining cabin, instead he imagined a rising grass slope, scythed smooth, called a glacis. Beyond the glacis was an eight foot drop into a granite faced, sheer-sided ditch twenty feet wide.

At the far side of the ditch his men would be faced with a ten foot climb that would lead to a gentle, inward-facing slope; the counterguard. The counterguard was like a broad target displayed to the marksman on the inner wall, the enceinte. Men would cross the counterguard, screaming and twisting as the balls thumped home, only to face a twelve foot drop into a flooded ditch that was sixteen feet wide.

34

By now the enemy would be dropping shells or even stones. A boulder, dropped from the twenty foot high inner wall, would crush a man's skull like an eggshell, yet still the wall would have to be climbed with ladders if the men were to penetrate into the Teste de Buch. Given a month, and a train of siege artillery, Sharpe could have blasted a broad path through the whole trace of ditches and walls, but he did not have a month. He had a few moments only in which he must save a frigate from the terrible battering of the fort's heavy guns.

'Major?' Abruptly the image of the twenty foot wall vanished to be replaced by Bampfylde's quizzically mocking smile. 'Major?'

'Sir?'

'We are talking, Major, of how many men would be needed to defend the captured fortress while we await reinforcements from the south?'

'How long will the garrison have to hold?' Sharpe asked.

Wigram chose to answer. 'A few days at the most. If we do find that Bordeaux's ripe for rebellion, then we can bring an Army corps north inside ten days.'

Sharpe shrugged. 'Two hundred? Three? But you'd best use Marines, because I'll need all of my Battalion if you want me to march inland.'

It was Sharpe's first trenchant statement and it brought curious glances from the junior naval officers. They had all heard of Richard Sharpe and they watched his weather-darkened, scarred face with interest.

'Your Battalion?' Wigram's voice was as dry as old paper.

'A brigade would be preferable, sir.'

Elphinstone snorted with laughter, but Wigram's expression did not change. 'And what leads you to suppose, Major, that the Prince of Wales's Own Volunteers are going to Arcachon?'

Sharpe had assumed it because he had been summoned, and because he was the de facto commander of the Battalion, but Colonel Wigram now disabused him brutally.

'You are here, Major, because you are supernumerary to regimental requirements.' Wigram's voice, like his gaze, was pitiless. 'Your regimental rank, Major, is that of captain. Captains, however ambitious, do not command Battalions. You should be apprised that a new commanding officer, of due seniority and competence, is being appointed to the Prince of Wales's Own Volunteers.'

There was a horrid and embarrassed silence in the cabin. Every man there, except for the young Captain Bampfylde, knew the bitter pangs of promotion denied, and each man knew they were watching Sharpe's hopes being broken on the wheel of the Army's regulations. The assembled officers looked away from Sharpe's evident hurt.

And Sharpe was hurt. He had rescued that Battalion. He had trained it, given it the Prince of Wales's name, then led it to the winter victories in the Pyrenees. He had hoped, more than hoped, that his command of the Battalion would be made official, but the Army had decided otherwise. A new man would be appointed; indeed, Wigram said, the new commanding officer was daily expected on the next convoy from England.

The news, given so coldly and unsympathetically in the formal setting of the *Vengeance*'s cabin, cut Sharpe to the bone, but there was no protest he could make. He guessed that was why Wigram had chosen this moment to make the announcement. Sharpe felt numbed.

'Naturally,' Bampfylde leaned forward, 'the glory attached to the capture of Bordeaux will more than compensate for this disappointment, Major.'

'And you will rejoin your Battalion, as a major, when this duty is done,' Wigram said, as though that was some consolation.

'Though the war,' Bampfylde smiled at Sharpe, 'may well be over because of your efforts.'

Sharpe stirred himself from the bitter disappointment. 'Single-handed efforts, sir? Your Marines are poxed, my

Battalion can't come, what am I supposed to do? Train cows to fight?'

Bampfylde's face showed a flicker of a frown. 'There will be Marines, Major. The Biscay Squadron will be combed for fit men.'

Sharpe, his belligerence released by Wigram's news, stared at the young naval captain. 'It's a good thing, is it not, that the malady has not spread to your sailors, sir? You seemed to have a full ship's company as I came aboard?'

Bampfylde stared like a basilisk at Sharpe. Colonel Elphinstone gave a quick, sour laugh, but Wigram slapped the table like a timid schoolmaster calling a rowdy class to order. 'You will be given troops, Major, in numbers commensurate to your task.'

'How many?'

'Enough,' Wigram said testily.

The question of Sharpe's troops was dropped. Instead Bampfylde talked of a brig-sloop that had been sent to watch the fortress and to question any local fishermen who put to sea. The presence of the American privateer was discussed and Bampfylde smiled as he spoke of the punishment that would be fetched on Cornelius Killick. 'We must regard that doomed American as a bonus for our efforts.' Then the talk went to naval signals, far beyond Sharpe's competence to understand, and again he wondered about that fortress. Even under-manned a fortress was a formidable thing, and no one in this wide cabin seemed interested in ensuring that he was given a proper force. At the same time, as the voices buzzed about him, he tried to assuage the deep pain of losing the command of his Battalion.

Sharpe knew the regulations disqualified him from commanding the Battalion, but there were other Battalions commanded by majors and the regulations seemed to be ignored for those men. But not for Sharpe. Another man was to be given the superb instrument of infantry that Sharpe had led through the winter's battles and, once again, Sharpe was adrift and unwanted in the Army's flotsam. He reflected, bitterly, that if he had been a Northamptonshire Sharpe, or a Wiltshire Sharpe, with an Honourable tag to his name and a park about his father's house, then this would not have happened. Instead he was a Middlesex Sharpe, conceived in a whore's transaction and whelped in a slum, and thus a fit whipping-boy for bores like Wigram.

Colonel Elphinstone, sensing that Sharpe was miles away again, kicked the Rifleman's ankle and Sharpe recovered attentiveness in time to hear Bampfylde inviting the assembled officers to dine with him.

'I fear I can't.' Sharpe did not want to stay in this cabin where his disappointment had shamed him in front of so many officers. It was a petty motive, pride-born, but a soldier without pride was a soldier doomed for defeat.

'Major Sharpe,' Bampfylde explained with ill-concealed scorn, 'has taken a wife, so we must forgo his company.'

'I haven't taken a wife,' Elphinstone said belligerently, 'but I can't dine either. Your servant, sir.'

The two men, Sharpe and Elphinstone, travelled back to St Jean de Luz in Bampfylde's barge. Elphinstone, swathed in a vast black cloak, shook his head sadly. 'Bloody madness, Sharpe. Utter bloody madness.'

It began to rain. Sharpe wished he was alone with his misery.

'You're disappointed, aren't you?' Elphinstone remarked. 'Yes.'

'Wigram's a bastard,' Elphinstone said savagely, 'and you're to take no bloody notice of him. You're not going to Bordeaux. Those are orders.'

Sharpe, stirred from his self-pity by Elphinstone's ferocious words, looked at the big Engineer. 'So why are we taking the fort, sir?'

'Because we need the *chasse-marées*, why else? Or were you dozing through that explanation?'

Sharpe nodded. 'Yes, sir.'

The rain fell harder as Elphinstone explained that the whole Arcachon expedition had been planned simply to release the three dozen *chasse-marées* that were protected behind the fortress guns. 'I need those boats, Sharpe, not to waltz into bloody Bordeaux, but to build a bloody bridge. But for Christ's sake don't tell anyone it's a bridge. I'm telling you, because I won't have you gallivanting off to Bordeaux, you understand me?'

'Entirely, sir.'

'Wigram thinks we want the boats for a landing, because that's what the Peer wants everyone to think. But it's going to be a bridge, Sharpe, a damned great bridge to astonish the bloody Frogs. But I can't build the bloody bridge unless you capture the bloody fort and get me the boats. After that, enjoy yourself. Go and ambush the high road, then go back to Bampfylde and tell him the Frogs are still loyal to Boney. No rebellion, no farting about, no glory.' Elphinstone stared gloomily at the water which was being pocked by the cold rain into a resemblance of dirty, heaving gunmetal. 'It's Wigram who's got this bee in his bonnet about Bordeaux. The fool sits behind a bloody desk and believes every rumour he hears.'

'Is it a rumour?'

'Some precious Frenchman pinned his ear back.' Elphinstone plucked his cloak even tighter as the barge struggled against the current sweeping about the sandbar. 'Michael Hogan didn't help. He's a friend of yours, isn't he?'

'Yes, sir.'

Elphinstone sniffed. 'Damned shame he's ill. I can't understand why he encouraged Wigram, but he did. But you're to take no notice, Sharpe. The Peer expects you to take the fortress, let bloody Bampfylde extract the boats, then come back here.'

Sharpe stared at Elphinstone and received a nod of confirmation. So Wellington was not unaware of Wigram's plans, but Wellington was putting his own man, Sharpe, into the operation. Was that, Sharpe wondered, the reason why he had lost his Battalion?

'It wouldn't matter,' Elphinstone went on, 'except that

we need the bloody Navy to carry us there, and we can't control them. Bampfylde thinks he'll get an earldom out of Bordeaux, so stop the silly bugger dead. No rising, no rebellion, no hopes, no glory, and no bloody earldom.'

Sharpe smiled. 'There'll be no fortress unless I have decent troops, sir.'

'You'll get the best I can find,' Elphinstone promised, 'but not in such numbers that might tempt you to invade Bordeaux.'

'Indeed, sir.'

The oarsmen were grunting with the effort of fighting the tide's last ebb as the barge rounded the harbour's northern mole. Sharpe understood well enough what was happening. A simple cutting out expedition, necessitating the capture of a coastal fort, was needed to release the *chasse-marées*, but ambitious officers, eager to make a name for themselves in the waning months of the war, wished to turn that mundane operation into a flight of fancy. Sharpe, who would make the reconnaissance inland, was ordered to blunt their hopes.

The steersman pointed the boat's prow towards a flight of green-slimed steps. The white-painted barge, in smoother water now, cut swiftly towards the quay. The rain became tempestuous, slicking the quay's stones darker and drumming on the top of Sharpe's shako.

'In oars!' the steersman shouted.

The white bladed oars rose like wings and the craft coasted in a smooth curve to the foot of the steps. Sharpe looked up. The harbour wall, sheer and black and wet, reared above him like a cliff. 'How high is that?' he asked Elphinstone.

The Colonel squinted upwards. 'Eighteen feet?' Then Elphinstone saw the point of Sharpe's question and shrugged. 'Let's hope Wigram's right and they've stripped the Teste de Buch of defenders.'

Because if the fort's enceinte was defended Sharpe would have no chance, none, and his men would die so that the naval officer could blame the Army for failure. That was a chilling thought for a winter's dusk in which the rain slanted from a steel-grey sky to pursue Sharpe through the alleys to where his wife sewed up a rent in his old jacket; his battle-jacket, the green jacket that he would wear to a fortress wall that waited for him in Arcachon.

CHAPTER 3

'I suppose,' Richard Sharpe said harshly, 'that the Army couldn't find any real soldiers?'

'That's about the cut of it,' the Rifle captain replied. 'Mind you, I suppose the Army couldn't find any real commanding officers either?'

Sharpe laughed. Colonel Elphinstone had done his best, and that best was very good indeed for, if Sharpe could not take his own men into battle, then there was no unit he would rather lead than Captain William Frederickson's men of the 60th Rifles. He took Frederickson's hand. 'I'm glad, William.'

'We're not unhappy ourselves.' Frederickson was a man of villainous, even vile, appearance. His left eye was gone and the socket was covered by a mildewed patch. Most of his right ear had been torn away by a bullet while two of his front teeth were clumsy fakes. All the wounds had been taken on the battlefield.

Frederickson's men, with clumsy and affectionate wit, called him 'Sweet William'. The 60th, raised to fight against the Indian tribes in America, was still known as the Royal American Rifles, though half the Company were Germans, a quarter were Spaniards enrolled during the long war, and the rest were British except for a single, harsh-faced man who alone justified his regiment's old name. Sharpe had fought alongside this Company two years before and, seeing the bitter face, the name came back to him. 'That's the American. Taylor, isn't it?'

'Yes.' Frederickson and Sharpe stood far enough from the two paraded Companies so their voices could not be overheard by the men.

42

'We might come up against some Jonathons,' Sharpe said. 'There's some bugger called Killick skulking in Arcachon. Will it worry Taylor if he has to fight his countrymen?'

Frederickson shrugged. 'Leave him to me, sir.'

Two Companies of the green-jacketed Riflemen had been given to Sharpe. Frederickson commanded one, a Lieutenant Minver the other, and together they numbered one hundred and twenty-three men. Not many, Sharpe thought, to assault a fortress on the French coast. He walked further along the quay with Frederickson, stopping by a fish cart that dripped bloody scales into a puddle. 'Between you and me, William, it's a mess.'

'I thought it might be.'

'We leave tomorrow to capture a fortress. It isn't supposed to be heavily defended, but no one's sure. After that, God knows what happens. There's a madman who wants us to invade France, but between you and me we're not.'

Frederickson grinned, then turned and looked at the two Companies of Riflemen. 'We're capturing a fort all by our little selves?'

'The Navy says a few Marines might be well enough to help us.'

'That's very decent of them.' Frederickson stared at the great bulk of the *Vengeance*. Barges, propelled by huge sweeps, were taking casks of water from the harbour to the huge ship.

'You'll draw extra ammunition,' Sharpe said. 'The First Division's paying for it.'

'I'll rob the bastards blind,' Frederickson said happily.

'And tonight you'll do me the honour of dining with Jane and myself?'

'I'd like to meet her.' Frederickson sounded guarded.

'She's wonderful.' Sharpe said it warmly, and Frederickson, seeing his friend's enthusiasm, hoped that a new wife had not sapped Sharpe's appetite for the bloody business that lay ahead at Arcachon.

*

Commandant Henri Lassan thought he detected sleet in the dawn, but he could not be sure until he climbed to the western bastion and saw how the flakes settled briefly on the great cheeks of his guns before melting into cold rivulets of water. The guns were loaded, as they always were, but their muzzles and vent-holes were stoppered against the damp. 'Good morning, Sergeant!'

'Sir!' The sergeant stamped his feet and slapped his hands against the cold.

Lassan's orderly climbed the stone ramp with a tray of coffee-mugs. Lassan always brought the morning guard a mug of coffee each and the men appreciated the small gesture. The Commandant, they said, was a gentleman.

Children ran across the courtyard and women's voices sounded from the kitchens. There should not be women in the fort, but Lassan had let the families of his gun crews take up the quarters vacated by the infantry who had gone to the northern battles. Lassan believed his men were less likely to desert if their families were inside the defences.

'There she is, sir.' The sergeant pointed through the sleeting rain.

Lassan looked over the narrow Arcachon channel where the tide raced across the shoals. Beyond the sandbanks the surging grey waves were torn by wind into a maelstrom of broken white water amidst which, beating southwards, was a little ship.

The ship was a British brig-sloop with two tall masts and a vast driver-sail at her stern. Her black and white banded hull hid, Lassan knew, eighteen guns. Her sails were reefed, but even so she seemed to plunge through the waves and Lassan saw how high the spray fountained from the brig's stem. 'Our enemies,' he said mildly, 'are having a disturbed breakfast.'

'Yes, sir.' The sergeant laughed.

Lassan cradled his coffee mug. There was something vulnerable about his face, a drawn and frightened look that made his men protective of him. They knew Commandant

44

Lassan wished to become a priest when this war ended and they liked him for it, but they also knew that he would fight as a soldier until the last shot of the war had been fired. Now he stared at the British brig. 'You saw her last night?'

'At sundown, sir,' the sergeant was certain. 'And there were lights out there at night.'

'He's watching us, isn't he?' Lassan smiled. 'He's seeing what we're made of.'

The sergeant slapped the gun as a reply.

Lassan turned to stare thoughtfully into the fort's court-yard. A warning had come from Bordeaux that he was to prepare for a British attack, but Bordeaux had sent him no men to reinforce his shrunken garrison. Lassan could man his big guns, or he could protect the landward walls, but he could not do both. If the British landed troops, and sent warships into the channel, then Lassan would be trapped between the hammer and the anvil. He turned back to stare at the British brig. If Bordeaux was right, that inquisitive craft was making a reconnaissance, and Lassan must deceive the watchers. He must make them think the fort was so thinly defended that a landing by troops would be unnecessary.

Lieutenant Gerard came yawning from the green-painted door of the officers' quarters. Lassan hailed him. 'Lieutenant!'

'Sir?'

'No flag today! And no washing hung to dry on the barracks' roof!' Not that anyone was likely to dry washing in this weather.

Gerard, his blue jacket unbuttoned above his braces, frowned. 'No flag, sir?'

'You heard me, Lieutenant! And no men in the embrasures, you hear? Sentries in the citadels only.'

'I hear you, sir.'

Lassan turned back to see the brig-sloop tack into the rain-sodden wind. He saw a shiver of sails, a spume of foam, and he imagined the cloaked officers, their braid tarnished by salt, staring at the grey, crouching fort through their spyglasses. He knew that such little ships, sent to spy on the French coast, often stopped the fishing boats that worked close inshore. Today then, and every day for the next week, only those fishermen whom Henri Lassan trusted would be allowed past the guns of the Teste de Buch. They would be encouraged to take English gold, and encouraged to drink a glass of dark rum in English cabins, and encouraged to sell lobsters to blue-coated Englishmen, and in return they would tell a plausible lie or two on behalf of Henri Lassan.

Then, with a roar from these great, passive guns that waited for employment, Henri Lassan would strike a blow for France.

He smiled, pleased with his notion, and went to breakfast.

Before dinner Sharpe faced a miserable and unhappy few moments. 'The answer,' he repeated, 'is no.'

Regimental Sergeant Major Patrick Harper stood in the small parlour of Jane's lodgings and twisted his wet shako in thick, strong fingers. 'I talked with Mr d'Alembord, sir, so I did, and he said I could come. I mean we're only sitting around like washer-women in a bloody drought, so we are.'

'There's a new colonel coming, Patrick. He needs his RSM.'

Harper frowned. 'Needs his major, too.'

'He can't lose both of us.' Sharpe did not have the power to deny the Prince of Wales's Own Volunteers the services of this massive Irishman. 'And if you come, Patrick, the new man will only appoint a new RSM. You wouldn't want that.'

Harper frowned. 'I'd rather be in a scrap if one's going, sir, and Mr Frederickson wouldn't take me amiss, nor would he.'

Sharpe could not be persuaded. 'No.'

The huge man, four inches taller than Sharpe's six feet, grinned. 'I could take sick leave, sir, so I could.'

'You have to be sick first.'

'But I am!' Harper pointed to his mouth. 'I've got a toothache something desperate, sir. Here!' He opened his mouth, jabbed with his finger, and Sharpe saw that Harper did indeed have a reddened and swollen upper gum.

'Does it hurt?'

'It's dreadful, so it is!' Harper, sensing a chink in Sharpe's armour, became enthusiastic about his pain. 'It's more of a throb, sir. On and off, on and off, like a great drumbeat in your skull. Desperate, it is!'

'Then see a surgeon tonight,' Sharpe said unsympathetically, 'and have it pulled. Then get back to Battalion where you belong.'

Harper's face dropped. 'Truly, sir? I can't come?'

Sharpe sighed. 'I'd rather have you along, RSM, than any dozen other men.' That was true a thousand times over. Sharpe knew of no man he would rather fight beside, but it could not be at Arcachon. 'I'm sorry, Patrick. Besides you're a father now. You should take care.' Harper's Spanish wife, just a month before, had given birth to a son that had been christened Richard Patricio Augustine Harper. Sharpe had found the choice of Richard an embarrassment, but Jane had been delighted when Harper sought permission to use the name. 'And I'm doing you a favour, RSM,' Sharpe went on.

'How would that be, sir?'

'Because your son will still have a father in two weeks.' Sharpe was seeing that black, sheer, wet wall and the image of it made his voice savage. Then he turned as the door opened. 'My dear.'

Jane, beautiful in a blue silken dress, smiled delightedly at Harper. 'Sergeant Major! How's the baby?'

'Just grand, ma'am!' Harper had formed a firm alliance with Mrs Sharpe that seemed aimed at subverting Major Sharpe's authority. 'And Isabella thanks you for the linen.'

'You've got toothache!' Jane frowned with concern. 'Your cheek's swollen.'

Harper blushed. 'It's only a wee ache, ma'am, nothing at all!'

47

'You must have oil of cloves! There's some in the kitchen. Come along!'

The oil of cloves was discovered and Harper sent, disconsolate, into the night.

'He can't come,' Sharpe said after dinner, when he and Jane walked back alone through the town.

'Poor Patrick.' Jane insisted on stopping at Hogan's lodgings, but there was no news. She had visited earlier in the day and thought the sick man was looking better.

'I wish you wouldn't risk yourself,' Sharpe said.

'You've said so a dozen times, Richard, and I promise I heard you each time.'

They went to bed and, just four hours later, the landlady hammered on their door. It was pitch dark outside and bitterly cold inside the bedroom. Frost had etched patterns on the small windowpanes, patterns that were reluctant to melt even though Sharpe revived the fire in the tiny grate. The landlady had brought candles and hot water. Sharpe shaved, then pulled on his old and faded Rifleman's uniform. It was the uniform in which he fought, stained with blood and torn by bullet and blade. He would not go into action in any other uniform.

He oiled his rifle's lock. He always carried a long-arm into battle, even though it had been ten years since he had been made into an officer. He drew his Heavy Cavalry sword from its scabbard and tested the fore-edge. It seemed odd to be going to war from his wife's bed, odder still not to be marching with his own men or with Harper, and that thought gave him a flicker of unrest for he was not used to fighting without Harper beside him.

'Two weeks,' he said. 'I should be back in two weeks. Maybe less.'

'It will seem like eternity,' Jane said loyally, then, with an exaggerated shudder, she threw the bedclothes back and snatched up the clothes that Sharpe had hung to warm before the fire. Her small dog, grateful for the chance, leaped into the warm pit of the bed.

'You don't have to come,' Sharpe said.

'Of course I'll come. It's every woman's duty to watch her husband sail to the wars.' Jane shivered suddenly, then sneezed.

A half hour later they went into the fish-smelling lane and the wind was like a knife in their faces. Torches flared on the quayside where the *Amelie* rose on the incoming tide.

A dark line of men, weapons gleaming softly, filed aboard the merchantman that was to be Sharpe's transport. The *Amelie* was no jewel of Britain's trading fleet. She had begun life as a collier, taking coal from the Tyne to the smoke thick Thames, and her dark timbers still stank thickly of coal-dust.

Casks and crates and nets of supplies were slung on board in the pre-dawn darkness. Boxes of rifle ammunition were piled on the quayside and with them were barrels of vilely salted and freshly-killed beef. Twice baked bread was wrapped in canvas and boxed in resinous pine. There were casks of water for the voyage, spare flints for the fighting, and whetstones for the sword-bayonets. Rope ladders were coiled in the *Amelie*'s scuppers so that the Riflemen, reaching the beach where they must disembark, could scramble down to the longboats sent from the *Vengeance*.

A smear of silver-grey marked the dawn and flooded slowly to show the filthy, littered water of the harbour. Aboard the *Scylla*, a frigate moored in the harbour roads, yellow lights showed from the stern cabin where doubtless the frigate's captain took his breakfast.

'I've wrapped you a cheese.' Jane's voice sounded small and frightened. 'It's in your pack.'

'Thank you.' Sharpe bent to kiss her and wished suddenly that he was not going. A wife, General Craufurd used to say, weakens a soldier. Sharpe held his wife an instant, feeling her ribs beneath the layers of wool and silk, then, suddenly, her slim body jerked as she sneezed again.

'I'm catching a cold.' She was shivering. Sharpe touched her forehead and it was oddly hot.

'You're not well.'

'I hate rising early.' Jane tried to smile, but her teeth were chattering and she shivered again. 'And I'm not certain the fish was entirely to my taste last night.'

'Go home!'

'When you're gone.'

Sharpe, even though a hundred men watched him, kissed his wife again. 'Jane . . .'

'My dear, you must go.'

'But . . .'

'It's only a cold. Everyone gets a cold in winter.'

'Sir!' Sweet William saluted Sharpe and bowed to Jane. 'Good morning, ma'am! Somewhat brisk!'

'Indeed, Mr Frederickson.' Jane shivered again.

'Everyone's aboard, sir.' Frederickson turned to Sharpe.

Sharpe wanted to linger with Jane, he wanted to reassure himself that she had not caught Hogan's fever, but Frederickson was waiting for him, men were holding the ropes that would swing the gangplank away, and he could not stay. He gave Jane a last kiss, and her forehead was like fire. 'Go home to bed.'

'I will.' She was shaking now, hunched and clenched against the bitter wind.

Sharpe paused, wanting to say something memorable, something that would encompass the inchoate, extraordinary love he felt for her, but there were no words. He smiled, then turned to follow Frederickson on to the *Amelie*'s deck.

The daylight was thin now, seeping through the hilly landscape behind the port and making the streaked, bubbling, heaving water of the harbour silver. The gangplank crashed on to the stones of the quay.

Far out to sea, like some impossible mountain forming on the face of the waters, an airy structure of dirty grey sails caught the morning daylight. It was the *Vengeance* getting under way. She looked formidably huge; a great floating weapon that could make the air tremble and the sea shake when she launched her full broadside, but she would be useless in the shoal waters by the Teste de Buch fort. That

50

would have to be taken by men and by hand-held weapons.

'He's signalling.' Tremgar, master of the *Amelie*, spat over the side. 'Means they'll be moving us off. Stand by, forrard!' He bellowed the last words.

A topsail dropped from the nearby *Scylla*'s yards and the movement, suggesting an imminent departure, made Sharpe turn to the quay. Jane, swathed in her powder-blue cloak, was still there. Sharpe could see her shivering. 'Go home!'

A voice shouted. 'Wait! Wait!' The accent was French and the speaker a dully-dressed man, evidently a servant, who rode a small horse and led a packhorse on a leading rein. '*Amelie!* Wait!'

'Bloody hell.' Tremgar had been packing a pipe with dark tobacco that he now pushed into a pocket of his filthy coat.

Behind the servant and packhorse and, stately as a bishop in procession, rode a tall, elegant man on a tall, elegant horse. The man had a delicate, sensitive face, a white cloak clasped with silver, and a bicorne hat shielded with oiled-cloth against the rain.

The gangplank was rigged again and the man, with a faint shudder as though the stench of the *Amelie* was too much for a gentleman of his fastidious tastes, came aboard. 'I seek Major Sharpe,' he announced in a French accent to the assembled officers who had gathered in the ship's waist.

'I'm Sharpe.' Sharpe spoke from the poop deck.

The newcomer turned in a movement that would have been elegant on a dance-floor, but seemed somewhat ludicrous on the battered deck of an erstwhile collier. He took a quizzing glass from his sleeve and, with its help, inspected the tattered uniform of Major Richard Sharpe. He bowed, somehow suggesting that he should have been the recipient of such an honour himself, then took off his waterproofed hat to reveal sleek, silver hair that was brushed back to a black velvet bow. He held out a sealed envelope. 'Orders.'

Sharpe had jumped down from the poop and now tore open the envelope. 'To Major Sharpe. The bearer of this note is the Comte de Maquerre. You will render him every assistance within your power. Bertram Wigram, Colonel.'

Sharpe looked into the narrow face that had been powdered pale. He suddenly remembered that Hogan, in his sick ramblings, had mentioned the name Maquereau, meaning 'pimp', and he wondered if the insult was a nickname for this elegant, fastidious man. 'You're the Comte de Maquerre?'

'I have that honour, Monsieur, and I travel to Arcachon with you.' De Maquerre's cloak had fallen open to reveal the uniform of the Chasseurs Britannique. Sharpe knew that regiment's reputation. The officers were Frenchmen loyal to the *ancien régime*, while its men were deserters from the French Army and all unmitigated scoundrels. They could fight when the mood took them, but it was not a regiment Sharpe would want on his flank in battle.

'Captain Frederickson! Four men to get the Frenchman's baggage on board! Quick now!'

De Maquerre tugged at his buttoned, kidskin gloves. 'You have quarters for my horse? And the packhorse.'

'No horses,' Sharpe said sourly, which only tossed the Comte de Maquerre into a sulky fit of protests in which the name of the Duc d'Angoulême, Louis XVIII, and the Lord Wellington featured prominently. In the meantime an angry message came from the *Scylla* demanding to know why the *Amelie* had not slipped her moorings at the flood tide, and finally Sharpe had to give way.

Which meant another delay as the Comte's two horses were coaxed aboard and a section of Frederickson's Riflemen were moved out of the forward hold to make way for the beasts. Trunks and cases were carried up the gangplank.

'I cannot, of course,' the Comte de Maquerre said, 'travel in this ship.'

'Why not?' Sharpe asked.

A wrinkle of the nostril was the only answer and a further delay ensued while a message was sent to the *Scylla* which demanded that His Excellency the Comte de Maquerre be allowed quarters on board the frigate or, preferably, the *Vengeance*.

Captain Grant of the *Scylla,* doubtless under pressure from the *Vengeance*, returned a short answer. The Comte, disgusted, went below to the cabin he would now have to share with Frederickson.

The light was full now, dissipated by clouds and showing the filth that floated yellow and black in the grey harbour. A dead dog bumped against the *Amelie*'s hull as the forward cables were released, then the aft splashed free, and from overhead came the menacing sound of great sails unleashing to the wind's power. A gull gave its lonely, harsh cry that sailors believed was the sound of a drowned soul in agony.

Sharpe stared at the golden-haired girl in the cloak of silver-blue and he blamed the wind for the tears in his eyes. Jane had a handkerchief to her face and Sharpe prayed that he had not seen the first symptoms of the fever in her. He tried to convince himself that Jane was right, and that she merely suffered from eating bad fish the night before, but goddamn it, he thought, why did she have to visit Hogan?

'Go home!' he shouted across the widening gap.

Jane shivered, but stayed. She watched the *Amelie* claw clumsily out beyond the bar and Sharpe, staring back to the harbour, saw the tiny signal of her white-waving handkerchief get smaller and smaller and finally disappear as a rain-squall seethed and hissed over the broken sea.

The *Vengeance* loomed over the other ships. The *Amelie*, pumps already working, took station astern while the *Scylla*, fast and impatient, leaped ahead into the squalls. The brig-sloops closed behind the *Amelie*, and the shore of France was nothing but a dark smear on a grey sea.

A buoy, tarred black and marking God alone knew what hazard in this empty waste, slipped astern and thus the expedition to Arcachon, amidst chaos and uncertainty, was under way.

CHAPTER 4

All day Commandant Henri Lassan watched the ships pass. He watched from within one of the fort's covered citadels and with the help of a brass-barrelled telescope that had belonged to his grandfather.

No flag flew from the fort. One of the local fishermen, trusted by Lassan, had taken his small boat to the Lacanau shoals where the British brig had taken the smack's wind and invited the captain aboard. Rum had been served, gold paid for fish, and the fisherman had solemnly informed the enemy that the fort was deserted entirely of its old garrison. They had gone north, he said, to serve the Emperor, and only a few local militia now patrolled the ramparts. If the lie was believed then Lassan might entice the British into the range of his heavy guns, and he had cause to think the lie had worked for the brig had flattened her sails into the wind and gone southwards.

Now, instead of the brig, a vast line of grey sails flecked the western horizon. Commandant Lassan guessed the ships were eight or nine miles out to sea and he knew that he watched a British convoy carrying men and weapons and horses and ammunition to their Army to the south.

The sight made Henri Lassan feel lonely. His Emperor was far away and he was alone on the coast of France and his enemy could sail with impunity down that coast in a massive convoy that would have needed a fleet to disrupt. Except there were no more French fleets; the last had been destroyed by Nelson nine years before and what ships were left rotted in their anchorages.

A few privateers, American and French, sailed the ocean,

but they were like small dogs yapping at the heels of a vast herd. Even Cornelius Killick, in his splendid *Thuella*, could not have taken a ship from that convoy. Killick would have waited for a straggler perhaps, but nothing less than a fleet could have broken that vast line of ships.

It was painful to see the enemy's power so naked, so unchallenged, so ponderous. In the great holds of those hull-down ships were the instruments that would bring death to Soult's army in the south, and Lassan could do nothing. He could win his small battle, if it came, but the greater struggle was beyond his help.

That thought made him chide himself for lack of faith and, in penitence, he went to the fort's small chapel and prayed for a miracle. Perhaps the Emperor, marching and counter-marching his men along the frost hardened roads of the north, could win a great victory and break the alliance that ringed France, yet the Emperor's desperation was witnessed by the fort's emptiness. France had been scraped for men, then scraped again, and many of the next class of conscripts had already fled into the woods or hills to escape the sergeants who came to take cannon-fodder still not grown to manhood.

A clash of boots, a shout, and the squeal of the gate hinges which, however often greased, insisted on screeching like a soul entering purgatory, announced a visitor to the fort. Lassan pocketed his beads, crossed himself, and went into the twilight.

'The bastards! The double-crossing bastards! Good evening, Henri.' Cornelius Killick, his savage face furious, nodded to the Commandant. 'Bastards!'

'Who?'

'Bordeaux! No copper! No oak! What am I supposed to do? Paste paper over the bloody holes?'

'Perhaps you'll take some wine?' Lassan suggested diplomatically.

'I'll take some wine.' The American followed Lassan into the Commandant's quarters that looked more like a library than a soldier's rooms. 'That bastard Ducos! I'd like to pull his teeth out through his backside.'

'I thought,' Lassan said gently, 'that the coffin-maker in Arcachon had given you some elm?'

'Given? The bastard made us pay three times the price! And I don't like sailing with a ship's arse made out of dead man's wood.'

'Ah, a sailor's superstition.' Lassan poured wine into the crystal glasses that bore his family's coat of arms. The last Comte de Lassan had died beneath the guillotine, but Henri had never been tempted to use the title that was rightfully his. 'Did you see all those fat merchantmen crawling south?'

'All day,' Killick said gloomily. 'Take one of those and you make a small fortune. Not as much as an Indiaman, of course.' He finished the glass of wine and poured himself more. 'I told you about the Indiaman I took?'

'Indeed you did,' Henri Lassan said politely, 'three times.'

'And was her hold crammed with silks? With spices? With treasures of the furthest East? With peacock's plumes and sapphires blue?' Killick gave his great whoop of a laugh. 'No, my friend. She was crammed to the gunwales with saltpetre. Saltpetre to make powder, powder to drive bullets, bullets to kill the British. It is kind of our enemies, is it not, to provide the powers of their own destruction?' He sat beside the fire and stared at the thin, scholarly-faced Lassan. 'So, my friend, are the bastards coming?'

'If they want the *chasse-marées*,' Lassan said mildly, 'they'll have to come here.'

'And the weather,' the American said, 'will let them land safely.' The long Biscay shore, that could thunder with tumbling surf, was this week in gentler mood. The breaking waves beyond the channel were four or five feet high, frightening enough to landlubbers, but not high enough to stop ships' boats from landing.

Lassan, still hoping that his deception would persuade the British that they had no need to land men on the

56

coast to the south, nevertheless acknowledged the possibility. 'Indeed.'

'And if they do come by land,' Killick said brutally, 'they'll beat you.'

Lassan glanced at the ebony crucifix that hung between his bookshelves. 'Perhaps not.'

The American seemed oblivious of Lassan's appeal to the Almighty. 'And if they take the fort,' he went on, 'they'll command the whole Basin.'

'They will, indeed.'

'And they'll take the *Thuella*.' Killick said it softly, but in his imagination he was seeing his beautiful ship captured by mocking British sailors. The *Thuella* would be sailed to England as a prize, and a sleek New England schooner, made to ride the long winds of empty oceans, would become an unloved coasting ship carrying British trade. 'By God, they will not take her!'

'We'll do our best,' Lassan said helplessly, though how four gun crews could resist a British attack was indeed a problem that called for a miracle. Lassan did not doubt that his guns could wreak damage, but once the British discovered the guns were manned they would soon land their Marines and surround the fort. And Lassan, because the Emperor had been greedy for men, could not defend the seaward and the landward walls at once.

The grim news made the American silent. He stared at the small fire, his hawk's face frowning, and when he finally spoke his voice was oddly tentative. 'What if we fought?'

'You?' Lassan could not hide his surprise.

'We can fight, Henri.' Killick grinned. 'And we've got those damned twelve-pounder guns in our hold.' He was suddenly filled with enthusiasm, seizing a map from Lassan's table and weighting its corners with books. 'They'll land south of Point Arcachon?'

'Undoubtedly.'

'And there are only two routes they can take north. The paths by the beach, or the road!' Killick's face was alight with the thought of action, and Lassan saw that the American was a man who revelled in the simple problems of warfare. Lassan had met other such men; brave men who had made their names famous throughout France and written pages of history through their love of violent action. He wondered what would happen to such men when the war ended.

'You're a sailor,' Lassan said gently, 'and fighting on land is not the same as a sea battle.'

'But if the bastards aren't expecting us, Henri! If the pompous bastards think they're safe! Then we ambush them!' Killick was certain his men, trained gunners, could handle the French artillery and he was seeing, in his hopeful imagination, the grapeshot cutting down marching files of British Marines. 'By God we can do it, Henri!'

Lassan held up a thin hand to stop the enthusiastic flow. 'If you really want to help, Captain Killick, then put your men into the fort.'

'No.' Killick knew only too well what the British would do to a captured privateer's crew. If Killick fought to save the *Thuella* then he must have a safe retreat in case he was defeated. Yet in his plan to ambush the British on their approach march he could not see any chance of defeat. The enemy Marines would be surprised, flayed by grapeshot, and the *Thuella* would be safe.

Henri Lassan, staring at the map, wondered whether the American's plan delineated the miracle he had prayed for. If the British did not capture the fort they could not take the *chasse-marées*, and without the *chasse-marées* they were trapped behind the rivers running high with winter's floodwaters.

Trapped. And perhaps the Emperor, bloodying his northern enemies, would march south and give the British Army a shattering defeat.

For, though Wellington had conquered every French Marshal or General sent to fight him, he had never faced the Emperor's genius. Lassan wondered if this big, handsome

American had found the small answer that would hold up the British just long enough to let the Emperor come south and teach the goddamns a lesson in warfare. Then a pang of realism forced Lassan's mind to contemplate failure. 'What will you do, *mon ami*, if the British win?'

Killick shrugged. 'Dismast the *Thuella* and make her look like a wreck, then pray that the British ignore her. And you, Commandant, what will you do?'

Lassan smiled sadly. 'Burn the *chasse-marées*, of course.' By so doing he would condemn the two hundred men of the crews and their families to penury. The mayor and *curé* had begged him to preserve the boats which, even in French defeat, would give life and bread to the communities of the Biscay coast, but in defeat Henri Lassan would do his duty. 'Let's hope it doesn't come to that,' he said.

'It won't.' Killick brandished his cigar to leave an airy trace of smoke like that made by the burning fuse of an arcing mortar shell. 'It's a brilliant idea, Henri! So let the buggers come, eh?'

They drank to victory in a winter's dusk while, far to the south, where they crossed the path of a great convoy tacking the ocean, Richard Sharpe and his small force came north to do battle.

It snowed in the night. Sharpe stood by the stinking tar-coated ratlines on the *Amelie*'s poop deck and watched the flakes whirl around the riding light. The galley fire was still lit forward and it cast a great sheet of flickering red on the foresail. The galley's smoke was taken northwards towards the lights of the *Vengeance*.

The *Amelie* was making good time. The helmsman said so, even Captain Tremgar, grunting out of his bunk at two in the morning, agreed. 'Never known the old sow to sail so well, sir. Can you not sleep, now?'

'No.'

'I'll be having a drop of rum with you?'

'No, thank you.' Sharpe knew that the merchant Captain was offering a kindness, but he did not want his wits fuddled by drink as well as sleeplessness.

He stood alone by the rail. Sometimes, as the ship leaned to a gust of wind, a lantern would cast a shimmering ray on to a slick, hurrying sea. The snow whirled into nothingness. An hour after Tremgar's brief conversation Sharpe saw a tiny spark of light, very red, far to the east.

'Another ship?' he asked the helmsman.

'Lord love you, no, sir!' The snow-bright wind whirled the helmsman's voice in snatches to Sharpe. 'That be land!'

A cottage? A soldier's fire? Sharpe would never know. The spark glimmered, sometimes disappearing altogether, yet then flickering back to crawl at its snail's pace along the dark horizon, and the sight of that far, anonymous light made Sharpe feel the discomfort of a soldier at sea. His imagination, that would plague him in battle, saw the *Amelie* shipwrecked, saw the great seas piling cold and grey on breaking timbers among which the bodies of his men would be whirled like rats in a barrel. That one small red spark was all that was safe, all that was secure, and he knew he would rather be a hundred miles behind the enemy lines and on firm ground than be on a ship in a treacherous sea.

'You cannot sleep. Nor I.'

Sharpe turned. The ghostly figure of the Comte de Maquerre, hair as white as the great cloak that was clasped with silver at his throat, came towards him. The Comte missed his footing as the *Amelie*'s blunt bow thumped into a larger wave and the tall man had to clutch Sharpe's arm. 'My apologies, Major.'

Steadied by Sharpe, the Comte rested his backside on one of the small cannon that had been issued to the *Amelie* for its protection.

The Comte, his hair remarkably sleek for such an hour of the morning, stared eastwards. 'France.' He said the name with reverence, even love.

'St Jean de Luz was in France,' Sharpe said in an ungracious attempt to imply that the Comte's company was not welcome.

The Comte de Maquerre ignored the comment, staring instead at the tiny spark as though it was the Grail itself. 'I have been away, Major, for eighteen years.' He spoke with a tragic intonation. 'Waiting for liberty to be reborn in France.'

The ship dipped again and Sharpe glimpsed a whorl of grey water that was gone as swiftly as it had been illuminated. The snow melted on his face. Everyone spoke of liberty, he thought. The monarchists and the anti-monarchists, the Republicans and the anti-Republicans, the Bonapartists and the Bourbons, all carried the word around as if it was a genie trapped in a bottle and they were the sole possessors of the world's corkscrew. Yet if Sharpe was to go down to the hold now and wake up the soldiers who slept so fitfully and uncomfortably in the stinking 'tween-decks of the *Amelie*, and if he was to ask each man what he wanted in life, then he knew, besides being thought mad by the men, that he would not hear the word Liberty used. They wanted a woman as a companion, they wanted cheap drink, they wanted a fire in winter and fat crops in summer, and they wanted a patch of land or a wineshop of their own. Most would not get what they desired.

But nor would Sharpe. He had a sudden, startlingly clear vision of Jane lying sick; sweating in the cold shivers of the killing fever. The image, so extraordinarily real in the freezing night, made him shiver himself.

He tried to shake the vision away, then told himself that Jane suffered from nothing more than an upset stomach and a winter's cold, but the superstition of a soldier suddenly gripped Sharpe's imagination and he knew, with an utter certainty, that he sailed away from a dying wife. He wanted to howl his misery into the snow-dark night, but there was no help there. No help anywhere. She was dying. That knowledge might have been vouchsafed by a dreamlike image, but Sharpe believed it. 'Damn your bloody liberty.' Sharpe spoke savagely.

'Major?' The Comte, hearing Sharpe's voice but no distinct words, edged down the ship's rail.

Jane would be dead and Sharpe would return to the coldly heaped soil of her grave. He wanted to weep for the loss.

'Did you speak, Monsieur?' the Comte persisted.

Sharpe turned to the Comte then. The Rifleman had been distracted by his thoughts, but now he concentrated on the tall, pale aristocrat. 'Why are you here?'

'Here, Monsieur?' de Maquerre was defensive. 'For the same reason you are here. To bring liberty to France!'

Sharpe's instincts were alert now. He was sensing that a new player had entered the game, a player who would confuse the issues of this expedition. 'Why?' he persisted.

De Maquerre shrugged. 'My family is from Bordeaux, Major, and a letter was smuggled to me in which they claim the citizens are prepared to rebel. I am ordered to discover the truth of the letter.'

God damn it, but his instincts were right. Sharpe was supposed to discover the mood of the French, but Wigram, knowing that Sharpe would return a gloomy answer, had sent this aristocrat at the very last moment. Doubtless de Maquerre would give Wigram the answer he wanted; the answer that would lead to madness. Sharpe laughed sourly. 'You think two Companies of Riflemen can provoke Bordeaux into rebellion?'

'No, monsieur,' the Comte de Maquerre paused as a wave lurched the ship sideways. 'I think two Companies of Riflemen, with the help of some Marines, can hold the fort at Arcachon until more men are carried north by *chasse-marée*. Isn't that why the boats are being collected? To make an invasion? And where better to invade than at Arcachon?'

Sharpe did not reply. Elphinstone had ordered him to scotch Wigram's desk-born ambitions, but now this foppish Frenchman would make that task difficult. It would be simpler, Sharpe thought, to tip the man overboard now.

'But if the city of Bordeaux is ready for rebellion,' de Maquerre was happily oblivious of Sharpe's thoughts, 'then we can topple the regime now, Major. We can raise insurrection in the streets, we can humble the tyrant. We can end the war!' Again Sharpe made no reply, and the Comte stared at the tiny glimmer of light in the cold darkness. 'Of course,' the Comte continued, 'if I do succeed in raising the city against the ogre I shall expect your troops to come to my aid immediately.'

Startled, Sharpe twisted to look at the pale profile of the Comte de Maquerre. 'I have no such orders.'

The Comte also turned, showing Sharpe a pair of the palest, coldest eyes imaginable. 'You have orders, Major, to offer me every assistance in your power. I carry a commission from your Prince Regent, and a commission from my King. When ordered, Major, you will obey.'

Sharpe was saved from a reply by the harsh clang of the ship's bell. He wondered, irritably, why sailors did not just ring the hour like other folk, but insisted on sounding gnomic messages of indeterminate meaning upon their bells. Feet padded on the deck as the watch was changed. The binnacle lantern flared bright as the lid was lifted.

'Your first duty, Major,' the Count ignored the dark figures who came up the poop-deck ladders, 'is to safely put my horses ashore.'

Sharpe had taken enough. 'My first duty, my Lord, is to my men. If you can't get your horses ashore then they stay here and I won't lift a goddamned finger to help you. Good day.' He stalked across the deck, a gesture somewhat spoilt by the need to stagger as the *Amelie* creaked on to a new course in obedience to lights that flared suddenly from the *Vengeance*'s poop.

The dawn crept slow from the grey east. The snow stopped and Sharpe could see, in the half-light, that none had settled on the land that proved surprisingly close. A brig was close inshore and signal flags hung bright from her mizzen yard.

'She wasn't with us yesterday.' Sweet William, looking disgustingly well-rested, nodded towards the signalling brig. He had brought Sharpe a mug of tea. 'She must have been poking around the fortress. Sleep sound?'

'No sleep.' Sharpe cradled the mug and sipped the hot, sour liquid. The shore looked barren. Sand dunes were grey behind the flicker of surf and beyond the dunes were the dark shapes of stunted pines. No houses were visible. Far inland there were the low, humped shapes of hills, and to the north there was a promontory of low, shadowed ground that jutted into the bleak waters.

Captain Tremgar pointed to the headland. 'Point Arcachon.' He turned away from the two Rifle officers and bellowed orders through a speaking trumpet. Sharpe heard the thumping rumble as the anchor cables snaked and whipped out of the hawse-holes. Sails, that a moment before had been filled with wind, flapped like monstrous bat wings as the topmen furled the stiff canvas on to the yards. The *Vengeance*, looming vast in the morning light, was already anchored, and already launching her first boats. 'Christ on his cross!' Sweet William vented a sudden anger. He was staring at the boats that huddled beside the *Vengeance*.

Sharpe took his spyglass from the sleeve-pocket on his overalls and extended the ivory barrels. The glass had been a gift from the Emperor of the French to his brother, the King of Spain, but the gift had been lost among the loot of Vitoria and was now carried by an English Rifleman.

'Jesus Christ!' Sharpe echoed Frederickson's blasphemy. The *Vengeance* had launched three longboats and each was filling with red-jacketed Marines. 'There must be a hundred of them!' He watched the men gingerly descend the tumble-home to step into the rocking boats. The sea, miraculously, was gentle this morning, heaving with the long swells of the ocean, but not broken into whitecaps. Sharpe raised the glass, cursing because the small movements of the *Amelie* made training the telescope difficult, and he saw yet more red-coated Marines waiting on the *Vengeance*'s maindeck. 'That bastard didn't need us at all!'

'Not to take the fort, perhaps,' Sweet William lit a cheroot, 'but a force of trained Riflemen will be damned useful for the march on Bordeaux.'

'Damn his bloody soul!' Sharpe understood now. Wigram had sent de Maquerre to force a decision, and Bampfylde had secreted the Marines to implement the decision. Come hell or high water Wigram and Bampfylde wanted to take Bordeaux, and Sharpe was caught in the middle. He watched the packed longboats pull towards the breaking surf and he felt a bitter anger at Bampfylde who had lied about a malady so that he could have trained skirmishers for his madcap scheme. Even the sun, showing through the clouds for the first time in weeks, could not alleviate Sharpe's anger.

'It's my belief,' Frederickson said, 'that he wanted you personally.'

'Me?'

'He probably has an exalted view of your ability,' Frederickson said drily. 'If the celebrated Major Sharpe fails, then no reasonable man could expect Captain Bampfylde to succeed. On the other hand, of course, who better than yourself to guarantee success?'

'Bugger Bampfylde,' Sharpe said.

The longboats landed their red-coated troops, then were launched back through the surf. The oarsmen, tugging against wind and tide, jerked like small marionettes to pull the heavy boats free of the shore's suction. They did not come to the *Amelie*; instead they went to the *Vengeance* where still more Marines waited for disembarkation.

The morning ticked on. A breakfast of gravy-dipped bread was passed around the Riflemen who waited on the *Amelie*'s deck. Those Marines already ashore formed up in ranks and, to Sharpe's astonishment, a half Company was marched off the beach towards the shelter of the dark pines. Sharpe himself was supposed to command the land operations, yet he was being utterly ignored. 'Captain Tremgar!'

'Sir?'

'Your boat can put me ashore?'

Tremgar, a middle-aged man wrapped in a filthy tarpaulin jacket, knocked the dottle from his pipe on the brass binnacle cover that was covered with tiny dents from just such treatment. 'Ain't got orders to do it, Major.'

'I'm giving you orders!'

Tremgar turned. One of the longboats was pulling away from the *Vengeance* and carrying, instead of Marines, a group of blue-cloaked naval officers. Tremgar shrugged. 'Don't see why not, Major.'

It took twenty minutes to lower the *Amelie*'s small tender into the water, and another five before Sharpe was sitting uncomfortably on the stern thwart. The Comte de Maquerre, seeing a chance to escape from the stinking collier, had insisted on sharing the boat. He had exchanged his British uniform for a suit of brown cloth.

From the *Amelie*'s deck the sea had appeared benign, but here, in the tiny boat, it swelled and threatened and ran cold darts of fear up Sharpe's back. The oars spattered him with water, the waves heaved towards the gunwales, and at any moment Sharpe expected the small rowboat to turn turtle. The Comte, wrapped in his cloak, looked seasick.

Sharpe twisted. The *Amelie*'s tar- and salt-stained hull reared above him. A cook jettisoned a bucket of slops over the side and gulls, screaming like banshees, swooped from the air between the yards to fight over the scraps.

The Comte, offended by Sharpe's cavalier treatment in the small hours, said not a word. Slowly, oar-tug by oar-tug, the four boatmen dragged the small craft away from the *Amelie* and the grumble of the surf, like the roar of a far-off, relentless battle, grew louder.

Sharpe instinctively touched his weapons. His rifle was muzzle-stopped against sea-water splashes, while the lock was wrapped in an old rag for protection. His sword was clumsy in the confines of the tiny boat. A surge heaved the boat up and ran it forward towards the breaking surf that betrayed itself to Sharpe as a spume of spray being whipped from a curling wave by the wind's flick, then the boat dropped into a valley of sliding, glassy grey water that was flecked with floating sea-weed.

This was the point of danger. This was the moment when the small boats must go from the sea's cradle into the broken forces where the waves battered at the shore. Years ago, on a beach like this in Portugal, Sharpe had watched the longboats broach in the combers and spill their men like puppets into the killing sea. The bodies, he remembered, had come ashore white and swollen, uniforms split by the swelling flesh, and dogs had worried at the corpses for days.

'Pull!' the bo'sun shouted. 'Pull, you bastards!'

The oarsmen pulled and, like a wagon loaded with cannon-shot, the boat fought the upward slope of the wave. The oars bent under the strain, then the vast power of the sea caught the boat's transom and it was running, suddenly free of all constraint, and the bo'sun was shouting at the men to ship oars and was leaning his full weight on the tiller behind Sharpe.

The bo'sun's shout seemed like a prolonged bellow that melded with the roar of the surf. The world was white and grey, streaked bottle green at its heart where the wave broke to carry the tiny boat surging forward. Sharpe's right hand was a cold and bloodless white where it gripped the gunwale, then the boat's bow was dipping, falling, and the water was smashing around Sharpe's ears in scraps of freezing white and still the shout echoed in his ears and he felt the panic of a man caught in a danger that is uncontrollable.

The bow caught, the boat twisted and shuddered, and suddenly she was running amidst bubbling sea-streaks beneath which the sand made a hissing noise as tons of beach were drawn backwards by the sucking water.

'Now!' the bo'sun shouted, 'now, you heathens!' and the bow-men were overboard, up to their knees in churning water and dragging the small boat towards the safety of the shelving beach.

'There, Major. That was easy,' the bo'sun said calmly.

Sharpe, trying not to show the terror he had felt, stepped forward over the thwarts. The two remaining oarsmen, grinning at him, helped his unsteady progress. Another wave, breaking and running up the beach, lifted the boat and shifted it sideways so that Sharpe fell heavily on to a huge black man who laughed at the soldier's predicament.

Sharpe stood again, balanced himself at the prow, then leaped into the receding wave. No firm ground, no lush soil of the most peaceful village green in England, had ever felt so good to him. He splashed to dry sand, breathing a silent thanks for safety as at last his boots crunched the small ridge of seaweed, shells, and timber scraps that marked the height of the winter tides.

'Major!' A voice hailed him. Lieutenant Ford, Bampfylde's aide, walked through the clinging sand. 'Welcome ashore. You're precipitate, are you not, sir?'

'Precipitate?' Sharpe, taking the rag off his rifle-lock, had to shout over the noise of wind and surf.

'You'd not been ordered ashore, sir.' Ford spoke respectfully, but Sharpe was certain the young lieutenant had been sent by Bampfylde to deliver this reproof. The captain himself, resplendent in blue, white and gold, directed affairs fifty yards down the strand.

'Let me remind you, Lieutenant,' Sharpe said, 'that proceedings ashore are under my command.'

The Comte de Maquerre, looking grey beneath the powder he had put on to his face, brushed at his cloak then stumped through the sand towards Bampfylde.

Ford glanced at the Comte, then back to Sharpe. 'You can see, sir,' the lieutenant could not hide his embarrassment, 'that our Marines have had a miraculous recovery.'

'Indeed.' There must have been hundreds of Marines on the beach and Sharpe had seen at least another fifty march inland.

'The captain feels,' Ford had carefully placed himself in a position that made it impossible for Sharpe to walk towards Bampfylde, 'that we can safely look after the matter ourselves.' He smiled, as though he had brought splendid news.

Sharpe stared at the young, nervous lieutenant. 'The matter?'

'The capture of the Teste de Buch,' Ford still smiled as if he could infect Sharpe with his good tidings.

Sharpe stared at Ford. 'You're standing in my path, Lieutenant.'

'Oh! My apologies, sir!' Ford stepped aside.

Bampfylde was greeting the Comte de Maquerre with evident familiarity, but, seeing Sharpe approach, he gestured for the Frenchman to wait, then stepped briskly towards the Rifleman. ''Morning, Sharpe! Quite a clever one, what?'

'Clever, sir?'

'The weather! God smiles on sailormen.' A gust of wind picked up particles of sand and rattled them against Sharpe's tall boots.

'Lieutenant Ford, sir, tells me you do not require my services.'

'Not at the Teste de Buch, certainly. One of our brigs quizzed a fisherman yesterday, Sharpe. Seems the Frogs have abandoned the fort! How about that, eh? There's a few fencibles left there, but I can't see you need to bother yourself with that sort of scum! I think the prudent thing, Major, is for you to march inland.'

'Inland, sir?'

'Weren't you planning to ambush the high road? But I want you back here, with your report, by the forenoon on Thursday. Is that clear?'

Sharpe looked past the plump, confident Bampfylde to see the Marines being paraded on the sand. They were in light order, having left their packs and greatcoats on the *Vengeance*. They also seemed to be in fine fettle and the sight angered Sharpe. 'Your men made a miraculous recovery, Captain?'

'Did they not, Major?' Bampfylde, in the heartiest of moods, smiled. 'A *ruse de guerre*, Major. You understand?'

Sharpe contained his fury. 'A ruse, sir?'

'We didn't want enemy agents in St Jean de Luz to suspect our plans. They'll have reported sick Marines and a tiny force of soldiery; scarce sufficient to round up a herd of sheep, let alone march on Bordeaux, eh?' Bampfylde saw Sharpe's disbelief and smiled at it. 'I've got more Marines afloat, Sharpe, if they're needed.'

'To capture Bordeaux?' Sharpe's voice was mocking.

'If Maquereau says it can be done, then we shall. He's riding direct to Bordeaux, Sharpe. A brave fellow, what? Your advice will be invaluable, of course, but Maquereau will be the judge of failure or success.' Bampfylde, on the brink of his triumph, was trying hard to be affable.

'Maquereau, sir?'

'Ah, the Comte de Maquerre. You mustn't use his nickname, Sharpe, it's not polite.' Bampfylde laughed. 'But you're on the verge of great events, Major. You'll be grateful for this opportunity.'

Sharpe's gratitude was lost in anger. Bampfylde had lied consistently. He had wanted Sharpe and the Riflemen for his dreams of glory, and now, on a cold French beach, Sharpe was exposed to the madness against which Elphinstone had warned him. 'I thought, sir, that the decision about Bordeaux was my responsibility.'

'And we've spared you that decision, Major. You can't deny that de Maquerre will be a more cogent witness?' Bampfylde paused, sensing Sharpe's anger. 'Naturally I shall take your advice, Major.' Bampfylde opened the lid of his watch as if to demonstrate that Sharpe was delaying his advance. 'Be back by Thursday, Major! That's when Maquereau should bring us the good news from Bordeaux. Remember now! Speed and surprise, Major! Speed and surprise!'

Bampfylde turned away, but Sharpe called him back. 'Sir! You believe the fisherman?'

Bampfylde bridled. 'Is it your business, Sharpe?'

'You'll send picquets ahead, sir?'

Bampfylde snapped his watch-lid shut. 'If I wish for lessons in the operations of military forces, Major, then I shall seek them from my superiors, not my inferiors. My boats will fetch your men now, Major Sharpe, and I will bid you good day.'

Bampfylde walked away. He did not need Sharpe to capture the fort, so he would not dilute his victory by having Sharpe's name mentioned in the despatch he would send to the Admiralty. That despatch was already taking shape in Bampfylde's head, a despatch that would be printed in the *Naval Gazette* and tell, with a modesty that would be as impressive as it was transparent, of a fortress carried, of a bay cleared, and of a victory gained. But that small victory would be but a whisper compared to the trumpeted glory when Bordeaux fell. Thus Bampfylde walked through the cloying, crunching sand and his head was filled with dreams of triumph and the sweeter dreams of victory's rewards that were fame and wealth beyond measure.

CHAPTER 5

Cornelius Killick spat coffee grounds into the fire that had been lit beneath the pine trees. The wind was chill, but at least it was not raining, though Killick suspected the lull in the foul weather would not last.

Some of his men slept, some clenched muskets, others played cribbage or dice. They were nervous, but they took comfort from their captain's blithe confidence.

Killick's confidence was a pretence. He was as nervous as any of his men, and regretting his impulsive offer to defend the fort's landward approaches. It was not that the American was afraid of a fight, but it was one thing to fight at sea, where he knew the meaning of every catspaw on the water and where he could use his skill at the *Thuella*'s helm to run confusion about his enemies, and quite another to contemplate a fight on dry land. It was, as his Irish lieutenant would say, a horse of a different colour, and Cornelius Killick was not sure he liked the colour.

He hated the fact that the land was such a clogging, cloying platform for a fight. A ship moved guns much faster than wheels, and there was nowhere to hide at sea. There, in the clean wind, a fight was open and undisguised, while here any bush could hide an enemy. Killick was keenly aware that he had never trained as a soldier, nor even experienced a battle on land, yet he had made the offer to Commandant Lassan, and so, in this chill wind, he was preparing to offer battle if the British Marines came.

Yet if Cornelius Killick had doubts to plague his confidence, he also had compensating encouragements. With him were the six twelve-pounder guns that had been swung out of the *Thuella*'s hold and mounted on their carriages. Their solidity gave Killick an odd comfort. The guns, so beautifully designed and yet so functional in their appearance, offered an implicit promise of victory. The enemy would come with muskets and be faced with these weapons that Napoleon called his 'beautiful daughters'. They were Gribeauval twelve-pounders, brute killers of the battlefield, massive.

To serve those guns Killick had sixty men; all of them trained in the use of cannon. The American knew well what fate the British might give to a captured privateer's crew, so Killick had not ordered his men to give battle, but had instead invited their help. Such was their faith in him, and such their liking for him, that only two dozen men had declined this chance. Thus Killick would be served this day by volunteers, fighters all. How, Killick asked himself, could impressed troops, led by arrogant, dandified officers, defeat such men as these?

A wind stirred the pines and drifted the fire's smoke towards the village. No one was visible on the far ramparts of the fort, nor did any flag show.

'Maybe the bastards won't come today.' Lieutenant Docherty poured himself some of the muddy coffee.

'Maybe not.' Killick leaned to the fire and lit a cigar. He felt a sudden pang that he should be forced to this unnatural fight or else lose his ship. He could not face losing the *Thuella*. 'But if they do come, Liam, we'll shock the bastards out of their skins.' That was Killick's third advantage; that he had the surprise of ambush on his side.

An hour later the first message arrived from Point Arcachon. Killick had posted four scouts, each one mounted on a lumbering carthorse, and the news came clumping northwards that Marines had landed safely and were already advancing along the tangle of sandy tracks that edged the beach.

'Did they see you?' Killick asked the gun-captain who brought the message.

'No.' The man was scornful of the Marines' watchfulness.

Killick stood and clapped his hands. 'We're moving, lads! We're moving!' The *Thuella*'s crew had waited with the guns at a point midway between the beach paths and the inland road. Now Killick knew which route the British were taking and so the guns had to be manhandled westwards to bar that route.

Other messages came as the guns were shifted. A hundred and fifty Marines had landed; they had neither artillery nor horses, and all marched north. Other men had followed the Marines ashore, but they had stayed on the beach. The scouts, all four of them, came back to the ambush site.

Henri Lassan had chosen the place, and chosen well. The guns were sited at the edge of a pine wood that topped a shallow ridge that jutted into a spreading, flat expanse of sand that edged the dunes of the beach. Two cottages had stood in the sandy space, but both had burned down in the last few years and their charred remains were all that broke up the area across which the Marines must march.

The gun emplacement also offered Killick's men protection. The twelve-pounders were shadowed by the pines, so that the grapeshot would blast, obscene and sudden, out of the darkness into the light. And even if the Marines were to counter-attack and brave the maelstrom of fire that would be slashing diagonally towards the sea they must climb a crumbling bank of sand that was six feet high and steep enough to demand the help of hands if it was to be negotiated.

Twenty men went back for the gun limbers, while the rest of Killick's men prepared the big guns for battle. The barrels had to be shifted on the carriages from their travelling position into the fighting stance, then trunnions must be clamped with iron capsquares as powder and grapeshot were rammed into cold muzzles. The grapeshot was adapted from the stocks taken from the *Thuella*'s magazine, and each canvas-wrapped bundle of balls would be propelled by four pounds and four ounces of French powder that came in a serge bag shaped to the cannon's breech. Vent-prickers slid into touch-holes to break the powder bags, then tin tubes filled with finely mealed powder were rammed down to carry the fire to the charge.

Killick stooped at the breech of one gun. He squinted through the tangent sights, set for point blank range, then gave the brass handle of the elevating screw a quarter turn. Satisfied, he went to each of the other guns and stared down the sights to imagine the tangling death he would cause to flicker above the clearing's sand. The guns' mute promise of terrible power gave Killick a welcome surge of confidence.

'The Commandant thanks you, Cornelius.' Lieutenant Liam Docherty had warned Commandant Lassan that the British had landed. 'He wishes you joy of the meeting.'

Killick gave his swooping, bellowing laugh as if in anticipation of victory. 'They'll not be here for six hours yet, Liam,' he paused to light a cigar, 'but we'll kill the sons of devils when they do come, eh?'

'We will indeed.' For Liam Docherty the coming battle would be one tiny shard of the vengeance he took on the British for their savagery in suppressing the rebellion of the United Irishmen. Docherty's father had been hanged as a rebel in Ireland, casually strung up beside a peat-dark stream with as little ceremony as might attend the death of a rabid dog, and the boy's mother, rearing him in America, would not let him forget. Nor did Liam Docherty wish to forget. He imagined the redcoats coming into the clearing and he relished the savage surprise that would be unleashed from the six gun barrels.

Some villagers, made curious by the strange happenings to the south, had come into the trees to watch the Americans prepare. Cornelius Killick welcomed them. In the night he had been besieged by fears, by imaginings of disaster, but now, when the shape of the enemy's approach was plain and the skilful placing of his ambush apparent, he felt sure of success and was glad that this victory would be witnessed by spectators. 'I wonder what they'd say in Marblehead if they could see us now,' he said happily to Docherty.

Liam Docherty thought that few people in Marblehead would be astonished by this new adventure of Killick's. Cornelius Killick had always had the reputation of being a reckless rogue. 'Maybe they'll name a street after you.'

'A street? Why not rename the bloody town?'

Only one thing remained to be done, and that was done with a due solemnity. Cornelius Killick unfurled the great ensign that he had fetched from the *Thuella*. Its stars and stripes had been sewn together by a committee of Marblehead ladies, then blessed by a Presbyterian Minister who had prayed that the flag would see much slaughter of the Republic's enemies. This day, Killick promised himself, it would. The flag, drooping in the windless space beneath the trees, would be carried forward at the first gunshot and it would stand proud as the gunners worked and as the enemy fell.

Cornelius Killick and the men of the *Thuella* were ready.

The beach was strangely deserted when the Marines were gone. The wind was cold as Sharpe's men tumbled uncertainly through the surf to drag their packs, greatcoats and weapons to the dunes.

'One more boat, sir,' Frederickson said unnecessarily.

Sharpe grunted. The clouds had hidden the sun again and he could see little inland through his telescope. On one far hill a track seemed to wind uncertainly upwards, but there was no visible village or church that might correspond to the scanty map that Frederickson spread on the sand. 'The captain said we were three miles south of Point Arcachon, here.'

Sharpe knew the map by heart and did not bother to glance down. 'There are no roads eastwards. Our quickest route is up to Arcachon then use the Bordeaux road.'

'Follow the web-foots on the beach?'

'Christ, no.' Sharpe did not care if he never saw Bampfylde again. 'We'll take the inland road.' He turned. The Comte de Maquerre was standing disconsolate by the tideline watching as his two horses, each given a long lead rope, were unceremoniously dumped overboard. The horses would have to swim now, tethered to the *Amelie*'s boat, and the Count feared for their loss.

Frederickson still stared at the map. 'How are you going to stop Bampfylde invading France?'

'By refusing to believe that prinked-up bastard.' Sharpe nodded towards the Frenchman. 'I should have heaved him overboard last night.'

'I could have an accident with a rifle?' Frederickson offered helpfully.

It was a cheerful thought for a cold morning, but Sharpe shook his head before turning to watch a working party of Riflemen wrestling supplies through the surf. 'We can jettison the bloody ladders,' Sharpe said sourly. He wondered how Bampfylde proposed crossing the ditches and walls of the Teste de Buch without scaling-ladders, then dismissed the problem as irrelevant now. Sharpe's job now was to go inland, ambush a military convoy on the great road that led southwards, and try to discover the mood of Bordeaux from the captives he would take. 'We'll split the supplies between the men. What we can't carry, we leave.'

'Yes, sir.' Frederickson folded the map and pushed it into his pouch. 'You'll leave the order of march to me?'

But Sharpe did not reply. He was staring at a group of seated Riflemen who sheltered from the icy wind in a fold of the sand-dunes. 'You!' he bellowed, 'come here!'

The Riflemen's faces, bland with the innocence that always greeted an officer's anger, turned to stare at Sharpe, but one man stood, shook sand from his green jacket, and started towards the two officers. 'Did you know?' Sharpe turned furiously on Frederickson.

'No,' Frederickson lied.

Sharpe looked towards the man he had summoned. 'You stupid bloody fool!'

'Sir.'

'Jesus Christ! I make you a bloody RSM and what do you do? You throw it away!'

Patrick Harper's cheek was even more swollen from the toothache and, as though it explained all, he touched the swelling. 'It was this, sir.'

The reply took the wind from Sharpe's anger. He stared at the huge Irishman who gave him a lopsided grin in return. 'Your tooth?' Sharpe asked menacingly.

'I went to the surgeon to have the tooth pulled, so I did, sir, and he gives me some rum against the pain, so he does, sir, and I think I must have taken a drop too much, sir, and the next thing I know is I'm on a ship, sir, and the bastard still hasn't touched the tooth, nor has he, sir, and the only explanation I can possibly think of, sir, is that in my legally inebriated condition some kind soul presumed I was one of Captain Frederickson's men and put me on to the *Amelie*.' Harper paused in his fluent, practised lie. 'It was the very last thing I wanted, sir. Honest!'

'You lying bastard,' Sharpe said.

'Maybe, sir, but it's the truth so help me God.' Patrick Harper, delighted with both his exploit and explanation, grinned at his officer. The grin spoke the real truth; that the two of them always fought together and Harper was determined that it should stay that way. The grin also implied that Major Richard Sharpe would somehow avert the righteous wrath of the Army from Harper's innocent head.

'So your tooth still isn't pulled?' Sharpe asked.

'That's right, sir.'

'Then I'll damn well pull it now,' Sharpe said.

Harper took a step backwards. He was four inches taller than Sharpe's six feet, with muscles to match his size, while on his shoulders were slung a rifle and his fearful seven-barrelled gun, but over his broad, swollen face there suddenly appeared a look of sheer terror. 'You'll not pull the tooth, sir.'

'I damn well will.' Sharpe turned to Frederickson. 'Find me some pincers, Captain.'

Frederickson's hand instinctively went to the pouch at his belt, then checked. 'I'll ask the men, sir.'

Harper blanched. 'Mr Sharpe! Sir! Please!'

'Quiet!' Sharpe stared at the huge Ulsterman. In truth he was relieved that Harper was here, but the Army was the Army and the relief could not be betrayed. 'You're a damned fool, RSM. What about your son?'

'He's a bit too young to fight yet, sir.' Harper grinned, and Sharpe had to look away so that he did not return the grin.

'No pincers, sir!' Frederickson sounded disappointed, though Sharpe suspected Sweet William had made no kind of real search for the implement. 'You'll want us under way, sir?'

'Inland. Sergeant Harper!'

'Sir?'

'Attach yourself to Captain Frederickson's Company and assume whatever rank he sees fit to give you.'

'Sir!'

Like beasts of burden the Riflemen shouldered packs, canteens, weapons, greatcoats and supplies. They went eastwards into the trees, then northwards on the country road that straggled between the few marsh hamlets of this barren coast.

It was not much of a road, merely a rutted cart track that wound between brush and pine and edged past great swamps where long-legged wading birds flapped slowly into the winter air as the Riflemen passed. The Green Jackets marched fast, as they were trained to march, and always, a quarter mile ahead, the picquets signalled back towards Sharpe that the road was clear.

It seemed strange to be this deep in France. This was the land of Bonaparte, the enemy land, and between Sharpe and Bordeaux, indeed between Sharpe and Paris, there were no friendly troops. A single squadron of enemy cavalry could cut this march into butcher's offal, yet the Green Jackets marched undisturbed and unseen.

'If we go at this pace,' Frederickson said, 'we'll overtake the Marines.'

'It had occurred to me,' Sharpe said mildly.

The eye-patched man stared at Sharpe. 'You're not thinking of taking the . . .'

'No,' Sharpe interrupted. 'If Bampfylde wants to take the fort, he can. But if the map's right we have to go close to Arcachon, so we might take a look at the fort before we turn eastwards.'

Patrick Harper carried the picquets' packs and coats as punishment, but the extra weight made no difference to his marching pace. His tooth bothered him; the pain of that was foul and throbbing, but he had no other cares in the world. He had followed Sharpe because it was unthinkable to stay behind when Sharpe went off on his own. Harper had seen that happen before and the Major had nearly killed himself in Burgos Castle as a result. Besides, Jane Sharpe, giving him the oil of cloves, had suggested he stowed away, Isabella had insisted he stay with the Major, and Captain Frederickson had turned his blind eye to Harper's presence. Harper felt he was in his proper place; with Sharpe and with a column of Riflemen marching to battle.

Their green jackets and dark trousers melded with the cloud-darkened pines. The 60th had been raised for just such terrain, the American wilderness, and Sharpe, turning sometimes to watch the men, could see how well chosen the uniform was. At a hundred paces an unmoving man could be invisible. For a moment Sharpe felt the sudden pride of a Rifleman. The Rifles, he believed as an article of his soldier's faith, were simply, indisputably, the finest troops in all the world.

They fought like demons and were made more deadly because they were trained, unlike other infantry, to fight independently. These men, in danger, would not look to an officer or sergeant for instruction, but would know, thanks to their training, just what to do. They were mostly squat and ugly men, toothless and pinched-faced, villainous and foul-mouthed, but on a battlefield they were kings, and victory was their common coin.

They could fight and they could march. God, but they could march! In '09, trying to reach the carnage of Talavera, the Light Division had marched forty-two hilly miles in twenty-six hours and had arrived in good order, weapons primed, and ready to fight. These men marched thus now. They did it unthinkingly, not knowing that the pace they unconsciously assumed was the fastest marching pace of all the world's armies. They were Riflemen, the finest of the best, and they were going north to war.

While to their west, on the less happy trails that edged the tumbled dunes, the Marines faltered.

It was not their fault. For months now, on a diet of worm-infested biscuit, rotting meat, foul water and rum, they had been immured in the forecastles of the great ships that weathered the Biscay storms. They were not hardened to marching, and the sand they crossed gave treacherous footing and chafed their boots on softened skin. Their muskets, all of the heavy Sea Service pattern, seemed to grow heavier by the mile. Their chest straps, whitened and taut, constricted labouring lungs. It was a cold day, but sweat stung their eyes while the muscles at the backs of their legs burned like fire. Some of the men were burdened by ropes and grapnel hooks that they would use to scale the fort's wall instead of the long ladders that Bampfylde had deemed unnecessary for the Marines.

'We shall call a halt.' Captain Bampfylde did not do it for the men's benefit, but his own. If they laboured, he suffered. His handmade boots had rubbed his right heel raw and raised blisters on his toes. The leather band of his bicorne hat was like a ring of steel and his white breeches were cutting into his crotch like a sawhorse.

The captain was regretting his intrepidity. He had been eager to lead these men into battle, and that could not be done from the deck of the *Vengeance* any more than it could be done from the quarterdeck of the *Scylla*. That frigate, under Captain Grant, would nose into the Arcachon channel to draw the fire of what few defenders might infest the fort's bastions. Once those defenders were occupied with the frigate, and while their gaze was fastened seawards, the Marines would assault the empty landward ramparts. It was that assault which would capture the imagination of the British public when it was printed in the *Naval Gazette*, not the old story of a ship bombarding a battery.

Captain of Marines Palmer saluted Bampfylde. 'We're behind time, sir.'

'God damn it, Palmer, if I require your contribution then I shall ask for it!'

'Sir!' Palmer was unmoved by Bampfylde's anger. Neil Palmer was ten years older than Bampfylde and too experienced to be worried by the petulance of yet another ambitious young captain who resented the fame gained by Nelson's band of brothers. 'I'll put picquets out, sir?'

'Do it!' Bampfylde subsided against the trunk of a tree. He wanted to haul off his precious boots and dabble his sore feet in the shallows of the sea, but he dared not betray such weakness in front of his men.

'Water, sir?' Lieutenant Ford offered a canteen.

'After you, Ford.' Bampfylde knew such behaviour was proper, and he was a man eager to be seen to behave heroically in all things.

He consoled himself that his discomfort was a small price to pay for the renown that he would win this day. The Marines might come late to the fortress, but the fortress would fall just the same, and the blisters on his feet would be forgotten in the blaze of glory. He opened his watch, saw they had already rested ten minutes, but decided a few more minutes could not hurt. He stretched out tired legs, tipped his hat forward, and polished the news of victory that he would write this night.

While a hundred yards away, standing on a sudden rise

of sandy soil that made a bare ridge through the thin pines, Captain Palmer stared at the countryside through a heavy, ancient telescope. Far to the north, beyond the fading ridges of sand and conifers, a rainstorm misted the land like a vast curtain. The rain lifted for a brief instant and Palmer thought he saw the malevolent, dark shape of the fort hull-down on the horizon, but, as the rain closed again on his view, he could not be certain of what he had seen.

He swung the glass inland. Two miles away, suddenly visible where the trees gave way to a stretch of marshy, glistening ground, he saw the tiny shapes of green jacketed Riflemen marching forward. Palmer was envious. He wished he was with them and not tied to Bampfylde's apron strings, but then a bark of command from the dunes made him collapse his glass and turn back towards his men.

'We'll attack,' Bampfylde told Ford and Palmer, 'at dusk.'

'Yes, sir.' Both men knew that the *Scylla* had been ordered into the channel two hours before sundown, but there was no hope of meeting that rendezvous. They must just march, on blistering, aching feet, and be consoled that the night would bring them victory, supplies from the ships, and blessed rest in the shelter of a captured stronghold.

In the Teste de Buch Commandant Henri Lassan told his beads, yet somehow could not shift from his thoughts a line from an essay by Montaigne that he had read the night before. It had said something about a whole man's life being nothing more than an effort to build a house of death, and he feared, without letting that fear affect his behaviour, that the Teste de Buch might be his house of death this day. He told himself that such fears were entirely natural in a man facing battle for the first time.

He knelt in the tiny whitewashed chapel that, in the early heady years of the Revolution, had been turned first into a Temple of Reason and then into a storeroom. The small red light of the Eternal Presence, that Lassan himself had caused to be placed in this shrine when he restored it as a chapel, took his thoughts back to prayer. If he should die today in this miserable, damp fort on the edge of France then that light was a sure promise of salvation. Beneath it a simple wooden crucifix stood on an altar that bore a frontal of plain white. It was an Easter frontal, used only because the fort had no other to put on the table beneath, yet somehow the Easter promise of resurrection was comforting to Commandant Henri Lassan as he rose from his knees.

He went into the courtyard. Rain had puddled the cobbles and streaked the inner walls dark. The fort seemed strangely empty. Lassan had sent the families of the garrison to the village so that no woman or child should be struck by enemy fire. The tricolour, that had not flown these past days, was wrapped on to the halyard ready to be hoisted when the first cannon slammed back on its carriage.

'Sir!' Lieutenant Gerard called from the western rampart.

Lassan walked up the stone ramp that made it easy for heated shot to be carried from the furnace to the guns. Not that he had enough men left to tend the fire, but cold shot should be sufficient for any vessel that tried to brave the narrow, shoal-ridden waters of the channel.

'There, sir.' The lieutenant pointed seawards where, westering from the horizon, came a British frigate. The warship's new topsails were as white as the bone in her teeth that was flashing bright as the wind drove the boat towards the channel entrance.

'That's the frigate that pursued the *Thuella*, isn't it?' Lassan asked.

'Yes, sir,' Gerard said. '*Scylla*.'

Beyond the frigate were other ships. One, Lassan could see, was a ship of the line; one of the great vessels that had put a noose around the Emperor's conquests. Lassan would rather be pouring his shot into that great belly than into the frigate's slender and fragile beauty, but the Commandant would take what targets he could in this day's fight for God and the Emperor. 'Wait till she passes the outer mark.'

'Sir.'

The *Scylla* moved closer, the giltwork of her figurehead gleaming, and Lassan knew the frigate had come to make him look one way while the Marines came from his rear, but he had an American warrior hidden in the woods and Lassan must put his trust in that unexpected ally. He knew that no Marine could pass Killick without shots being fired, and even if the Americans were pushed back then the noise of their battle would give Lassan a chance to man the ramparts by the fortress gate. For the moment that rampart was only garrisoned by three sick men.

If the *Scylla*'s attack was timed properly, Lassan thought, then the Marines must be close. Lassan looked south, but could see nothing untoward beyond the village, then he turned back seawards in time to watch the frigate's flying-jib shiver as it turned towards the channel. At the same time the *Scylla*'s great battle-ensign unfurled from an upper yard.

Lassan's men crouched by their guns. Their portfires seeped grey smoke into the air and Lassan knew how dry their mouths were and how fragile their bellies felt. On the frigate's forepeak he could see men clustered around the chasing guns. The officers on the quarterdeck, Lassan knew, would have donned their best uniforms in honour of their enemy while, deep in the frigate's bowels, the surgeon would be waiting by his razor-sharp scalpels.

The fortress waited. A corporal stood by the flagpole ready, at the first bellow of the guns, to hoist the standard of France. A gull, wide wings still, rode the soft wind above the channel.

Lassan imagined the red coats of Marines in the Americans' gunsights, then forgot what happened to his south because the frigate's graceful profile was changing and the white wave at her bows was cutting into the fretted, churning tiderace of the channel.

The frigate seemed to shudder as she met the full force of the Arcachon ebb, then the bellying sails plunged her on-wards and the long, reaching spar of the *Scylla*'s bowsprit bisected the tarred elm pole that marked the inner shoal and Lieutenant Gerard's voice, harsh and proud, shouted the order to fire.

The French gunners touched portfires to vents, and the battle of Arcachon had begun.

CHAPTER 6

The bellow of the guns rolled like thunder over the rain-sodden land. Instinctively, without any orders, the Riflemen knelt as if to shelter from artillery.

Sharpe ran. His metal scabbard flapped at his side, his rifle slipped from his shoulder to dangle at his elbow, and his pack thumped on to the small of his back.

Sergeant Rossner, leading the small picquet that spied the route ahead, was crouching by a straggle of furze that lined the roadside at the crest of a gentle rise. He gave a Germanic grunt as Sharpe dropped beside him then a jerk of his half-shaven chin to indicate the source of the thunder.

Not that Sharpe needed any such indication. Darkly streaked smoke billowed from the landscape a mile and a half ahead and to Sharpe's left. Directly ahead of him, and reaching across the whole view, lay the silvered waters of the Arcachon basin, made visible suddenly by this rise in the road, but Sharpe stared only at the fortress, seemingly half-buried in the encroaching sand, and at the white-sailed frigate that coughed her own billow of whiter smoke to meld with the fort's darker gusts. 'Marines, eh?' The German sergeant showed his disgust by spitting on to the road.

Sharpe took out his telescope as Frederickson crouched beside him. From this landward side the Teste de Buch fort looked hardly formidable. It was built low within its protective glacis of packed earth and sand off which, as Sharpe watched, the small shot of the frigate bounced like cricket balls.

The smoke from the fort's guns drifted northwards, leaving the channel clear for the gunners' aim. Four guns only were working, but they were served with a quick skill that betrayed the presence of real gunners. God damn Bampfylde's fisherman, Sharpe thought, for the Teste de Buch was lethal still. It was doing the *Scylla* damage, while the frigate could make small impression on its massive walls.

Sharpe trained the telescope left. He paused as he saw a throng of people, drably dressed, then realized, from the heavy skirts worn by most of the crowd, that he watched the villagers who, in turn, watched the uneven battle from the crest of the dunes beside the channel. Sharpe looked further south, seeking the bright coats of the Marines, then checked the glass again.

He saw another small crowd of people, but these were not watching the frigate's struggle, but instead seemed to be crowded at the edge of a group of dark pines. Some, a few, had strolled further north to watch the battle in the channel, but they had chosen a poor vantage point to witness a sight that must be rare in their harsh lives.

'Why?' he spoke aloud.

'Sir?' Frederickson asked.

Sharpe was wondering why villagers, witnessing a contest that would be told to their grandchildren as a great happening in the village's history, chose such a strange place to watch the event. Most of the villagers had gone to the dunes, seeking the best view, yet a sizeable few were huddled there at the wood's edge. He stared at them, making out a shape beneath the tree shadows. 'William? That wood, where the people are, tell me what you see?'

Frederickson took the precious glass and trained it. He stared for twenty seconds, then shook his head. 'It looks like a bloody limber!'

'Doesn't it?' Sharpe took the glass back and, his guess reinforced by Frederickson's puzzled confirmation, saw more clearly the box shape slung between the high wheels. He had seen those objects before; the small carts that carried the ready ammunition to French guns. 'Bloody Bampfylde,' he said as he stared at the shape beneath the trees, 'has been

88

wrong about everything. The fort is defended, they're not bloody militia, and I'll wager you a year's pay they've got a damned ambush waiting for the web-foots.' Sharpe swept the telescope right again to look at the fort. He could just see the gunners working on the water-bastion. Above them, sluggish in the falling breeze, the tricolour was bright, while closer, on the ramparts above the fort's gate, he could see no one.

He lowered the glass a fraction. It was hard to tell from this low vantage-point, but the approach to the fort seemed to go through a humped landscape of wind-drifted dunes. One thing was certain; which was that all French eyes were glued seawards. 'I think we ought to have a snap at it.'

Frederickson grinned. 'No ladders?' He mentioned it not to discourage Sharpe, but to encourage a solution.

Sharpe raised the glass. 'They've kept the drawbridge down.' Where the approach road crossed the inner ditch a solid wooden bridge was suspended by chains. It led to a closed gate. The fact of the drawbridge being down reinforced Sharpe's suspicion that another French force was hidden in the woods. If that force was pushed backwards by the Marines then their horses would drag the field guns over the bridge and into the fort's safety.

Sharpe closed the telescope and slid the brass shutters over its lenses. What he planned was risky, even foolhardy, but the Marines marched into ambush and the fort would never again be so unprepared for a surprise attack. Once the hidden field guns opened fire then the garrison would know the enemy was at their rear and men would hurry to the land defences and slide their muskets over the wall.

The road ahead dropped to a stone mill that stood beside a small stream. Beyond that were pale, poor meadows where broken byres served a handful of thin cattle. Beyond that again were the masts of the coastal shipping huddled where another village, betrayed by smoke from its chimneys, lay at the basin's edge. The Riflemen must cross the stream, slip through the scant cover of the meadows, then work their way into the sandy waste about the fort. Sharpe smiled. 'To be truthful I don't know how we get over the bloody wall.'

'Knock on the front door?' Frederickson suggested.

Sharpe pushed his telescope into the tin box that protected it from harm, then into his pocket. 'Send two good men south to warn Bampfylde. Then we go down the slope in small groups. Open order. Rendezvous at the first cattle shed.' He had a growing suspicion that this was a task best left to a small group, a very small group. Sharpe turned. 'Sergeant Harper!'

The huge Irishman, grinning with anticipation, loped up the road. 'Sir?'

'You wanted to be killed, so come with me.'

'Yes, sir.'

Sharpe and Harper were going to war.

The guns of the Teste de Buch fired shot weighing thirty-six pounds, each shot propelled by ten pounds and two ounces of black powder. The iron balls, striking the *Scylla*, splintered oak like matchwood, threw cannon barrels off carriages, and made carnage among the gun crews.

They were deadly weapons that graced Lassan's semi-circular water-bastion. Each was mounted on a traverse and slide. The traverse was hinged at the embrasure in the fort's wall, and wheeled at its rear so that the crew could swivel the whole gun to face anywhere within its designated arc of fire. The traversing wheels, iron bound, had ground deep, semi-circular grooves into the stone. For this battle the guns were slewed right to fire south-west and Lassan's men had hammered iron pegs into holes drilled in the curving grooves so that the traverses, under the guns' recoil, did not swing out of true.

The recoil was soaked up by the slide. A field gun, or a gun aboard a ship, was mounted on wheels and the hammer of the shot's explosion in the breech would drive the weapon fiercely backwards. After each shot the crew must manhandle the gun forward again, aim it again, and all the time the crews were swabbing out and reloading, but not with these guns. Lassan's great weapons also had wheels, but the wheels fitted over wooden ramps that sloped up towards the rear of the traverse. The recoil slammed the guns backwards and gravity ran them down into place again. And again, and again, and another thirty-six pound ball of iron shivered the *Scylla* as Lassan's monsters belched flame and smoke across the waters of the channel.

The smoke of the guns drifted northwards, but, in that strange phenomenon that all gunners knew and none could ever explain, the very firing of the guns seemed to still the wind. The smoke thickened before the embrasures, making a filthy-smelling fog that obliterated the target from the gunners' view.

The blinding fog did not matter. Henri Lassan had thought long about the science of gunnery and had ordered white lines painted on the granite bastions. A similar pattern of lines was painted on the barracks' roof from where, unobstructed by the smoke, a sergeant watched the target and shouted out the alignment. 'Three!' he bellowed, and 'three!' the gun captains shouted, and four handspikes wrenched the eye-pins from the drilled holes and four other handspikes levered the traverses about until the iron wheel was flush with the white-line marked with the numeral three, then the pins were dropped into new holes and the guns, despite the fog of war, hammered their shot with deadly accuracy.

'Two!'

The shout told Lassan that the target was moving and he guessed, correctly, that the frigate was bearing away. He walked southwards, away from his gunsmoke, to see the two-decked *Vengeance* raise her gunports. That battleship was beyond Cap Ferrat and far beyond range. He watched. The great slab-side, chequered black and white, disappeared in one great clap of smoke, but, as Lassan had suspected, the broadside fell uselessly into the sea. 'Keep firing!'

'One!' the sergeant shouted from the roof and the crews levered at the vast guns as the boys ran up the stone ramp with more charges. A ball from the frigate rumbled overhead, another struck the stone of the embrasure nearest Lassan with a crack that made his heart pulse warm fear through his chest, but most of the frigate's shots were uselessly striking the sea wall or glancing off the southern glacis.

'She's gone!' the sergeant shouted.

'Cease fire!' Lassan shouted, and the thunder ended suddenly. The smoke cleared with painful slowness to show that the frigate, sorely wounded, had gone south beyond the arc of the big guns. Lassan contemplated manning some of the twenty-four pounders on his southern ramparts, then saw the shot-torn foresails fill with air again and knew that the British captain, under orders to keep the fort's gunners busy, was heading back into the channel. The sight of those torn sails and flying severed cables made Lassan think that some of his shots had been going high.

'Lower the barrels, Lieutenant!' Lassan wanted to pump his shots into that fragile hull.

The *Scylla*'s guns were run out, ready to fire when the frigate wore, but the bow-chasers, long-nines, barked defiance. The balls cracked on the bastion's stone, doing no damage, then the sergeant on the barrack roof again had the enemy in his line of aim. 'One!' the sergeant shouted.

'Fire!' Gerard bellowed. The great barrels jerked back and up, the wheels rumbled as they rolled back down the slide, and the smoke, that stank like rotten eggs, pumped again into the cold air. Lassan's garrison might have been stripped to the bone, he might not even have crews for every gun, but he would do his duty and he would show the British that an under-manned fort could still hurt them and still, by the grace of the good God and in the service of the French Emperor, win battles.

*

The handcart was made of splintered, fragile wood that was held to uncertain unity by bent, rusted nails and with lashings of thin, frayed, black twine. Some of the wheel-spokes were broken.

Sharpe pulled the handcart out of the cattle byre and listened to the ghastly screech of the wooden axle that ran through two ungreased wooden blocks. He supposed that the cart was used to take hay from these meadows into the village, or perhaps bedding straw to the fort, but it had been abandoned through the frost months to lie in this byre where the spiders had made thick webs on its spokes and handles. 'It could work.' Sharpe tested the small bed of the cart and it seemed solid enough. 'Except we don't speak French.'

'Sweet William does, sir,' Harper said, then, seeing Sharpe's face, corrected himself. 'Captain Frederickson croaks Frog, sir.'

A group of armed men, approaching a fort, invited hostility, but two men, pushing a wounded comrade on a handcart, posed no threat.

'Jesus.' Frederickson's voice was awed when, arriving at the cattle byre, he heard Sharpe's plan. 'We're supposed to walk up and ask for a bloody sawbones?'

'You suggested knocking on the front door,' Sharpe said. 'So why not?'

The Riflemen still drifted down the gentle slope. They came in scattered groups, spread out in the chain formation they would use in battle, and no alarm had been raised at the sight. Sharpe doubted whether any Frenchman had even seen the dark shapes flit down the slope. Once on the lower ground, over the tiny stream and hidden by the ditches that were edged by straggling blackthorn hedges, the Riflemen were invisible. The fort still thundered its huge noise.

'What we need,' Sharpe said, 'is blood.' He was reckoning that the fort would not refuse entry to a mortally wounded man, but mortal wounds were usually foul with blood and, in search of it, both officers looked instinctively to Patrick Harper.

Who stared back with a slow and horrified understanding. 'No! Holy Mother, no!'

'It has to come out, Patrick.' Sharpe spoke in a voice of sweet reason.

'You're not a surgeon, sir. Besides!' Harper's swollen face suddenly looked cheerful. 'There's no pincers, remember?'

Sweet William unbuckled his pouch. 'The barber-surgeons of London, my dear Sergeant, will pay six shillings and six pence for a ten-ounce bag of sound teeth taken from corpses. You'd be surprised how many fashionable London ladies wear false teeth taken from dead Frogs.' Frederickson flourished a vile-looking pair of pincers. 'They're also useful for a spot of looting.'

'God save Ireland.' Harper stared at the pincers.

Captain Frederickson smiled. 'You'll be doing it for England, Sergeant Harper, for your beloved King.'

'Christ, no, sir!'

'Strip to the waist,' Sharpe ordered.

'Strip?' Harper had backed into the corner of the filthy byre.

'We need to have your chest soaked in blood,' Sharpe said as though this was the most normal procedure in the world. 'As soon as the tooth's pulled, Patrick, let the blood drip on to your skin. It won't take long.'

'Oh, Christ in his heaven!' Harper crossed himself.

'It doesn't hurt, man!' Frederickson took out his two false teeth and grinned at Harper. 'See?'

'That was done with a sword, sir. Not bloody pincers!'

'We could do it with a sword.' Sharpe said it helpfully.

'Oh, Mary mother of God! Christ!' Harper, seeing nothing but evil intent on his officers' faces, knew that he must mutiny or suffer. 'You'd be giving me a wee drink first?'

'Brandy?' Frederickson held out his canteen.

Harper seized the canteen, uncorked it, and tipped it to his mouth.

'Not too much,' Frederickson said.

'It's not your bloody tooth. With respect, sir.'

Frederickson looked at Sharpe. 'Do you wish to play the surgeon, sir?'

'I've never actually drawn a tooth.' Sharpe, in front of the curious Riflemen who had gathered to watch Harper's discomfiture, kept his voice very formal.

Frederickson shrugged. 'We should have a screw-claw, of course, but the pincers work well enough on corpses. Mind you, there is a knack to it.'

'A knack?'

'You don't pull.' Frederickson demonstrated his words with graphic movements of the rusted pincers. 'You push the tooth towards the jawbone, twist one way, the other, then slide it out. It's really not hard.'

'Jesus!' The big Irish sergeant had gone pale as rifle-cartridge paper.

'I think,' Sharpe said it with some misgivings, 'that as Sergeant Harper and I have been together so long, I ought to do the deed. Push, twist, and pull?'

'Precisely, sir.'

It took five minutes to persuade and prepare Harper. The Irishman showed no fear in battle; he had gone grim-faced into the carnage of a dozen battlefields and come out victorious, but now, faced with the little business of having a tooth pulled, he sat terrified and shaking. He clung to Frederickson's brandy as if it alone could console him in this dreadful ordeal.

'Show me the tooth.' Sharpe spoke solicitously.

Harper eventually opened his mouth and pointed to an upper tooth that was surrounded by inflamed gum. 'There.'

Sharpe used a handle of the pincers and, as gently as he could, tapped the tooth. 'That one?'

'Jesus Christ!' Harper bellowed and jerked away. 'Bloody kill me, you will!'

'Language, Sergeant!' Frederickson was trying not to laugh while the other Riflemen were grinning with keen enjoyment.

Sharpe reversed the pincers. The jaws, somewhat battered

and rusted, were saw-toothed for better purchase. It was a handy instrument for burglary and doubtless ideal for the procurement of false teeth from mangled corpses, but whether it was truly suitable for a surgical operation Sharpe could not yet say. 'It can't be worse than having a baby,' he said to Harper. 'And Isabella didn't make this fuss.'

'Women don't mind pain,' the Irishman said. 'I do.'

'Don't grip the fang too hard,' Frederickson observed helpfully, 'or you might smash it, sir. It's the devil of a job to fetch out the remnants of a broken tooth. I saw it happen to Jock Callaway before Salamanca and it quite spoilt Jock's battle. You remember Jock, sir?'

'The 61st?' Sharpe asked.

'Died of the fever next winter, poor fellow.' Frederickson stooped to see what was happening.

The word 'fever' shot through Sharpe's head like a death-knell, but this was no time for such thoughts. 'Open your mouth, Sergeant.'

'You'll be gentle?' Harper's voice was sullen and mutinous.

'I will be as gentle as a new-born lamb. Now open your bloody gob.'

The huge mouth with its yellowed teeth opened. The Irishman's eyes were wary and a faint groan, half a moan, escaped as Sharpe brought the pincers up.

Slowly, very slowly, doing his utmost not to jar the offending tooth, Sharpe closed the vicious jaws on that part of the tooth not hidden by the swollen gum-tissue. 'That's not too bad, is it?' he asked soothingly. He gripped the handles tight, but not too tight, and felt a faint tremor run through the huge man. 'Ready?'

He pushed upwards. He could smell Harper's breath and feel the rank fear from the man. He sympathized with it. Sharpe had once had a tooth pulled in India and he remembered the pain as vividly as any wound taken in battle. He pushed harder. The tooth did not move, though

Harper quivered as he loyally tried to push against Sharpe's pressure.

'Harder,' Frederickson muttered.

Sharpe pushed harder, the metal jaws slipped up into the swollen gums, and the pincers were wrenched away as Harper bellowed and flailed to one side. 'Jesus and his bloody saints! Christ!' The sergeant had his hands to his mouth that was trickling blood. 'God in heaven!' He was keening with the sudden agony.

'It slipped,' Sharpe said in apologetic explanation.

'Bloody near killed me!' Harper swallowed more brandy, then spat a potent mixture of blood and alcohol on to the ground. 'Jesus!'

'Perhaps I should try,' Frederickson offered. Lieutenant Minver, like his men, grinned.

'God damn all officers! All!' Harper was in a blaze of anger now. 'Bloody murdering bastards!' He picked up the pincers, opened his mouth, and probed with a finger.

He flinched.

Sharpe drew back. The Riflemen, no longer laughing, watched as the huge, bare-chested man put the pincers over his own tooth. The big hand closed and Harper's blue eyes seemed to grow wider. He pushed and Sharpe heard a distinct crack, like gristle snapping, then the pincers were being twisted right and left, Harper was moaning, and again there were the tiny sounds of tissue parting or bone grating.

Sharpe held his breath. No one moved. A French child of ten could have taken these prize troops captive at this moment as the bare-chested Harper, shaking with the pain and cold, began to pull.

The Irishman's hand trembled. A bead of blood pulsed at his lower lip, another, then in a great groan and a gush of pus and blood, the huge tooth tore free. Scraps of flesh were attached to its branching roots, but blood, bright red blood was pouring on to Harper's chest in great rivulets that steamed in the cold air.

'Get him on to the wagon!' Sharpe ordered.

'Christ in his heaven!' The pain had brought tears to Harper's eyes. He stood, coughing blood, a fearful sight. He was weeping now, not out of weakness, but in anger and pain. He was blood smothered; steaming with warm blood, coughing blood, his face and chest soaked in blood.

'You shouldn't go,' Frederickson said to Sharpe, meaning that it was foolish for the two senior officers to risk themselves at the same time.

Sharpe ignored the well-meant advice. 'Lieutenant Minver. As soon as we have the gate open, you charge! Swords fitted!'

'Sir.' The lieutenant, a thin dark man, smiled nervously. Harper lay on the cart, shivering.

'Take your men to the edge of the sand,' Sharpe said as he took off his pack, his officer's sash, snake-buckled belt, his Rifleman's jacket, and his shako. Frederickson was doing the same. 'Sergeant Rossner? You bring this equipment.'

'Sir!'

Harper's seven-barrelled gun, loaded and primed, was put beside the Irishman's bloodstained right hand. His rifle was on the left side of the cart where Sharpe's sword, drawn from the scabbard, lay easily to hand. Sharpe wanted to give the impression of three men bringing the victim of an accident from the ambush party. Yet success depended on the French guards seeing only the dreadful blood on Patrick Harper.

Harper, lying belly up on the cart, was in danger of choking on his own blood. He spat a thick gob, turned his head, and spat again. 'Spit onto your chest! Don't waste it!' Sharpe said. Harper growled in mutiny, then spat a satisfying lump of blood down to his navel. Sharpe took one handle of the cart, Frederickson the other, and Sharpe nodded. 'Move.'

The firing from the fort had stopped which meant, Sharpe knew, that either the frigate was out of range or else was sinking. There was no sound from the ambush site.

The cart screeched foully on the rough track that led past scrawny alders towards the Teste de Buch. Far away, over the houses and beyond the dunes, Sharpe saw a shiver of white which he knew must be the frigate's topsails, then heard a bellow of thunder and saw a blossom of smoke which told him Grant had opened fire again. Captain Grant, at least, was doing his duty. Even at the cost of his ship and men he was drawing the fort's fire, and his success was measured by the sudden clap of thunder as the huge fortress guns opened their own fire again.

The cart axle screeched fit to wake the dead, bounced on the uneven road, and Harper groaned. His right hand, streaked with bloody rivulets, groped for his seven-barrelled gun and Sharpe, seeing the movement, knew the huge Irishman was recovering. 'Well done, Sergeant.'

'Didn't mean to be rude to you, sir.' Harper choked on blood as he said the words.

'Yes, you did,' Frederickson cheerfully answered for Sharpe. 'So would any man. Now shut up. You're supposed to be dying.'

Patrick Harper said nothing more as the cart slewed round a corner, over a muddy rut, and up on to the harder track that led straight to the bridge over the fort's inner ditch. The wind gusted, bringing the stench of powder smoke in its cold touch. No sound came from the south and Sharpe knew the Marines were still far from Arcachon. If the *Scylla* was to be saved from further punishment, then the Rifles would have to do the job.

They were already within cannon-range of the fort, but no gunners stared from the deep embrasures. 'Run,' Sharpe said. 'Run as if he's dying.'

'He is,' Harper groaned.

Sharpe had to push hard to keep up with Frederickson's pace and he saw a head appear on the fortress wall, he saw the tricolour lift to the smoke-fouled wind, then Sweet William, beside him, was shouting in breathless French and Sharpe knew that it was madness for three men to take on one of the coastal forts of mainland France, but he was committed now, inside musket range, and all they could do was push on, pray, then fight like the soldiers that they were; the best.

CHAPTER 7

They stopped ignominiously on the sand-gritted planks of the drawbridge.

The gates did not open, they could go no further, and Sharpe and Frederickson, chests heaving and breath misting into great plumes from the effort of pushing the obstinate cart with Harper's weight, could only stare up at a puzzled face which appeared on the ramparts.

Frederickson shouted to the sentry in French, an answer was made, and Harper, fearing a sudden musket blast from above, groaned horribly on the cart. The blood on his huge chest was drying to a cracked crust.

'He wants to know,' Frederickson spoke to Sharpe with astonishment in his voice, 'whether we're the Americans.'

'Yes!' Sharpe shouted. 'Yes, yes!'

'Attendez!' The guard's head disappeared.

Sharpe turned to look through the notch made where the approach road cut through the glacis. He stared at the place where the villagers stood by the trees and where he had dimly discerned the shape of a gun's limber among the pines. 'The Americans are manning those guns?' He too sounded astonished.

Frederickson shrugged. 'Must be.'

Sharpe turned back, his boots making a hollow sound on the thick planks of the drawbridge. To right and left the flooded inner ditch stretched. The ditch water, fed by a rivulet from the millstream, seemed shallow enough, but it would still be a cloying obstacle to men trying to assault the gaunt, rough-faced wall of the fort's enceinte.

The fortress guns bellowed to Sharpe's left, jetting smoke

and flame towards the frigate that was now beyond Cap Ferrat. The battle had become a long-range duel as Grant teased the fort and, doubtless, cursed the land force for their late arrival.

'What's the crapaud bastard doing?' Harper growled softly.

'Gone to fetch the officer of the guard?' Sharpe guessed. Harper shivered. The light was dying in the west, a cold evening promised frost in the night, and the huge Irishman was stripped to the waist. 'Not long now,' Sharpe said, the words spoken more in nervousness than for comfort.

Suddenly a bolt clanged, scraped, then a bar thudded to the ground from its brackets.

'Christ!' Frederickson's voice betrayed relief that their ruse, so quickly devised and then made possible by Harper's pain, was working.

'Wait for my word.' Sharpe said it softly as he saw Harper's muscles, beneath their crazed and shivering quilt of dried blood, suddenly tense.

The hinges of the gate squealed like a tormented soul. Lieutenant Minver, two hundred yards away, would see the huge door leafing open and should already be moving. 'Now,' Sharpe said.

The French guard was eager to help the wounded man. The guard himself was injured, his leg setting in plaster, and he gestured at the cast as if to explain the slowness with which he tugged the huge, iron-studded gate open.

Harper, rolling from the cart, did not see the thick plaster on the man's leg, nor did he see the welcoming, reassuring smile; he only saw a man in an enemy jacket, a man who barred a door that must be opened, and Harper came up from the roadway with a sword-bayonet in his right hand and the Frenchman gave a horrid, pathetic sigh as the twenty-three inch blade, held like a long dagger, ripped into his belly. Sharpe saw the blood spilling like water on the cobbles of the archway as he pushed his full weight on to the half-opened gate.

Harper twisted the bayonet free and left the guard bleeding and twitching on the drawbridge. He kicked the man's musket into the ditch, then fetched his rifle and seven-barrelled gun from the cart. Frederickson, sword in hand, dragged the empty handcart into the tunnel that pierced the ramparts. No one had seen them, no one raised the alarm; they had taken the garrison utterly by surprise.

Sharpe bolted both doors open. His rifle was slung, his sword naked, and at any second he expected a shout of alarm or a musket shot, but the three Riflemen were undetected. They smiled at each other, made nervous by success, then their ears were punched by the shattering pulse of air as the fortress guns fired towards the *Scylla*. Harper hefted his seven-barrelled gun. 'I'll teach those bastards how to fire guns.'

'Sergeant!' Sharpe called, but Harper was already running, gun cocked, towards the courtyard.

A shout sounded from the sand-dunes and, at the same instant, two muskets coughed above Sharpe. He realized there must be other guards on the gate's roof, men who could see Minver's assault approaching, and Sharpe looked for a route that would take him to the ramparts. A low, arched doorway lay to his right and he ducked through it.

He found himself in a guardroom. A wooden musket rack, varnished and polished, held eight muskets upright. A table was littered with playing cards before a black-leaded pot-bellied stove that silted smoke from an ill-fitting chimney pipe. Stairs climbed through an arch on the far side of the room and, exchanging his sword for the rifle, Sharpe took the steps at a rush.

He could hear, above him, the rattle of ramrods in barrels. The stairs turned a right angle, the sky was grey overhead, then a moustached face, just ten feet away, turned towards the sound of feet on the stairs and Sharpe pulled the rifle's trigger and saw the man twitch backwards. More blood.

A movement to his left as he cleared the stairs made Sharpe twist round. A second man was desperately pulling a ramrod free of his musket's long barrel, then, seeing that he could not free his weapon of the encumbrance, the Frenchman just raised the gun to his shoulder.

Sharpe fell and rolled to his right.

The musket banged and flamed and the ramrod, which could have impaled Sharpe like a skewer, cartwheeled across the inner courtyard to clang against the stone ramp.

'Non! Non!' The man was backing away now as Sharpe, unscathed, rose from the stones with his sword in his right hand.

'Non!' The guard dropped his musket, raised his hands, and Sharpe accepted the man's surrender by the simple expedient of tipping him over the ramparts into the flooded ditch twenty feet below. Minver's Riflemen, pouches, scabbards, canteens and horns flapping as they ran, were on the road now; the fastest men already close to the glacis.

Sharpe turned towards the sound of the fortress guns. He could see an empty wall on which vast, cold guns stood mute. At the wall's end was a small stone citadel, little more than a covered shelter for sentries, and beyond that was the semi-circular bastion that jutted into the waters of the Arcachon channel and from which the heavy guns fired. The French artillerymen, stunned, deafened and half blinded by their own firing, had still not seen the small slaughter at the gate. They swabbed and charged their vast weapons, intent only on the frigate that dared to defy them.

Then a voice screamed defiance at them. Some turned. The others, losing the rhythm of their tasks, twisted to see what had interrupted the work.

Patrick Harper had shouted at them in a voice that would have silenced hell itself, a voice that had called Battalions to order across the vast spaces of windy parade grounds, and the gunners stared with astonishment into the courtyard below where a blood-boltered giant seemed to hold a small cannon in his hands.

'Bastards!' Harper screamed the word, then pulled the seven-barrelled gun's trigger. The half-inch balls flayed up and out, fanning to strike the left hand gun crew. Two men fell, then Harper dropped the massive gun and unslung his rifle.

'Patrick!' Sharpe had seen a Frenchman on the barrack roof who knelt, carbine in hand, to aim downwards. 'Cover!'

Harper rolled right, looked up, and ran.

A French officer, commanding the big gun battery, stared at the blood-streaked giant, then to Sharpe, and the Rifleman saw the look of sheer surprise on the thin, pale face. Frederickson, sword in hand, was crossing the yard, careless of the carbine above him, and shouting to the gunners to surrender.

The French officer suddenly jerked, as though waking to find a nightmare real, and shouted at his men to forsake their cannons and snatch their carbines from racks beside the embrasures. Sharpe had forgotten how French gunners carried long-arms and he bellowed at Frederickson to take cover, then saw the flicker of movement as the Frenchman on the roof changed aim.

Sharpe twisted away, knowing the shot was aimed at himself. He had a glimpse of the foreshortened stab of flame with its aureole of smoke, then the carbine ball slashed across his forehead. One half inch closer and he would have been dead, killed by fragments of skull driven into his brain, but instead he staggered, stunned, and his vision was suddenly sheeted with scarlet as he twisted, fell, and heard the sword clang as it bounced on the rampart's stones. His head felt as if a red-hot poker had been slashed across his face. He was blind.

A pitiless stab of pain lanced in his head, making him moan. The blindness was making him panic, and his dizziness would not let him stand. He slumped against the wall and tasted thick, salty blood on his tongue. He scrabbled vainly for his fallen sword.

A French shout of command made him turn his face left, but he could see nothing. Carbines fired. A ball fluttered overhead, another slapped the wall beside him, then a Baker rifle's quick crack, that Sharpe had heard a million times before, sounded to his right and he could hear the scrape of boots on stone as the riflemen came into the courtyard. Another crack, a scream, and another Baker rifle had found a victim, then Frederickson was shouting orders.

A volley splintered the dusk, sparking pricks of flame from rifle muzzles, then half the Green Jackets went forward, their comrades covering them, and the long sword-bayonets were carried up the stone ramp and Sharpe heard them cheer and knew that the fort was taken. He was blind.

Slowly, fearfully, Sharpe raised a hand to his throbbing head and gouged at his right eye. He scraped blood away and saw a shimmer of light. His eyes were thick with blood, sealed by it, and he spat on a filthy hand and scraped at the gore to clear his right eye and dimly saw Frederickson's men scouring the water-bastion with their bayonets. He felt a pang of relief, clear as spring water, that he could see. He could see the enemy leaping from the embrasures, abandoning fort and guns, and he saw a shot from the *Scylla*, that had been firing vainly for ninety minutes, take the head from a Rifleman on the western ramparts. The body, streaming blood like a squirting wine-bag, tumbled down on to the courtyard's cobbles.

'Get the flag down!' Sharpe bellowed it. He was on his hands and knees, blood soaking his shirt and threatening to close his right eye again. 'The flag!'

Lieutenant Minver, understanding, cut the halyard with his sword so that the tricolour fluttered down. That would stop the *Scylla*'s guns.

'Close the gate!' Sharpe shouted again, and the effort lanced such quick agony through his skull that he sobbed. He shook his head, trying to clear the pain, but it pulsed like a needle of fire behind his eyes.

A massive volley sounded to the south and Sharpe, his head hurting with every move, twisted round to see the blossom of smoke from the grove of trees. 'Captain Frederickson! Captain Frederickson!'

Frederickson took the stairs to the upper rampart three at a time. 'Jesus!' He stooped beside Sharpe and tried to wipe the blood away from his face, but Sharpe, still on his hands and knees, twisted away. 'Minver's Company to the ramparts. Take yours and clear those damned American guns.' He saw Frederickson hesitate. 'Go!'

Frederickson went and Sharpe, the pain suddenly dreadful, realized that the *Scylla* had ceased fire and that the field guns had ended their fusillade. He leaned against the wall, closed his good eye, and let the pain come. He had captured a fort.

Cornelius Killick could have happily taken Nicolas Leblanc and wrung his damned French neck.

It was Leblanc's factory, at St Denis near Paris, that manufactured the potassium nitrate that was mixed with charcoal and sulphur to make gunpowder.

It was not that Cornelius Killick had ever heard of Nicolas Leblanc, but the American knew powder, and he knew, the instant that his guns fired, that French powder was fit only for July the Fourth fire-crackers. The potassium nitrate, saltpetre, was at fault, but that again Killick could not know, but he did know when a gun coughed instead of banged. He had charged the guns as he would his own guns, and as if he was using American powder, but he should have elevated the guns to compensate for the poor quality of the charges.

He had elevated the barrels slightly, knowing that the first shots, fired through cold metal, would go low, but he could never have guessed how low. The first blast of grapeshot, instead of taking the red-coated Marines in a storm of metallic death, spattered into the sand. Some of the balls bounced upwards, but Killick did not see a single body struck by grape.

Killick swore, for his troubles multiplied. The bastards must have known he was there. He had seen the first red jackets ten minutes before and waited for them to march unsuspecting into the clearing, but instead they had lined the trees at the far side and Killick, tired of the delay, had fired his opening volley at that tree line. And he had wasted it. He swore again.

His men were sponging out, ramming, and levering the guns back into their positions. A British musket fired and Killick heard the ball flicker through the pines above. Then more flames stabbed from the shrubs at the clearing's far side and the musket balls thudded into the sandy bank or thumped on trees or rained pine needles down on to the gunners.

Killick ran left. If the Marines were to attack him they would come this way, flitting through the trees, and the dusk would make their scarlet coats hard to see. He shouted at the left hand gun to slew round and cover the approach, then stared into the gathering darkness. He could see nothing.

Cornelius Killick was nervous. His men were nervous. This was not warfare as he knew it. Killick's war was out where the wind gave the advantage to the better man and where the dead went to the cleansing sea. It was not in this damned vale of shadows where the enemy could skulk and hide and creep and murder.

A twig cracked, he twisted, but it was only Marie from the village who stared with huge, worried eyes at him. 'Go back,' Killick barked.

'The fort,' Marie said.

'What about it?' Killick was searching the southern shadows, watching for the flicker that might betray an enemy movement.

'The flag's gone,' Marie said.

'Shot away,' Killick said, then ignored the girl's news because British muskets sparked and the far tree-line was puffed with clouds of powder smoke. 'Go back, Marie! Back!'

Some of the *Thuella*'s crew fired back, using the French muskets that were sold so widely in America. If only the bastards would show themselves, Killick thought, then his six guns could tear the guts out of them. 'Liam! Liam!' he shouted.

'Sir?'

'Do you see anything?' Killick ran through dead pine-needles towards his main battery.

'Only their bloody smoke. Bastards won't show themselves!'

A soldier, Killick thought, would know what to do at this point. Perhaps he should throw men into the trees, cutlasses and muskets ready, but what good would that do? They would simply become meat for the Marines' muskets. Perhaps, he thought, another volley would stir the bastards up. 'Liam? Aim high and fire!'

'Sir!'

The brass elevating screws were turned and the portfires touched vent tubes and the fire slipped down to the coarse powder that hammered more grapeshot to slice into the undergrowth across the clearing. A bird squawked and flapped heavily away from the shredded trees, but that was the only visible result of the volley.

Smoke drifted over the clearing. Good sense told Cornelius Killick that this was the moment to run like hell. He had lost his greatest weapon, surprise, and he risked losing much more, but he was not a man to admit failure. Instead he imagined victory. Perhaps, he thought, the bastards had gone. No muskets fired across the clearing now, no redcoats moved, nothing showed. Perhaps, astonished and shredded by the volleys of grape, the yellow-bellied bastards had turned and run. Killick licked dry lips, tested the surprising thought, and decided it must be the truth. 'We've beaten the bastards, lads!'

'Not these bastards, you haven't.'

Killick turned with the speed of a snake, then froze. Standing behind him was a one-eyed man whose face would have terrified an imp of Satan. Captain William Frederickson, in grim jest, always removed his eye-patch and false teeth before a fight and the lack of those cosmetics, added to the horror that was his eye-socket, gave him the face of a man come from a stinking and rotting grave. The Rifle officer's voice, Killick noticed in stunned astonishment, was oddly polite while, behind him and moving with fast confidence, green-jacketed men whose guns were tipped with long, brass-handled bayonets slipped between the trees.

Killick put a hand to his pistol's hilt and the one-eyed man shook his head. 'It would distress me to kill you. I have a certain sympathy for your Republic.'

Killick gave his opinion of Frederickson's sympathy in one short and efficacious word.

'It is the fortune of war,' Frederickson said. 'Sergeant Rossner! I want prisoners, not dead 'uns!'

'Sir!' The Riflemen, taking the Americans from the rear, and coming so unexpectedly with weapons ready, gave the *Thuella*'s crew no chance to fight. Docherty drew his sword, but Taylor's bayonet touched the Irishman's throat and the feral eyes of the Rifleman told the lieutenant just what would happen if he raised the blade. Docherty let it fall. Some of *Thuella*'s crew, unable to retreat into the clearing that was covered by the Marines' muskets, dropped their weapons and ran to shelter with the startled villagers.

'Who the hell are you?' Killick asked.

'Captain Frederickson, Royal American Rifles. You're supposed to offer me your sword.'

Killick succinctly gave his view of that suggestion, and Frederickson smiled. 'I can always take it from you. Do you command here?'

'What if I do?'

Killick's truculence only made Frederickson more patient. 'If you want to fight my lads, then I assure you they'll welcome the chance. They've been fighting for six years, and about the only consolation our Army offers to them is the plunder from dead enemies.'

'Shit,' said Killick. There was no fight to be had, for the Riflemen were already herding his gun crews back. One of the green-jacketed bastards, the one who had taken Liam

Docherty prisoner, was folding the Stars and Stripes into a bundle. Some of his men, Killick saw, were edging away with the villagers, but they had abandoned their weapons so as not to be taken for combatants. Cornelius Killick felt the impotence of a sailor doomed to fight out of water. He could have wept in anger and impotence and for the shame of seeing his flag taken. Instead, clinging to a shred of dignity, he plucked his sword from his scabbard and offered it, hilt first, to Frederickson. 'If you'd fought me at sea . . .' Killick began.

'. . . I would be your prisoner,' Frederickson politely finished the sentence. 'And if you give me your word that you will not attempt to escape, then you may keep your sword.'

Killick dutifully slid the blade back into its scabbard. 'You have my word.'

Frederickson took a silver whistle from the loop on his crossbelt and blew six blasts on it. 'Just to let our web-footed friends know that we've done their job.' He opened his pouch and took out an eye-patch and false teeth. 'You'll forgive my vanity?' Frederickson asked as he tied the eye-patch in place. 'Shall we go back now?'

'Back?'

'To the fort, of course. As my prisoner I can assure you that your treatment will be that of a gentleman.'

Killick stared at the Rifleman whose face, even with patch and teeth restored, was hardly reassuring. Cornelius Killick expected a British officer to be a supercilious poltroon, all airs and graces and high-spoken delicacies, and he was somewhat shaken to be faced with a man who looked as hard-bitten as this Rifleman. 'You give me your word we'll be treated properly?'

Frederickson frowned, as though the question were indelicate. 'You have my word as an officer.' He smiled suddenly. 'I can't speak for the food tonight, but doubtless there'll be wine in abundance. This is, after all, the Médoc, and the harvest was good this year or so I believe. Sergeant!' He gave a shrug of apology to Killick for thus turning away. 'Leave the guns to the web-foots! Back to the fort!'

'Sir!'

Cornelius Killick, who had hoped to be as successful on land as he was at sea, had met a Rifleman, and all he could do was light a cigar and console himself that, for a sailor, there was no disgrace in being bested ashore. But it irked all the same, God, how it irked!

And the Arcachon Basin, in which the *Thuella* was stranded, had fallen.

Henri Lassan, seeing his men cornered in their bastion and recognizing the import of the feared Green Jackets and their long, glittering bayonets, had known there was no future in fighting. 'Over! Over!' He pointed over the bastion and down to the strip of wind-drifted sand that edged the fort's western ramparts. Here, on the fort's seaward facing flank, there was no flooded ditch for the tidewater was better than any moat, and his gunners leaped from the embrasures to tumble heavily on the sand. Lassan, as he jumped, felt a sudden, keen pang for the loss of his books, then the wind was driven from him by the jar of his landing. Two of his men twisted their ankles, but they were safely helped into the dune's cover from where, the wounded men assisted by their comrades, Lassan led his men north. Two rifle bullets followed them, but a bark of command ordered the ceasefire.

The fortress had fallen, not to Marines, but to Green Jackets, and Lassan wondered how they had come so silently, and how they had pierced the defences without his knowledge, but that was useless speculation today, when he had failed in his task.

He had lost the Teste de Buch, but he could yet frustrate his enemy. He supposed they had come for the *chasse-marées* and Lassan, stumbling in the cloying sand, would go to Le Moulleau and there burn the boats.

Falling night brought cold rain to pit the sand with

tiny dark craters. The track wound through dunes, past discarded fish traps and the black ribs of rotted boats. The fishing village lay two miles north and Lassan could see the dense tangle of masts and yards where the *chasse-marées* had been moored by his orders. The owners of the boats mostly lived aboard, waiting and grumbling until they could be released back to their trade.

Vestiges of cannon smoke sifted north with Henri Lassan. The tide, he saw, was turning. Tiny waves rolled over the beds where mussels and oysters thrived. No more would the women bring him the flat baskets of shellfish and stop to gossip about the prices in the Arcachon town market or to whisper, with pretended shock, of the bedtime exploits of the American captain. Lassan wondered what had happened to Killick, but that speculation was as useless as wondering how the Teste de Buch had fallen. Commandant Henri Lassan, sword at his waist and pistol in his belt, had a task to do, and he went north in the gathering darkness to perform it.

And at Le Moulleau the *chasse-marée* crews mutinied. They gathered outside the white-painted Customs House, disused these many years because of the Royal Navy blockade, but still manned by two uniformed men who opened their heavy door to listen to the commotion outside. Behind the crews were the wooden pilings that edged the sheds where the shellfish were broken open and where the murmur swelled into an angry protest. The ships were their livelihoods. Without the ships they would starve, their children would starve, and their women would starve.

Lassan's men, embarrassed by their predicament, stared at the ground. Torches flared in brackets on the Customs House façade, casting a red light on angry faces. Rain spat from the south. Lassan, a reasonable and kind man, raised his hands. 'My friends!' He explained why the boats were needed, how the English would use the craft to make a bridge or to land their Army north of the Adour. 'What of your children then? What of your wives, eh? Tell me that?'

There was silence, except for the running of the tide and the hiss as rain hit the torches. The faces were suspicious. Lassan knew that the French forces were disliked by the French peasantry, for the Emperor had decreed that French troops could take what rations they wanted and not pay for them. Lassan himself had refused to obey that decree, but the disobedience had been funded from his own pocket. Some of these men knew that, knew that Lassan had always been a decent officer, but still he threatened them with hunger.

'The English,' a voice shouted from the anonymity of the crowd, 'are offering twenty francs a day. Twenty!'

The murmur started again, grew, and Lassan knew he would have to use force to keep these men from interfering with his duty. He had tried reason, but reason was a feeble weapon against the cupidity of peasants, so now he must be savage in his duty. 'Lieutenant Gerard!'

'Sir?'

'You will fire the boats! Start at the southern moorings!'

A jeer went up and Lassan instinctively reached for his pistol, but his sergeant touched his arm. 'Sir.' The sergeant's voice was sad.

A creak sounded, then another. There was the squeak of an oar in its thole, then there were splashes and Lassan could see, in the darkness, the white marks of blades touching water. He still watched and, in the glistening darkness where the torchlight touched the water into ripples, he saw the ghostly shapes of white-painted boats.

On the flowing tide the British had rowed up channel and Lassan, listening to the ridicule of his countrymen, saw the blue-jacketed sailors, cutlasses in their hands, swarming from their longboats on to the *chasse-marées*. The French crews, welcoming English gold, applauded.

Lassan turned away. 'We go east, Lieutenant.'

'Sir.'

Henri Lassan, with his little band of gunners, stumbled away from the village. He would follow the Arcachon's southern shore, then head inland to Bordeaux to report to his superiors that he had failed, that Arcachon was lost, and that the British had taken their boats.

And thus the battle of Arcachon, that had begun with such high hopes for its defenders, ended in a rain-cold night of bleak defeat.

CHAPTER 8

Five French dead and one dead Rifleman were laid in the fort's chapel, not out of reverence, but simply because it was the most convenient place for the corpses to lie until there was time to bury them. Lieutenant Minver stripped the white frontal from the altar and ordered two of his men to tear it into strips for bandages; then, being a well-trained young man who had been told constantly by his parents never to leave a light burning in an empty room, he pinched out the flame of the Eternal Presence before going back to the courtyard.

The Teste de Buch was in chaos. Riflemen manned the ramparts while Marines and sailors seethed in the courtyard. The six field guns, with their limbers, had been dragged into the fort where they were objects of much curiosity to the seamen. The *Scylla*, her flanks riven by the heavy shot, was moored beneath the silent guns.

The Marines' packs and supplies were being ferried from a brig anchored below the *Scylla*, then slung over the fort's wall by a system of ropes and pulleys. The Marines had marched in light-order, but had still reached the fort two hours after Sharpe's Riflemen.

'I must thank you, Major Sharpe.' Captain Bampfylde limped on blistered feet into the room where Sharpe was being bandaged by a naval surgeon. Bampfylde flinched at the sight of so much blood on Sharpe's face and shirt. 'My dear fellow, permit me to say how sorry I am?'

The surgeon, a drunkard of morose disposition, answered in place of Sharpe. 'It's nothing, sir. Head wounds bleed like a stuck pig.' He finished the bandaging and gave

Sharpe's head a light buffet. 'I'll warrant you've got a head like a bloody bass drum, though.'

If the man meant painful, then he was right, and the friendly tap had not helped, but at least Sharpe's sight had come back as soon as the blood was washed from his eyes. He looked up at Bampfylde whose young, plump face looked tired. 'The fort wasn't exactly deserted.'

'So it seems!' Bampfylde crossed to the table and examined a bottle of wine abandoned by the French garrison. He plucked out the cork and poured a little into a convenient glass. He smelt it, swirled it around, examined it, then sipped it. 'Very nice. A trifle young, I'd say.' He poured more wine into the glass. 'Still, no bones broken, eh?'

'I lost one man dead.'

Bampfylde shrugged. '*Scylla* lost sixteen!' He said it as if to show that the Navy had taken the greater punishment.

'And the Marines?' Sharpe asked.

'Two men were scratched,' Bampfylde said airily. 'I always thought that clearing was the most likely place for an ambuscade, Sharpe. If they want to catch the likes of us, though, they'll have to show a livelier leg, what?' He laughed.

Bampfylde was a lying bastard, Sharpe thought. The two Riflemen sent by Frederickson had warned the Marines of the field guns, and Marine Captain Palmer had already thanked Sharpe for the service. But Bampfylde was speaking as though he had both detected and defeated the ambush, whereas the bloody man had done nothing. Bampfylde finished the wine. 'Some of the Americans escaped?' He made the question sound like an accusation.

'So I believe.' Sharpe did not care. Bampfylde had thirty American prisoners to send to England, and surely that was enough. The fort was taken, seamen from the *Scylla* had gone up channel to find the *chasse-marées*, and no man could have expected more of the day.

'So you'll go inland in the morning, Sharpe?' Bampfylde peered at Sharpe's head wound. 'That's only a scratch, isn't it? Nothing to slow your reconnaissance?'

Sharpe did not reply. The fort was taken, Elphinstone would get the extra *chasse-marées* he needed, and the rest of this operation was farcical. Besides, he did not care whether Bordeaux was seething with discontent or not, he only cared that Jane should not die while he was away. Sharpe twisted round to look at the surgeon. 'What's the first symptom of fever?'

The surgeon was helping himself to the wine. 'Black-spot, Yellow, Swamp? Walcheren? Which fever?'

'Any fever,' Sharpe growled.

The surgeon shrugged. 'A heated skin, uncontrolled shivering, a looseness of the bowels. I can't say you have any pyretic symptoms yourself, Major.'

Sharpe felt a horrid dread. For a second he felt a temptation to claim that his wound was incapacitating and to demand that he was returned to St Jean de Luz by the first ship.

'Well, Sharpe?' Bampfylde was offended that Sharpe had ignored his questions. 'You will be marching inland?'

'Yes, sir.' Sharpe stood. Anything rather than endure this bumptious naval captain. Sharpe would march inland, ambush the road, then return and refuse to have any further part of Bampfylde's madness. He knew he should dry his sword if it was not to have rust spots by morning, but he was too tired. He had not slept last night, he had marched all day, and he had taken a fortress. Now he would sleep.

He pushed past Bampfylde and went to find a cot in an empty room of the barracks. There, surrounded by the small belongings of a gunner evicted by his Green Jackets, he lay down and slept.

It was night now, a cold night. Sentries shivered on the ramparts and the flooded ditch had a skin of thin ice. The wind dropped, the rain had died, and the clouds thinned to leave a sky pricked by cold, white, winter-bright stars above the shimmering, glittering, ice-edged marshes.

Across those silent marshes, and from the silvered, steel-flat waters of Arcachon, a glimmer of mist was born. The mist skeined slow in a still night, a night of frost and white vapour beyond a fort where the blood spilt in a skirmish froze hard in the darkness.

Torches flared in the courtyard of the Teste de Buch. Breath smoked to vapour. Frost touched the cobbles white and rimed the gun barrels on the ramparts.

Bampfylde had ordered the Green Jackets to rest and replaced them with Marines whose scarlet coats and white crossbelts seemed bright in the starlit night.

Nine French prisoners, one of them the sergeant who had fired at Sharpe from the barrack roof, were locked in an empty ready magazine. They would be taken by Bampfylde's ships to the rotting prison hulks in the Thames or else to the new stone jail built by French prisoners in the wilds of Dartmoor.

The other prisoners were locked in the spirit store that Bampfylde had ordered emptied of its brandy and wine. Thirty men were crammed into a space fit for no more than a dozen. They were the Americans.

'At least they claim they're Americans!' Bampfylde, his bootless feet propped on an ammunition box, sat in front of a fire that had been lit in Lassan's old quarters. 'But I'll warrant half of them are our deserters!'

'Indeed, sir.' Lieutenant Ford knew that American ships, both Navy and civilian, were heavily crewed by seamen who had run from the harsh discipline of the Royal Navy.

'So have the bastards out one at a time.' Bampfylde paused to bite into a chicken leg that should have been a part of Henri Lassan's dinner. He sucked the bone clean then tossed it at the fire. 'And talk to them, Lieutenant. Use two reliable bo'sun's mates, understand me?'

'Aye aye, sir.' Ford understood very well.

'Any man you believe is a deserter, put in a separate room. The real Americans can go back to the store.'

'Aye aye, sir.'

Bampfylde poured more of the wine. It might be a young vintage, but it was very, very hopeful. He made a mental note to have all the crates shipped to the *Vengeance*. He had also found some fine crystal glasses, incised with a coat of arms, that would look very fine in his Hampshire house. 'You think I'm being too particular with the American prisoners, Ford?'

Ford did. 'They're all going to hang, sir.'

'True, but it is important that they hang in the proper manner! We can't have a pirate flogged, can we? That would be most uncivil!' Bampfylde laughed at his small jest. Those crewmen of the *Thuella* who were suspected of being British seamen and deserters would face the worst fate. They would be placed in a ship's boat and rowed past all the ships of Bampfylde's command. In front of each ship, under the gaze of the crews, they would be lashed with the cat o' nine tails as a visible, bloody warning of the price a deserter must pay. The knotted thongs would flay their skin and flesh to the bone, but they would be restored to consciousness before they were hanged from the *Vengeance*'s yardarm. The others, the Americans, would be hanged ashore, without a flogging, as common pirates.

Lieutenant Ford hesitated. 'Captain Frederickson, sir . . .' he began nervously.

'Frederickson,' Bampfylde frowned. 'That's the fellow with the beggar's face, yes?'

'Indeed, sir. He did say they were his prisoners. That he'd guaranteed them honourable treatment.'

Bampfylde laughed. 'Perhaps he thinks they should be hanged with a silken rope? They are privateers, Ford, pirates! That makes them the Navy's business, and you will oblige Captain Frederickson to keep his opinions to himself.' Bampfylde smiled reassurance at his lieutenant. 'I shall talk to the American officers myself. Send me my bargemen, will you?'

The capture of Cornelius Killick had given Captain Bampfylde a particular and keen pleasure. American seamen had twisted the Royal Navy's tail, winning single-ship battles with contemptible ease, and men like Killick had become popular heroes to their countrymen. The news of his capture and ignominious death would teach the Republic that Britain could lash back when it so wished. Their Lordships of the Admiralty, Bampfylde knew, would be well pleased with this news. Not many enemies still defied Britain on the waves, and the downfall of even one, even though he be a common pirate, would be a rare victory these days.

'I am not,' Cornelius Killick said when he was brought into Bampfylde's presence, 'a pirate.'

Bampfylde's fleshy face showed ironic amusement. 'You're a common and vulgar pirate, Killick, a criminal, and you'll hang as such.'

'I carry Letters of Marque from my government, and well you know it!' Killick, like Lieutenant Docherty, had been stripped of his sword and his hands were bound behind his back. The American was chilled to the bone, furious and helpless.

'Where,' Bampfylde looked innocently at Killick, 'are your Letters of Marque?'

'I got 'em, sir.' Bampfylde's bo'sun produced a thick fold of papers that Killick had carried in a waterproof pouch on his belt. Bampfylde took, opened, and read the papers with scant interest. The Government of the United States, in accordance with the customary laws, gave permission to Captain Cornelius Killick to wage warfare on the enemies of the Republic wherever on the High Seas those enemies might be found, and extended to Captain Killick the full protection of the said Government of the United States.

'I see no Letters of Marque.' Bampfylde threw the document on to the fire.

'Bastard.' Killick, like every privateer, knew that such letters offered small protection, but no captain liked to lose his papers.

Bampfylde laughed. He was scanning the other papers

that were certificates of American citizenship for the *Thuella*'s crew. 'A fanciful name for a pirate ship, *Thuella*?'

'It's Greek,' Killick said scornfully, 'and means storm-cloud.'

'An American educated in the classics!' Bampfylde mocked the fine looking man. 'What miracles this young century brings!'

Bampfylde's bo'sun, the man who governed the captain's private barge, elbowed Lieutenant Docherty in the ribs. 'This one's no Jonathon, sir, he's a bloody Mick.'

'An Irishman!' Bampfylde smiled. 'Rebelling against your lawful King, are you?'

'I'm an American citizen,' Docherty said.

'Not any longer.' Bampfylde threw all the certificates on to the fire where they flared bright, then shrivelled. 'I smell the whiff of the Irish bogs on you.' Bampfylde looked back to Killick. 'So where's the *Thuella*?'

'I told you.'

Bampfylde was not sure he believed Killick's story that the *Thuella* was stranded, stripped, and useless, but tomorrow the brigs could search the Bassin d'Arcachon and make certain. Bampfylde also hoped that the rest of the privateer crew could be hunted down and brought to his justice. 'How many of your crew are British subjects?' he asked Killick.

'None.' Killick's face glared defiance. Fully one-third of his men had once served in the Royal Navy and Killick well knew what ghastly fate awaited them if they were discovered. 'Not one.'

Bampfylde took a cigar from his case, cut it, then held a twisted paper spill made of a page torn from Lassan's copy of Montaigne's *Essays* in the fire. 'You're all going to hang, Killick, all of you. I could claim that you're all deserters, even you!' He lit his cigar, then dropped the flaming spill. 'You fancy a thrashing, Killick? Or would you prefer to tell me the truth?'

Killick, whose cigars had been stolen from him by a

Marine, watched enviously as the British captain drew on the glowing tobacco. 'Piss on you, mister.'

Bampfylde shrugged, then nodded to the bo'sun.

There were seven bargemen, all favourites of their captain, and all strengthened by their time at the oars. They were also veterans of countless brawls in dockside taverns and of the fights they had won when part of a press gang, and two bound men, however strong, were no match for them.

Bampfylde watched impassively. To him these two Americans were pirates, pure and simple, who wore no recognized uniform and their fate did not disturb him any more than he might worry about the rats in the *Vengeance*'s bilge. He let his men hit them, he watched the blood smear from split lips and noses, and not until both men were on the floor with bloodied faces and bruised ribs did he raise a hand to stop the violence. 'How many of your men, Killick, are deserters?'

Before Killick could make any reply the door opened. Standing there, and with taut fury on his face, was Captain William Frederickson. 'Sir!'

Bampfylde twisted in his chair and frowned at the interruption. He was not concerned that the Rifleman should witness this beating, but it offended Bampfylde that the man had not had the simple courtesy to knock first. 'It's Frederickson, isn't it? Can't it wait, man?'

It was evident that Frederickson was struggling to control his temper. He swallowed, drew himself to attention, and forced civility into his face. 'I gave Captain Killick my word, as a gentleman, that he would be treated with respect and honour. I demand that my word is kept.'

Bampfylde was truly astonished at the protest. 'They're pirates, Captain!'

'I gave my word.' Frederickson stood his ground stubbornly.

'Then I, as your superior, have rescinded it.' Bampfylde's voice was suddenly infused with anger at this soldier's impertinence. 'They are pirates and in the morning they will hang from a gallows. That is my decision, Captain Frederickson, mine, and if you say one more word on it, just one, then by God I will have you put under arrest like them! Now get out!'

Frederickson stared at Bampfylde. For a second he was tempted to dare Bampfylde to make good his threat, then, without a word, he turned and stalked from the room.

Bampfylde smiled. 'Shut the door, Bo'sun. Now, where were we, gentlemen?'

In the fort's yard, carpenters from the *Scylla* hammered six inch nails into beams that, when all the work was done, would be raised to make a gallows for the morning where Cornelius Killick, instead of dancing scorn about the Navy, would dance attendance on a rope.

Thomas Taylor, the Rifleman from Tennessee who had so far done his duty without murmur or protest, stopped Captain Frederickson close to the busy hammers. 'Sir?'

'It'll stop, Taylor, I promise you.'

Taylor, satisfied because of the fury on his captain's face, stepped back. The air about the fort was ghostly with a mist that blurred the stars and touched frigid on Frederickson's scarred skin. He saw his own anger mirrored in Taylor's eyes and knew that loyalties were being stretched in this cold night. 'It will stop,' he promised again, then went to wake Sharpe.

Sharpe struggled out of a dream in which he saw his wife as a flesh-rotted skeleton presiding at a tea-party. He groped for his sword, flinched from a stab of pain that seared in his bandaged head, then recognized the eye-patched face in the light of the horn-lantern that Frederickson carried. 'Dawn already?' Sharpe asked.

'No, sir. But they're beating the hell out of them, sir.'

Sharpe sat up. It was piercingly cold in the room. 'They're doing what?'

'The Americans.' Frederickson told how the seamen were

being dragged before Ford, while the officers were being entertained by Captain Bampfylde. Rifleman Taylor had woken Frederickson with the news, now Frederickson woke Sharpe. 'They've found two deserters already.'

Sharpe groaned as his head split with pain. 'The deserters will have to hang.' His tone conveyed that such men deserved nothing else.

Frederickson nodded agreement. 'But I gave my word to Killick that he would be treated like a gentleman. They're half killing the poor bastard. And they're all to hang, Bampfylde says, deserters or no.'

'Oh, Christ.' Sharpe pulled his boots on, not bothering to tuck his overall trousers into the leather. He put his arms into his jacket, then stood. 'Bugger Bampfylde.'

'Page nine, paragraph one of the King's Regulations might be more appropriate, sir.'

Sharpe frowned. 'What?'

'"Post Captains,"' Frederickson quoted, '"commanding Ships or Vessels that do not give Post, rank only as Majors during their commanding such Vessels."'

Sharpe buttoned his jacket then buckled the snake hasp of his sword belt. 'How the hell do you know that?'

'I took care to look up the respective pages before we left, sir.'

'Jesus. I should have done that!' Sharpe snatched up his shako and led the way downstairs. 'But he's commanding the *Vengeance*! That gives Post and makes him a full Colonel!'

'He's not on board,' Frederickson said persuasively, 'and the *Vengeance* is a half mile offshore. If he commands anything, it's the *Scylla*, and frigates aren't Post.'

Sharpe shrugged. The quibble seemed dubious grounds for taking command from Bampfylde.

Frederickson clattered down the stairs behind Sharpe. 'And may I remind you of the next paragraph?'

'You're going to anyway.' Sharpe pushed open a door and went into the pitiless cold of the courtyard. The air stung his cheeks and brought tears to his eyes.

'"Nothing in these regulations is to authorize any Land Officer to command any of His Majesty's Squadrons or Ships, nor any Sea Officer to command on Land."' Frederickson paused, raised his heel, and slammed it down on the iced cobbles. 'Land, sir.'

Sharpe stared at Frederickson. The carpenter's mauls sounded like small cannons thumping to increase the throbbing agony of his skull. 'I don't give a damn, William, if they hang Killick. The bloody Americans shouldn't be butting into this bloody war anyway, and I don't give a tuppenny damn if we hang every mother's son of them. But you gave your word?'

'I did, sir.'

'So I give a damn that your word's kept.'

Sharpe did not bother to knock on Bampfylde's door, instead he kicked it in and the crack of the swinging wood slamming against the wall made Captain Bampfylde jump in alarm.

This time there were two Rifle officers, both scarred, both with faces harder than rifle butts, and both displaying an anger that was chilling in the fire-heated room.

Sharpe ignored Bampfylde. He crossed the room and stooped to the fallen men who had been further punched and kicked since Frederickson had left. Sharpe straightened and looked at the bo'sun. 'Untie them.'

'Major Sharpe . . .' Bampfylde began, but Sharpe turned on him.

'You will oblige me, Captain Bampfylde, by not interfering with my exercise of command on land.'

Bampfylde understood instantly. He knew a quotation from the Regulations and he knew a lost battle. But a battle was not a campaign. 'These men are the Navy's prisoners.'

'These men were captured by the Army, on land, where they were fighting as auxiliaries to the Imperial French Army.' Sharpe was making it up as he went along. 'They are my prisoners, my responsibility, and I order them untied!' This last was to the captain's barge crew who, startled by the sudden shout, stooped to the bound men.

Captain Bampfylde wanted these Americans, but he wanted to preserve his dignity more. He knew that in a struggle over precedence, a struggle fuelled by legalistic interpretations of the Regulations, he would barely survive. He also felt the disarming touch of fear in the presence of these men. Bampfylde well knew what reputations came with Sharpe and Frederickson, and their ruffianly looks and scarred faces suggested that this was a battle Bampfylde could not win by force. Instead he would have to use subtlety, and in that knowledge he smiled. 'We shall discuss their fate in the morning, Major.'

'Indeed we will.' Sharpe, somewhat surprised by the ease of his victory, turned to Frederickson. 'Order the other Americans into proper confinement, Mr Frederickson. Use our men as guards. Then clear the kitchen and ask Sergeant Harper to join me there. Bring them.' He nodded at the American officers.

In the kitchens, Sharpe offered an awkward apology.

Cornelius Killick, who was tearing a loaf of bread apart, cocked a bloodied eyebrow. 'Apologize?'

'You were given an officer's word, and it was broken. I apologize.'

Patrick Harper pushed open the kitchen door. 'Captain Frederickson said you wanted me, sir?'

'To be a cook, Sergeant. There's some Frog soup on the stove.'

'Pleasure, sir.' Harper, whose face was almost back to its normal size and who seemed remarkably well recovered from his self-inflicted surgery, opened the stove's fire-box and threw in driftwood. The kitchens were blessedly warm.

'You're Irish?' Lieutenant Docherty suddenly asked Harper.

'That I am. From Tangaveane in Donegal and a finer piece of God's country doesn't exist. It's fish soup, sir,' Harper said to Sharpe.

'Tangaveane?' The thin-faced lieutenant stared at Harper. 'Then you'd be knowing Cashelnavean?'

'On the road to Ballybofey? Where the old fort would be?' Harper's face suddenly took on a look of magical happiness. 'I've walked that road more times than I remember, so I have.'

'We farmed on the slopes there. Before the English took the land.' Docherty gave Sharpe a sour, challenging look, but the English officer was leaning against the wall, apparently oblivious. 'Docherty,' Docherty said to Harper.

'Harper. There was a Docherty,' Harper said, 'who had a smithy in Meencrumlin.'

'My uncle.'

'God save Ireland.' Harper stared in wonder at the lieutenant. 'And you from America? Do you hear that, sir? He has an uncle that used to tinker my ma's pans.'

'I heard,' Sharpe spoke sourly. He was thinking that he had stuck his neck out and to small avail. He had saved these men for twelve hours, no more, and there were times, he thought, when a soldier should know when not to fight. Then he remembered how Ducos, the Frenchman, had treated him in Burgos and how a French officer had risked his career to save Sharpe, and Sharpe knew he could not have lived with his conscience if he had simply allowed Bampfylde to continue his savagery. These men might well be pirates, they probably did deserve the rope, but Frederickson had pledged his word. Sharpe walked to the table. 'How are your wounds?'

'I lost a tooth,' Killick grinned to show the bloody gap.

'That's a fashion these days,' Harper said equably from the range.

Sharpe pulled a bottle of wine towards him and knocked the neck off against the table. 'Are you pirates?'

'Privateer,' Killick said it proudly, 'and legally licensed.'

Frederickson, shivering from the cold in the yard, came through the door. 'I've put the rest of the Jonathons in the guardroom. Rossner's watching them.' He looked towards the seated Americans. 'I'm sorry, Mr Killick.'

'Captain Killick,' Killick said without rancour, 'and thank you for what you did. Both of you.' He held out a tin mug for wine. 'When they dangle us at a rope's end I'll say that not every Britisher is a bastard.'

Sharpe poured wine into Killick's cup. 'I saw you,' he said, 'at St Jean de Luz.'

Killick gave a great, hoarse whoop of a laugh that reminded Sharpe of Wellington's strange merriment. 'That was a splendid day!' Killick said. 'We had them wetting their breeches, right enough!'

Sharpe nodded, remembering Bampfylde's fury in the dining-room as the naval captain had watched the American. 'You did.'

Killick felt in his pocket, realized he had no cigars, and shrugged. 'Nothing in peace will offer such joy, will it?' Sharpe made no reply and the American looked at his Lieutenant. 'Perhaps we ought to become real pirates in peacetime, Liam?'

'If we live that long.' Docherty stared sourly at the Rifleman.

'For an Irishman,' Killick said to Sharpe, 'he has an unnatural sense of reality. Are you going to hang us, Major?'

'I'm feeding you.' Sharpe avoided the question.

'But in the morning,' Killick said, 'the sailormen will want us, won't they?'

Sharpe said nothing. Patrick Harper, by the stove, watched Sharpe and took a chance. 'In the morning,' he said softly, 'we'll be away from here, so we will, and more's the pity.'

Sharpe frowned because the sergeant had seen fit to interrupt, yet in truth he had asked for Harper's presence because the good sense of the huge Ulsterman was something that he valued. Harper's words had served two purposes; first to warn the Americans that the Riflemen could not control their fate, and secondly to tell Sharpe that the consensus, among the Green Jackets at least, was that a hanging would not be welcome. The Rifles had captured these Americans, had done it without bloodshed to either side, and they felt bitterly that the Navy should so high-handedly decide to execute opponents whose only fault had been to fight with unrealistic hopes.

No one spoke. Harper, his pennyworth contributed, turned back to the stove. Docherty stared at the scarred, stained table, while Killick, a half smile on his bruised face, watched Sharpe and thought that here was another English officer who did not match the image encouraged by the American news-sheets.

Frederickson, still by the door, thought how alike Sharpe and the American were. The American was younger, but both had the same hard, good-looking face and both had the same savage recklessness in their eyes. It would be interesting, Frederickson decided, to see whether such similar men liked or hated each other.

Sharpe seemed embarrassed by the encounter, as if he was uncertain what to do with this exotic and unfamiliar enemy. He turned to Harper instead. 'Isn't that soup ready?'

'Not unless you want it cold, sir.'

'A full belly,' Killick said, 'to make us hang heavier?' No one responded.

Sharpe was thinking that in the morning, once the Riflemen were gone, Bampfylde would string these Americans up like sides of beef. Ten minutes ago that thought had not upset Sharpe. Men were hanged in droves every day, and a hanging was prime entertainment in any town with a respectable sized population. Pirates had always been hanged and, besides, these Americans were the enemy. There were good reasons, therefore, to let the *Thuella*'s crew hang.

Yet to reason thus, in cold blood, was one thing, and it was quite another to look across a table-top and apply that chilling reason to men whose only fault had been to pick a fight with Riflemen. There were French soldiers grown old in war who would have hesitated to take on Green Jackets, so should a seaman hang because of optimism? Besides, and though Sharpe knew this was not a reasonable objection, he found it hard to think of men who spoke his own language as enemies. Sharpe fought Frenchmen.

Yet the law was the law, and in the morning Sharpe's orders would take him far from this fort, and far from Cornelius Killick who would, abandoned to Bampfylde's mercies, hang. That, Sharpe decided, was certain and so, unable to offer any reassurance, he poured wine instead. He wished Harper would hurry with the damned soup.

Cornelius Killick, understanding all of Sharpe's doubts from the troubled look on the Rifleman's bandaged face, spoke a single word. 'Listen.'

Sharpe looked into Killick's eyes, but the American said nothing more. 'Well?' Sharpe frowned.

Killick smiled. 'You hear nothing. No wind, Major. There's not a breath of wind out there, nothing but frost and mist.'

'So?'

'So we have a saying back home, Major,' the American was staring only at Sharpe, 'that if you hang a sailorman in still airs, his soul can't go to hell. So it lingers on earth to take another life as revenge.' The American pointed at Sharpe. 'Maybe your life, Major?'

Killick could have said nothing more helpful to his cause. His words made Sharpe think of Jane, shivering in the cold sweat of her fever, and he thought, with sudden self-pity, that if she could not be saved then he would rather catch the fever and die with her than be in this cold, ice-slicked fort where the mist writhed silent about the stones.

Killick, watching the hard face that was slashed by a casual scar, saw a shudder go through the Rifleman. He sensed that Docherty was about to speak and, rather than have their situation jeopardized by Irish hostility, he kicked his lieutenant to silence. Killick, who had spoken lightly enough before, knew that his words had struck a seam of feeling and he pressed his advantage with a gentle voice. 'There's no peace for a man who hangs a sailorman in a calm.'

Their eyes met. Sharpe wondered whether the American's words were true. Sharpe told himself it was nonsense, a superstition as baseless as any soldier's talisman, yet the thought was irresistibly lodged. Sharpe had been cursed years before, his name buried on a stone, and his first wife had died within hours of that curse. He frowned. 'The deserters must hang. That's the law.'

No one spoke. Harper waited for the soup to seethe and Frederickson leaned against the door. Docherty licked bloodied lips, then Killick smiled. 'All my men are citizens of the United States, Major. What they were before is not your business, nor my President's business, nor the business of the bloody law. They all have citizens' papers!' Killick ignored the fact that the certificates had been burned by Bampfylde.

'You give those scraps of paper to anyone who volunteers; anyone!' Sharpe said mockingly. 'If a donkey could pull a trigger you'd make it into a citizen of the United States!'

'And what do you give to your volunteers?' Killick retorted with an equal scorn. 'Everyone knows a murderer is forgiven his crime if he'll join your Army! You expect us to be more delicate than your own service?' There was no reply, and Killick smiled. 'And I tell you now that none of my men deserted the Royal Navy. Some may have fouled-anchor tattoos, some may have English voices, and some may have scarred backs, but I tell you now that they are all, every last jack of them, free-born citizens of the Republic.'

Sharpe looked into the hard, bright eyes. 'You tell me? Or do you swear to me?'

'I'll swear on every damned Bible in Massachusetts if you demand it.' Which meant that Killick lied, but that he lied to protect his men, and Sharpe knew that he himself would tell just such a lie for his own men.

'Thomas Taylor is American,' Frederickson observed mildly to Sharpe. 'Would you approve of him being hanged if the tables were turned?'

And if he let them go, Sharpe thought, then the Navy would complain to the Admiralty and the Admiralty would huff and puff to the Horse Guards and the Horse Guards would write a letter to Wellington and all hell would break loose about Major Richard Sharpe's head. Men like Wigram, the bores who worshipped proper procedure, would demand explanations and decree punishments.

And if he did not let the Americans go, Sharpe thought, then a girl might die, and he would go back to St Jean de Luz to be shown the fresh, damp earth of her grave. Somehow he believed, with the fervour of a man who would cling to any hope, that he could buy Jane's life by not hanging a sailorman in still airs. He had lost one wife by a curse; he could not risk it again.

He was silent. The soup boiled and Harper shifted it from the flames. Killick, as if he did not care what the outcome of this meeting was, smiled. 'A flat calm, Major, and the ice will mask our dead faces just because we fought like men for our own country.'

'If I were to let you go,' Sharpe spoke so quietly that, even in this night's uncanny silence, Killick and Docherty had to lean forward to hear his voice, 'would you give me your word, as American citizens, that neither of you, nor any man in your crew, here or absent, will take up arms against Britain for the rest of this war's duration?'

Sharpe had expected instant acceptance, even gratitude, but the tall American was wary. 'Suppose I'm attacked?'

'Then you run.' Sharpe waited for a reply that did not come, then, to his astonishment, found himself pleading with a man not to choose a hanging. 'I can't stop Bampfylde hanging you, Killick. I don't have the power. I can't escort you into captivity; we're a hundred miles behind enemy lines! So the Navy has to take you away from here and the

Navy will string you up, all of you. But give me your word and I'll release you.'

Killick suddenly let out a great breath, the first sign of the tension he had felt. 'You have my word.'

Sharpe looked at the Irishman. 'And you?'

Docherty stared in puzzlement at Sharpe. 'You'll let all of us go? All the crew?'

'I said so.'

'And how do we know . . .?'

Harper spoke in sudden Gaelic. His words were brief, harshly spoken, and a mystery to every man in the room except to himself and Docherty. The American lieutenant listened to the huge Irishman, then looked back to Sharpe with a sudden, unnatural humility. 'You have my word.'

Cornelius Killick held up a hand. 'But if I'm attacked, Major, and can't run, then by Christ I'll fight!'

'But you won't seek a fight?'

'I will not,' Killick said.

Sharpe, his head splitting with pain from the bullet-strike, leaned back. Harper brought the cauldron to the table and splashed soup into five bowls. Frederickson came and sat down, Harper sat beside him, and only Sharpe did not eat. He looked at Killick instead, and his voice was suddenly very weary. 'Your boat's wrecked?'

'Yes,' Killick told the lie glibly.

'Then I suggest you go to Paris. The American Minister there can arrange passage home.'

'Indeed,' Killick smiled. He spooned soup into his mouth. 'So what now, Major?'

'You finish your soup, collect your men, and go. I'll make sure there's no trouble at the gate. You forfeit your weapons, of course, except for officers' swords.'

Killick stared at Sharpe as though he could not believe what he was hearing. 'We just go?'

'You just go,' Sharpe said. He pushed his chair back and walked to the door. He went into the yard, stared upwards, and sure enough the Union flag that the sailors had raised to the flagpole's peak was hanging utterly limp in the still, misting air.

It was a flat calm, an utter stillness; no airs in which to hang a sailorman, and so Richard Sharpe would let an enemy go and he would say he did it for honour, or because the war was so close to ending that there was no need for more death, or because it was just his pleasure to do it.

He felt tears in his eyes that had been earlier closed with blood, then walked to the gate to make sure that no man stopped the *Thuella*'s crew from leaving. His wife would live and Sharpe, for the first time since the *Amelie* had sailed, felt that he, just like the Americans, was free.

CHAPTER 9

'Be Pleased to acquaint the Lords Commissioners of the Admiralty,' wrote Captain Horace Bampfylde as he drafted his first despatch to the Secretary of the Admiralty, which gentleman would not only acquaint the Lords Commissioners, but also the unlordly editor of the *Naval Gazette* who was in a position to do much honour to Captain Bampfylde, 'that judging it to be of Consequence that their Lordships should have as early Information as possible of the Defeat of the French Forces in the Basin of Arcachon, I have this day ordered the *Lily* cutter to sail with this Despatch.' The *Lily* was waiting in the roads outside.

'I had established,' Bampfylde's quill squeaked on the thick paper, 'from picquets sent ahead, that an Artillery Fortification, of Breastwork, Ditch, and Emplacements, in which six pieces of artillery were arrayed, which pieces were defended by musketeers, had been constructed against just such an approach as I had the honour to make.' Bampfylde had decided not to reveal that the 'breastwork' was manned by American sailors, for victory over such opponents would not be considered as praiseworthy as a triumph over French land forces. By default, therefore, Bampfylde would allow the Lords Commissioners to believe that he had faced and overcome a part of Napoleon's Army.

He refought the battle with quill and ink, not as it had actually taken place, but as he was convinced it ought to have taken place; indeed in a manner that precisely described what Bampfylde believed would have happened if Major Sharpe had not disobeyed his orders and assaulted the Teste de Buch instead of marching inland. The quill paused and Bampfylde persuaded himself that he did Major Sharpe a favour by not writing a description of the Rifleman's disobedience, and further persuaded himself that it might be better, all round, if Sharpe's name did not appear in the description of the fort's capture at all. Why raise the subject of a fellow-officer's failure to follow orders?

'Going forward with a file of men under Lieutenant of Marines Fytch,' Bampfylde resumed, 'I succeeded in drawing the Enemy fire and thus marking the position of the skilfully hidden battery to my flanking force that was under the command of Captain Palmer. The Guns were taken at point of cutlass and sword. Due to the Temerity and Masterful Gallantry shown by the men under my command our losses were trifling.' That seemed eminently just to Bampfylde. After all the guns had been physically taken by the Marines and it seemed hardly necessary to spell out the trifling point that the gun crews had already been captured. Guns were guns, and next to enemy flags, were valuable trophies. That thought gave Bampfylde pause. He had already sequestered the French tricolour that had flown over the Teste de Buch, but his Midshipman had so far failed to find the American ensign. That must be diligently sought, Bampfylde thought, as he bent again to his literary labours.

'At this time, the *Scylla*, Captain Duncan Grant, was, as per my orders, fully engaging the guns of the fort with her main batteries. Thus distracted, the defenders were disconcerted by the sudden appearance from the woods, of my land force. Deeming the moment opportune, I went forward to the Escalade. It is with the Greatest Pleasure and Satisfaction that I make known to Their Lordships the Very Gallant Behaviour of Lieutenant Ford, who with the Utmost Intrepidity, was at the Forefront of the attack. In the crossing of two ditches, two walls, and the enceinte of the enemy position, Lieutenant Ford showed a True British spirit, as did the Marines who followed us in the Assault.' Bampfylde frowned, wondering whether he had over-egged the pudding a little, but it was important that Ford, who had noble connections in London, should feel pleased with this despatch. Bampfylde, still frowning, was concerned that their Lordships would realize that Ford, who had been described as so very gallant, was at all times at Bampfylde's side and that the enconium so generously penned should, in reality, be read as applying to the author.

Captain Bampfylde was not certain that meaning was entirely plain, yet he knew their Lordships to be subtle men, and he must trust to their perspicacity. Again he scanned his words as a test for truth. He and Ford had indeed crossed two ditches and walls, all of them thanks to the drawbridge which had been captured by Sharpe's Riflemen, but it would do no harm for the word 'escalade' to suggest a desperate struggle.

'Taken in the rear, their Defences broken, the Enemy retreated to the Inner Galleries of their Fortress where, with Fortitude and Determination, the Marines I had the Honour and Happiness to command, overpressed the Foe. Great Carnage was done upon the Enemy before a Surrender was accepted, whereupon I had the Privilege of Raising His Majesty's Flag upon the Captured Mast.' Bampfylde had indeed ordered the flag raised, and it handily gave the impression that he had been present when the fort was captured.

And in all honesty, Bampfylde persuaded himself, he had captured the Teste de Buch. It had been his plan, his execution, and, though the Rifles had undoubtedly reached the fort first and taken possession of the gate and ramparts, the Marines, in exploring the labyrinthine tunnels and store-rooms, had discovered six French gunners hiding in a latrine. The existence of those men proved that the Rifles had not possessed all the fortress, and that it had been the Marines, under Bampfylde's command, who had achieved that task. Captain Bampfylde felt certain that his account, far from being unfair, was a model of generous objectivity.

'Among the prisoners taken were the crew of the American

Privateer, *Thuella*, which crew included in their numbers some Deserters from His Majesty's Navy.' Writing that line gave Captain Bampfylde particular satisfaction. Tomorrow he would have those men hanged. Sharpe would be leaving, and when Sharpe was gone Captain Bampfylde would show his men how a privateer's crew was treated.

A knock sounded on the door. Bampfylde scowled at the interruption, but looked up. 'Come!'

'Sir?' An astonished Lieutenant Ford stood there. 'They're letting them go, sir. The Americans.'

'Go?' Bampfylde stared with disbelief at his lieutenant.

'Gone rather, sir.' Ford shrugged helplessly. 'Major Sharpe's orders, sir.'

Bampfylde felt a pulse of hatred so fierce and so deep that he thought that never could he assuage such a feeling. Then he knew he must try. 'Wait.'

He dipped his quill into ink, and the nib emerged coated with vitriol. 'Those prisoners, condemned for Desertion or Piracy, were Released, without my Knowledge nor Consent, by Major Richard Sharpe, Prince of Wales's Own Volunteers, whom we had Conveyed to the Teste de Buch, together with a small Force of soldiery, for Operations in the interior. As yet, with all the Attendant Duties that this Victory brings, and in the Business of anticipating the Prizes that will lie open to His Majesty's ships Tomorrow, I have had neither opportunity nor time to Demand of Major Sharpe his Reasons for this,' Bampfylde paused, then swooped, 'Betrayal. But be Assured that such Reasons will be sought and Conveyed to their Lordships by Your Most Humble and Obedient Servant, Horace Bampfylde.'

He sanded the despatch, folded it, then sealed it. Ford would wrap it in waxed paper, then take it to the *Lily* to wait for the winds that would speed this message back to London to the greater glory of Horace Bampfylde and to the deserved damnation of Major Richard Sharpe.

*

The mist thickened slowly, just as the ice on the marshes thickened. There was no wind as dawn silvered the Bassin d'Arcachon and as Cornelius Killick, with his men, finished their frozen march to the village of Gujan where the *Thuella* was grounded.

Liam Docherty was astonished by the night's events. First his life had been spared by an Englishman, then, as he left the fort, a savage-faced Rifleman had thrust a cloth bundle into his arms. That bundle proved to be the *Thuella*'s ensign and, to Docherty, a further proof that some supernatural force had given the *Thuella*'s crew protection in the cold, still night.

Cornelius Killick took their release more carelessly, as though he knew his time on this earth was not yet finished. 'There never was a saying, Liam, that hanging a sailorman in still airs brought revenge. But it seemed worth an attempt, eh?' He laughed softly. 'And it worked!' He stared up at his beached schooner, knowing that it needed days of work before it could float. 'We'll patch with the elm and hope for the best.'

'At least the bastards won't find us in this mist,' Docherty said hopefully.

'If the wind doesn't spring.' Killick stared over the saltings beyond the creek and saw how the slow, creeping whiteness was thickening into a vaporous shroud that might yet be his schooner's salvation. 'But if we burn her,' he said slowly, 'the British can't.'

'Burn her?' Docherty sounded appalled.

'Get the topmasts down. I want the bowsprit off her. Make her look like a hulk, Liam.' Killick, despite his sleepless night, was suddenly full of demonic energy. 'Then set smoke fires in the hold.' He stared up at the sleek bulge of the careened hull. 'Streak it with tar. Make her look abandoned, burned, and wrecked.' For if the British saw a canted, mastless hull, seeping a smudge of smoke, they would think the *Thuella* beyond salvage. They would not know that men carefully tended the smoke-rich fires, or that the topmasts, guns and sails were held safe ashore. 'Do it, Liam! Fast now, fast!'

Killick grinned at his men, filling them with hope, then stalked back to the small tavern where Commandant Henri Lassan, wet and disconsolate, huddled before a smoking fire. 'You'll not stay with us, Henri?'

Lassan was wondering what fate had attended upon his small and valuable library. No doubt it would be burned. The British, in Lassan's grim view, were entirely capable of burning books, which made it all the more surprising that they had released the Americans. 'What was the name of the officer?'

'Sharpe.' Killick, with relief, had found some of his cigars safe amongst the baggage stored at Gujan. He lit one now, noticing that the mist was thickening to fog.

'Sharpe?' Lassan frowned. 'A Rifleman?'

'Green Jacket, anyway.' Killick watched as Lassan scribbled in a small notebook. The French officer, resting in Gujan on his eastward journey, wanted to know all that Killick could tell him about the British force and the American, considering the request, decided that the giving of information did not break his promise to Sharpe. 'Does it matter who he is?'

'If he's the man I think he is, yes.' Lassan sounded dispirited by his defeat. 'You've met one of their more celebrated soldiers.'

'He met one of America's more celebrated sailors,' Killick said happily. He wondered if this unnatural calm presaged a storm. He saw Lassan's pencil pause, and sighed. 'Let me think now. I'd guess a hundred Riflemen, maybe a few more.'

'Marines?' Lassan asked.

'At least a hundred.' Killick shrugged.

Lassan looked through the window, saw the fog, and knew he must find a horse, any horse, and take his news to those who could best use it. The British had come, had won their victory, but they had not yet left Arcachon, so Lassan would go to Bordeaux and there find the men who could organize revenge on a Rifleman.

Fog writhed about the low walls of the Teste de Buch, utterly obscuring the ramparts from the courtyard where Sharpe, in the dawn, paraded his Riflemen.

'He's not best pleased with you,' Captain of Marines Palmer spoke hesitantly. Sharpe replied with his brief opinion of Captain Bampfylde that made the tough Marine smile. 'I'm to give you this.' Palmer handed Sharpe a sealed paper.

Sharpe supposed the paper was a reprimand or protest from Bampfylde, but it was merely a reminder that Major Sharpe was expected back at the Teste de Buch by noon on Thursday. Doubtless Bampfylde was unwilling to face Sharpe in person, and Sharpe did not care. His head was aching, sometimes pulsing with a stab of dark agony, and his mood was bleak.

'We're marching with you,' Captain Palmer said. He had fifty Marines on parade. He had also taken two of the captured gun-limbers, each harnessed behind a pair of cart-horses that had been discovered in a meadow by the village and which now drew the Marines' packs and supplies. 'The men aren't hardened to marching,' Palmer explained.

'You're attached to us?' Sharpe asked with surprise.

Palmer shook his head. 'We're supposed to be hunting your Americans.'

'If they've got any sense,' Sharpe said, 'they'll be long gone.'

The gate squealed open, boots slammed on the cobbles, and the small force that was intended to cut the French supply-road marched into the cold whiteness of the fog. If his map was right Sharpe reckoned they faced a full day's march. First they would follow the main road, keeping to its ruts in the blinding fog as far as a bridge at a village called Facture. There they would turn south-east and follow the River Leyre until they reached the supply road. One day on the road to cause what chaos he could, then one day for the return journey.

The Riflemen again outstripped the Marines. Gradually the sound of the horses' trace-chains faded behind and Sharpe's men marched amidst the clinging, soft wet fog as if in a silent cloud.

Nothing stirred in Arcachon. The fog half obscured the buildings, the shuttered windows stayed shuttered, but the road led straight through the market-place.

'I wanted to thank you,' Frederickson said, 'for your actions last night.'

Sharpe had been lost in the private pain of a stabbing headache. He had to think to remember the events of the night, then he shrugged. 'For nothing.'

'I doubt that Bampfylde feels it's nothing?'

Sharpe gave a dutiful smile. He flinched as a dart of pain stabbed behind his bandaged forehead.

Frederickson saw the flinch. 'Are you well, sir?'

'I'm well.' It was said curtly.

Frederickson walked in silence for a few paces. 'I doubt Captain Palmer can find the fugitives in this fog.' He spoke in the tones of a man who openly changed the subject.

'Bampfylde's got the *chasse-marées*,' Sharpe said, 'what the hell else does he want?'

'He wants the American schooner for prize money. Did you ever meet a naval captain who didn't want prize money?' Frederickson sounded scornful. 'The web-foots fight a battle and spend the next ten years in litigation over the division of the spoils. The Navy's made the legal profession wealthy!'

It was an old Army complaint. A naval captain could become rich for ever by capturing an unarmed enemy merchantman, while a soldier could fight a score of terrible engagements and never see a sixpence for all the crammed warehouses he might capture. Sharpe could hardly complain, for he and Harper had stolen their wealth off a battlefield, but the old soldier's envious habit of despising the Navy for legalizing theft persisted. The Army did award prize money; a saddle horse, taken in battle, fetched three shillings and ninepence, but that sum shared between a Company of infantry made no man wealthy and no lawyers fat. Sharpe forced a smile and fed Frederickson's resentment. 'You can't be rude about the Navy, William; they're the heroes, remember?'

'Bloody web-foots.' Frederickson, like the rest of the Army, resented that the Navy received so much acclaim in Britain while the Army was despised. The jealous grousing, so well practised and comforting, kept Frederickson voluble through the long morning's march.

In the afternoon the Riflemen marched clear of the fog which hung behind them like a great cloud over the Bassin d'Arcachon. Wisps of mist, like outriders to the fog bank, still drifted above the flat, marshy landscape over which the road was carried on an embankment shored by plaited hurdles. Widgeon, teal and snipe flapped away from the marching men. Harper, who loved birds, watched them, but not so closely that he did not see the twisted rope handle of an eel-trap. Two eels were inside and the beasts were chopped up with a sword bayonet and distributed among the Riflemen.

It was cold, but the march warmed them. By late afternoon, within sight of two small villages, they reached a miserable, plank bridge rotting over a sluggish stream. 'I suppose this could be Facture.' Sharpe stared at the map. 'Christ knows.'

He sent Lieutenant Minver with six men to discover the names of the closest villages, and with them went a bag of silver French francs to buy what food could be prised from the peasants. The ten-franc silver coins were forgeries, made at Wellington's command by counterfeiters recruited from the Army's ranks. The Peer insisted that all supplies in France were paid for with good coin, but French peasants would not touch Spanish silver, only French, so Wellington had simply melted the one down to make the other. The silver content was good, the coins indistinguishable from those minted in Paris, and everyone concerned was happy.

'They're bloody poor, sir.' Minver returned with five loaves, three eels, and a basket of lentils. 'And this is the River Leyre, sir.'

'No meat?' Frederickson was disgusted. Each of the Riflemen carried three days' supply of dried beef in their packs, but Frederickson, Sharpe knew, was very fond of freshly-killed pork.

'No meat,' Minver said. 'Unless they're hiding it.'

'Of course they're bloody hiding it,' Frederickson said scathingly. 'You want me to go, sir?' He looked hopefully to Sharpe.

'No.' Sharpe was staring back the way they had come where, in the distance, a straggle of redcoats appeared. Sharpe was cold, his head was hurting like the devil, and now he had the Marines on his coat-tails. 'Bloody hell!'

'I was hoping you'd be here, sir,' Palmer greeted Sharpe.

'Hoping?'

'If Killick went inland, which seems likely, then we're better following you. Or going with you.' Palmer grinned, and Sharpe realized that the Marine captain had no intention of hunting Killick and only wanted to be a part of Sharpe's expedition. Setting an ambush on a high road of France was, to Captain Palmer, a taste of real soldiering, while following some half-armed fugitives in a scramble over a cold marsh was just a waste of time. Palmer's lieutenant, a thin, vacant youth called Fytch, hovered close to his seniors to overhear Sharpe's decision.

'I presume, Captain,' Sharpe said carefully, 'that you were given a free hand in your search for Captain Killick?'

'Indeed, sir. I was told not to come back till I'd found the scoundrel. Not till Thursday, anyway.'

'Then I can't stop you accompanying me, can I?' Fifty muskets would be damned useful, so long as the Marines could keep pace with the Riflemen. 'We march that way.'

Sharpe pointed south-east into the damp water-meadows that edged the Leyre.

Palmer nodded. 'Yes, sir.'

They marched, and if it had not been for his piercing, spiking headache, Sharpe would have been a happy man. For three days he was free to cause chaos, to carry the war, which the French had carried throughout Europe, deep into the heart of France itself. He would dutifully question his prisoners, but Sharpe already knew that he would not recommend an advance on Bordeaux and, if de Maquerre returned with such a recommendation, Sharpe, as senior land officer, would forbid the madness. He felt relieved of care, he was free, he was a soldier released from the leash to fight his own war; to which end, and reinforced with fifty footsore Marines, he marched south-east to set an ambush.

'I expected an answer to my letter,' Ducos said, 'I hardly expected you to come yourself.'

The Comte de Maquerre was chilled to the marrow. He had ridden across freezing marshland, and through low, vine-covered hills where the wind had been as bitter as a blade of ice; and all to be thus ungraciously received in a capacious room lit by six candles on a malachite table. 'My news is too important to be entrusted to a letter.'

'So?'

'A landing.' De Maquerre crouched by the fire, holding his thin hands to its small flames. 'At Arcachon. The fort's probably taken already and more men can be shipped north within a week.' He twisted to stare at Ducos' thin face. 'Then they'll march on Bordeaux.'

'Now? In this weather?' Ducos gestured towards the uncurtained windows where the wind beat a sharp tattoo of freezing rain on the black glass. Only that morning Ducos had found three sparrows frozen to death on the balcony of his quarters. 'No one could land in this weather!'

'They already have landed,' de Maquerre said. 'I was

with them. And once they hold the Bassin d'Arcachon they'll have sheltered waters to land a bigger force.' The Comte thrust impotently at the glowing coals, trying to rouse fierce flames, then described how he was supposed to return to Bampfylde with an encouragement for the British plans. 'If I say the city will rebel, then they'll ship their troops north.'

'How many?'

'The First Division.'

Ducos trimmed the wick of a smoking candle. 'How do you know all this?'

'Through a man called Wigram, a colonel . . .'

'. . . on the staff of the British First Division.' Ducos' knowledge of the enemy was encyclopaedic, and he loved to display it. 'A painstaking man.'

'Indeed,' de Maquerre shivered violently, 'and a man who will offer indiscretions in return for an aristocrat's company. Even a French aristocrat!' de Maquerre laughed softly, then twisted to face the table. 'Hogan's sick.'

'How sick?' Ducos' interest was quickened by the news.

'He'll die.'

'Good, good.' Pierre Ducos stared at his maps. He had the answer he had so desperately sought, but, like a man brought a priceless gift, he began to doubt the generosity of the giver. Suppose this news had been planted on de Maquerre? Suppose, after all, the British planned a bridge across the Adour, but wished the French to concentrate troops at Arcachon? Or suppose the invading force flooded ashore at the mouth of the Gironde? The answer had brought him no relief, merely more doubts. 'How many troops are already ashore?'

'Three Companies of Marines, two of Riflemen.'

'That's all!' Ducos snapped the words.

'They think it's enough,' de Maquerre said mildly. 'They plan to take the fortress, then ambush the supply road.'

'Ambitious of them,' Ducos said softly.

'They've got an ambitious bastard doing it,' de Maquerre

147

said viciously. 'A real bastard. It would be a pleasure to bury him.'

'Who?' Ducos asked in polite interest. His attention was on the map where his finger traced the thin line of the River Leyre. If such an ambush was planned, then that would be the closest stretch of road to the British landing.

'Major Richard Sharpe, Prince of Wales's Own Volunteers. He's really a Rifleman. God knows why he fights in a line Battalion.'

'Sharpe?'

Something in Ducos' voice made Maquerre turn. 'Sharpe.'

A spasm showed on Ducos' face, a twist of hatred that went almost as soon as it appeared, but was nevertheless a rare revelation of the real man behind the careful mask.

Richard Sharpe. The man who had mocked Ducos, who had once broken Ducos' spectacles, and who had destroyed all Ducos' careful plans in Spain.

Sharpe. A brute, a mindless barbarian whose sword had wrecked so many careful, elegant schemes. Sharpe, whom Ducos had once had at his mercy in Burgos Castle, except that the Rifleman had filled a small room with blood from which Ducos had fled in horror. Sharpe.

'You know him?' de Maquerre asked tentatively.

Know him? Did Ducos know Sharpe? If Pierre Ducos had been a superstitious man, which he prided himself on not being, he would have believed that Sharpe was his personal devil. How else did the Rifleman crop up so often to ruin his meticulous plans?

For Ducos was a man who laid careful, almost mathematical plans. He was a soldier whose rank bore no relation to his responsibility, a secretive man who drew together the strands of politics and soldiering, police-work and spying, all to the Emperor's glory. Now, in Bordeaux, Ducos was responsible for defending France's southern flank by forecasting the enemy's plans and, for once, the mention of Sharpe's name brought him relief.

If Sharpe had been sent to Arcachon, then doubtless de

Maquerre's news was correct. Wellington would not waste Sharpe on a diversion. Ducos' enemy had been delivered into his hands. Sharpe was doomed.

The exultation in that thought made Ducos pace to the window. A few lights flickered in the city that the Major so despised. The merchants of Bordeaux were suffering from the British blockade, their warehouses and quays were empty, and doubtless they would welcome a British victory if it swelled their bellies again and filled their strongboxes. 'You've done well, Comte.'

De Maquerre acknowledged the praise with a shrug.

Ducos turned. 'You leave tomorrow. Find Sharpe. I'll tell you where, and order him to Bordeaux.'

'If he obeys,' de Maquerre sounded dubious.

Ducos laughed; a strange, sudden yelp of a sound. 'We'll entice him! We'll entice him! Then go to Arcachon and give the very opposite message. You understand?'

De Maquerre, huddled by the fire, smiled slowly. By telling Bampfylde that there would be no rebellion in Bordeaux he would spike the British hopes for a landing, while, at the same time, he could maroon Sharpe in France. De Maquerre nodded. 'I understand.'

Ducos repeated his odd laugh. General Calvet's demi-brigade was billeted in Bordeaux on their journey south to Soult's Army. One half Battalion had already left with the cumbersome supplies, but Calvet must have at least two thousand men remaining who could destroy Sharpe at Arcachon. Ducos would ruin the British hopes for a march on Bordeaux and he would also hunt his own enemy, his own most hated enemy, to death on the marshes of France. Revenge, the Spanish said, was a dish best eaten cold, and this revenge, in this winter, would be as cold and thorough as any man, even the implacable Pierre Ducos, could wish.

CHAPTER 10

There was small sleep to be had that night for either Riflemen or Marines. The dawn was cold; bitter cold. Wraiths of mist drifted above the meadows frosted crisply white.

Sharpe woke with a stinging headache behind his bandaged forehead. He sat with his back against a pollarded willow and felt a louse in his armpit that must have come from the *Amelie*, but he was too tired and too cold to hunt for it.

'Jesus, Jesus, Jesus.' Frederickson, teeth chattering with the cold, crouched by Sharpe. 'Nothing passed yesterday.'

Dim in the mist, a hundred yards upstream, a handsome stone bridge with carved urns marking the limits of its balustrades, arched over the Leyre. Next to the bridge, and on the western bank down which Sharpe and his small force had marched last night, there stood a stone-built house from which a trickle of chimney smoke tantalized the senses with its promise of a warm fire.

'It's a toll-house,' Frederickson said, 'and the bugger wouldn't give us coffee.'

No doubt, Sharpe reflected, the toll-keepers of France were as disobliging as their English counterparts. There was something about that job to bring out the surliness in a man. 'If we had enough powder we could break that damn bridge.'

'We don't,' Frederickson said unhelpfully.

Sharpe struggled to his feet. Frederickson had taken the last watch and his picquets were set double-strength about the margins of the water-meadow where the small force had bivouacked. It had been a miserable bivouac. Some of the Marines had sheltered beneath the scanty cover of the

150

limbers, but most of Sharpe's men had simply rolled themselves in greatcoats, pillowed their heads on packs, and shivered through the slow, small hours.

A cow, on the further bank, bellowed softly and watched the two men who walked beside the river. A cow at pasture in February suggested a softer climate than England, but it was still damned cold. A swan, beautiful and ghostly, appeared beneath the bridge, followed a moment later by its mate, and the two birds, disdaining the unnatural movement in the fields, glided gently downstream. 'Luncheon,' Frederickson said.

'I never liked their taste,' Sharpe said, 'like stringy water-weeds.' He flinched as a sudden stab of pain lanced in his head. He wondered if the naval surgeon had been wrong, and if his wound was more serious than the mere bloody scrape of a carbine ball. He seemed to remember that Johnny Pearson of the Buffs had taken such a wound at Busaco, sworn it was nothing, then dropped dead a week later.

A rickety wooden fence, untended and draped with frost-whitened thorn, barred the steep embankment that carried this High Road of France southwards. Sharpe climbed to the carriageway that was formed of a white, flinty stone which had been rammed hard to smoothness, but which was nevertheless rutted and puddled with ice. No weeds grew on the surface, which bespoke constant use. To the south, where the road disappeared in the mist, he could see the shapes of houses, a church, and tall, bare poplars. The river curved here, and doubtless that small town was where the old road crossed the river, while this bridge, newer and wider, had been built in the meadows outside the town so that the hurrying armies would not have to negotiate narrow, mediæval streets on their urgent journeys to Spain. Down this carriageway, for the last six years, the guns and men and ammunition and horses and blades and saddles and all the countless trivia of war had been dragged to feed the French armies. And up this same road, Sharpe thought, those same armies would trudge in defeat. 'What's in the town?'

Frederickson knew Sharpe's question meant what enemy forces might be in the town. 'The toll-keeper says nothing.'

Sharpe turned to look north. 'And up there?'

'A stand of beeches a quarter mile up and an excuse for a farm. It'll do.'

Sharpe grunted. He trusted Frederickson absolutely, and if Frederickson said that the beeches and farm were the best site for an ambuscade, then Sharpe knew it would be pointless to look elsewhere.

A violent screech, a flapping of wings, and a sudden curse betrayed that the swans had been purloined for food. Captain Palmer, scratching his crotch and yawning, climbed the fence. ''Morning, sir.'

''Morning, Palmer,' Sharpe said. 'Cold enough for you?'

Palmer did not reply. The three officers walked towards the toll-house that was marked by a white barred gate across the road. A black and white painted board, just like those on the toll-houses of England, announced the crossing charges. There was a ford to the right of the bridge, but the ford had been half blocked with boulders so that no carriage or waggon could escape payment of the toll.

The toll-keeper, peg-legged and bald, stood truculently by his gate. He spoke to Frederickson, who, in turn, spoke to Sharpe. 'If we haven't got the *laissez-passer* then we have to pay six sous.'

'Lacy-passay?' Sharpe asked.

'I rather gave him to think we're German troops fighting for Bonaparte,' Frederickson said. 'The lacy-passay allows us to escape all tolls.'

'Tell him to go to hell.'

Frederickson conveyed Captain Sharpe's compliments to the toll-keeper who answered by spitting at Sharpe's feet. '*Trois hommes*,' the man said, holding up three fingers in case these heathen German troops did not understand him, '*six sous*.'

'Bugger him.' Sharpe raised the black-painted metal latch that held the gate shut and, from above him, a click sounded and he looked up to see the toll-keeper's wife leaning from an upper window. She was a woman of squat, startling ugliness, her hair bound with a muslin scarf, and, more to the immediate point, armed with a vast, brass-barrelled blunderbuss that covered the three officers.

'Six sous,' said the toll-keeper stoically. Life held few surprises for toll-keepers, and strange troops were nothing new to him.

Captain Palmer, who held Major Richard Sharpe's reputation in some awe, was now astonished to see the Rifleman grudgingly take out a ten-franc silver piece. A delay ensued while the toll-keeper went indoors, unlocked his iron-bound chest, found the right change, then gave Sharpe a written receipt which, Frederickson explained, would enable reimbursement to be made at the District Headquarters in Bordeaux.

'I can't have that bugger charging for all of us,' Sharpe said. 'Rather than disarm his Grenadier, William, we'll march the men through the ford.'

'Yes, sir.' Frederickson was highly amused by the whole transaction.

'Shouldn't we . . .?' Palmer began hesitantly.

'No,' Sharpe said. 'We're under orders not to agitate civilians, Captain. No stealing, no raping. If anyone breaks that order he'll be hanged. By me. Instantly.' His headache had made him speak more sharply than he had intended.

'Yes, sir.' Palmer sounded subdued.

They walked to the stand of beeches that Frederickson had patrolled in the night. 'It's the right place,' Sharpe said grudgingly, 'if anything travels today. Which I doubt.' Any sensible man would stay indoors on this cold day.

The beeches lay to the right of the road, the farm to the left. The farm was a miserable hovel of a place; merely a mud-walled cottage surrounded by frosted slush with two dilapidated outbuildings where chickens lived in filthy straw.

A pigsty lay beyond a low hedge. Sharpe broke a piece of cat-ice with his heel, then swivelled to look where the road passed between the beeches and the farm's hedgerow. 'We use your Marines there, Palmer. You stop them, and the Rifles will kill them.'

Palmer, not wanting to show any lack of understanding, nodded. Frederickson understood instantly. By using the Marines, with their heavy firepower of quick-loading muskets, as the stop in the bottle, Sharpe would force an enemy to scatter left and right to outflank the road-block. On those flanks they would run into the hidden Riflemen. It would be quick, bloody, and effective. 'What if they come from the south?'

'Leave them.' Sharpe knew that any northward-bound convoy would be travelling empty.

It took two hours to set the trap. No one could be visible, and so Minver's Company of Riflemen and Palmer's Marines were somehow crammed into the tiny farm buildings. Frederickson's Company, drawing the short straw because Sharpe trusted their officer, were in the more exposed beech wood. Harper, with two of Frederickson's Riflemen, was a half mile to the north as look-out.

The farmer, with his wife and daughter, crouched in a corner of their kitchen that was filled with big, stinking men armed with the heavy Sea-Service muskets. The daughter was waif-like and, beneath her stringy, dirty hair, pretty in a winsome and frightened way. The Marines, starved of women for months, eyed her hopefully.

'One flicker of trouble,' Sharpe warned Palmer, 'and I'll kill the man responsible.'

'Yes, sir.'

Sharpe visited the Riflemen in the small barn. The barn's outside end wall, as in England, served as the countryman's museum. A stoat was nailed to the wood, its old, dry fur pricked with frost. Ravens decayed there, and an otter skin hung empty. The Riflemen, despite their cold breakfast and shivering night, grinned at Sharpe.

He walked north along the hedgerow. He saw two men strolling down the road with a dog at their heels. A quarter of an hour later a woman drove a skeletal cow north, doubtless to sell the beast at market to raise enough cash to see the winter through. None of them saw the Rifleman.

It seemed extraordinary to Sharpe that he could be here, deep in France, unchallenged. Only the Navy, he supposed, could make such a thing possible. The French, bereft of a fleet, could never set such a trap on a Hampshire road. But Sharpe could come here, strike like a snake, and be gone by the next sundown, while Bampfylde's flotilla, riding at the mouth of the Arcachon Channel, was as safe as if it was anchored in the River Hamble.

Sharpe turned back towards the farm. The cold weather and the emptiness of the road made him doubt whether any convoy would travel today. His head hurt foully and, safe from any man's gaze, he flinched with the pain and rubbed a cautious hand over his bandaged forehead. Johnny Pearson, he remembered, had just pitched forward into a dish of hot tripe; no warning, no sound, just stone dead a few seconds after he had cheerfully said it was time to take the bandage off his scalp. Sharpe pressed his forehead to test whether the bone grated. It did not, but it hurt like the very devil.

Back in the farm hovel a cauldron boiled on the open fire and the Marines had pooled their tea to fill the small room with a homely smell. The girl, Sharpe noticed, was now giving the strangers shy smiles. She had catlike, green eyes, and she laughed when the men tried to talk to her.

'Take some tea to the barn,' Sharpe ordered.

''Twas our leaves,' a voice said from the back of the room.

Sharpe turned, but no one pressed the objection and the tea was taken out to the Riflemen.

The frost melted outside. The mist cleared somewhat, showing the poplars to the north where Harper lay hidden in a ditch. A grey heron, enemy of trout fishermen, sailed with slow, flapping wings towards the north.

Sharpe, as the morning wore on and as the Marines beguiled the green-eyed girl into giggling flirtation, decided the day was being wasted. Nothing would come. He crossed to Frederickson's men to find them hidden deep beneath the thick drifts of dead leaves and told Sweet William that, if nothing appeared within two hours, they would start to withdraw. 'We'll march to Facture and billet the men warm tonight.' That would leave a short crisp distance for the morning march to Arcachon where Sharpe would insist that the nonsense about taking Bordeaux be abandoned.

Frederickson was disappointed that this journey might be in vain. 'You wouldn't wait till dusk?'

'No.' Sharpe shivered inside his greatcoat. He was sure nothing would come now, though he partly suspected that he rather hoped nothing would come so that he could begin the homeward journey. Besides, his head was splitting fit to burst. He told himself he needed a doctor, but he dared not reveal the extent of his pain to Frederickson. Sharpe forced a rueful smile. 'Nothing's going to come, William. I feel it in my bones.'

'You have a reliable skeleton?'

'It's never wrong,' Sharpe said.

The enemy came at midday.

Harper and his two men brought news of it. Twenty cavalry, walking rather than riding their horses, led six canvas-covered wagons, two coaches, and five Companies of infantry. Sharpe, trying to ignore the searing stabs in his head, considered Harper's report. The enemy was coming in strength, but Sharpe decided that surprise would nullify that advantage. He nodded to Palmer. 'Go.' He ran to the barn and ordered Minver's Riflemen to their hidden positions. 'If I blow "withdraw",' he said, 'you know where to go.'

'Over the bridge.' Minver drew his sword and licked his lips. 'And cover the retreat.'

Sharpe doubled back, Harper with him, to where the

Marines crouched behind the hedge. 'You see the milestone?' Sharpe said to Palmer.

Palmer nodded. Fifty yards up the road was a milestone that had been first defaced of its number of miles, then re-inscribed with the strange kilometres that had recently been introduced in France. The stone recorded that it was 43 kilometres to Bordeaux, a distance that meant nothing to Sharpe. 'We don't move till they reach that stone, understand?'

'Yes, sir.' Palmer blanched to think of letting the enemy come that close, but raised no objection.

Normally all Sharpe's presentiments, any gloom, would have vanished at the first sight of the enemy, but the pain in his skull was a terrible distraction. He wanted to lie down in a dark place, he wanted the oblivion of sleep, and he tried to will the pain away, but it was there, tormenting him, and he forced his attention past the stabbing ache to watch the cavalry appear from the last wisps of mist. Through his glass he could see that the cavalry horses were winter-thin. The British Army, in their tiny corner of France, had not even brought the cavalry over the Pyrenees, knowing that until the spring grass had fattened the horses the cavalry would be a burden rather than an advantage. But the French had always been more careless of their horses. 'If a horse gets close to you,' Sharpe told the Marines who, he thought, might not have experienced cavalry before, 'hit it in the bloody mouth.' The Marines, shivering in the lee of the hedge, grinned nervously.

Behind the cavalry, squealing as such waggons always squealed, the heavy transport waggons lumbered on the roadway. Each was hauled by eight oxen. Behind the waggons were the infantry, and behind the infantry the two carriages that had their windows and curtains tight closed against the cold.

Sharpe pushed his telescope back into his pocket. In the beech wood, he knew, Frederickson's killers would be sliding loaded rifles forward. This was like shooting fish in a barrel, for the enemy, deep in their homeland, would be marching with unloaded muskets and absent minds. They would be thinking of sweethearts left behind, of the next night's billet, and of the enemy waiting at the far, far end of the long road.

A French cavalry officer, brass helmet shielded with canvas and with a black cloak covering his gaudy uniform, suddenly swung up into his saddle. He spurred ahead of the convoy, doubtless drawn to the town beyond the river where wineshops would be open and fires burning in brick hearths.

'Damn.' Sharpe said it under his breath. The man could not help but see the ambush and he would spring it fifty yards too soon. But nothing went as planned in war, and the disadvantage must be taken, then ignored. 'Deal with the bugger, Patrick. Wait till he sees us.'

'Yes, sir.' Harper thumbed back the cock of his rifle.

Sharpe looked at Palmer. 'On my order we advance. Two files.'

'Yes, sir.'

'No shouting, no cheering.' French and Spanish troops cheered as they advanced, but the silence of a British attack was an eerie and unsettling thing. The Marines, white-faced, crouched low. One crossed himself, while another, his eyes shut, seemed to be praying silently.

The French officer kicked his horse into a trot. The man had a cigar which dribbled smoke, and his broad, open face looked cheerfully at the sodden, misty countryside. He glanced at the farm, bent to pluck his cloak loose of his stirrup leather where it had wrapped itself as he mounted, then saw the red coats and white crossbelts where the Marines were concealed in the hedge-shadow that was still white with frost.

He was so astonished that he kept coming, mouth opening to shout an inquiry, and when he was still some fifteen yards short of the hedgerow, Harper shot him.

The rifle bullet struck a cuirass hidden by the cloak. The ball, squarely hitting the steel, punctured the armour and deflected upwards, through the Frenchman's throat and into his brain. Blood, bright as dawn, fountained from the man's open mouth.

'In line!' Sharpe bellowed. 'Advance!'

The horse, terrified, reared.

The Frenchman, still incongruously holding his cigar, toppled backwards in the saddle. He was dead, but his knees still gripped the horse's flanks and, when the beast plunged its forefeet back down, the corpse nodded forward in a grotesque obeisance to the Marines who were scrambling from the ditch to form a double-line across the road.

'Forward!'

The horse turned, eyes showing white, and the dead Frenchman seemed to grin a bloodshot grin at Sharpe before the horse whirled the ghastly face away. The body slumped to the left, fell, but the man's boot was fast caught in the stirrup and the corpse was dragged, bouncing, behind the bolting horse.

'Hold your fire!' Sharpe cautioned the Marines. He wanted no nervous man to waste a musket shot. He drew his sword. 'Double!'

The remaining cavalry had stopped, appalled. The waggons, with their vast weight, still trundled forward. The infantry seemed oblivious of the ambush's opening shot.

The Marines, their breath misting, ran up the road that was marked with great splashes of blood. Sharpe's boot crushed the dead cavalry officer's fallen cigar.

Two cavalrymen hauled carbines from their saddle holsters. 'Halt!' Sharpe shouted.

He stood to one side of the road. 'Front rank kneel!' That was not entirely necessary, but a kneeling rank always steadied raw troops and Sharpe knew that these Marines, for all their willingness, had small experience in land fighting. 'Captain Palmer? Fire low, if you please.'

Palmer, a naval cutlass in his hand, seemed startled at Sharpe's sudden courtesy in allowing him to give the order to fire. He cleared his throat, measured the distance to the enemy, saw how the handful of cavalry were already climbing into saddles and spreading on to the verges, and shouted the order. 'Fire!'

Fifty musket balls crashed out of fifty muzzles.

'Reload!' a sergeant shouted. Lieutenant Fytch, a heavy brass-hilted pistol in his right hand, jiggled up and down on the balls of his feet with excitement.

Harper had gone right to clear the filthy, yellowish cloud of musket smoke. He saw six horses down, legs kicking on the roadway's stone. Two men had fallen, while two others crawled towards the beechwood. An ox from the leading waggon was bellowing with pain.

A carbine banged, then another. Far to the convoy's rear the French infantry were hurrying down the verges, officers shouting. The ox-waggons, brake blocks squealing, were juddering to a clumsy halt.

Harper was looking for officers. He saw one, a cavalryman with drawn sabre, who was bellowing at his men to form line and charge.

It took Harper twenty seconds to reload the Baker Rifle. Another Marine volley hammered forward, this one doing less damage because the redcoats, unsighted by their musket smoke, fired blind. Harper had the rifle at his shoulder, the officer in his sights, and he pulled the trigger.

Black powder flared, flaming debris lashed his cheek, then he unslung the seven-barrelled gun and jumped sideways again. The officer was turning away, hand clasped to a shoulder, but a half dozen cavalrymen were coming forward, sabres drawn and spurs slashing back at thin flanks.

''Ware cavalry, sir!' Harper shouted to Palmer then, hearing the wooden ramrods of the Marines still rattling in barrels, he fired his volley gun.

The impact threw him backwards, but the noise of the seven-barrelled gun, like a small cannon, seemed to stun the tiny battlefield. Two cavalrymen were snatched from their saddles, a horse swivelled to throw its rider, and the cavalry's small threat was finished. Then, beyond the wounded horses and the scatter of the day's first dead, the leading two

Companies of French infantry appeared in front of the waggons. Their muskets were tipped with bayonets.

Frederickson opened fire.

The volley, stinging from the flank, flayed into the first infantry ranks, and Frederickson was bellowing commands as though he held more men under orders. The French were glancing nervously towards the beechwood as Captain Palmer loosed his third volley.

The mist remnants were thick with smoke now. The stench of blood mingled with powder-stink.

Sharpe had joined Harper. Minver's men, slower to deploy, were firing from the left.

'Stop loading!' Sharpe shouted at the Marines. 'Front rank up! Fix swords!' The headache was forgotten now in the greater urgencies of life and death.

'Bayonets, sir,' Harper muttered. Only Green Jackets, who carried the sword bayonet, used the order to fix swords.

'Bayonets! Bayonets! Captain Palmer! I'll trouble you to go forward!'

Sharpe could sense this whole battle now, could feel it in his instincts and he knew it was won. There was an exultation, an excitement, a feeling that no other experience on God's earth could bring. It could bring death, too, and wounds so vile that a man would shudder in his sleep to dream of them, but war also gave this supreme feeling of imposing the will on an enemy and taking success in the face of disaster.

The French outnumbered Sharpe by three or four to one, but the French were dazed, disorganized, and shaken. Sharpe's men were keyed to the fight, ready for it, and if he struck now, if he behaved as though he had already won, then this half stunned enemy would break.

Sharpe looked at the Marines. 'Advance. At the double! Advance!'

The cavalry was gone, destroyed by the seven-barrelled gun and by Frederickson's sharpshooters. Dead and wounded horses lay in the fields, dropped by rifle-fire, and their surviving riders had fled to the safety of the waggons that offered some small shelter from the bullets. In front of the waggons a rabble of infantry was being shaken into line and Sharpe's Marines, coming from the smoke with muskets tipped with bayonets, charged them.

If the enemy held, Sharpe knew, then the Marines would be slaughtered.

If the enemy held, then each Marine would be faced with three or four bayonets.

It would only take one enemy officer, one of those blue-coated men on horseback, to survey Sharpe's feeble charge and the Marines were done for.

'Charge!' Sharpe shouted it as though the volume of his voice alone would breed extra men to face down the enemy line that, uneven though it was, bristled with blades.

'Fire!' Frederickson, good Frederickson, had understood all. He had formed his Company into ranks, taken them from the trees' cover and now, at sixty yards range, poured a controlled volley of rifle fire into the infantry's flank.

That volley, with Sharpe's stumbling charge, broke the French. Just as scared Frenchmen began to see the paucity of the attacking force, so another enemy appeared and another voice was shouting charge, and then the sight of the bayonets, as it so often did, engendered panic.

The French infantry, mostly young conscripts who had no stomach for a fight, broke and fled. An officer beat at them with the flat of his sabre, but the French were running backwards. The officer turned, drew a pistol, but a rifle bullet buried itself in his belly and he folded forward, eyes gaping, and one of Frederickson's Riflemen grasped the bridle as the officer fell sideways to the cold earth.

'Form at the first waggon's rear!' Sharpe yelled it to Palmer as they ran forward. The Marines' line was now broken by the necessity for men to step around the dead and dying on the ground. Harper, who could not bear to see an animal suffer, picked up a fallen French pistol and shot a wounded, screaming horse between the eyes.

A carbine, fired by a dismounted cavalryman, threw down a Marine. Minver's men shot the cavalryman, six bullets striking at once and flinging him down like a puppet that lay suddenly still and bloodied on the pale grass.

There were fugitives under the first waggon. One still had a musket and Sharpe, thinking it loaded, struck with his sword to knock it clear. The boy, terrified, screamed, but Sharpe had gone on, jumping blue-jacketed dead. Ahead, in a foul panic, a mass of infantry tumbled in pell mell retreat. An officer, emerging from a coach, shouted at them, and some, braver than the rest, slowed, turned, and formed a new line.

'Captain Frederickson!'

'I see them, sir!'

Sharpe ran behind the rear of a waggon. On this left side of the road, where Minver's men stayed in hiding, a full Company of French infantry was formed in three ranks. '60th!' Sharpe had to shout twice to Minver as Frederickson's volley drowned his first shout. 'Flank attack! Flank attack!'

Palmer's Marines were panting. Some had reddened bayonets, and others stabbed at Frenchmen cowering beneath the heavy waggon, but Palmer and his sergeants pushed them into line and shouted at them to load muskets.

The French Company fired first.

The range was seventy yards, too long for muskets, but two Marines were down, a third was screaming, and the others still thrust with wooden ramrods at powder and bullets. Sharpe supposed the Marines used wooden ramrods because metal rods would rust at sea, then forgot the idle speculation as more enemy bullets thumped into the heavy timber of the waggons. Stragglers from the first Company had joined the ranks where French muskets tipped up as the enemy began to reload.

'Aim!' Palmer shouted.

'Hold your fire! Hold your fire!' Sharpe took station at the head of the Marines. He made his voice steady. There was a time to rouse men in battle and a time to calm them. 'Marines will advance. At the march! Forward!' Sharpe was taking the Marines down the left flank of the waggons, leaving Frederickson to control the right side of the road.

Minver's Riflemen were showing themselves on this French flank, green-jacketed men who appeared from behind trees and farm buildings, men who worked forward in the skirmishing chain, each man covering his partner, and their fire nibbled at the flank of the French Company.

A French officer looked sideways, judging whether to turn a file to flick the Riflemen away with a controlled volley, then he looked forward to where the redcoats advanced.

This was no mad charge, meant to panic, but a slow, steady advance to show confidence. Sharpe wanted to close the range, he wanted this volley of musketry to kill. He watched the enemy's movements. Ramrods, new and bright-metalled, flashed as they were raised. He heard the scraping rattle as they plunged downwards into muskets held between clenched knees. 'Marines! Halt!'

The boots of the men who advanced on the road crashed to attention. The sound seemed unnaturally loud.

Minver's men still fired, their bullets spinning constantly from the flank. Carbine bullets, fired by dismounted cavalrymen, buzzed past Sharpe. An ox, oblivious of the carnage around, staled on the road and the smell of the steam pricked at Sharpe's nostrils. 'To your front! Aim!' Sharpe wanted this slow and sure. He wanted the Frenchmen to see the shape of their death before it came. He wanted them scared.

The Marine line seemed to take a quarter turn to the right as the muskets went into the shoulders. One or two men who had not yet cocked their pieces pulled back the flints and the clicks seemed ominous.

Sharpe walked to the flank of the Marine formation and raised his sword. Some of the French were priming their muskets, but most were staring nervously at the small line of redcoats who seemed so deliberate and savage. Sharpe lct them wait, giving their imaginations time to torment them.

Harper came to stand alongside Sharpe. He had his rifle loaded, aimed, and he waited for the order. To Harper's eyes these Frenchmen were boys, the scrapings of a countryside to bring Napoleon's armies up to strength. These were not the moustached, experienced veterans who had died in the appalling Spanish battles, but conscripts dragged unwilling from school or farm to die in a cause that was doomed anyway.

The conscripts primed their pieces. Some had forgotten to take their ramrods out of their musket barrels, but it did not matter.

'Aim low!' Sharpe's voice was harsh. He knew most troops fired high. 'Aim at their balls! Fire!' The sword swept down.

The volley smashed out, the sound of the muskets deafening as the heavy weapons leaped back into bruised shoulders. The smoke, stinking of rotten eggs, made its fog.

'Lie down!' Sharpe shouted. He saw astonished faces and his voice rose in anger. 'Lie down! Lie down!'

The Marines, puzzled, dropped flat. Sharpe knelt to one side of the rolling, poisonous cloud of musket smoke.

The French Company had shaken as the volley struck home. Just like a man punched in the belly the whole Company seemed to fold, then the officers and sergeants, shouting orders, pushed the ranks back into placc and Sharpe saw how the rear files had to step over the writhing and the dead left by the Marine's well-aimed volley.

The French commander ignored the Riflemen on his flank. They could be dealt with after the redcoats. '*Tirez!*'

For a new Company, unblooded, it was a good response. Sixty or seventy muskets fired at the gunsmoke, but the Marines were flat and the conscripts fired high.

'Go for them! Go!' Sharpe was triumphant now. This one Company had been the last danger, but hc had drawn their sting by laying his men flat. 'On your feet! On your feet!

Go! Cheer, you bastards!' This was the moment for noise, the moment for terror.

The Marines, who a second before had been the target for a controlled, tight volley, scrambled unscathed to their feet and charged. They yelled as if they were boarding an enemy ship. Lieutenant Fytch fired his pistol wildly, then tried to drag his heavy sword from its scabbard.

The conscripts, staring through their own musket-smoke, saw the unharmed enemy coming with long bayonets and, like the first two Companies at the convoy's head, broke.

Some were slow, and those the Marines caught and pinned to the ground with bayonets. A mounted officer, scarlet-faced and furious, charged at the redcoats, but Sharpe lunged with his sword, caught the horse's hindquarters and the beast turned, teeth snapping, as the officer hacked down with his infantry sword.

The blades met, clashed, and the shock ran up Sharpe's arm. The horse reared, lashed with its hooves as it was trained to do, but Sharpe backswung the sword into the beast's mouth as he was trained to do.

The animal twisted, the officer kicked his feet out of the stirrups and, as the horse fell to one side, nimbly threw himself clear. The horse collapsed off balance, lips bleeding, then scrambled to its feet as if nothing was amiss.

'Surrender,' Sharpe said to the officer.

The reply, whatever it meant, did not signify surrender. The Frenchman's sword blade flickered out in an expert lunge. The man's horse was now cropping the grass and the Frenchman reached with his spare hand for its bridle.

Sharpe lunged, knew that the man would counterattack, so immediately stepped back. The blade duly came for him, skewered thin air, and Sharpe's heavy blade cracked down on to the sword hilt, driving the weapon down, and Sharpe stepped forward, brought his knee up, then used the ugly, iron guard of his sword to punch the officer's face. 'Surrender, you crapaud bastard!'

The officer was on the grass, sword forgotten and hands clutched to his crotch. He was gasping for breath, moaning, and Sharpe decided that constituted a surrender. He kicked the man's sword into the ditch, pulled the horse towards him, and hauled himself clumsily into the saddle. He wanted the extra height to see what happened on his small, well-chosen battlefield.

The French had run. A Company of them were being organized a quarter mile north, but they posed no immediate problem. A few survivors still clung to the waggons, some died from bayonet thrusts, but most were being taken prisoner. The waggons were otherwise abandoned and Sharpe guessed their drivers, with other fugitives, had fled into the beech woods. 'Captain Palmer?'

Palmer seemed astonished to see Sharpe on horseback. 'Sir?'

'One squad of men into the beech trees. Flush the damn place clear. Don't be cautious about it! Scare the bastards!'

'Yes, sir.'

'Captain Frederickson!' Sharpe twisted the horse towards the far side of the road. 'Keep that Company busy!' Sharpe pointed to the north. 'Take half Minver's men and press them, William, press them!'

There were picquets to be set on the flanks, the wounded to take into the shelter of the waggons, and the waggons themselves to explore. The two coaches, harness-horses shivering, were brought forward. One was empty, the other contained two women who sat, terrified, with smelling salts uncapped. 'Put a guard on them, Captain Palmer! Unharness the horses.' Sharpe would leave the women where they were, but the horses, like the oxen, would be scattered into the meadows. Some men would have advised killing the animals to deprive the French of their future use, but Sharpe could not bear to give that order.

The oxen lumbered away, protesting under the prodding of the bayonets. One beast, wounded by a musket bullet in the small battle, was slaughtered and Sharpe watched two

Marines cutting up the steaming, warm flesh that would make a fine supper tonight.

Other Marines swarmed over the waggons, ripping the canvas covers away and slashing the tie-ropes. Barrels and boxes were uncovered and thrown to the road's verges where the prisoners, shivering and terrified, sat under guard.

It had taken twenty-five minutes of savagery, of fire and smoke and bluff and blood, and a French convoy, deep in France and guarded by a half Battalion of troops, was taken. Better still, and even more inexplicable, Sharpe's headache was entirely gone.

CHAPTER 11

Lieutenant of Marines Fytch, to whom Sharpe had hardly spoken since they had marched inland, brought the civilians to Major Sharpe. The Lieutenant herded them at pistol-point until told by Sharpe to put his damned toy away. Fytch, his martial ardour offended by the Rifleman, gestured at the four stout and worried looking men. 'They're from the town, sir. Buggers want to surrender.'

The four men, all dressed in good woollen clothes, smiled nervously at the mounted officer. They each wore the white cockade which was the symbol of the exiled King Louis XVIII and thus an emblem of anti-Napoleonic sentiment. The sight of the cockade, and the evident willingness of the four men to embrace a British victory, were uncomfortable reminders to Sharpe of Bampfylde's hopes. Perhaps Bordeaux, like this small town, was ripe for rebellion? He should, Sharpe knew, have interrogated a captured French officer by now, but his determination to obey Elphinstone's privately given orders, had made him ignore the duty.

'Kindly ask them,' Sharpe said to Fytch who evidently had some French, 'if they still wish to surrender when they understand that we will be leaving here this afternoon and may not be back for some months?'

The Mayor's monarchical enthusiasm evaporated swiftly. He smiled, bowed, fingered the cockade nervously, and backed away. But he still wished to assure the English milord that anything the town could offer his men would be available. They had only to ask for Monsieur Calabord.

'Get rid of him,' Sharpe said. 'Politely! And get those damned civilians off the bridge!' Townspeople, hearing the crackle of musketry, had come to view the battle. The one-legged toll-keeper was vainly trying to make them pay for the privilege of their grandstand view.

Frederickson's rifles snapped from the north as he harried the broken infantry away from the scene of their defeat. Two waggoners and four cavalrymen, hands held high, were being prodded from the beech trees towards the disconsolate prisoners. Marines were piling captured muskets in a pile.

The luckiest Marines were rifling the waggons. Much of the plunder was useless to a looter. There were vats of yellow and black paint that the French mixed to colour their gun-carriages, and which now the Marines spilled on to the road to mingle with the blood and ox-dung. Two of the waggons held nothing but engineer's supplies. There were coils of three inch white-cable, sap forks, cross-cut saws, bench-hammers, chalk-lines, scrapers, felling-axes, augers, and barrels of Hambro' line. There were spare cartouches for the infantry, each bag filled with a wooden block drilled to hold cartridges. Other waggons held drag-chains, crooked-sponges, relievers, bricoles, wad-hooks, sabot-bracers, and hand-spikes. There were garlands for the stacking of round-shot and even band instruments including a Jingling Johnny that a proud Marine paraded about the stripped waggons and shook so that the tiny bells mounted on the wooden frame made a strangely festive sound in the bleak, cold day. Another man banged the clash-pans until Sharpe curtly ordered him to drop the bloody cymbals.

On one waggon there were crates of tinned food. The French had recently invented the process and it was a miracle to Sharpe how such food stayed fresh over weeks or even months. Bayonets prised open lids, and jellied chickens and joints of lamb were hacked into portions so that men's faces, already blackened by powder smoke, were now smeared with grease. Sharpe accepted a leg of chicken and found it delicious. He ordered two dozen of the tins put aside for Frederickson's Riflemen.

And in the centre two waggons, strapped down by three

inch cable and covered by a double wrapping of tarpaulin, was powder. Barrels of black powder that were destined for the mortars at Bayonne, and coils of quick-match to be cut into shell-fuses. 'Lieutenant Minver!'

'Sir?'

'These waggons! Drag them to the bridge. I want the powder packed in the roadway.' It would not be a scientifically controlled explosion, as Hogan so long ago had taught Sharpe to devise, but it might seriously weaken the new stone structure with its proud, carved urns, and the purpose of Sharpe's incursion was to slow the French supplies. A blown bridge, demanding a detour through an old town, would cause a temper-fraying delay. 'And pack all the other waggonloads round it!'

That would take at least two hours. In the meantime captured spades dug graves in the cold soil of the water meadows. A French cavalryman, wearing the odd plaited pigtails at his temples, the *cadenettes*, was buried first. French prisoners did the work for the twenty-two dead Frenchmen, while the Marines dug graves for their three dead.

'Congratulations, sir,' Palmer said.

'Your men did well, Captain.' Sharpe meant it. He had been impressed by the steadiness of the Marines, and by their swiftness to reload muskets. Those qualities won battles, and battles changed history.

Patrick Harper, a tinned chicken in one hand, brought Sharpe a leather bag taken from the abandoned carriage. 'It's all Frog scribble, sir.'

Sharpe looked through the papers and suspected they were just the kind of thing Michael Hogan prayed for. Hogan might be dead now, but the papers would be a goldmine to whoever had succeeded to his job.

'Guard them, Patrick.'

Harper had also helped himself to a fine, silver-chased pistol that had been discarded in the carriage.

The sun, paled to a silver disc by new cloud and mist, was low. A cold wind, the first wind since Sharpe had spared

Killick's life, sighed chill over the graves. A scream came from the farm, and a cheer went up from the Marines searching the last waggon as they found wine bottles packed in sawdust. A corporal brought a bottle to Sharpe. 'Sir?'

'Thank you, Corporal.' Sharpe held the bottle out to Harper who obligingly struck the neck with the blade of his sword-bayonet. The scream sounded again. A girl's scream.

Sharpe dropped the wine and put his heels back. Prisoners twisted aside as the horse plunged down the bank, jumped a shallow ditch, then Sharpe reined the beast right, ducked under a bare-branched apple tree, and twisted left. Pounding feet sounded behind him, but all Sharpe could see was a man running away, running towards the river and Sharpe put his heels back again.

The man was a Marine. He was clutching his red jacket loose in one hand and holding up his unbuttoned breeches with his other. He looked over his shoulder, saw Sharpe, and dodged to his right.

'Stop!'

The man did not stop, but ducked through a gap in the thorn hedge that tore his jacket from his grasp. He abandoned it and began running across the field. Sharpe forced his horse at the gap, kicked it through, and drew his sword. The man was stumbling, flailing for balance on the tussocks of the meadow, then the flat of the heavy sword, swept down in a clumsy curve, took him on the side of the head. He fell, uncut by the blade, and Sharpe circled the horse back to the fallen man.

It was all because of the farm girl; the green-eyed, pale, shivering girl whom the man had dragged into the scanty hay-store and attacked. She was now sitting, trembling, with the scraps of her torn clothing drawn around her thin body.

'She asked for it,' the Marine, taken back to the dung-stinking farmyard, said.

'Shut your face!' Harper had appointed himself Master-at-Arms. 'She wouldn't be bloody screaming and you wouldn't be bloody running, would you?'

'Fetch her some clothes,' Sharpe snarled at one of the Marines who had formed a circle about the prisoner. 'Captain Palmer! You warned this man?'

Palmer, pale-faced, nodded.

'Well?' Sharpe insisted on a verbal acknowledgement.

'Aye, aye, sir.' Palmer swallowed. 'But the girl wasn't raped, sir.'

'You mean she screamed too loudly. But you know what the orders are, don't you?' This question was addressed to all the Marines who stared with undisguised hostility at the Rifle Officer who threatened to hang one of their own comrades. There was silence as Sharpe rammed his sword home. 'Now back to your duties! All of you!' He jumped off the horse.

Captain Palmer, a Marine sergeant, Harper and Sharpe stayed with the prisoner. The story came slowly at first, then quickly. It had been attempted rape. The girl, the Marine said, had encouraged him, but her screams and the bruises and scratches on her thin arms told a different story.

'Matthew Robinson's a steady man, sir.' Palmer walked with Sharpe to the end of the farmyard. Sharpe could see that Minver's Riflemen had managed to get the first powder waggon to the end of the bridge, but, faced with the slope of the roadway, could get it no further. They were now rolling the powder barrels to the crown of the arch.

'You know what the Standing Orders are,' Sharpe said bleakly.

'It won't happen again, sir.' Palmer sounded contrite.

'I know damned well it won't happen again!' Sharpe, hating the necessity of the moment, snapped the words. 'That's why we're hanging the bastard!'

'I mean we don't need Robinson's death as an example, sir,' Palmer pleaded.

'I'm not doing it as an example.' Sharpe turned and gestured towards the farmer and his wife. 'I'm doing it for them! If the French people think we're savages, Palmer, then they'll fight us. You know what it's like having *guerrilleros* up your backside when you fight? Every waggon we send up from the coast will have to be guarded by a Battalion! Every one! That's how we beat the French out of Spain, Captain, not just by hammering the bastards in battle, but because half their armies were guarding waggons against Spanish peasants. Peasants like them!' Again he pointed to the French couple.

'The girl wasn't harmed, sir,' Palmer said stubbornly. 'And we've proved by our action here that we can offer protection.'

'And the story is spread about,' Sharpe said, 'that a man can rape a girl and his officers will condone it.'

Palmer stood his ground. 'If Robinson was one of your men, sir, one of your Riflemen, would you . . .'

'Yes,' Sharpe said, and knew instantly that if he was Palmer, and Bampfylde was the officer demanding the hanging, then Sharpe would fight just like Palmer for the life of his man. God damn it, but, years before, Sharpe had even defended the most useless man in his Light Company in just this same situation.

Palmer saw Sharpe's hesitation. 'Robinson fought damned well, sir. Doesn't your Field Marshal mitigate punishment for bravery in the field?'

Wellington had been known to cancel a half-dozen hangings because the prisoners' Battalions had fought well. Sharpe swore, hating the decision. 'Orders are orders, Mr Palmer.'

'Just as I believe we're ordered to hang privateers and deserters, sir?' Palmer said it bluntly, daring Sharpe's wrath.

'Damn your insolence.' Sharpe said it without conviction, almost as a sop to the weakness he was showing. 'You will apologize to the girl and to her parents. Give them this.' He took two of the forged silver ten-franc pieces from his pouch.

'Thank you, sir.' Palmer beamed as he took the coins.

'I'm not done with him,' Sharpe warned. 'RSM Harper!'

Harper pretended not to notice his restoration to Regimental Sergeant Major. 'Sir?'

'Take Marine Robinson and the girl's father round the back of the barn. I want you at the bridge in ten minutes!'

'Do I need a rope, sir?'

'No. But give the father his chance.' God damn it, Sharpe thought, but he had broken orders again. First he spared a damned American, now a Marine, and what was the point of orders if sentimentality weakened a man into disregarding them?

'Thank you, sir,' Palmer said again.

'You won't thank me when you see what Patrick Harper can do to a man. You'll be carrying Robinson home.'

'Better than burying him, sir.'

The incident put Sharpe into a sour mood, worsened by the feeling that he had shown weakness. Twice now he had backed out of an execution and he wondered if it was because he had taken a respectable wife. Old soldiers claimed that marriage did weaken a man, and Sharpe suspected they were right. His foul mood was not helped by the agonizing slowness with which the powder was being crammed between the bridge's balustrades. Lieutenant Fytch had ordered the toll-keeper and his wife out of their house and the woman, who had earlier threatened Sharpe with her blunderbuss, was now weeping for the loss of her home. Her husband, stumping on his wooden leg, was dragging belongings out to the road.

The sound of Frederickson's rifle fire had finished and Sharpe saw the Company marching back towards the bridge. That meant the French had gone altogether, though he knew Sweet William would have left picquets to guard against their return.

Using the Marines to help, the Riflemen hastened the setting of the explosives. The other supplies, destined for Soult's army, were heaped about the powder barrels. Frederickson sounded his whistle to pull in the picquets, while a squad of Minver's men pushed the townspeople further away from the bridge. It was getting dark, and Sharpe wanted to be moving.

'Sir!' Patrick Harper, who had silently reappeared at the bridge, pointed northwards. 'Sir!'

Two horsemen had appeared. They had not come by the road, but instead, perhaps forewarned by the retreating infantry, had made a wide detour through the fields. Now, with white handkerchiefs skewered to their sword-tips as makeshift flags of truce, they galloped their horses towards the bridge.

They were good horses, corn fed and with strong hind-quarters. Both took the soft, plunging ground like thorough-breds and were scarcely blowing as they were curbed beside Sharpe who waved down the cautious rifles of Frederickson's newly arrived Company.

The Comte de Maquerre, dressed in his *Chasseurs Britannique* uniform beneath his pale cloak, nodded cautiously at Sharpe. The other rider was a slim, middle-aged man in civilian clothes. He had a face of such startling and pleasant honesty that Sharpe's weariness and self-disgust seemed to vanish like frost beneath the rising sun. The man was so calm and self-composed that Sharpe instinctively smiled in response to his greeting, which consisted of mild astonishment at the evidence of carnage on the road and a frank expression of admiration for Sharpe's success.

The man was French, but spoke good English, and his loyalty was proclaimed by the white cockades that he wore, not only on his brown cloak, but also on his bicorne hat. 'I am Jules Favier, assistant to the Mayor of Bordeaux.' He spoke as he climbed from the saddle. 'And I am at your service, Major.'

The Comte de Maquerre stayed on horseback. His thin face, reddened by the cold, seemed nervous. 'Bordeaux has risen, Major.'

Sharpe stared up at the Comte. 'Risen?' This was the news Sharpe most feared, the spur into what Elphinstone had described as madness.

'Risen for the King!' Favier said happily. 'The Bonapar-tistes have been ejected!' Favier, contentment suffusing his honest, cold-chapped face, smiled. 'The rising ended when the garrison came over to our side. The white flag of Bourbon flies, the defences are manned by subjects of his most Christian Majesty, King Louis XVIII, whom God bless.'

'Indeed,' Sharpe said. The news explained why the Comte de Maquerre could wear an enemy's uniform deep in France, but the news meant much, much more. If it was true that the third city of France had rebelled against Bonaparte and persuaded its garrison troops to forsake their Imperial allegiance, then Sharpe was hearing of the end of this war. Wigram and Bampfylde would be proved right. Sharpe knew he should feel an elation, a great soaring of spirit that all the sacrifices had been worthwhile and that twenty-one years of relentless savagery had been brought to peace by Napoleon's fall, but he could raise nothing more than a grim smile to meet Favier's enthusiasm.

'We have come,' de Maquerre said, 'for your help.' He spoke lamely, almost as if what he said gave him embarrassment.

Favier took a paper from his saddle-bag. 'If you will accept this, *monsieur*, on behalf of the Provisional and Royalist Government of Bordeaux.' He handed the paper to Sharpe, then gave a small bow.

The paper was entirely in French, and was decorated with an elaborate seal. Sharpe saw that his name had been spelt wrong; without its final 'e'. 'What is it?'

'You have no French?' Favier sounded politely surprised. '*Monsieur*, it is a commission that appoints you a Major General in the forces of his most Catholic Majesty, King Louis XVIII of France, whom God bless.'

'God bless him,' Sharpe said automatically. 'A Major General?'

'Indeed.' De Maquerre spoke from his saddle. It had been Ducos' idea that a soldier as ambitious as Sharpe could not resist such a lure.

Sharpe was wondering what Wellington would make of the appointment, and imagined that aristocrat's grim amusement that a one time private should be offered such a rank. 'I . . .' he began, but Favier interrupted him.

'Our citizens have taken Bordeaux, *monsieur*, but their confidence needs the presence of an ally. Especially an ally as famous and redoubtable as yourself.' Favier softened his flattery with an honest smile. 'And once it is known that Allied troops are in the city, then the whole countryside will rise with us.' Favier spoke with an enthusiasm and confidence that was entirely lacking in the Comte.

Sharpe thought of the local Mayor who had already tried to surrender. Doubtless France was filled with men and women eager to disavow their Napoleonic past and declare for the winning side, but Sharpe was equally sure that Napoleon's fanatical supporters were not so ready for surrender. The nearest allied forces to Bordeaux, besides Sharpe, were a hundred miles away and there was Marshal Soult with a French army screening their advance. 'I don't,' Sharpe said, 'have orders from my General that would allow me to help you.' He held the commission out to Favier.

'You have orders,' de Maquerre said coldly, 'to give me every assistance.'

Favier seemed upset by de Maquerre's hostile tone. He smiled at Sharpe. 'Your Field Marshal, I think, would admire a soldier who grasped the moment?'

'Maybe.'

'And you have a reputation, *monsieur*, as a man not afraid of great risks?'

Sharpe said nothing. He had been secretly charged by Elphinstone with scotching Bampfylde's high hopes. One part of Sharpe, that part which had so often dared impossible things, drew him towards Bordeaux, but the soldier within him could imagine his men besieged in that city and surrounded by a population that, with a brigade of Soult's veterans pressing close, might well decide that their change of allegiance had been premature. 'I cannot, sir.' He held out the commission again. 'I'm sorry.'

A look of disappointment, suggesting personal hurt,

crossed Favier's face. 'I understand, Major, that your expedition is commanded by Captain Bampfylde, of His Britannic Majesty's Navy?'

Sharpe paused, thinking that on land Bampfylde held an equal rank to himself, but, merely by boarding the *Vengeance*, Bampfylde magically arose to become the equivalent of a full colonel, and so, in that knowledge, Sharpe reluctantly nodded. 'He does command, yes.'

Favier shrugged. 'Would it offend you, Major, if the Comte and I sought to countermand your refusal by seeking Captain Bampfylde's approval?'

'I can't stop you,' Sharpe said ungraciously, 'but I must tell you that I'm starting the return march within an hour. I expect to be at Arcachon this time tomorrow.'

The Comte de Maquerre, as though eager to be on his way, had turned his horse away from Sharpe. Favier, leaving the forged commission in Sharpe's hand, collected his horse's reins and pulled himself into the saddle. 'I hope to meet you in the morning, Major, with orders that will reverse your march. God save King Louis!'

'God save him.' Sharpe watched as the two Frenchmen put their horses to the ford. As they threaded the boulders Favier twisted in his saddle to give a parting wave, then put his heels back.

'What did they want?' Frederickson, unashamedly curious, asked Sharpe.

'To make me into a Major General,' Sharpe said. He tore the commission into shreds of paper and tossed them into the River Leyre. 'They said Bordeaux's risen and declared itself for fat Louis.' Sharpe watched the horsemen disappear in the dusk. The two men evidently knew a cross-country route to Arcachon for they disdained the river bank up which Sharpe had marched the night before. 'They wanted us to go there.'

'So bloody Bampfylde's right?' Frederickson uttered the suspicions that Sharpe feared to face.

But Sharpe was wondering why the Comte de Maquerre

had left most of the talking to the Mayor's assistant. Aristocrats did not usually defer to bureaucrats. And why, if there were French troops on this road, even defeated French troops, had Maquerre been so confident as to wear his *Chasseurs Britannique* uniform?

'I think they were lying,' Sharpe said, 'and I'm not going near Bordeaux.'

Sweet William shrugged. 'Perhaps the war's over, sir?'

'Maybe.' A cold wind suddenly gusted over the scattered remnants of the French convoy. Tiny flames had been lit in the carriage lamps of the coach in which the two Frenchwomen were safely sheltered. 'But we'll still blow the goddamned bridge,' Sharpe said, 'because no one's told us not to.'

It was almost dark when the small force of Riflemen and Marines was at last assembled in the river meadow. They were weighed down with plunder, with joints of the dead oxen, with captured wine illicitly stuffed into packs and with enemy weaponry that all soldiers delighted to keep, but inevitably threw away as soon as the marching became heavy and tedious. Most of the surviving French horses had been rounded up, bridled and were being used to carry packs or wounded men, among whom was Marine Matthew Robinson whose face looked as if it had received the full recoil of a twelve-pounder field-gun. The French prisoners, their braces and belts and bootlaces cut, had been released on the river's far bank.

Sharpe looked around for the last time. The captured quickfuse snaked from the explosives, past the toll-house, down the bank, through the rickety fence, and reached to the centre of the meadow. The townsfolk were far back, the prisoners a half mile up the road, and only the stupid oxen were close to the gunpowder. Sharpe nodded to Minver. 'Light it.'

Flint struck on steel, half-charred linen kindling was blown to life, and the flame was lowered to the fuse.

'Wait! Wait!' A dozen Marines were shouting suddenly.

Minver looked to Sharpe, who nodded, and the flame was blown out. Men were staring north-east, across the river, and in the twilight Sharpe saw a small slim figure, clothed in white, running frantically towards the bridge.

It was the girl, green-eyed and slender, who had been scratched and punched when Robinson tried to rape her. Desperately, her skirts catching the sudden wind like moth-wings, she scrambled over the bridge's parapet, past the powder, then jumped down into the meadow. She ran on, past Sharpe, past Frederickson's Company who would form the rearguard, running to the man with the battered face who had forced her into the byre and torn at her clothes.

'Jesus Christ,' Sharpe said. The girl was holding one of Robinson's hands, staring up at him, speaking in fast French, but the expression on her face was one of adoration.

Captain Palmer, as astonished as Sharpe, laughed. 'Strange things, women.' He watched the girl pulling herself up to share Robinson's saddle. 'An unmarried girl, sir, wants nothing but a husband.'

'And once she's got one,' Sharpe said sourly, 'she wants everything. It would have been better for both of them if I'd hanged the bastard.' He looked at Minver. 'Light it, Lieutenant.'

Flint struck steel again, the flame flickered to illuminate the fuse laying in the grass, then the powder caught, sparked, and fizzed its swift way towards the bridge.

'March!' Sharpe turned to his heavily-laden force and pointed the way home. 'March!'

'It's a hulk, sir.' Lieutenant Tom Martin, of the brig-sloop *Cavalier*, twisted his bicorne hat in both his hands.

'A hulk?' Bampfylde frowned. They were in Commandant Lassan's old quarters where, because of a lack of firewood, Bampfylde's steward warmed his master with volumes taken at random from the shelves. The books were in French, which made them unreadable, so both the steward and his

181

master considered that no great harm was being done.

Martin dropped his hat and showed Captain Bampfylde where, on the chart, the *Thuella* had been found. The schooner was ashore at the end of the tidal creek that led to the village of Gujan. 'She's dismasted, sir, aground, and derelict.'

'You fired at her?'

'Aye, sir.' Martin, when at last the damned fog had cleared, had spotted the *Thuella* far across the shoals. The tide was low, and still falling, so the most he could do was fire at long range. Two or three shots had crashed into the *Thuella*'s timbers, but at that range, and with such small calibre guns as the *Cavalier* carried, the damage was slight.

'Derelict, you say?' Bampfylde asked.

'Bottomed, emptied, stripped, scorched, dismasted, and smoking.' Martin delivered the gloomy words in hope that they would be sufficient. The glass was falling ominously and all the experienced sailors wanted to be at sea before the storm struck, but if Captain Bampfylde believed that the *Thuella* was salvageable then he might be tempted to stay at Arcachon and God alone knew what damage a storm could wreak on a brig in these enclosed waters.

'Smoking?'

'Looked as if the Jonathons tried to fire her, sir. Must be damp wood, though, 'cos she hadn't burned through.'

'You could,' Bampfylde said sourly, 'have sent a party to burn her properly, Mr Martin. That would have made sure of her.'

'They've made a battery ashore, sir. Mounted all her guns to face the water.' Thomas Martin sensed that perhaps he should have informed Captain Bampfylde of that salient fact earlier. 'They didn't return fire, sir, but we saw them.'

Damn Sharpe, Bampfylde thought. The *Thuella* existed, her crew had made themselves a fortress on land, and it would take two days to extirpate that nest of pirates. Bampfylde might not have the two days. The weather was surly, threatening a Biscay storm. For two days fog had shrouded the Bay, and now, when at last the fog lifted, all prudent seamen were advising Bampfylde to give his squadron sea-room. 'Can they refloat her?'

'No, sir. Looks to me as if they've ripped out what's good and abandoned the rest.' Captain Cornelius Killick would have loved to hear that statement, for he had worked hard to give just that impression. He had careened the schooner hard over, streaked her timbers and copper with pitch to suggest scorch marks, and lit smoking fires of damp grass to suggest smouldering embers deep in an abandoned hold. 'And they've cut away her figurehead,' Martin added hopefully.

'Ah!' That nugget of information pleased Bampfylde. No sailor would take away a figurehead if a ship still had life in her. 'It sounds as if she's done for! And doubtless the storm will finish her off.'

'Indeed, sir.' Martin, dismissed, shuffled from the room.

The storm, not the *Thuella*, was Bampfylde's chief worry. The still air was being stirred now by a strangely warm wind and every look at the weatherglass confirmed that the mercury shrank inside its four-foot tube. The continued existence of the American privateer, even if grounded and abandoned, was a nuisance, but it was palliated by Bampfylde's success in having found two splendid French brigs that were both now his prizes and already on their way to England. The *chasse-marées* had gone south, the fort was garrisoned by Marines and, apart from the Americans, Captain Bampfylde could count his job well done. All that was needed now was for de Maquerre to confirm that Bordeaux was ready to surrender.

But the Comte de Maquerre had not returned and Bampfylde dared not sail until the news from Bordeaux was received. If de Maquerre did not return till Thursday, then the storm would be on the flotilla and it would take seamanship of genius to claw off this shoaled coast.

But at least, if he must wait till Thursday, Bampfylde

could send the remaining Marines by longboat to attack the Americans across the Gujan shoals. That thought made Bampfylde frown. Palmer should have searched the village of Gujan, so where was the damned Captain of Marines? Captured? Lost in the fog? Damn the bloody man! Damn and damn again. Bampfylde stared at the chart. If the two brigs covered Killick's land-battery with gunfire, then the Marines could go in with powder barrels, pitch-blende, and Chinese lights to torch the *Thuella* down to charred ribs. If the weather held. If.

He climbed to the ramparts of the Teste de Buch where warm rain came ominous and heavy to aggravate his fear. An east wind, he thought, would be best. That would take his ships well offshore to the wide seas where they would be safest in a hard blow, but a west wind would destroy him and no amount of boastful despatches would forgive a captain who lost his 74 on a lee shore. Bampfylde paused to stare northwards where tiny lights flickered in a village. If de Maquerre came in the morning then Bampfylde would leave a strong garrison in the fort, sail his flotilla out to weather the storm at sea, then return to lead the advance on a rebellious Bordeaux. The storm might delay that glorious moment for two days, but it would also finish off the wounded American schooner.

Yet, in the ominous night of falling mercury, Captain Bampfylde's hopes of glory were mercilessly dashed. Lieutenant Ford woke the captain at half past three. 'Sir!'

Bampfylde, struggling out of a dream, noticed that the wind was stronger, gusting as it had before the fog had come down. 'What is it?'

'The Comte de Maquerre, sir. With a man from the Mayor's office in Bordeaux. They say their news is urgent.'

Urgent or not, Bampfylde insisted on dressing properly, and it was a half hour before, in the finery of a naval captain, he greeted the two Frenchmen. Both Favier and de Maquerre showed the tiredness of men who had ridden good horses half to death, who were weary in every bone and soaked to the skin. Their news sent a shiver through Captain Bampfylde.

'Major Sharpe is taken.' De Maquerre spoke first.

'Taken?' Bampfylde could only repeat the word.

'The Bonapartistes,' Favier picked up the tale, 'knew of your coming here, Captain. A brigade was deployed. It was delayed, but it will be here by tomorrow midday.'

'A brigade?' Bampfylde, who had gone to sleep congratulating himself on the coming success of this expedition, stared at the kindly faced Favier. 'A French brigade?'

Favier wondered what other kind this plump young man expected. 'Naturally, *monsieur*. They have defeated Major Sharpe, the Marines who were with him, and now come to capture your good self.'

Bampfylde was overwhelmed. 'Marines?' He seemed only capable of snatching single words from the disastrous flood of news.

'Marines, Captain,' Favier said sympathetically.

So that was where Palmer had got to! Swanning off with the Rifles! Bampfylde made a note to tear out Captain Palmer's guts and wrap them round his neck, except that Palmer was a prisoner now. Or dead. 'Coming here? A brigade?'

Favier nodded. 'We warn you at some risk to ourselves, Captain. Bordeaux was in ferment, you understand, and our Mayor would support the return of King Louis, but alas!' Favier shrugged, 'the tyrant's heel is again upon our necks and we must, as ever, submit.'

Bampfylde, as his daydreams of glory collapsed, stared at the Comte de Maquerre. 'But you said Bordeaux had no fighting troops!'

'They do now,' de Maquerre said grimly.

'And Sharpe's captured?' Bampfylde snatched at another scrap in the fuddling flood.

'Or dead. There was appalling slaughter.' Favier frowned. 'General Calvet's men are veterans of Russia, Captain, and such fiends are pitiless. They think nothing of drinking their enemies' blood. I could tell you stories,' Favier shrugged, as though the stories were too awful for a naval captain's ears.

'And they're coming here?'

'Indeed.' De Maquerre wondered how many times it must be said before this fool believed them. 'By midday tomorrow.' He repeated the lie. He doubted whether Calvet's troops could reach Arcachon in the next forty-eight hours, but Ducos wanted Sharpe's escape route cut, and the urgency of fear might hasten Bampfylde's evacuation.

Bampfylde stared aghast at the two Frenchmen. His hopes, fed by Colonel Wigram, of leading a successful landing that would lance into Bordeaux were evaporating, but for the moment Bampfylde had other, more pressing worries. He twisted round to tap the glass and the column of mercury sank perceptibly. 'You'll come with us, of course?'

Jules Favier, a colonel in the French Army and one of Ducos' most trusted men, felt a sudden leap of exultation. It had worked! 'I cannot, *monsieur*. I have a family in Bordeaux. Should I leave, then I fear for their fate.'

'Of course.' Bampfylde imagined warriors, hardened by the Russian carnage, slashing into the fortress.

'I have no business here.' De Maquerre desperately wanted to stay in France, but Ducos had insisted he return to the British Army to leak news of whatever scheme replaced the landing at Arcachon. 'So I will sail with you, Captain.'

Bampfylde tapped the glass again as if to confirm the bad news. There would be a storm, a ship-killing storm, but this welter of news had severed his last need to stay at Arcachon. He looked at the Comte. 'We leave on the morning tide.'

Favier's tiredness was suddenly washed away. Ducos' daring scheme had been more successful than Favier had dared hope and, thanks to a growling wind and a falling glass, and thanks to some well-told lies, a Rifleman would be marooned in France, and the trap-jaws would clash home. On Sharpe.

CHAPTER 12

Jules Favier slept. It no longer mattered whether Sharpe was turned back towards Bordeaux or continued on to the coast; either way the Rifleman was stranded and the British plan to end the war by a killing stroke into the belly of France was defeated.

A wind rose as Favier slept. It shrieked over the ramparts, dying sometimes to a low moan, then gusting again to a fearsome frenzy. The waters of the channel, normally too enclosed to be stirred by anything other than a fretting tide, were whipped to whitecaps in the dawn's first light. The flotilla's smaller craft snubbed at their anchors while, out beyond the Cape, the *Vengeance*'s great bellying bows shuddered through the waters in towering, wind-lashed sprays of white.

Boat after boat rowed into the channel. Supplies were taken from the fort, stripping it of food and wine. Two Marines were sent to corrall a cow, which they did with difficulty, and the poor beast was prodded back to the fort where it was shot, messily butchered, and the bloody cuts of its carcass were crammed into barrels for seamen's meat. The flagpole was cut down, and the Marines and sailors were ordered to use the garrison's deep well as a latrine so that the brackish water would be fouled. Two seamen, hulking men with muscles hardened by years of service, took axes to the fort's main gates and reduced them to splintered baulks that were then fired. The drawbridge was hauled up close to the burning gates so that it too would be reduced to ashes.

The *Vengeance*'s sailing-master, one eye on the glass and

the other on the low scurrying clouds that sometimes spat heavy rain on to the burning timbers of the gate, counselled speed, but Bampfylde was determined to do this task properly. The Comte de Maquerre's news meant that no landing could be made at Arcachon; therefore the fort would be abandoned, but not before it had been made untenable for the French. The Teste de Buch would be slighted.

Men were ordered to the ramparts where they hammered iron spikes into the touch-holes of the huge thirty-six pounder guns. The spikes were sawn through and filed flat so that no pincers could gain sufficient purchase to draw them free. Teams of seamen, using tackles, blocks and ropes from the *Cavalier*, eased the vast gun barrels from their slides and tipped them, in tumbling crashes, into the channel. The twenty-four pounders, like the six field guns that should have been delivered to Baltimore, were likewise spiked, turned off their carriages, and jettisoned into the flooded ditch. The twelve-pounder carriages were rammed into the burning gate, then Chinese Lights, signalling confections of nitre, sulphur, antimony and orpiment, were tossed among the carriages to encourage the blaze.

Those Marines who had remained at the Teste de Buch were the first men to leave the slighted fortress. They were rowed to the brig and, on their way, tipped muskets from the fort's armoury into the corroding seawater. The Comte de Maquerre, after an emotional farewell to the newly woken Favier, went to the *Scylla*.

By ten in the morning only a handful of sailors were left ashore. Quickfuses were laid into the fort's magazines, while another was taken to a stack of powder barrels that had been piled in the kitchens beneath the barracks block. The spare rifle ammunition, left by Sharpe to await his return, was piled on to that stack. Jules Favier, who had taken his horse safely beyond the drawbridge before the destruction began, shook Bampfylde's hand. 'God save King George, Captain.'

'God bless King Louis.'

Favier used a naval ladder to descend the western battlements, then picked his way through the sand to where his horse was tethered. He waved a last time to Captain Bampfylde who, surrounded by his acolytes, walked to his waiting boat. A lieutenant paused, turned at the fuse's end, and Favier saw the snap of light as flint struck steel.

There was a pause as fire ate up the worsted quick-match that had been soaked with a liquid solution of mealed powder, spirits of wine, and isinglass. Bampfylde was being rowed through choppy waves towards the *Cavalier*. Spits of rain pitted the sand while gulls, wheeling effortlessly, rode the strong wind that blew from the hills towards the sea. Favier mounted his horse.

The quick-match, hissing sparks, darted into an embrasure of the Teste de Buch. The first brig had hoisted its anchor and was already, under sails blown to a flat hardness, beating towards the channel's mouth. The *Scylla*, *Amelie*, and *Vengeance*, sails reefed, were already hull down.

Captain Bampfylde climbed the *Cavalier*'s tumblehome. The brig's sidesmen twittered their pipes, the anchor was lifted, and Lieutenant Martin ordered sheets hauled tight. He was to take Captain Bampfylde to the *Vengeance* and it would be a pretty piece of seamanship to transfer the captain in this weather.

Bampfylde, grinning with anticipation like a raw midshipman, stood at the rail of the *Cavalier*'s small quarterdeck. 'It should be a picture, Ford!'

'Indeed it should, sir.' Ford opened his watch and saw that it was still an hour short of midday, the time when the French brigade should arrive. Now they would come to find a fortress destroyed.

The two men waited. The rain striking the *Cavalier*'s vast driver sail made a rapping tattoo that was matched by the quiver of Bampfylde's excited fingers.

Lieutenant Ford was nervous. 'Perhaps, sir, the rain's . . .'

But even as he spoke the fuse-borne fire bit home.

A lance of light, white and sharp and straight as a blade, pierced into the low cloud from the very centre of the Teste de Buch. It was followed by smoke; roiling greasy smoke shot through with red flames that spat outwards in sudden, angry dashes.

Then came the noise; the rolling, grumbling, hammering sound of the powder magazines exploding, and in the noise came another roar as the explosives in the barracks caught the fire and Captain Bampfylde clapped his hands with delight as stones, tiles, and timbers shattered upwards.

The single flame vanished, to be replaced by a horror of dirty smoke that carried ashes, made sodden by the rain, far out to sea. A few flames flickered bright above the unscathed ramparts, then, dampened by the squalls, disappeared. Bampfylde, pleased with his work, smiled. 'The French nation is deprived of one fortress, Ford. That is a consolation to us.'

'Indeed, sir.'

Bampfylde turned. 'I shall use your cabin, Mr Martin. Pray send me some coffee or, failing that, tea.'

'Aye aye, sir.'

The brigs turned where the shoals marked the limit of Cap Ferrat and were swallowed in the rising sea and the squalls of rain. The coast was left deserted, its fort empty and shattered, and the squadron was gone.

Sharpe's last sight of the bridge over the Leyre was of the powder billowing flame and smoke outwards, of stones from the balustrade making vast splashes in the shallow water, of the toll-keeper's windows smashing inwards, and of four toppling stone urns. The bridge still stood, but it was weakened and no artilleryman would dare take the weight of guns over that stone roadway until a competent engineer, fond of life, volunteered to stand beneath the blackened arch as the guns trundled overhead.

The Riflemen and Marines bivouacked after a mere five

miles, leaving the river bank to go to an enormous house standing in a vast garden of lawns and lakes. The house remained shut despite all the hammering on its doors and, though Sharpe saw dark figures, silhouetted by candlelight, who folded shutters on the upper floor, no one appeared to inquire who the soldiers were. A carved escutcheon over the main door suggested that the house had been, and maybe still was, the residence of aristocrats.

There was a barn at the house's rear that was more than an adequate bivouac. There was straw, kindling for fires, and blessed shelter against the rain that had started to sweep in great gust-borne swathes over the garden.

Sharpe ate tinned chicken with the cheese Jane had packed for him, and washed both down with wine taken from the ambushed convoy. Frederickson squatted beside him at the end of the barn that had been designated officer's territory.

'She said,' Frederickson told Sharpe, 'that she didn't mean to scream. She's called Lucille. She's rather fetching, don't you think?'

'She's not ugly,' Sharpe allowed. He watched the pale girl who sat shyly with her man at the barn's far end. 'But Robinson's a Marine! Marines can't take wives on to ships.'

'She says he paid for her. Twenty francs.' Frederickson sucked a wing-bone clean. 'That's a very fair price for a bride in these parts.'

'I paid that!' Sharpe protested.

'I suppose she's yours, then,' Frederickson laughed.

'What's he going to do? Kiss her goodbye at Arcachon? Does she know he's a Marine?'

'I told her,' Frederickson said.

Sharpe shrugged. Any troops marching through the countryside seemed to end with a tail of women, but it was one thing to be a soldier, rooted on land, and quite another to be a Marine who could offer a wife no home. 'Can they ship her to England?' Sharpe asked Palmer.

'No.' Palmer was cleaning the vent of his pistol. 'Anyway,

Robinson's already married. Got a wife and two nippers in Portsmouth.' He blew dust away from the touch-hole.

'I suppose when he's finished with her,' Frederickson said, 'she'd better go to one of my men. We can smuggle her on to the *Amelie*.' No one demurred. It was a normal enough solution to a routine problem, and there were always men willing to take on a discarded or widowed woman. Sharpe remembered, after Badajoz, meeting a weeping woman who had just lost her husband in the dreadful slaughter of that fight. She did not weep for the loss, but because she had precipitately accepted another man in marriage and then been asked for the same favour by a sergeant who would have been a much better catch.

Sharpe slept seven hours, waking to the predawn darkness and the hiss of rain on the wooden roof. Sergeants stirred sleepers awake with boot toe-caps and the first flames flickered to boil water.

Sharpe went outside and stood against the barn wall where Frederickson companionably joined him.

'He's gone,' Sweet William said.

Sharpe yawned. 'Who's gone?'

'Marine Robinson. He buggered off with his Lucille. Another of Cupid's walking wounded.'

'Bloody hell.'

'Palmer's not best pleased.' Frederickson buttoned his breeches.

'Did the picquets see anything?'

'They say not.' Frederickson walked with Sharpe to a fire where Sergeant Harper was stewing tea. ''Morning, Sergeant! It's my guess,' Frederickson looked back to Sharpe, 'that the picquets were asked to look the other way.' The Marines had provided the guard last night.

'Or he gave them a canter on the filly,' Harper said. 'I've known that a good few times.'

'You should write your memoirs,' Frederickson said cheerfully. He looked into the wet landscape where Robinson had disappeared. 'We'll not see him again.'

Nor did they. Love had struck, as callous in its target as a musket ball fired at a Battalion, and a man ran for freedom while Sharpe marched his force into the rain-smeared dawn, going to the ships, going to his own woman whom he had married with as little forethought as Marine Robinson had shown in his desertion, and going home.

At first Sharpe thought a ship must have burned at its moorings, then he thought it a rick-fire, then he assumed Bampfylde must have torched the village. Finally, in the half gale that blew his straggling force along the embanked road of the marshes, he saw that there were no masts in the channel and that the smoke, grey and hazy in the evening light, came from the fortress.

'Jesus wept,' Frederickson said.

'God save Ireland!' Patrick Harper stared at the gaping hole that had been the entrance to the fort. 'Were they captured?'

'Frogs would still be here.' Sharpe turned to stare at the village, at the trees to the south, but nothing moved in the landscape. A few villagers stood watching them, but nothing more.

'They've gone!' Palmer spoke with horror in his voice.

It was a nightmare. It took minutes to establish that there truly were no ships, not one, that not a single mast reared above a sand-dune, that no brig lay up channel and no frigate beat the stormy waters off the Cape. They had been abandoned.

The gate of the fort was a smoking wreckage, tangled with the charred remains of gun carriages. The drawbridge was dangling chains, scorched by fire, and grey-edged, blackened beams that had fallen into a ditch to lay across the twelve-pounder gun barrels that were half sunk in muddy water.

Two of the Marines splashed over the ditch and one heaved the other up to the stone platform to which the drawbridge had been hinged. The two men disappeared into the fort and came back with the beams that had been intended to be the gallows from which the Americans would hang. The timbers were long enough to bridge the ditch and, by that precarious means and with the horses abandoned to a meadow, Sharpe and his men went into the Teste de Buch. Its granite walls still stood, and the offices were untouched, but precious little else remained.

There were no guns. There was no powder. The arched doorways to the magazines were blasted black. The barracks were a heap of damp ashes. Frederickson, suspicious that the brass-banded well bucket had been left in place, smelt the water. 'Fouled.'

Sharpe went to the highest rampart and stared with his telescope to sea. The ocean was an empty, heaving, grey mass whipped to white flecks by the wind. Empty. The broken, charred damp trail of a burned quick-match showed where the fuse had been laid. He swore uselessly.

'We never saw those Frogs again!' Harper said.

'Maquereau.' Sharpe spoke the nickname aloud, recalling his suspicions that the tall aristocrat had been nervous at their last meeting. Not that it mattered now. The bleak truth was, that with less than two hundred men and with no more ammunition than those men carried in their pouches, he was marooned on the French coast a hundred miles from safety. His Riflemen could march that in four days, but could the Marines? And what of the wounded? And if they were caught, Sharpe knew, they would be finished. Even the poorly mounted French cavalry would make short work of a hundred and seventy men.

Those men slumped in the courtyard, made even more miserable by the buffet of wind and rain. 'Captain Palmer!' Sharpe's voice bellowed through the squall. 'I want billets found for everyone! Clear out the galleries. Send a squad to cut firewood!'

He would make them busy. Men could make a new gangway over the ditch, and other men were sent to cut down pines that would barricade the gaping archway. Such forestry would be slow work with bayonets, but better than no work at all. Other men dragged two of the twelve-pounder barrels from the ditch and dropped them into two of the carriages that had merely been scorched rather than burned. The big guns, the ship-killers tipped into the shallow waters at the channel's edge, were too heavy to tackle.

'Lieutenant Fytch! Search every damned room in the place. Bring every cartridge, ball, or powder barrel to the ready magazine.'

Some men were set to cooking, others went to the ramparts where they kept watch in the twilight. The wind raged at them, the rain slopped in bucketfuls from stone walls, but fires burned in galleries bored deep inside stone ramparts and ox-meat cooked in iron pots dragged from the wreckage of the kitchens. Frederickson used the limbers to collect barrels from the village that he filled with clean water from the small stream.

'We don't know what's happened,' Sharpe spoke to the officers in Lassan's old quarters that still had a few books left on the shelves, 'so it's no use speculating. Bampfylde's gone, we're here.'

'And who is in Bordeaux?' Frederickson asked slowly.

'God only knows. If it's Boney's men then we have to assume they'll hear of us and come after us. If the city really has declared for Louis then they'll help us. I want two of your best men, William, to ride that way in the morning. They're to stay out of trouble, observe, and come back by nightfall with any news. And I want you to question the villagers tomorrow.'

'Yes, sir.'

Sharpe looked at Palmer. 'You take your men to all the local villages tomorrow, and to Arcachon. Search every house! Bring every grain of powder and scrap of lead you can find.'

Palmer nodded. 'And the Standing Orders about not upsetting the populace?'

'Write them promissory notes. You'd better bring food, too. Everything you can find.'

Frederickson tossed another newly cut piece of pine on to the fire that spluttered with resin. 'You think we'll stay here?'

'We can't march south, not if the Frogs are after us, and I'd rather be behind walls than in open country. Besides, if the Navy does come back for us then we'd better be where they can find us.' That seemed the likeliest answer to Sharpe, that this weather had driven the ships offshore and that, as soon as the sea was calmer and the wind more gentle, the great sails would appear again. Yet second thoughts suggested otherwise. Why had Bampfylde slighted the fort? Why had he not left a handful of Marines in place? And why no letter nailed to a door? Those questions indicated to Sharpe that Captain Horace Bampfylde had run. He had abandoned his jejune plans for invading France and scuttled away. The more Sharpe thought about it, the less likely it seemed that the sails of Bampfylde's flotilla would reappear. 'And if we do stay here, gentlemen, then we may have to fight for it.'

Fytch and Minver looked somewhat pale, while Frederickson gave a slow smile, then a chuckle, and finally made the sign of the cross on his faded green jacket. 'As Patrick Harper would say, God save Ireland.'

'Shouldn't we have a flag, sir?' Minver asked.

'A flag?'

'In case a naval ship happens past, sir. Something they can recognize.'

'See to it. Cut a new flagpole tomorrow.'

There was silence for a few seconds. The fire flared bright, then faded again. Lieutenant Fytch smiled nervously. 'Perhaps the peace has come?'

'Perhaps the moon will sprout wings and deliver us some artillery,' Sharpe said, 'but until someone in British uniform tells me to stop fighting, I'm going to hold this place and you're going to help me do it.'

'Yes, sir.'

'So get to work.'

Outside there was a full gale blowing, shrieking over the water and driving rain in stinging blasts. Sharpe and Frederickson ran to the shelter of one of the small citadels where they settled back to watch the flicker of movements that betrayed sentries. Both officers had work to do, but they had instinctively come to this place to say what could not be said in open council. 'Would you say,' Sharpe asked quietly, 'that we've got nine hundred and fifty feet of ramparts here?'

Frederickson sucked his cheroot into a bright glow. 'I'd say a few feet more. A thousand?'

'That's over five feet of wall to every man.' Sharpe had been working it out and hating the arithmetic. 'If they come, William, and they attack everywhere at once, they'll crucify us.'

'The crapauds never attack everywhere at once,' Frederickson spoke scornfully. Crapauds against the goddamns. That was the soldier's slang for French against British. The French had always called the British the goddamns and Sharpe, like many men in Wellington's Army, liked the nickname. There was a reckless touch to it which spoke of French respect for the enemy, a touch entirely lacking in the scornful crapaud or toad. He took Frederickson's cheroot and sucked smoke deep into his lungs. 'Remember the Gateway of God?'

'We won that.' Frederickson took back the proffered cheroot.

'So we did,' Sharpe said. 'I wonder what happened to those Americans?'

'Buggered off if they've got any sense. Lucky bastards have probably got a whore apiece in Paris.'

'If we could find a boat tomorrow,' Sharpe said speculatively.

Frederickson gave the suggestion short shrift. 'In this weather? And can you sail a boat? Even if it was flat calm

197

we'd be up to our arses in water and confusion within minutes.'

'The Marines might be able to sail.'

'Web-foot soldiers don't sail,' Frederickson said. 'Besides, any boat big enough for us will have been scooped up by Bampfylde. He's a naval officer, remember. He has a patriotic duty to become rich.'

Sharpe shrugged in the darkness. 'We'll just have to hold this place, won't we? Beat the bastards ragged and then rip the guts out of Bampfylde.' The last few words were spoken so savagely that even Frederickson shivered.

Sharpe reached up to his scalp and took off the bandage that had been there since the fort had been captured. He tossed the bloody rag into the darkness. 'For two sous, William, I'd march south tomorrow. Take our goddamned chances.'

'It's a bare country,' Frederickson said, 'with few places to hide. And the wounded would slow us down.'

'So we'll stay.' Sharpe was matter of fact again. 'You'll command the south and east walls and I'll give you half the Marines as a tow-row Company.' He meant Grenadiers, the shock troops. 'Palmer can have Minver's Company and the other Marines for these walls. I want six of your best men. I'm taking the same from every Company.'

'You, Harper, and the pick of the bunch?' Frederickson smiled.

'In case there's a tender spot.' Sharpe stood. 'Try and get some sleep, William. Tomorrow's likely to be a long day.'

'And the last peaceful one for a while?'

'If the Frogs know we're here, yes.' Sharpe slapped the granite wall of the citadel. 'Bloody silly place to die, isn't it?'

'That'll teach 'em to fight us.'

'Yes.' Sharpe laughed, walked away, then stopped. His voice came out of the darkness. 'What does Teste de Buch mean, William?'

'I don't know. But I know what *Tête de Buche* would mean.'

It sounded the same to Sharpe. 'What?'

'Woodenhead, blockhead, idiot.'

'Goddamn,' Sharpe was amused, for only a blockhead would find himself in this predicament, yet in the morning the blockhead must make his goddamns ready to fight, and not just fight, but win. Here, on the edge of France, in the dead days of winter, they must take victory from disaster and hold the fort.

CHAPTER 13

Major Pierre Ducos rode his horse along the shabby, damp, dispirited lines of conscripts. A few, precious few, veterans stiffened these ranks, but most of the faces were young, pinched and terrified. No wonder, for yesterday some of these youths had been blooded and savaged, and their tale had spread gloom amongst the rest of the demi-brigade. 'The enemy was a Battalion strong,' a Chef de Battalion spoke nervously to Ducos, 'with skirmishers added.'

'There were less than two hundred men, Colonel.' Ducos' voice was pitiless. 'You were six hundred.' Dear God, but how Ducos despised soldiers! Braggarts and drum-thumpers all, until the enemy knocked the wind out of their bellies, after which they whined that they had been outnumbered, or that the sun had dazzled them, or that their powder had been damp. God only knew why politicians resorted to soldiers as a final instrument of policy; it was like wagering on a cockfight to decide the fate of empires. 'And now, Colonel, you will face those same few enemy with upwards of two thousand men. You think it will be enough?' Ducos made the inquiry with a mocking solicitousness.

'They're behind walls,' the colonel spoke nervously.

'In a fortress that has been slighted,' Ducos said acidly, 'and is without cannon and has very little musket ammunition.' Pierre Ducos allowed himself a moment's pleasure that Richard Sharpe was stranded and trapped. It would, of course, have been far more elegant if Favier had tricked Sharpe into marching through open countryside towards Bordeaux, but the ploy of the forged Bourbon commission had failed and Ducos acknowledged that Favier and de

Maquerre had done well. The squadron of ships was gone and Sharpe was bereft. A threatened British landing had been averted, and within a few hours Major Richard Sharpe would be surrounded by bayonets and menaced by two batteries of artillery. Commandant Henri Lassan also marched with the besieging force and, though the Commandant had been disgraced by the loss of his command, restitution had been promised if his intimate knowledge of the Teste de Buch's defences made General Calvet's recapture of the coastal fort swift.

At least, Ducos consoled himself, the general of this demi-brigade knew his business. Calvet was an old soldier of France, a veteran of the Revolutionary wars, and a hard man risen from the ranks in the hard way. He had made his name in Russia where, amidst the retreat of the Grand Army, he had held his brigade together. Other men starved, froze, or were hacked to bloody ruin by the Cossacks, but Calvet's men, fearing their general more than the enemy or the weather, held to their ranks. To this day, it was said, Calvet's wife slept on a pillow stuffed with the hair cut from the Cossacks her husband had killed with his own sword. It was a rare flash of imagination in a man known for his direct, straightforward, and bloody mode of fighting. General Calvet was a brute, a butcher, a tough man in a bloody profession, and Ducos, if he had believed in a God, would have given thanks that such an instrument was at his hand.

Jules Favier, restored to uniform and in high spirits, walked his horse alongside Ducos' mount. 'Calvet,' he said in mild warning, 'has never fought goddamns.'

'Goddamns,' Ducos retorted, 'have never fought Calvet.'

Colonel Favier acknowledged that truth, then looked at the sky. 'The seamen said there'd be a storm.'

'They were wrong,' Ducos said. And indeed the weather, that all night had grumbled with thunder and blown foul and hard, had this morning settled into a gusty, calming mood. Intermittent sunshine glowed on the floodwaters that stretched from overflowing ditches into the fields. Cavalry had gone south across those fields in case Sharpe decided to march to safety down the coast, but Ducos was certain that the Rifleman would stay in the fortress and wait in hope for the return of his ships. 'Calvet will settle his hash,' Ducos said with a rare smile on his pinched, scholar's face.

The gun-wheels rumbled louder than thunder on the plank-bridge at Facture, then the force was on the marshes proper, the Bassin d'Arcachon stretched vast to their right, and the fortress of Teste de Buch lay a half day's march in front.

Calvet, Ducos, and retribution were coming for a Rifleman.

In the night a stab of lightning, its forked branches wide enough to embrace the whole northern sky, had slashed down to sheen the waters of the bay with a steel-hard light that had glittered and gone. The wind had raged at the fort, but in the dawn, that was ragged with clearing cloud, the wind had strangely dropped and the air was suddenly warmer. Patrick Harper, scraping with a blunt razor at the stubble on his face, declared there was even a touch of spring in the February air. 'The baby will be two months old today, so he will,' he declared to Sharpe.

'And better off if you'd stayed with the Battalion,' Sharpe growled.

'Not at all!' Harper was relentlessly cheerful. 'The ships will come, sir, so they will.'

One of the wounded men was put on the western ramparts to watch for those ships, while another was placed on the eastern walls to look for the enemy. Two of Frederickson's Germans, solid reliable men, were sent inland on captured cavalry horses to glean what tidings they could. Another, a silent corporal with a flat, hard face, was sent south on the best of the captured horses. 'I'm sorry to lose him,' Sweet William said, 'but if he can make it in three days, then we might survive.' The man, a volunteer, had been sent to try and thread the enemy lines and carry news of Sharpe's predicament to the British Army. Sharpe doubted if the man would ever be seen again, but the possibility that ships could be sent north on a rescue mission was not to be discarded.

The calm, warmer weather raised the men's spirits. Uniforms, soaked by the last few days' exertions, were hung to dry on ramparts, giving the Teste de Buch a comfortingly domestic air. Palmer's Marines, stripped to the waist, took axes and billhooks from the villagers and went to the woods where tree after tree was felled and dragged back to the fort for fuel and barricades. Small boats were broken up and their timbers brought within the walls. Every container that could hold water, from rain-barrels to cooking pots, was carried to an empty, scorched magazine and stored in safety.

It was no time to be careful of French opinion. Houses were searched for food, powder and weapons. Smoked hams and bacon were brought to the fort, cattle were slaughtered, and winter stores of wheat, pathetically hidden, were dragged in heavy sacks up the sandy road.

To one of the merlons, a jutting stone stub between two embrasures, a stripped pine trunk was lashed tight. It had been the tallest tree in the woodlands and now, at its tapering tip, it carried a crude flag.

The flag was not the Union flag, for Minver's men could not find sufficient blue cloth to make such a thing. Instead it was the flag of England; the red cross of St George made from the sleeves of Marines' uniforms and sewn on to a white field that had previously served as a tablecloth in the house of the Customs Inspector at Le Moulleau. A red cross on white, the flag of the man who had slain the dragon, and though few of Sharpe's men would hold allegiance to England, coming as they did from Germany or Ireland or Scotland or Wales or Spain, the flag was oddly comforting. It streamed in the wind-gusts as a signal to an empty sea.

The defences were Sharpe's concern. There were four ramparts, and at the corners of the fort were higher citadels, little more than guerites for the shelter of sentries, but the citadels effectively blocked swift movement from one rampart to the next. A soldier, wishing to go from the north wall to the east, must thread the two doorways of the north-east citadel and, to make a swifter passage, Sharpe had walkways of rough pine lashed together then bridged diagonally across the corners.

The courtyard was not square, but made into an irregular shape by the buildings that were sheltered beneath the ramparts. The burned barracks filled the square of the north-eastern corner, while the garrison offices and the officers' quarters filled the south-western. The gap between them was crudely but thickly barricaded with an abatis of untrimmed pine trees. If the enemy penetrated the courtyard then they would be faced by the thick hedge of bristly pine.

Sharpe's greatest worry was ammunition. Lieutenant Fytch, set to count the cartridges left to the Marines, gloomily reported that each man had scarce thirty shots left. The Riflemen, who always carried more into battle, had over sixty, but the grim total was less than nine thousand cartridges in the fort. A Battalion could fire as much in the first five minutes of a battle, and Frederickson, scratching calculations on a bastion with a spare rifle flint, grunted. 'I reckon we've got enough for an eighteen-minute battle. After that we'll be throwing blacking-balls at them.'

'We've got the powder in the horns.' Sharpe was speaking of the fine powder that every rifleman carried in a horn. The powder was kept for the special shots, when marksmanship might be spoiled by the coarser powder of cartridges, but Sharpe knew that, even if spare bullets could be found, the extra powder would not be sufficient for more than six or seven hundred rounds.

So more men were sent out to search for powder. The villagers had duck guns, therefore there must be powder in the countryside, and Sharpe gave the men permission to pull walls down to find hidden supplies. He would be lucky, hc thought, to even double his ammunition supply, so other means of killing Frenchmen must be devised.

Lieutenant Fytch had a dozen men sharpening pine stakes that had first been hammered into the bed of the wet ditch. The stakes, whittled to points with knives and bayonets, were hidden beneath the water in those places Sharpe judged the most dangerously exposed to French assaults. Above the stakes, heaped on the ramparts, were piles of masonry that had been loosened by Bampfylde's explosions. A building stone, dropped from the firestep, would kill a man as effectively as any bullet, yet the piled masonry seemed a pathetic weapon to prepare against whatever might come from the east.

'Perhaps they won't come,' Patrick Harper said.

'There aren't supposed to be many troops in this area,' Sharpe said hopefully.

'I suppose they was ghosts we were fighting two days ago?' Harper asked innocently. 'And perhaps we won't need this bastard.' He slapped the breech of one of the two twelve-pounder guns rescued from the ditch. Harper had taken it upon himself to make the guns battleworthy. Presently there was not enough powder to fire even one cannon, but Harper prayed enough propellant would be scraped up from the local village. Like many an infantryman he was fascinated by cannon and wanted desperately to make at least one of these guns capable of firing a shot. With a gentleness that was surprising in such a huge man, and with a tenacity Sharpe had seen before in the Irishman, Harper was using a narrow-bladed awl to dig the iron spike, scrap by bright scrap, out of the vent-hole.

'Can it be cleared?' Sharpe asked.

Harper's pause seemed to suggest that the job might be expedited if officers did not insist on asking him damn-fool questions, then he shrugged. 'I'll clear the bastard if it takes all day and night, sir.'

By the afternoon Sharpe fervently hoped that the cannons could be made to work, for Lieutenant Minver had struck gold. Or rather, in the strongroom at the back of the Customs House at Le Moulleau, he had found eight barrels of black powder.

'It's filthy stuff, sir,' Minver said dubiously.

Sharpe fingered some of the powder in his right hand. It was old, it smelt damp, and it was the worst kind of black powder; that made from the dusty leavings of finer powder and adulterated with ground pit-coal, but it was still gunpowder. He put a pinch into the pan of his rifle, snapped the flint on to the frizzen, and the powder fizzed dirtily. 'Mix it with the other captured powder. And well done.'

A laboratory was made in the chapel where three men tore pages from Lassan's remaining books and twisted the paper into crude cartridges that were filled with the coarse powder. They lacked bullets as yet, but Frederickson had a squad of men ripping the lead from the church at Arcachon and Sergeant Rossner was stoking a fire in the furnace that had once heated the French shot and Lieutenant Fytch was the possessor of a pistol that came complete with a mould for bullet-making which, though slightly smaller in calibre than the muskets or rifles, would still make a usable missile. Some undamaged bullets were raked out of the burned barracks where, Sharpe supposed, his spare ammunition had been exploded by Bampfylde.

More powder still came from Arcachon and from the villages of Le Teste, Pyla and Le Moulleau. There were leather bags of powder, boxes of powder, and small barrels of powder. There were even musketoons, an ancient matchlock, six blunderbusses, eight duck guns, and a fine duelling pistol that had yet another bullet mould in its wooden case.

The men were busy and, as ever, purposeful activity made them content. When a cheer announced that Patrick Harper had succeeded in making one of the twelve-pounders battleworthy, that contentment soared into a confidence that belied the desperation of their predicament. Harper started on the second twelve-pounder gun. 'Unless you'd like me to work on one of the big buggers?' he asked Sharpe hopefully.

Sharpe declined the offer. He did not have enough men to raise one of the vast thirty-six pounders from the channel, nor could he spare the powder needed to fire one of the huge guns. Even these smaller field guns, if they could both be fired, would not be used more than once or twice. They were weapons for emergency only.

'Sir!' The wounded man watching inland waved to Sharpe. 'Visitor, sir!'

Sharpe ran to the gate, walked across the precarious plank bridge, and saw a tall, long-haired man walking towards the glacis.

It was Cornelius Killick, and the sight of the American astonished Sharpe. He had thought Killick would have long gone inland, yet here was the privateer captain looking for all the world as though he merely took an afternoon stroll. Sharpe met the American beyond the glacis. 'I thought you'd gone to Paris, Mr Killick.'

Killick ignored Sharpe's greeting, staring instead at the work being done to barricade the fort's blackened archway. 'You look as if you're expecting trouble, Major.'

'Maybe.'

'Stranded, are you? A modern Robinson Crusoe?'

'Maybe.'

Killick laughed at Sharpe's evasive answers, then allowed himself to be drawn away from the fort. 'I'm doing a bit of repair work myself.'

'You are?'

'I'm putting an elmwood arse on an oak-built ship.' The American grinned. 'The *Thuella* wasn't quite as knocked up as I thought. You want passage, Major Sharpe?'

'To America?' The thought amused Sharpe.

'We make fine whisky, Major,' Killick said persuasively, 'and fine women!'

'If you say so, but I'll refuse just the same.'

The two men walked to the sand dunes by the channel where the American opened a leather bag and offered Sharpe an oyster. 'Ever eaten a raw oyster, Major?'

'No.'

'Perhaps you'd better not. You might accuse me of breaking my promise not to fight Englishmen.' Killick laughed, broke a shell open with a clasp knife, and tipped the oyster into his mouth. 'So you're in trouble.'

'I can't deny it.'

Killick sat and, after a moment's hesitation, Sharpe sat beside him. He suspected the American had come here for some purpose, though Killick was at pains to make the visit seem casual. The purpose could be simply to spy on Sharpe's preparations, but Killick had made no real effort to enter the fort and seemed content to have Sharpe's attention. The American tossed empty shells on to the sand. 'Some of my men, Major, being less civilized than myself, ain't happy with me. All because of my oath, you understand. If we can't fight, then we can't make money.'

'Is that why you fight?'

Killick shrugged. 'It's a business, Major. The *Thuella* cost my principals one hundred and sixty-three thousand new-fangled dollars. They've made a profit, but have you ever known a merchant content with a simple profit? And if my men don't take prizes, my men starve, so they're unhappy.'

'But alive,' Sharpe observed drily.

'There is that,' Killick allowed. 'But their pride is hurt. They had to squat in Gujan while a British brig put a couple of roundshot into their boat and I wouldn't let them fire back. I'm now being accused of cowardice, lack of patriotism, bastardy, even atheism! Me!' Killick's tone suggested that he could more than cope with the grumbles of his crew.

'I'm sorry.'

Killick gave Sharpe a long, pensive look. 'I suppose you wouldn't release me from my promise?'

Sharpe smiled at the innocence with which the question had been asked. 'Why on earth should I?'

'I can't think of a good reason,' Killick said cheerfully, 'except that it irks me. Oh, it was fair! I grant you that. And

I'd take it again if it would save my excellent hide for another few years, but it irks. This is my only war, Major, and I am damned good at it. Damn good.' The statement was not a boast, but a bleak fact and it reminded Sharpe of that noontide at St Jean de Luz when this big, confident man had made a monkey out of the Navy. Killick shrugged. 'I want to be released from that oath. It keeps me awake at nights, it itches like the pox, it irks.'

'The answer's still no.'

Killick nodded, as though he had known he could not change Sharpe's mind, but had nevertheless made a dutiful effort. 'Why did those bastards run out on you?'

'I don't know.'

The American cocked an eye towards the sky. 'It might have been the weather. I thought we were in for one hell of a blow, but the damn thing disappeared. Strange weather here, Major. You expecting them back?'

'Maybe.'

'But they haven't come today, my friend, so my bones tell me you're in trouble.' Killick gave a slow, friendly grin. 'You're between the devil and the deep blue sea, aren't you?'

'Maybe.'

The American laughed. 'You could always join my crew, Major. Just march your men to Gujan and I'll sign you all on. You want to be an American citizen?'

Sharpe laughed. The teasing was good-natured, and came from a man that Sharpe instinctively liked. If Killick had been British, Sharpe thought, and dressed in a green jacket, he would have made a damn fine Rifleman. 'Perhaps you'd like to sign your men up in the Rifles? I could start you off as a corporal.'

'I've had my bellyful of land fighting,' Killick said with a rueful honesty. He gave a wistful glance towards the open sea, then looked again at Sharpe. 'I'll be sorry to see you defeated, Major.'

'I don't intend to be.'

'And I'm mindful,' the American continued as though Sharpe had not spoken, 'that you saved my life. So even if you won't release me from my oath I reckon I owe you something. Isn't that right, Major?'

'If you say so.' Sharpe spoke with the caution of a man wary of an enemy bringing a gift.

But this enemy smiled, shucked an oyster, then tossed the shell halves on to the sand in front of Sharpe. 'They used to collect tons of those things out of the bay. Tons! Used to take them to a place at the end of the channel,' Killick jerked a thumb north, 'and burn them, Major. Burn them. They stopped a few years back because they couldn't ship the stuff out any more, but there's a stone barn full of it up there. Full of it.' Killick smiled.

Sharpe frowned, not understanding. 'Full of what?'

'Major! I may bring you breeches, but I'm damned if I'm going to pull them up for you.' Killick twisted another oyster apart with his blade, then shrugged. 'Always think I'm going to find a pearl in these damn things, and I never do. Lassan was pretty astonished you spared our lives, Major.' The last sentence was said as casually as his remark about pearls.

'Lassan?' Sharpe asked.

'He was the commandant here. Scrupulous sort of fellow. So why did you, Major?'

The question was evidently asked seriously, and Sharpe thought carefully about his answer. 'I find it hard to hang people, even Americans.'

Killick chuckled. 'Squeamishness, eh? I was hoping I'd talked my way out of a hanging. All that guff about never hanging a sailorman in still airs.' Killick grinned, pleased with his cleverness. 'It was all bally-hoo, Major. I just made it up.'

Sharpe stared at the American. For days Sharpe had believed, with all the force a superstition could command, that by showing mercy to Killick he had saved Jane's life. Now it was bally-hoo? 'It isn't true?'

'Not a word, Major.' Killick was pleased with Sharpe's shock reaction. 'But I thank you anyway.'

Sharpe stood. 'I have work to do.' His hopes were sliding into a bleak despair. 'Good day to you.'

Killick watched the tall figure walk away. 'Remember, Major! Oyster shells! Halfway between here and Gujan, and that ain't bally-hoo!'

Sharpe went into the fortress. He wanted to speak with no one. Suddenly all the preparations he had made against siege seemed useless, contemptible, and pathetic. The hay-rakes, taken from the villages, seemed feeble instruments with which scaling-ladders could be knocked aside. The two guns, made ready by Harper, were toys to swat at a monster. The pine abatis was a bauble, no more of an obstacle than a sheep hurdle. Jane was dying. Sharpe could not see beyond that fact.

'Sir!' Frederickson ran up the stone ramp. 'Sir!'

Sharpe, who had been sitting in one of the embrasures that faced the channel, looked up. 'William?'

'Two thousand of the buggers, plus two batteries of artillery.' Frederickson's mounted Riflemen had returned on lathered horses with the grim news.

Sharpe looked down again, wondering what purpose the white lines on the rampart, each numbered, had served.

'Sir?' Frederickson frowned.

Sharpe's head jerked up again. 'Two thousand, you say?'

'At least.'

Sharpe forced himself to attend to the news. 'How far?'

'Three hours.'

'They'll arrive in darkness,' Sharpe spoke softly. Somehow he did not care if it was two or twenty thousand.

'Sir?' Frederickson was puzzled by Sharpe's mood.

'Tell me,' Sharpe suddenly stood, 'what happens when you burn oyster shells?'

'Oyster shells?' Frederickson frowned at the strange question. 'You get quicklime, of course.'

'Lime?' Sharpe told himself he could not wallow in self-pity. He had men to defend and an enemy to defy. 'It blinds people?'

'That's the stuff,' Frederickson said.

'Then we've got three hours to fetch some.' Sharpe was shaking himself back to normal. He passed on Killick's directions and ordered one of the limbers taken north.

Two hours later, when the light was nothing but a glow above the western horizon, eight barrels of quicklime were carried into the fortress. Like the powder from the Customs House it was old and damp through too long storage behind the lime-kilns and it clumped in great dirty-white fist-sized lumps, but Frederickson took the barrels to the gallery where the cooking fires were lit and levered off the barrel tops so that the powder would start to dry. 'It's a nasty weapon,' he said to Harper.

'It's a nasty war,' Harper crumbled one of the lumps, 'and if the Frogs decide not to fight, sir, we can always paint the bloody place white.'

From the courtyard outside came the sound of stones whispering on steel as the bayonets were sharpened. The job was being done with the obsessiveness of men who knew that careful preparation could fractionally tip the casual scales of life and death in their favour. Sharpe, listening to the hiss of steel, tried to guess what his enemy planned.

The French, he decided, would be mostly raw troops. They would arrive in weary darkness and head for the village that promised shelter and water. Yet their General would know that a surprise night assault could bring him swift victory. If Sharpe was that General he would assemble his veterans and send them on a silent march to the north, from whence, while the defenders were distracted by the noise of the troops in the village, those veterans would strike.

So Sharpe must strike first.

Except that, sitting in the gathering dusk, Sharpe was assailed by bleak and horrid doubts. One hundred and seventy men, desperately short of ammunition, faced over ten times their own number. The enemy brought guns, while Sharpe only had the two twelve-pounders that were loaded, like the duck-guns, with scraps of stone and metal. It was madness to fight here, yet unthinkable to surrender without a fight.

Captain Frederickson, his face smeared black with dampened soot scraped from the shattered kitchen chimney, crouched beside Sharpe. 'I've chosen a dozen men, sir. Including Harper.'

'Good.' Sharpe tried to imbue his voice with enthusiasm, but could not succeed. 'I don't understand, William, why the bastards are fighting us. Why not let us rot here? Why waste men on us?'

'Christ knows, sir.' Frederickson obviously did not care. He only anticipated a rare fight. 'You'll want a prisoner, no doubt?'

'It would be useful, William.' Sharpe stared eastwards, but there was still no sign of the approaching French forces. 'I wish I could come with you.'

'You can't, sir.'

'No.' This was one of the sacrifices of command; that Sharpe must delegate. In years past he would have liked nothing better than to have led a raiding party against the enemy, but now he must stay in the fortress where the nervous garrison could see and take confidence from his calm demeanour.

He walked with Frederickson to the north-west corner of the fort where, with the aid of a fishing net hung from an embrasure, the Riflemen climbed down to the night-shadowed sand. The shining metal of their weapons and uniforms had, like their faces, been blacked. They carried no packs, no canteens, only ammunition, bayonets, and firearms. They were Sharpe's best and if he lost them tonight he would lose this battle.

When they had disappeared into the darkness Sharpe turned and walked, feeling suddenly lonely, to the eastern ramparts. He waited there, staring inland, until at last the sounds came from the darkness.

'Sir?' A Marine sentry spoke nervously.

'I hear it, lad.' Sharpe heard the chink of trace chains, the thump of wheels, the noise of artillery drawn behind horses. He heard, too, the soft thunder made by boots. The French had come.

For a long time he could not see the enemy. There was no moon and the land was dark. He heard the noises, he heard the voices raised in sudden orders, then a flash of lantern light showed, another, and slowly, dimly, Sharpe made out the darker mass that seemed to mill into the village to the south.

The enemy had come and the second battle of Arcachon was about to begin.

CHAPTER 14

General Calvet sat in a miserable hovel in a miserable village on the miserable edge of an increasingly miserable France. 'You say this Sharpe is good?'

'Lucky,' Ducos said scornfully.

'The Emperor,' Calvet said, 'will tell you a soldier needs luck more than brains. He came up from the ranks?'

'Like yourself, General,' Ducos replied.

'Then he must be good.' Calvet rubbed his hands in gleeful anticipation. The general had a broad, scarred face, burned with powder stains like dark tattoos. He wore a bushy, black veteran's moustache. 'Favier! You've fought the English, what are they like?'

Favier knew this was a time for truth, not bombast. 'Unimaginative in attack, rock-solid in defence, and quick with their muskets, very.'

'But these scoundrels are short of ammunition.' The general had heard how the British had scoured the local villages for powder. Calvet sat at a scarred table with a map drawn by Commandant Lassan beside the bread and cheese that was his supper. 'So the quicker they are with muskets, the sooner they'll exhaust their powder.' Calvet stared at the map. A double ditch, one of them flooded, surrounded three sides of the fort, but the fourth side, that which faced the channel, had no flooded ditch. The main bastion stood in the tidal shallows, but the northern half of the western wall was edged with sand as far as the moat's outflow. That was the vulnerable place.

The moat's outflow was a sluice gate in a small, masonry dam at the fort's north-western corner. That dam would act as a bridge leading to the ramparts' base, and the trick of this attack, Calvet knew, would be to draw the defenders' attention away from that spot.

'You'll attack tonight?' Ducos asked eagerly.

'Don't be a damned fool, man. That's what he's expecting! He's got his men on alert! They'll have a bad night and I'll make it worse, but I won't attack.' Calvet saw the disapproval on Ducos' face and, knowing what sinister power Ducos sometimes wielded with the Emperor, the big general deigned to explain himself. 'I've got raw troops, Ducos, nothing more than bloody farm-boys. Have you ever attacked at night? It's chaos! A bloody shambles! If they're repulsed, and they will be, they'll taste defeat and a new conscript should always be given a victory. It makes him feel invincible! No. We attack tomorrow. The goddamns have had no sleep, they'll be nervous as virgins in a Grenadiers' barracks, and we'll crush them.' Calvet leaned back in his chair and smiled about the crowded room. 'Tomorrow night we'll have Major Sharpe as our dinner guest.'

An aide lit a new candle. 'If he's alive, sir.'

'If he's not, we'll eat him.' Calvet laughed. 'We ate enough men in Russia. Human flesh tastes like skate, did you know that, Ducos? Next time you eat skate, remember it.'

'Thank you, sir.' Ducos did not smile.

'Boiled buttock of corporal, well-peppered,' Calvet mused. 'I've dined on worse. What's the range of their damned rifles?'

'Two hundred paces,' Favier said, 'but they can be a nuisance up to four hundred.'

'Then we'll put the howitzers here.' Calvet's thumb smeared the pencil marks that showed the village on the map. 'I want them bedded down as mortars.'

'Of course, sir,' the Artillery colonel said.

'And the other guns here,' the thumb stabbed down again, leaving a scrap of cheese by the watermill. 'Make embrasures in the wall, but don't open fire tonight. Tonight I want muskets up on the glacis. Lots of them. Keep the bastards worried. I want noise, bangs, shouts.' He was looking at one of his Battalion colonels. 'Pick a different spot every few minutes, don't make it regular. You know how to do it.'

'Yes, sir.'

'Make 'em use up some of their precious ammunition. But keep clear of this place.' Calvet pointed to the dam. 'I want that left alone.'

'Yes, sir.'

'And at dawn I want no one in sight, no one.' Calvet stood. He was a huge man, with a paunch like a ready-barrel of howitzer powder. He stretched his arms, yawned, and turned to the straw mattress that was laid by the fire. 'Now I'm sleeping, so get out. Wake me at five.'

'Yes, sir.'

'When we do attack,' the general's rumbling voice checked the exodus of uniformed officers, 'we do it quickly, efficiently, and right. Any man who lets me down will have to explain himself, alone, to me.' He raised one clenched fist the size of a small cannon-ball. 'Now bugger off and keep the bastards hopping.'

The waves broke and sucked on the beach at the channel entrance, the wind rattled pine branches and sighed over the ramparts, and the picked men of the best French Battalion went to their night-time task while the others slept. And General Calvet, head on a haversack and boots ready by his bed, snored.

'Hold your fire!' Sharpe bellowed the order, heard it echoed by a sergeant, then ran down the southern rampart.

Six or seven musket shots had cracked from the glacis, the balls hissing uselessly overhead, and two Marines and a Rifleman had instinctively returned fire. 'You don't fire,' Sharpe said, 'unless you're ordered to fire or unless the bastards are climbing the wall! You hear?'

None of the three men replied. Instead, crouching beneath the battlements, they reloaded their weapons.

Sharpe sent Fytch around the ramparts with a new warning that no man was to fire. The French, Sharpe guessed, were trying to provoke just such defensive fire to see which parts of the rampart responded most heavily. Let the bastards guess.

Sixty men were in the old garrison offices, fully armed, but told to catch what sleep they could. When the attack came, and Sharpe did not expect it till the deadest hours of the night, those men could be on the ramparts in minutes.

He crouched in an embrasure. The wind fingered cold on the scabbed blood on his forehead, and the sigh of it in his ears made listening difficult. He thought he heard the scrape of a boot or musket butt on the glacis, but was not sure. Whatever the sound was, it was too small to presage a full attack. Sharpe had crouched beyond a fortress's defences, throat dry and fear rampant, and he knew what sudden commotion was made by a mass of men moving to the escalade. There would be ladders bumping forward, the chink of equipment, the scrape of hundreds of boots, but he could hear nothing but the wind and see nothing but the blackness.

He went to the eastern wall and crouched beside Sergeant Rossner. 'Anything?'

'Nothing, sir.' The German sergeant had his shako up-ended on the firestep and half-filled with cartridges. Beside him was a roped mass of hay. If an attack came the hay would be lit then slung far over the walls to illuminate targets. No lights were allowed in the courtyard or on the walls of the Teste de Buch, for such lights could only silhouette the defenders for the convenience of French marksmen.

Sharpe moved on, crouching to talk with men, offering them wine from his canteen, always giving the same message. There was nothing to fear from random shots, or from the shouts that sometimes sounded in the darkness. The French were trying to fray the defenders' nerves, and Sharpe would have done the same. Once there was the sound of massed feet, shouts, and a fusillade of musketry that flattened on the walls, but no dark shapes appeared beyond the glacis lip. Jeers and insults came from the darkness, more shots, but Sharpe's men, once the first fear had subsided, learned to ignore the sounds.

In Commandmant Lassan's old quarters two Marines, one who had been a surgeon's mate and another who had trained in the butcher's trade, laid out carpenter's tools, shaving razors, and sewing kits on a table. They had no clamps, instead there was a cauldron of boiling pitch with which to cauterize a stump. They had no camphorated wine, nor any solution of lead acetate, so instead they had a barrel of salt-water to wash wounds, and a pot filled with spider-webs that could be stuffed into deep cuts. Patrick Harper, the big Irishman, had recommended maggots for cleaning wounds, but the dignity of their new-fetched professional pride would not allow the two Marines to accept the nostrum. They listened to the shots in the night, sipped the brandy that was supposed to dull wounded men's pain, and wondered when the first wounded would be brought for their attention.

Captain Palmer, trying to sleep where the sixty men were held in reserve, knew that there would be small rest tonight. Musket shots and sudden shouts came faint to the old offices, but not so faint that they did not cause men to stir and reach for their muskets or rifles. 'I wish the bastards would come,' one Marine muttered, and Palmer held the same belief. Better to get it over, he thought, than this damned waiting.

A Spanish Rifleman on the southern wall sent for Sharpe. 'Can you hear it, señor?' The man spoke in Spanish.

Sharpe listened. Faint, but unmistakable, came the sound of picks and spades thudding into earth, then the ring of a crowbar on stone. 'They're making a battery,' he replied in Spanish.

'In the village?' The Rifleman made it half a guess and half a question.

Sharpe listened again. 'I'd say so.'

'They'll be in range, then.' The Spaniard slapped the woodwork of his rifle.

'Long range,' Sharpe said dubiously.

'Not for Taylor,' the Spaniard said. The American's marksmanship was a legend to Frederickson's men.

But Taylor, this night, was in the darkness; gone with Harper and Frederickson, gone to spread terror among the men who tried to keep a garrison awake with clamour, gone to the kill.

Not a man made a sound. They lay flat to let their eyes adjust to the darkness.

The sky was not so dark as the land. There was no moon, but a spread of stars showed between patches of cloud and that lighter sky might betray a silhouette from ground-level and so the Riflemen lay, bellies on the sand, unmoving.

They were the best. Each man was a veteran, each had fought in more battles than could be casually recalled, and each had killed and gone past that point where a man found astonishment in the act of giving death to another human being.

William Frederickson, whose passion was for the architecture of the past and who was as well educated as any man in Wellington's Army, saw death as a regrettable but inevitable necessity of his trade. If wars could be won without death Frederickson would have been content, but so far mankind had devised no such process. And war, he believed, was necessary. To Frederickson the enemy was the embodiment of Napoleon's Imperial ambitions, the foe of all that he held most dear, and while he was not so foolish, nor so blind, as to be unaware of their humanity, it was nevertheless a humanity that had been pointed in his direction with orders to kill. It was therefore necessary to kill more swiftly and more efficiently than the enemy.

Thomas Taylor, Frederickson's American, reckoned death as commonplace as a meal or a woman. It was part of being alive. From his youngest days he had only known cruelty, pain, sickness, poverty, and death, and he saw nothing strange in any of those things. If it had made him heartless, it had also given him a pride in surviving in the valley of the shadow. He could kill with a rifle, a knife, a sword bayonet, or his bare hands, and he was good with all of them. He was a man of great resentment, and small remorse. He resented a fate that had driven him from his own land, that had doomed him to an Army he did not love, but his pride would not let him be a bad soldier.

For Patrick Harper killing was a soldier's trade and an act that provoked equal measures of regret and pride. By nature the Irishman was a gentle, pacific man, but there was a rage in him that could be touched by battle and turn him into a warrior as fearsome as any celebrated in Celtic song. Only battle seemed to touch that rage.

Sometimes, thinking of the men he had killed and whose faces he had seen show the last emotion of life, Harper might wish the blow withdrawn, the bayonet unthrust, or the trigger unpulled, but it was always too late. Other times, when he looked about the men he led, he was proud that he was of the best, that his deeds were celebrated, and that his name was never spoken with disdain. He loved the men he fought alongside, and their deaths hurt him, so he fought for them like a demon. He was a soldier, and he was a good one, and now he lay in the sand and was aware of the Green Jackets lying to his left and right and of the small sounds that came from the dunes ahead.

For an hour or more the French had been sniping at the fort, teasing the defenders, but always from a safe distance. They had done it to the southern and eastern ramparts, and now dark figures showed in the dead ground to the north where Frederickson's men lay.

Sweet William clicked his tongue softly, held a hand up so that it was silhouetted on the dark sky, and slowly gestured further north.

Thirteen shadows moved in the sand. They had blackened

faces, blackened hands, and darkened weapons. Their rifles were slung taut across their backs for Frederickson, knowing the value of fear driven into an enemy's heart, wanted this night's killing to be silent. They would use blades, not bullets, and the thirteen men moved with the skilled silence that presages death. Each Rifleman had spent time in daylight on this very ground and, though the dunes looked different under the night's cloak, the remembered knowledge was an advantage not given to their enemies.

A squad of ten Frenchmen gathered under the fold of a dune that edged on to the saw-grass of the glacis. They were one of six such parties abroad this night and they were enjoying their work. No danger seemed to threaten them, not even random musket fire from the dark ramparts that showed above the glacis. For the first hour of their excursion, treading into unknown darkness, they had gone cautiously and nervously, but the night's innocent silence had lulled their fears and made them bold.

Fifty yards to their left Lieutenant Piellot's squad suddenly yelled like savages and blasted shots at the fort. The men in the shelter of the dune grinned. Their own officer whispered that they could rest a moment and one sergeant made a cave about his head with his greatcoat and, under its hooding darkness, struck a flint on steel, blew tinder to life, and lit his short pipe.

Five yards away, unseen, Thomas Taylor eased himself along the sand on his elbows. In his right hand, blackened with a ball of boot-blacking, was a twenty-three inch sword bayonet that had been honed and sharpened to a razor's fineness.

The French officer, a captain of skirmishers, clambered to the top of the dune, careless of the small noises made by the cascading sand. Lieutenant Piellot was making enough racket to wake the dead and the small laughter and low voices of his own squad caused the captain no concern. He stared at the fortress and thought he saw a figure move on the ramparts. At night the eyes played tricks and he stared at the place where he thought he had seen movement and decided he was wrong. He hoped the British would surrender swiftly. The captain, who had a fiancée in Rheims and a mistress in Bordeaux, did not relish dying for the Emperor in a useless escalade on this shabby fortress.

Piellot's men fired a volley and the noise slammed over the dunes in two waves; the first from the muskets and the second the echo from the fortress wall. The squad shouted insults, rattled their ramrods in hot barrels, and the captain knew there was no point in his own men startling the enemy until Piellot's men quit their entertainment. He slid down the sand, calling to his men to relax, but suddenly his feet were seized, tugged hard, and the captain slithered down the dune, sprawling and flailing, until a boot slammed into his belly and a knee dropped on to his chest and a voice was hissing in fluent French that unless he kept very silent the knife at his throat would cut through to his spine. The captain kept very silent.

He could see nothing, but he could hear grunts and scuffles. One of his men's muskets banged into the air and, in the muzzle's red flash, the captain had a glimpse of black shapes rising and falling, of blades dripping, and suddenly the smell of raw blood was in his nostrils. Flesh sucked on steel, a blade grated on bone as it was withdrawn, men breathed heavily, then there was a respite from the sound of butchery.

'One,' Frederickson, kneeling on the captain, whispered the word into the sudden silence.

'Two,' Harper hissed.

'Three,' said a German from Mainz who kept a count of the Frenchmen he killed in battle.

'Four,' Thomas Taylor.

'Five,' a youth who was reputed to have stabbed his mother in Bedford then fled to the Army before the law could catch him.

'Six,' a Spaniard recruited in Salamanca to swell ranks depleted by war. The numbers went to thirteen. All

Frederickson's men were present, none was wounded, and, of the enemy, only the French captain was alive.

That captain, feeling he had shown insufficient valour this night, pushed his hand down to his belt where a pistol was holstered. The knife pressed on his throat. 'Don't move,' the voice said. The captain froze.

Frederickson ran his free hand over the captain's body, found pistol and sword, and drew both free. He pushed the pistol into his jacket, then used his knife to cut the Frenchman's small ammunition pouch free. The Riflemen were slashing at the dead men's cartouches. French musket balls, being fractionally smaller than the British issue, could be used by the Marines and Riflemen in their weapons, whereas captured British ball was useless to the French.

'RSM Harper?' Frederickson backed away from his captive. 'Take the bugger back.' Sweet William, careless of the conventions of this war, first tied a gag about the officer's mouth. 'Tommy? John? Go with Mr Harper.' Frederickson was careful to give Harper the honorific due to a Regimental Sergeant Major.

It took twenty minutes before the French officer was hauled by a loop of rope to the battlements on the western face, followed by nine precious cartouches of ready ammunition, and it was another ten minutes before Harper and his escort were back with Frederickson. They made themselves known with the harsh call of a nightjar, were answered in kind, then went on to the east where more Frenchmen waited in the darkness.

'He says, sir,' Lieutenant Fytch was acting as interpreter, 'that there won't be an attack tonight.'

'He does, does he?' Sharpe kept his eyes on the captured French officer who shook in the corner of the room.

Sharpe did not blame the man. The French captain had been brought to the makeshift surgery to answer questions and the man doubtless believed the ranks of pincers, saws, probes, and razors were to be used on him. Each slow, burping bubble of the simmering pitch made Captain Mayeron shudder.

'Ask him who's in command,' Sharpe ordered. He half listened to the ensuing conversation as he probed through Mayeron's belongings. There was a fine watch with a chased silver lid that told Sharpe it was quarter past three in the morning. There was a bundle of letters, tied in a green ribbon, all written from Rheims and signed Jeanette. There was a miniature painting, enclosed in a leather wallet and presumably of the same Jeanette who simpered artfully at the beholder. There was a handkerchief, a clasp knife, three walnuts, an unwashed fork and spoon, a flask of brandy, a pencil stub, and a small, leather-clad diary that contained sketches of the countryside and a clumsy, heavy-jowled, pencil-drawn portrait of a girl called Marie. In the same page was a slip of pasteboard on which was glued some dried flowers and signed, evidently with love, by the same Marie.

'Calvet,' Fytch said. 'A general.'

'Never heard of him. Ask him if Bordeaux has risen for the King?'

The question elicited an indignant, long answer that translated simply as 'no'.

Sharpe was not surprised by the answer, but he probed further. 'Ask him if there was any trouble in the city recently?'

Captain Mayeron, prompted by a particularly rich burst of bubbling from the cauldron of pitch, said there had been some bread riots at Christmas, but no political trouble except the usual grumbling of merchants made poor by the blockade. And no, the garrison had not rebelled, and no, he did not think the population was ready to rebel against the Emperor. He seemed to think about the last answer, shrugged, then repeated it.

Sharpe listened to the translation and began to understand the treachery of the Comte de Maquerre. Hogan, in his feverish babbling, had used the man's name, together with the name of Pierre Ducos, and now Sharpe suspected he was a victim of the clever Frenchman's scheming.

Or was he? In these last few hours, alone with his thoughts, Sharpe had begun to suspect a deeper, more secret scheme. Why would Wellington allow men like Wigram and Bampfylde to harbour grandiose schemes of invasion? Neither staff colonels nor naval captains had the authority to authorize such adventures, yet neither man had been slapped down except by Elphinstone who was of their own rank. Wellington or the Admiral of the Biscay Squadron could have ordered the two men to stop their scheming, yet they had been allowed to indulge their dreams of madness. And why had the Comte de Maquerre been sent to Bordeaux? Surely the answer was that Wellington wanted the French to believe in an Arcachon landing. General Calvet's presence at Arcachon meant that he could not oppose a bridge across the Adour. So the victim was not Sharpe, but the French, yet de Maquerre's treachery had still abandoned Sharpe to this fate in a slighted fortress.

Captain Mayeron, fearful because of the boiling pitch, suddenly spoke.

'He asks,' Fytch translated, 'whether he can be exchanged.'

'For whom?' Sharpe asked. 'They haven't taken any of us prisoner! Give him his belongings back, then lock him in the liquor store.'

Sharpe returned to the ramparts and there stood down half of his men and sent them to get some precious sleep. The captured Captain Mayeron had convinced Sharpe that the enemy he faced, though overwhelming in numbers, was half-trained and incapable of a night-time escalade. The Frenchman had also convinced Sharpe that he was not caught in a trap, but was an unwitting part of a greater trap. But that was no consolation, for in the morning the French guns would begin their fire and the time of trial would begin.

*

Frederickson first led his squad eastwards, then south through the tangle of small meadows. He was drawn by a rhythmic, clanging sound that came from the direction of the watermill.

He paused in the black-shadowed shelter of the byre where Harper had drawn his own tooth. There was the beat of owl-wings overhead, then silence again except for the ring of picks or crowbars on the watermill's stones.

Frederickson waved his men into hiding, then stared at the mill. There was the faintest glow of light limning the doors and windows, suggesting that men worked inside the big stone building by the light of shielded lanterns.

'They're putting guns in there,' Harper offered his opinion in a hoarse whisper.

'Probably.' Artillery placed in the mill would be protected by stone walls from rifle fire, and would be able to rake the southern and eastern flanks of the beleaguered fortress.

Frederickson turned towards the village where the bulk of the enemy forces had gone. More half-shielded lights showed among the small buildings, but he could see no movement between the village and the mill. He wondered how many picquets guarded the big stone building that straddled the stream. 'Hernandez?'

The Spanish Rifleman from Salamanca appeared beside Frederickson. He moved with an uncanny silence; a stealth learned when he was a *guerrillero*, and a stealth much prized by Captain Frederickson. The Spaniard listened to his Captain's quick orders, showed a white grin against blackened skin, and went southwards. Hernandez, Frederickson believed, could have picked the devil's own pockets and got clean away.

The other Riflemen waited for twenty minutes. A French squad fired from the glacis, shouted insults at the ramparts, but no defender fired back. A dog barked in the village, then yelped as it was kicked into silence.

Frederickson smelt Hernandez before he saw him, or rather he smelt blood, then heard two thumps as the Spaniard seemed to materialize out of the shadows. 'There are four men on the track from the mill to the village,' Hernandez whispered, 'and there were two guarding the bridge.'

'Were?'

'*Si, señor.*' Hernandez gestured to the ground and thus explained the curious double thump that had presaged his return.

Frederickson's voice was gentle with reproof. 'You didn't cut their heads off, did you, Marcos?'

'*Si, señor.* Now they cannot give the alarm.'

'That's certainly true.' Frederickson was glad that the darkness cloaked the horrors at his feet.

He led his squad south, following the path reconnoitred by Hernandez, a path that led to the small bridge beside the mill. Once at the bridge they were close enough to see the shapes of men working inside the building. One group of men, using crowbars, sledgehammers and picks, were making loopholes in the thick outer wall of the mill, while others cleared the mill's machinery to leave a space for the guns. 'There were twenty French bastards inside,' Hernandez whispered.

'Guns?'

'I didn't see them.'

One of the lantern shields was lifted as a man stooped to light a cigar. Frederickson thought he saw the shape of a French field gun in the recesses of the mill, but it was hard to tell exactly what lay in the deep shadows. But Frederickson knew that at least twenty men worked inside, and another four Frenchmen were close to the mill. Sweet William had thirteen men, but his were Riflemen. The odds therefore seemed stacked against the French, in which case there was small point in waiting, so Frederickson, sword drawn, led his men to the attack.

General Calvet was not unduly annoyed, he was even amused. 'So he's good! That makes him a worthy foe. I'll take another egg.' Another rifle crack and another scream betrayed that some fool had shown himself on the northern edge of the village. 'Four hundred paces!' Calvet looked at Favier.

'They have some marksmen,' Favier said apologetically.

'I've never understood,' Calvet broke off a piece of bread with which to mop up his egg-yolk, 'why the Emperor won't use rifles. I like them!'

'Slow to load,' Favier ventured.

'Tell that to the poor bugger who's on his way to the surgeons.' Calvet grunted scant thanks as his servant tipped another runny egg from the pan on to the plate. 'Where's the bacon?'

'The British took it all to the fort.'

'So they're eating bacon for breakfast and I'm not,' Calvet growled, then looked at Ducos who sat in the corner with a pen and notebook. 'Tell your master, Ducos, that we lost thirty-four dead, six wounded, and had one twelve-pounder scorched. We lost two limbers of ammunition. That's not a big loss! I remember a night we got in among the Ivans at Vilna. I had two of them on this sword! One behind the other like chickens on a spit! And the one in front was grinning at me and jabbering away in his heathen language. Remember that?' He twisted to look at his aide. 'How many guns did we take?'

'Four, sir.'

'I thought it was six.'

'Six it was,' the aide said hastily.

'Six guns!' the general said happily, 'and Sharpe didn't take one last night! Not one! He just scorched a carriage!'

The mill had burned, but the stone walls were still intact and the guns were being emplaced behind the finished, scorched embrasures. Calvet acknowledged that the British troops had done well in the night. They had scoured the mill of its work-party, exploded the limbers, but they could have done much better. Sharpe, in Calvet's book, had made a mistake. He had only sent out a small force and, though that force had committed butchery, they had done not nearly so much damage as a major sortie from the fortress might have achieved. Calvet chuckled. 'He thought we were going to pounce, so he kept most of his men at home.' The general spooned half the fried egg into his mouth, then went on talking despite the mouthful. 'So we'll just have to surprise this half-clever bugger, won't we?' He wiped egg yolk from his chin with his sleeve, then looked at Favier. 'Go and have a talk with this Sharpe. You know what to say.'

'Of course, sir.'

'And tell him I'd be obliged for some bacon. The fat sort.'

'Yes, sir.' Favier paused. 'He'll probably want some brandy in return.'

'Give it to him! I'll get it back by the end of the day, but I do feel like some fat bacon for lunch. Right, gentlemen,' Calvet slapped the table to show that the pleasantries were over, and that the siege proper could begin.

CHAPTER 15

The moment Colonel Favier removed his hat, Sharpe recognized the man who had spoken to him at the bridge over the Leyre. Favier smiled. 'My general sends his congratulations.'

'Give him my commiserations.'

The French corporal holding the white flag of truce stood miserably beside Favier's horse, while Favier stared along the ramparts. There was no one but Sharpe to be seen. Favier smiled. 'My general informs you that you have acquitted yourself nobly and that you may march out with all the honours of war.' Favier shouted far louder than was necessary for just Sharpe to hear; he wanted the hidden garrison to listen to this offer. 'You will be imprisoned, of course, but treated as honourable and brave opponents.'

'I'll give you my answer,' Sharpe said, 'at midday.'

Favier, who knew all the rules of this game, smiled. 'If your answer is not forthcoming in ten minutes, Major, we shall presume that it is a rejection of our most generous terms. In the meantime may we remove our dead from the north ground?'

'You can send six men, unarmed, and one light cart. You should know that Captain Mayeron is our prisoner.'

'Thank you.' Favier calmed his horse that had suddenly skittered sideways on the road that led through the glacis. 'And you should know, Major, that your ships believe you to be defeated and captured. They will not return for you.' He waited for a response, but Sharpe said nothing. Favier smiled. 'You and your officers are invited to take lunch with General Calvet.'

'I shall give you that answer with the other,' Sharpe said.

'And General Calvet begs a favour of you. He would be appreciative of some fat bacon. He offers this in return.' Favier held up a black, squat bottle. 'Brandy!'

Sharpe smiled. 'Tell the general that we have all the food and drink we need. When you come for your answer I'll give you the bacon.'

'It's a pity for brave men to die!' Favier was shouting again. 'For nothing!'

Eight minutes later Sharpe gave Favier the answer that the Frenchman expected, a rejection of the offered terms, and also tossed down a muslin-wrapped leg of bacon that the flag-carrier had to pick up from the broad ledge of the counter-guard. Favier waved a friendly farewell, then turned his horse away.

To the north a small waggon was still picking up the dead left in the dunes by Frederickson's men. Sharpe wanted the French conscripts to see those corpses and to fear the night. The French could rule the day, but his Riflemen could make the environs of the Teste de Buch into a nightmare.

Yet within minutes of Favier's departure Sharpe had some evidence that the Frenchman had planted some fear into his own men. Lieutenant Fytch, albeit sheepishly, wanted to know whether there was any hope in a fight.

'Who rules the waves, Lieutenant?' Sharpe asked.

'Britannia?'

Sharpe pointed to the sea. 'So that's our territory. Any moment, Lieutenant, a ship could appear. When it does, we're safe. How would you feel if we surrendered and a naval squadron appeared an hour later?' The very fact that the question had been asked was cause for worry. Sharpe did not fear for the morale of his Riflemen, but the Marines had not been fighting the French so consistently and, bereft of their ships, they felt the flickers of fear that could gnaw into a man's confidence. 'We've sent a message south, the Navy patrols this coast, we only have to hold on.'

'Yes, sir.'

Yet, in truth, Sharpe might have shared the tremor of despair that the lieutenant's question had shown. There were no ships in sight, even though the waters beyond Cap Ferrat had settled to a gentle, sun-glittering chop. He waited on the ramparts, wondering what surprises the French general planned, and found himself contemplating the very thing Favier had encouraged; surrender.

Sharpe told himself that he was trapped, out-numbered, and with limited supplies of food, water and ammunition. When one of those things gave out, he was doomed.

Yet to be made a prisoner was to be taken far away from this part of France, to be marched north to the grim fortress town of Verdun and he would be even further from Jane. He had told his men they fought in hope of rescue, but he had lied.

Sharpe's troubled thoughts were interrupted by Frederickson climbing the ramp. 'I thought you were sleeping,' Sharpe said.

'I slept for three hours.' Frederickson stared out to sea. These western ramparts were the safest, the only wall not covered by the French forces, and the two officers could lean in a gun embrasure and stare at the waves.

'There's something I should have told you,' Sharpe said uncertainly.

'You have an unnatural passion for my beauty.' Frederickson blew steam from a mug of tea. 'I understand it.'

Sharpe smiled a dutiful appreciation. 'Jane.'

'Ah.' Frederickson, abandoning jest, turned and leaned his rump on the stone. 'Well?'

'She has the fever.'

Frederickson's one eye considered Sharpe. 'She was well the night before . . .'

'The symptoms appeared next morning.'

Frederickson sighed. 'I wish I could express my sorrow properly, sir.'

'It's not that.' Sharpe was embarrassed into incoherence. 'I just think I'm fighting here because I can't bear to leave her. If she dies, and I'm not there. You understand? If I surrender,' he waved feebly towards the north, 'I'll be taken away from her.'

'I understand.' Frederickson took a cheroot from his pocket. He only had six left and had rationed himself to one a day. He lit it, and drew the smoke into his lungs. He watched Sharpe, knowing what Sharpe wanted to hear, but unable and unwilling to express it. He was saved an immediate reply by the presence of three Riflemen carrying a barrel of lime to one of the citadels.

Frederickson did not know Jane. He had met her just once, and he had discovered a girl of startling prettiness, but that did not make her special. Many girls, to one degree or another, were pretty. Marine Robinson's green-eyed drab, for whom Robinson risked a deserter's death, would be as pretty as any society girl if she was washed, dressed properly, and taught the monkey-antics of the salon. Frederickson had noted that Jane had a sweet-natured smile and a pleasant, vivacious personality, but such things were the stock-in-trade of the young woman seeking matrimony. Any father from the middling sort in Britain, and hopeful of marrying his daughter into the better classes, made sure his child was tricked out with such allurements. And as for intelligence, which Jane seemed to have, in Frederickson's view the largest part of female humanity so blessed inevitably wasted the gift on cheap novels, gossip, or evangelical religion.

So to suffer for such a girl, as Sharpe was evidently suffering, did not touch a nerve in Frederickson's soul. He allowed that Jane Sharpe might one day prove to be above the common ruck, might even prove to have a distinction and character that would outlast the fading of her beauty, and doubtless Sharpe saw those possibilities within her, but Frederickson, not knowing her, did not. To agonize over a wife was therefore beyond Sweet William's comprehension; indeed for a soldier to take a wife was beyond his comprehension. Whores could scratch that itch, and so Frederickson

234

found he could say nothing that would be of comfort to his friend. Instead, abandoning sympathy, he posed a question. 'If you died this morning, God forbid, then I'd take over?'

'Yes.' Sharpe knew that Frederickson's commission was senior to Palmer's.

'Then I,' Frederickson said stonily, 'would fight the bastards.'

'Why?'

'Why!' Frederickson stared at Sharpe with amazement. 'Because they're crapauds! Because they're slimy Frogs! Because as long as they're fighting us they can't go south and give the Peer a headache! Because the English have a God-given duty to rid the world of the French! Because it's what I'm paid to do. Because I've got nothing better to do! Because Napoleon Bonaparte is a foul little worm who grovels in his own excrement! Because no one's ordered me to surrender just because the odds are unhealthy! Because I don't want to live under French rule and the more of those bastards I kill the more the rest of them will slowly comprehend that fact! Do you need more?' He watched Sharpe. 'If you weren't married, would you surrender?'

'No.'

'So being married has weakened you. It does, you know. Saps a man.' He grinned to show that he did not want to be taken seriously, even if he had spoken with real conviction. 'I'm sorry about Jane, I truly am. But her fight isn't here and you are.'

'Yes.' Sharpe felt ashamed of himself. He wanted to tell Frederickson about the superstition that had kept him going through the ambush and how Killick, unwittingly, had taken that strength away from him, but he could say nothing. 'I'm sorry.'

'You need a good fight,' Frederickson said cheerfully. 'Nothing like a good fight to raise the spirits. And two weeks from now, my friend, we'll open a bottle and be embarrassed this conversation ever took place.'

'Yes.' Sharpe had expected some sympathy, and had found none. 'They came for a parley.'

'So I heard.'

'They said that Bampfylde was told we'd been defeated. That's why the Navy buggered off.'

'Clever.' Frederickson blew smoke into the wind.

It was de Maquerre, Sharpe thought. Perhaps Hogan had known de Maquerre was a traitor, but no one else had known. But now Sharpe knew and he vowed, should he survive this siege, that he would seek the Frenchman out. Then the first howitzer shell cracked apart and both men twisted towards the explosion even as the shards of broken shell casing, humming and fizzing from the smoke, spattered about them.

A howitzer was merely a short-barrelled cannon useful for the firing of exploding shell. The loss of accuracy occasioned by the stunted barrel was compensated by the diameter of the shell's explosion.

Their proper use, in battle, was to lob shells over the heads of friendly troops. Thus, unlike the long-barrelled cannons, they were fired at a gentle upward angle.

Yet General Calvet did not want to use a shallow trajectory. Instead he wanted his four howitzers to fire as mortars; firing almost vertically so their shells would plummet straight down into the killing confines of the fortress walls.

So each eight hundred and eighty pound barrel had to be wrestled from its carriage and laid in a specially made cradle of timbers laid in the gunpits. The timbers were levered and sawn from the village houses, notched to take the howitzer's trunnions, then wedged solid with wooden quoins. Now, angling up to the sky, they would arc their shells high over the walls. Or so the theory went.

The problems, apart from the shifting and settling of the timbers beneath the hammer blows of each shot, were twofold. First, the gunner must precisely gauge the weight of powder that would send the ball neatly into the courtyard of the Teste de Buch. A quarter ounce too much would send the shell searing far beyond the enemy. Second, the duration of the ball's flight had to be estimated and one of the five fuses selected as appropriate. It was a science fleshed out with instinct, and the very first guesses of the French artillery colonel were a tribute to his experience.

He ordered five ounces of powder used, far less than a mortar would take for the same distance, and he selected the middle fuse. The first gun, firing its experimental shot, hammered down into the timbers and squirted a quoin loose, but the colonel, watching the tiny trace of smoke from the burning fuse, saw the shell arc sweetly towards the fort, then fall, faster and faster, to provoke a cracking, dirty-smoked explosion in the very centre of the enemy.

The shell was a sphere of cast-iron filled with powder. When the fuse burned to the powder, the shell exploded and fragments of iron whistled out to fill a circle, twenty yards in diameter, with possible death. The shells dropped almost vertically.

'Take cover!' Sharpe shouted through the smoke.

Two men were down, one screaming and clutching his belly, the other motionless.

A second shell hit the ramparts, bounced, and trickled down the stone ramp. Sharpe waited for the explosion.

A third shell tore through the rafters of the garrison's offices and exploded on the upper floor. Lieutenant Fytch, shooting out of the door like a rabbit pursued by a ferret, shouted for water.

The fourth shell buried itself in the ashes and blackened timber of the burned barracks and vented those relics up and out as it coughed its dark explosion.

'We've got one dead, sir!' A Rifleman pointed to the second shell which had come to rest on the ramp. No smoke came from the reed which held the fuses, but Sharpe had seen such things explode quite inexplicably.

'Stay clear of it!'

There was a pause in which, Sharpe knew, the enemy was realigning the guns and ladling black powder into the swabbed barrels. Sharpe was furious with himself. For some reason he had not anticipated mortar fire and the shock of it stunned him.

'I suppose,' Frederickson said, 'we're going to have to endure it for a while.'

'I imagine so.' But the powder laboratory was threatened, as was the surgeon's room, and Sharpe shouted for Lieutenant Minver to make up a work-party to remove both to safer places deep in the stone galleries.

Six men ran with fouled water from the well and handed their buckets into the offices where other men fought the fire. Two Marines carried the wounded man towards the surgery, while a Rifleman dragged the dead man to the side of the yard. Sharpe saw, with approval, how the dead man's ammunition was rescued.

Two more guns fired, this time with a different sound, and Sharpe whipped round to see that two of the enemy's twelve-pounder guns, Napoleon's 'beautiful daughters', were successfully embrasured in the scorched watermill. They were firing heavy canister, presumably to scour the defenders from the ramparts, and the heavy balls thudded on stone or whispered overhead. 'Rifles! Watch those bastards!' The gunners, five hundred yards away to the south-east, just might show themselves in a window of the mill, though the smoke of their guns provided a sheltering screen against the Rifles' aim. Then, in a shattering beat of sound, the six other twelve-pounders, some inside the mill and the others sheltered by a stone wall that ran alongside the stream-race, opened fire.

A howitzer shell screamed down, this one exploding five yards above the courtyard's cobbles, and a fragment of its casing took the skulltop from one of the men who had crouched for shelter behind the furnace. Bullet-making had been interrupted by the attack and molten lead, tipped by the shell's blast, poured slow and obscene on to the dead face.

Another shell landed on the eastern ramparts and tossed a Rifleman down into the courtyard. The next shell overshot, cracking apart in the dry northern ditch, while the last of this second volley, its fuse damp, bounced, span, smoked, and Patrick Harper, magnificently casual as he emerged from a powder gallery, checked the spin with his boot, licked forefinger and thumb, then bent down and plucked the burning fuse free. 'Good morning, sir!'

'Good morning, RSM. Thank you for last night.'

Harper cocked an ear to the morning's sounds. 'Doesn't seem to have discouraged the bastards, sir.'

Sharpe left just a dozen men in the shelter of the citadels, mostly Riflemen, and the rest were put deep in the safe galleries of the fort. The offices would have to burn.

Sharpe stayed on the ramparts, as did Captain Palmer, but Frederickson was ordered unwillingly into shelter. The heavy canister balls rattled and scraped on the stones, bounced spinning from the glacis, and tore at the makeshift flag. Once a French gunner showed himself beside the mill, four rifles spat, but the man, with a derisive gesture, leaped to safety.

The shells had to be endured. They came with a horrid frequency, no longer spaced in batches of four because each French gun, finding its rhythm, fired at its own pace. Sometimes two or three would land together, sometimes there would be a pause as long as thirty seconds when no shell landed, but the morning seemed to Sharpe to be an unending thunder. Again and again the explosions cracked and shook and rumbled and the foul-smelling smoke soured the air and flames started again in the destroyed barracks to match the flames that shot up above the ramparts from the burning offices. Six men, led by Minver, had helped move the makeshift surgery into a ready magazine while another six, led by Harper, rescued the laboratory with its precious load of half-made cartridges.

A young Marine, crouching beside Sharpe in the dubious safety of the south-east citadel, flinched each time a shell exploded. 'Bastards,' he said, 'bastards.' Fragments of shell casing scrabbled on stone; one fragment came through the citadel door and dropped, still smoking, at Sharpe's feet.

'Bastards,' the Marine said. A shell hit the citadel roof, making a noise like the ringing crack of a sledge-hammer, and Sharpe heard the shell scrape as it slid down the stone roof towards the ditch and he knew if it exploded outside the loopholes the iron would scythe this casement clean like a butcher's cleaver swept at waist level, but the shell splashed harmlessly into the ditch.

'Bastards,' the Marine said.

The fortress shook with the explosions, the air thumped with them, the cobbles were scorched by them. One of Harper's cannon, so lovingly restored, was blown from its carriage. A corpse, hit in the belly by an exploding shell, spattered flesh and blood on the walls. One of Sharpe's walkways, circumventing the citadels, was lifted from its place and dropped into the barracks' rubble. Another, at the south-western corner, was burned by the flames that climbed from Lassan's offices.

The twelve-pounders, seeing no movement on the walls, changed to solid shot and the hammer blows rang like harsh bells throughout the Teste de Buch. At five hundred yards, over open sights, the gunners could not miss. Their iron shot skimmed the glacis to crack into the ramparts and the stones, laid with poor mortar, began to shift.

'Bastards.' The Marine's knuckles, gripping the stock of his heavy musket, were white.

'What's your name?' Sharpe asked.

The Marine, who looked about sixteen years old, blinked. 'Moore, sir.'

'Where are you from?'

'Exminster, sir.'

'Where's that?' Sharpe was peering through the loophole,

watching for an attack, but when the boy did not reply, he turned to him. 'Well?'

'Near Exeter, sir. In Devon.'

'Farmers?'

'Father's a publican, sir. The Stowey Arms.'

Two shells exploded, filling the air with smoke, thunder and the hot breath of flame, and Marine Moore, for once, did not swear.

'One day,' Sharpe said, 'you and I will drink some pots of ale at your Stowey Arms in Exminster and no one will believe the tales we tell.'

The boy grinned. 'Yes, sir.'

'Is it a good alehouse?'

'The best, sir.'

'And the ale?'

'Rare stuff, sir. Better than the muck you get here.'

'French beer,' Major Richard Sharpe said authoritatively, 'is pissed by virgins.' He saw the boy grin as he was supposed to, and slapped his shoulder. 'You, Marine Moore, look through that hole. You see anything move, sing out. Understand?'

'Yes, sir.'

'I'm relying on you.' Sharpe, hiding his own terror that was quite as keen as Moore's, stepped out of the citadel's shelter. He straightened his jacket and sword, then walked down the southern rampart. He saw the destruction in the courtyard, heard a roundshot shiver a merlon not six paces away, but walked on calmly. Men, sheltering in the archways opening from the courtyard or crouching in the rampart's citadels, should see him now. He must look calm in the face of this terror, he must let them know that the shells and shot, however loud, were not the end of the earth. He remembered how he, as a younger soldier, had watched his officers and sergeants and how he had believed that if they could take the murderous sounds, then so could he.

He stood at the midpoint of the rampart and stared south.

He felt all the old symptoms of fear. His heart thumped in his ribcage, his belly seemed to be sinking, his throat was dry, he felt a muscle trembling in his thigh that he could not still, and sweat, though it was a cold day, pricked at his skin. He told himself he should not move from the spot until he had counted to twenty, then decided that a brave man would count to sixty.

He did this so his men would see him, not because he thought it safe. A roundshot glanced off the cordon of the parapet, and Sharpe knew the twelve-pounders, barrels heated, were firing higher. The mortars, he noticed, were both less frequent and less accurate and he guessed the wooden beds had shifted in the sandy soil. He reached fifty in his count, decided he was deliberately hurrying the numbers, so made himself start again from forty.

'Sir! Mr Sharpe!' It was Moore. The boy was pointing south-east, inland, and Sharpe, staring at that direction, saw the mass of men who had been drawn up behind the village and who now, drums beating and colours held high, emerged into plain view. The mortars, Sharpe realized with surprise, had stopped firing. He looked towards the field guns and those weapons, all eight of them, were silent. Their gunsmoke drifted over the meadows. He noticed that there was a touch of spring in the air and something beautiful in the way the sun glittered on the water.

Sharpe turned. 'Captain Frederickson! To your places! All of you!' He blew his whistle, watched as men debouched at a run from the stone tunnels, then turned back to see what his enemy might do.

The assault was coming.

General Calvet, a flitch of fat bacon in one hand and a watch in the other, grinned. 'You think they'll have manned the ramparts by now, Favier?'

'I'm sure, sir.'

'Give the signal, then. I'll go back to lunch.'

242

Favier nodded to the trumpeter, who made the call, and the infantry immediately sat down.

The gunners, who had been hammering quoins into the shaken howitzer beds, leaped back as the portfires were lit and as the barrels thudded down again.

'Lie down!' Sharpe was furious. He had fallen for a trick like a raw officer fresh out of school and he had brought his men into the open, just as the French had wanted him to do, and now the shells were wobbling at the top of their arc, spiralling smoke, then were plunging towards the fort. 'Lie down!'

The field guns fired, the shells exploded, and the night-mare of fire and banging and skull-splitting shrieks and flame and whistling fragments began again.

A solid shot, striking an embrasure, drove stone scraps into a man's eyes. A shell, landing on the western wall between two Marines, took the belly of one and left the other unscathed but screaming.

'They did that neatly,' Frederickson said.

'And I fell for it,' Sharpe said with bitter self-digust.

Frederickson peered through an embrasure. The French infantry lay by the millstream as though on a holiday. 'They'll attack the gate when they do come.'

'I imagine so.'

'Confident bastards, letting us know.' Both officers ducked as a roundshot shivered dust and dry mortar from the stones above them. The great masonry block had been shifted a full inch by the blow.

Sharpe stared at the far rampart. 'Lieutenant Minver!'

'Sir?'

'Get some bread and cold meat sent round!'

Minver, somewhat aghast at being ordered to brave the courtyard where most of the shells exploded, nodded. Sharpe would leave his men exposed for he had no way of telling just when the attack of massed infantry would start forward. They would come from the south-east and the howitzers could keep firing until the French were actually at the

243

ramparts. The field guns, firing very close to the line of advance, would have to cease fire long before the attack struck home.

Sharpe wanted them to come. He wanted to hear the Old Trousers, the drummers' *pas de charge*, he wanted to hear the screams of attacking men, the banging of muskets, for that would be preferable to this helpless waiting. He suddenly wanted to echo young Moore and swear uselessly at the gunners who sweated and fired and swabbed and fired again.

Harper, waiting on the western wall with Sharpe's picked squad, went to the screaming Marine and slapped him into silence. 'And shovel that mess over the side, lad.' He gestured at the spilt guts of the dead man. 'You don't want flies here, do you?'

'Flies in winter?'

'Don't be cheeky, lad. Do it.'

One of the Marines with Harper seemed untroubled by the shelling. He drew a stone along the fore-edge of a cutlass, doing it again and again in search of the perfect cutting blade. Another, leaning against the abandoned timber slide of one of Lassan's guns, read a small book with evident fascination. From time to time he looked up, saw that his services were not yet required, and went back to the book. Captain Palmer, staring north and east from his allotted station, thought he saw movement in the dunes but when he examined the place with his spyglass he saw only sand and grass.

For a half hour more the bombardment continued. Screaming shells blasted apart in black ruin, flames roared from the rafters that collapsed in a shower of sparks into the ruins of the offices, and iron shards spat dirty death into the corners of the garrison. Men shivered. They stared at stone an inch before their face, they cursed the French, their officers, their luck, the whole rotten world that had brought them to this eye of a manmade hell, until at last, at long, long last, the trumpets sounded thin through the thunder's noise and the far cheer betrayed that a mass of men moved towards the attack and the men in the fort, men in red and green and men with drawn and dirtied faces, prepared themselves to fight.

CHAPTER 16

Two Marines from Sharpe's squad, judging the intervals between the fall of howitzer shells, darted around the court-yard to retrieve those shells that had not exploded. There were six. The fuses of two had failed to ignite in the howitzer barrels, two had half burned-fuses, while two had simply failed to explode. The four with usable fuses were carried to the bastion above the gatehouse where Lieutenant Fytch licked nervous lips and fingered the hilt of his pistol.

Bread and cold meat had been distributed, but most men found it hard to chew or swallow the food. As the French column came closer and the threat of its drums louder, the bread was abandoned beside the upturned shakoes that served as cartridge holders.

A shell, landing in the flooded ditch, fountained water on to an embrasure. A man laughed nervously. A sparrow, made bold by winter hunger, pecked at one of the discarded lumps of bread then flew off.

Marine Moore, for the twentieth time, lifted the pan lid to check that his musket was primed. For the twentieth time it was.

The French drums sounded clearly inside the fort, punctu-ated only by the fire of the big guns. Between the rattled passages of drumbeats there was a pause filled by hundreds of voices. '*Vive l'Empereur!*'

'Funny thing to hear for the first time,' Fytch said.

'I've heard it more times than I can remember,' Sharpe said truthfully, 'and we beat the buggers every time.' He looked at the column, a great mass of men that advanced implacably over the sandy esplanade. It had been French columns like this, so huge and seemingly so irresistible, that had terrified half the nations of Europe into surrender, but it was also a formation that was designed to contain half-trained troops who could, therefore, be scared and bloodied into defeat. French skirmishers were deploying on the glacis and one of them put a bullet within six inches of Sharpe's face. A rifle cracked and Sharpe saw the Frenchman slide back behind his mist of musket smoke.

Sharpe had drawn all his Riflemen to the southern or eastern walls. He waited till the enemy was two hundred paces away, then filled his lungs. 'Rifles! Fire!'

More than a hundred rifles spat fire.

Perhaps a dozen men in the leading rank of the French column keeled over. Immediately, with a shiver, the column stepped over the bodies. A slow ripple seemed to move down the column as the succeeding ranks negotiated the dead and wounded.

Riflemen concentrated on reloading; working with fast, practised hands, ramming ball and wad and powder down clean barrels, aiming again, firing again, reloading again.

At a hundred paces Sharpe blew two blasts on his whistle. Those Riflemen whose places were on the other ramparts ran back to their stations.

The field guns stopped firing.

It seemed oddly quiet. The drumming and shouting still continued, but the ear-hammering percussion of the twelve-pounders was over. The howitzers, firing still, made a more muffled, coughing sound. A wounded man, under the razor, screamed from the surgery tunnel and a Marine, for no apparent reason, vomited.

'At this range,' Sharpe walked down the line of Marines and kept his voice as matter-of-fact as a drill-sergeant, 'aim two feet above the target.' He glanced at the enemy. 'Take aim!'

The red-coated men pushed their muskets over the embrasures.

'Fire! Reload!'

247

A Frenchman crawled across the sand of the glacis, trailing blood.

A Marine, hit by a skirmisher's musket ball, spun backwards, teetered on the edge of the firestep, then fell into the burning branches of the pine abatis.

'Fire!'

A howitzer shell cracked on the firestep beside Sharpe and span into the courtyard where its explosion made a ball of filthy smoke shot through with red flames.

'Fire!' Lieutenant Fytch shouted. He pointed his pistol at a French officer not fifty yards away and pulled the trigger. The gun rammed a shock up his arm and blotted his view with smoke.

A Marine's musket hangfired and he threw the gun into the courtyard and picked up the weapon of a dead man. The ammunition left in the pouch of the corpse who had fallen into the burning abatis began to explode.

The Riflemen, knowing that survival depended on the speed of their work, no longer rammed shots home, but tap-loaded their guns by rapping the butts on the rampart then firing the weapon into the gap between the glacis' shoulders. Musket balls and rifle bullets spat into the enemy, but still the column came forward. Sharpe, who had seen it so often before, was again amazed at how much punishment a French column would endure. Three of the Marines, issued with civilian blunderbusses taken from the surrounding villages, poured their fire into the column's head.

The shape of the attack was clear now.

At the front of the column the French general had put raw recruits, musket-fodder; boys whose deaths would not damage the Empire and he had invited the British to slaughter them. Now, pushed by officers and sergeants, the survivors of those conscripts spread along the counter-guard or sheltered in the dry ditch and banged their muskets at the smoke-wreathed wall above them.

Behind were the veterans. Twenty or more men carried great fascines of roped branches, great mattresses of timber that sheltered them from bullet strike and which would be thrown into the ditch where the drawbridge should have been. Behind them, moustached faces grim, came the Grenadiers, the assault troops.

Frederickson had lit a candle sheltered in a lantern. He used a spill to take the flame from the candle to the first unexploded mortar shell. He watched the fuse hiss, waited till the fire had burned into the hole bored in the casing, then, with a grunt, heaved it over the edge.

'Fire!' Lieutenant Fytch, his pistol reloaded, wasted the bullet into a fascine.

The shell bounced on the road, disappeared beneath the leading rank, then exploded.

A hole seemed to be punched in the men carrying the great bundles, but as soon as the smoke cleared, the hole filled, and a French sergeant kicked dead men and discarded bundles into the ditch.

'Patrick! The gate!' Sharpe had waited till the last moment, believing that the volume of fire from the walls would hold the column's head back, and now he wondered if he had waited too long. He had meant to attack with his own squad, but he preferred now to control this fight from the ramparts and he knew that any attack headed by Harper would be driven home with a professional savagery.

'Fire!' Frederickson shouted and a score of bullets thudded downward. Some spurted dust from the road, one span a Frenchman clear round, but the rest seemed to be soaked up in the surging, pushing mass that strained to reach the shelter of the archway. That arch was blocked by pine trees, but the barricade had been knocked about by roundshot, and the leading attackers, throwing their fascines down and jumping on to their uncertain footing, could see footholds among the branches.

One man toppled from the makeshift bridge and fell on to the hidden spikes. His screams were cut off as water flowed into his mouth.

Another mortar shell was thrown to explode on the roadway. The air was hissing with bullets, endless with the noise of muskets firing and the rattle of ramrods.

'Now!' Sharpe shouted at Sergeant Rossner.

The sergeant, hiding beneath the ramparts at the south-eastern corner of the fort, had a wooden baker's peel which he dug into a barrel of lime. He scooped shovel-load after shovel-load of the white powder over the edge.

'Fire!' Frederickson shouted.

Lieutenant Fytch, aiming his pistol, was shot in the chest and thumped back, astonishment on his face and blood on his crossbelt. 'I'm . . .' He could not say what he wanted to say, instead he began to gasp for breath; each exhalation a terrible, pitiful moan.

'Leave him!' Sharpe bellowed at a Marine. This was no time to rescue wounded men. This was a time to fight, or else they would all be wounded. 'The whole barrel, sergeant!'

Rossner stooped, lifted the barrel, and tipped it over the rampart. Two bullets struck it, but the powder spumed and fell, was caught by the wind, and Sharpe saw it, like musket smoke, drifting on to the assault troops.

Some of whom, safely over the moat, were dragging with their hands at the branches in the archway.

'Fire!' Harper bellowed the order to his squad and pulled the trigger of his seven-barrelled gun.

Bullets tore through pine and threw men backwards.

'Spike the bastards!' Harper dropped the gun and unslung his rifle. He rammed its bayonet forward, between two branches, and twisted the blade in a Frenchman's arm.

Attackers were coughing, screaming, and clutching at their eyes as the lime drifted among the Grenadiers.

'Fire!' Sharpe yelled and a score of muskets hammered down into the crowd below.

The conscripts on the counterguard fired at the fort, but most fired high. Some balls struck. A Marine corporal, hit in the shoulder, went on loading his musket despite the pain.

'You've got them beat!' Frederickson hurled a third shell that exploded among half-blinded men. 'Now kill the bastards, kill them!' Men loaded as fast as cut, grazed hands would work. Bullet after bullet spat down into the French mass that was still pushed forward by the rear ranks.

Sharpe fired his own rifle down into the chaos. 'Cheer, you buggers! Let them know they've lost! Cheer!'

Lieutenant Fytch, blood filling his mouth, tried to cheer and died instead.

'Fire!' Frederickson shouted over the cheer.

The area about the gate was flames and smoke and bullets heavy with death. Men screaming, men blinded, men bleeding, men crawling.

'Fire!'

Men stumbled, the pain in their eyes like fire, to fall from the makeshift causeway on to the spikes. Blood drifted on the muddy waters.

'Fire!'

Harper's men, the lodgement beneath the archway cleared, knelt with reloaded weapons and poured bullets at point-blank range into defeated men. 'Fire, you bastards, fire!' Harper was keening with the joy of battle, lost in it, revelling in it, spitting hatred at men he had never met, men he would drink with on a summer's day if life had been different, but men who now folded over his bullets and shed bright blood onto a blood-soaked road. 'Fire!'

The last shell was thrown far to explode where the road-way narrowed between the glacis' shoulders and the men at the column's rear, at last sensing that the front ranks had recoiled in screaming agony, faltered.

'Fire!' Rifles spat at conscripts on the counterguard. Farm-boys, who five weeks before had never seen an army musket, now choked their blood on to sand.

'Cheer! Cheer!' Men whose mouths were dry with gritty powder raised a cheer.

'Keep firing! Drive them back!'

Men's faces were black with powder. Their nails bled where they had dragged at cartridges, levered stiff frizzens, and torn on flints. Their teeth, showing skull-white in the powder-dark faces, grinned as if in rictus. Breath came short. The whole world now was a few smoky yards, stinking of fire, in which a man rammed and loaded, fired and killed, rammed and loaded and other men screamed and some men crawled bleeding along the ramparts and another man slipped in spilt brains and swore because his musket fell into the courtyard.

The French inched back. The bullets cracked at them, thudded into flesh and still the bullets came. No troops fired muskets faster and no troops had been given such a target.

'Fire!' Sharpe, his rifle re-loaded, pulled the trigger. The smoke of his men's weapons obscured individuals, but he knew where the enemy was and his bullet twitched the smoke as it flashed through.

Harper, no more enemy visible, shouted for his men to hold their fire. He hauled a pine tree aside, crouched, then beckoned to Taylor. 'Ammunition.'

They went to the edge of the ditch, found the men they had killed, and cut their cartridge bags away. They tossed the bags through the archway then went back and re-blocked the arch. There had been no time to run the one remaining cannon into a firing position and Harper, regretting the lost chance, went to check that the quickfuse still led through the cleared venthole to the charge. It was safe and, reassured, he began the laborious process of re-charging the seven-barrelled gun.

A French officer, galloping his horse across the esplanade to see why the attack had faltered, was seen by two riflemen from the south-western bastion. They both fired. Man and horse shuddered, blood spat to sand, then the wounded horse, screaming and tossing, dragged its dead master in a great circle towards the column's rear.

'Fire!' Frederickson shouted and more heavy bullets tore into the smoke and drove the column further back. The drums hesitated, a single rattle sounded defiance, then was silent.

'Hold your fire! Hold it!' Sharpe could see the enemy

going, running, and though he wished he could have fired till the last enemy was out of sight, he had ammunition to conserve. 'Hold your fire! Hold your fire!' He felt the wild elation of a battle won, of an enemy broken. The space before the fort's gate was foul with dead and wounded men, and smeared with a great, white smudge of lime that was mixed with blood. 'Cease firing!'

At which point Calvet's real attack burst on to the north-western corner of the Teste de Buch.

Black clouds were coming from the north. Captain Palmer had watched them, had seen the grey blur of rain beneath them and judged that by this night the Teste de Buch would once again be crouching beneath dirty weather. Biscay, he thought, was living up to its reputation for sudden storms and uneasy calms.

Then the attack had struck at the fort's gate.

Men on the northern rampart turned to watch. It seemed to them that a cauldron boiled around the gate, a cauldron that billowed smoke into the sky.

The musketry had fused into a single, sustained crackle. Screams punctuated it. The smell of rotten eggs, powder smoke stench, came over the courtyard. Palmer saw Fytch struck, saw him fall, imagined him dying. Blood, flowing from the lieutenant's mouth, trickled to the firestep's edge then, with obscene slowness, ran down the inner wall.

Palmer watched Harper's group sprint across the court-yard, trampling the useless, burned abatis, and fire like men possessed into the darkness of the arch.

The fort stank of blood and smoke, the soldier's smell.

Palmer, grateful that the coughing shells no longer fell into the fort, turned back towards the north. Gulls fought above the channel's beach a quarter mile away. The rain seemed no closer. Beneath the diving, screaming gulls two men in a rowing boat planted fish traps of woven willow.

The noise and carnage at the Teste de Buch might have been a whole world away for all they seemed to care.

The sea was empty. Not one grey sail offered hope.

Palmer was thinking of a wife left in Gravesend, of two children who went hungry three days out of seven, of his hopes for that family when this war ended. An orchard, he thought, far from the sea and never fouled with smoke, would be a fitting place. Somewhere with a small cottage, not too big, but with a room where the children could sleep, another for himself and Betty, and a room where his few books could justify the name of study. A horse, for no gentleman walked where he could ride, and perhaps his father-in-law, who had mightily disapproved of Betty marrying a Marine, might lend some money to make the Marine into a market-gardener.

'Sir?' A Rifleman close to Palmer stared towards the channel.

'What is it?'

'Thought I saw something.'

Palmer stared, saw nothing, and put it down to gulls fighting by the fish-traps.

He was sure, thinking about it, that his eldest child's feeble health was due to living in a town. Gravesend was filthy with coal-smoke and in winter the sea-fog could lie heavily on a small chest. Two of Palmer's children had died as infants and were buried in the pauper's graveyard, for a Marine officer had no money to spare on lavish funerals for the barely baptized. An orchard would be a place to grow up, Palmer thought, an orchard heavy with apples and with espaliered pear-trees growing against a sun-warmed crinkle-crankle wall.

A cheer from the gate made him turn. The men on the ramparts still fired, but the cheer told Palmer that this round was won. God alone knew how, except that the Marines and Riflemen had loaded and fired in practised frenzy and the cheer swelled again and suddenly there was an unnatural silence because all the muskets had gone quiet and there was just the wind sighing over cold stone, the crying of the injured, and a sudden, startled shout from Palmer's right. He ran.

Three hundred Frenchmen had left the village before dawn and groped their way in the darkness. They had marched in a great circle, east and north and west, to come, an hour after first light, to the channel's edge north of the fortress.

One hundred of the men were new conscripts, brought along to fire their muskets when ordered.

The other two hundred were among the best in Calvet's force. They were led by a Captain Briquet whose warlike name, meaning sabre, gave the force an odd confidence. They were guided to their assault by Henri Lassan who saw, in this attack, his chance of redemption.

Briquet, though a junior officer compared to many in Calvet's force, had a reputation. He was brave, thorough, and a firebrand.

His task was to approach the fort once the larger battle began. Under the cover of its noise, and trusting to the distraction offered by its existence, he planned to come close beneath the fort's vulnerable north-western corner. Lassan had promised the approach could be made unseen because the sand-dunes offered hiding, and Lassan had been proved right.

Once in place, hidden close to the fortress, a Forlorn Hope would charge across the masonry bridge of the dam, put ladders to the closest embrasures, and climb. The Hope, who expected death, would be led by Briquet who expected to be a major when the sun went down.

The conscripts, under experienced sergeants, would flay the walls left and right of the assault with musket fire.

The Forlorn Hope, gaining the ramparts, would hold a small section while the other veterans, with more ladders, flooded on to the sand strip between the fort and the channel to place more ladders. Briquet, knowing that the ramparts facing the channel would have the fewest defenders, aimed to take that wall. The stone ramp, that Lassan had drawn on his careful plan, would then lead into the heart of the Teste de Buch.

Two hundred men, Briquet said, could capture this fort. It would take, if the first lodgement was successful, no more than twenty minutes.

Yet for that lodgement to work the British sentries must be drawn to look the other way, and in that cause men must die at the main gate. General Calvet had ordered it thus, but Captain Briquet's fear, for he was a man who thirsted for glory, was that the larger attack would pierce the fortress before his Forlorn Hope could rush the stone dam. The colonel leading the main attack, Briquet knew, was desperate to succeed and there was not a man marching with the drummers who did not believe that the British would be swept ignominiously aside once the fascines were in place and the *moustaches* stormed over the ditch.

Briquet's force, with stealth and care, crept southwards between the dunes and the water. Two men, ostensibly planting fish-traps from a tiny boat, gave warning when faces appeared at the fort's north-western corner, but their warnings were few.

Briquet listened to the turmoil at the gate. Not once did he raise his head to look at the fort, not once did he risk discovery. That could wait for the last moment, the dash over the dam.

'This is as close as we can get unseen,' Lassan said.

The firing at the main gate was dying and Briquet knew this was the moment or there would be no moment at all. '*Venez!*'

His feet scrambled for footing in the sand, a sergeant shoved him upwards, and suddenly the fort loomed above him and Briquet had an impression that no men guarded the ramparts, but he dared not search for the enemy because there was a task to do. He saw the stone dam, exactly as Lassan had described it, and he leaped the small wooden fence that straggled to the sea, then his bootnails were loud on the stone that was lightly covered with sand.

A musket banged somewhere, then another, but Briquet took no notice. He jumped the rusted cogs of the sluice-gear and steadied himself with a hand on the fortress wall. 'One!' He pointed right, 'Two!' Left.

The ladders, carried with such care down the channel's edge, were dragged forward. There were four men to each ladder, two planted the rails in the sand and the others swung the ladders up and over so that the timbers crashed on to the stonework. Briquet shouldered a sergeant aside with a snarl and climbed the first ladder as if the dogs of hell were at his heels.

A man appeared above him, startled, but a musket shot from below dissolved the man's face in blood and Briquet, spattered by the gore, spat as his head cleared the embrasure's lip.

He reached up, grasped the top of a merlon, and heaved himself over. He tripped on an empty gun slide, recovered, and already the sergeant was beside him.

Briquet drew his sword, the steel whispering at the scabbard's throat. 'Follow me!'

Men poured up the ladders. More men, cheering, followed with new ladders and Briquet, leading his charge along the western walls, knew that the fort was his.

He had achieved surprise, he had gained the wall, and he would be a major by sundown.

Captain Palmer saved the north wall. The pine-lashed walkway was still in place, circumventing the citadel, and he seized the timbers, grunted, then shoved the heavy pinetrunks into the courtyard beneath. Now the only access was through the citadel that was blocked by a barrel of lime.

'Fire!' Palmer, crammed into the tiny sentry-chamber with five Marines, fired over the barrel at the blue uniforms who had appeared with such suddenness on the gun-platform.

'William! Stay!' Sharpe needed a man above the gate. If the French, sensing that the defenders were being stripped away by the new threat, attacked again, then it would need a man like Frederickson to hold them.

'Marines! Marines!' He shouted the word like a battle-cry.

Sharpe was running towards the western wall. 'Marines!' The Marines, trained for the bloody business of boarding enemy ships, were the troops he needed now. The Rifles could defend the 'gate, but the Marines could show their worth in the close-quarter work. 'Marines!'

Sharpe threw down his rifle and tugged the Heavy Cavalry sword from its ungainly scabbard. How in Christ's name had the French sneaked into the fort? A musket ball snicked the wall beside him, fired by a Frenchman on the west wall. Sharpe could see red uniforms bunched at the far citadel, showing that the north wall held. Sharpe's job, and the task of the Marines who ran behind him, was to throw the enemy off the western bastions.

The walkway across the corner of the ramparts was gone, burned by the fire, so Sharpe must lead his men through the zig-zag of the citadel. The enemy would know it, their muskets would be waiting for men coming from that narrow doorway, but it was no use dwelling on fear. Sharpe saw a French officer, sword drawn, leading his men in a rush down the western rampart and Sharpe knew it would be a race to see who reached the citadel first and he ran harder, ammunition pouch bouncing, then slammed through the door to check his speed by thumping on the inner wall.

Frederickson, left with the Riflemen, sent a volley at the French who had climbed the ladders. At this range, across the angle of the fort, the rifle fire was deadly.

Marines crushed into the citadel and Sharpe, trusting they would follow him, jumped through the doorway. 'Come on!'

He emerged into winter sunlight to see a space of five

empty, stone-flagged yards beyond which, screaming and threatening, the front rank of the French charged at him.

The enemy had the impetus here. They were running, and Sharpe had just emerged from the obstacle of the citadel. This was the second of pure, naked fear prompted by the sight of steel, then Sharpe snarled his challenge and hissed his blade in a glittering arc to check the French rush.

'Bayonets!' Sharpe shouted at the two men who had followed him on to the ramparts. Other Marines pushed behind, but it was up to Sharpe to clear a space for them. 'Now kill them!' He jumped forward to anticipate the French attack. The French officer, a short man with a fierce face, lunged with his sword. The man was flanked by moustached giants with bayonets.

The Heavy Cavalry sword, a butcher's blade, swept one musket aside. The French officer's sword skewered past Sharpe's swerve and a Marine, instinctively seizing the blade, screamed as Briquet withdrew and cut the Marine's fingers to the joints.

Sharpe hit the soldier nearest him with the guard of the sword, then sawed the blade downwards on to the officer. Briquet, sensing the flash of steel, ducked, but a Marine's bayonet thumped on his ribs and the Heavy Cavalry sword took him in the side of the neck to end his hopes of glory.

A boot kicked at Sharpe's groin and struck his upper thigh. His sword was tangled in the officer's fall, but he ripped it clear and drove it forward with both hands so that the point was in his assailant's throat.

A bayonet tried to reach Sharpe from the second French rank.

There were men grunting and kicking and slashing around him. He could smell their sweat, their breath, and he needed space. A musket fired, the noise huge, but it was impossible to tell which side had fired the shot.

The French, by sheer weight of numbers, were pressing the tiny handful of British backwards. Sharpe had a half yard of space behind him, stepped back, and screamed the war cry as he swung the great sword in a fearsome downwards swing. A man ducked, Sharpe twisted his wrist to lunge the sword, stamped forward, and a Frenchman moaned as the big blade gouged at his belly.

'Marines! Marines!' One Marine was down, coughing and bleeding, but two others forced their way over his body and thrust into the fight with bayonets. Two more came behind them. This was gutter fighting, something learned in a hard childhood and never taught by drill sergeants. Here men clawed and kicked and smelt the breath of the men they killed.

A Marine tripped over Captain Briquet's body and a French bayonet lunged into his back. Immediately another Marine, screaming like a banshee, drove his blade into the Frenchman's face. The bodies were like a barricade now, but the Marines kicked them down to the smouldering embers of the burned offices, and carried their wet blades forward.

Sharpe was using the sword to press men back. He watched the enemy's eyes and, though he did not know it, he smiled. He lunged, parried, stamped forward, lunged, and every action was now a reflex. Nineteen years of battle had come to this moment.

A musket exploded close to Sharpe and the bullet thumped at his chest like a prize-fighter's blow. A French lieutenant, blood on his face and jacket, twisted into the enemy's front rank and hissed his slim flexible blade towards Sharpe's face. Sharpe knocked the blade aside and rammed his own heavier sword at the officer's eyes. 'On! On!'

They were holding. A dozen Marines were on the rampart now and the French, the impetus of their first charge checked, were wary of the bayonets. Some of the French, seeing their way blocked, turned to flood into the semi-circular bastion where the thirty-six pounders had stood. Others ran down the stone ramp into the courtyard.

Frederickson had brought a dozen Riflemen halfway down the southern rampart and he drilled them as if they were on the training ground at Shorncliffe. Aim, load, fire, aim, load, fire, and every volley flailed into the French who still swarmed up the ladders on to the battlements.

The French on the rampart, hearing a cheer as their comrades spilt down the ramp, gave ground before Sharpe. If the courtyard was taken then there would be no need to fight this savage Rifleman whose face was black with powder. His eyes glittered against darkened skin and his teeth were bared.

Sharpe sensed that the fight on the rampart was dying as men, on both sides, let their fear of cold steel bring them caution. He dared not let it die. He shouted his Marines to charge again, trampled over the French lieutenant's body, and stabbed a French sergeant, wrenched the blade free of the clinging flesh, and his Marines drove into the newly made gap with blades jabbing at the enemy in quick, professional lunges.

Shots sounded in the courtyard. There was a scream, then the bellow of a vast gun that told Sharpe Harper was in action.

Another volley came from Frederickson.

The rampart's stones were slick with blood. A Marine slipped and a tall Frenchman, carrying an engineer's axe, killed the fallen man with a single blow. The axeman gave the enemy new spirit and drove deep into Sharpe's men.

Sharpe knew the fort was lost if the axeman lived. He lunged at the man and his sword rammed itself between the man's ribs, grated, then a French hand gripped Sharpe's blade, blood showed at his fingers, but the man held on, tugged, and another man clawed at Sharpe's face. A bayonet stabbed his thigh, Sharpe fell backwards, sword lost in the melée, and a Frenchman's breath was in his face and fingers were at his throat. Sharpe was on his back now, driven there by two Frenchmen. He brought up his knee and clawed his fingers at the man who tried to choke him. The man screamed as Sharpe's fingers closed in his left eye.

There was no skill left, no order, just a bitter mass of men who ripped at each other with blades, kicked and clawed and stabbed again. A Marine sergeant, shouting an incomprehensible challenge, bayoneted one of Sharpe's assailants and kicked the other in the face. The axeman, choking on blood in his lungs, fell sideways and two Marines grunted as they forced bayonets into his trunk. Somewhere a man sobbed, and another screamed.

Sharpe twisted up and, his sword lost, picked up the wide-bladed axe. The Marine sergeant did not hear Sharpe's thanks, but just drove on with his bloodied bayonet.

A Frenchman tripped on a gunslide, an opening appeared and Sharpe hacked down with the axe blade, then screamed the challenge to drive the enemy a full two paces back.

An explosion hammered in the courtyard, a sound that echoed like a drumbeat of hell in the echoing walls of the Teste de Buch. Smoke billowed.

Harper had turned the cannon, then fired it with its charge of stone-shards, nails, and lead scraps into the French who came down the stone ramp. The cannon's recoil had thrown it back five yards. 'Now kill them!' Harper charged.

Minver's Riflemen, on the north wall, fired down at the French who were left in the courtyard. Some of the Riflemen, wanting loot from the dead, jumped down to risk broken ankles. The long sword bayonets, brass-handled, hunted forward.

Sharpe swung the axe underhand, screaming the challenge and the blade buried itself in a body, wrenched free in a gush of blood and he went forward again.

He saw a movement to his left, ducked, and a man jumping from a ladder tripped on Sharpe's back and sprawled into the Marines. One hit him a hammer blow of a musket butt, killing him as clean as a rabbit chopped on the neck.

Sharpe turned, protected by the embrasure, and saw the

262

French firing from the dunes. Another man neared the ladder's head and Sharpe swung the axe into his face, heard the scream, then took an upright of the ladder, pushed it away and sideways, and heard the shouts as the ladder tumbled.

'Behind you!' The voice warned him, Sharpe ducked, and a bayonet slid over his back. He drove the axe handle into the Frenchman's belly then stepped back, reversed the weapon, and brought the head down in a vicious swing to bury it into the man's ribs. The axe stuck there.

A French musket, tipped with a bayonet, lay at his feet. It felt unnatural, but it served. He jabbed it forward as he had learned so many years ago. Forward, twist, back, right foot forward, lunge, twist, back.

If he shouted orders he did not know it. If he screamed with rage, he did not know it. He just fought to clear a wall of enemy.

There was the strange sensation that he had noticed before in battle, the odd slowing of the world as though the men around him were puppets under palsied fingers. He alone seemed to be moving fast.

A Frenchman, eyes wide with terror, lunged, and it seemed a simple matter to knock the man's musket aside and drive the bayonet into the man's belly, to twist, to draw it free then stamp the foot forward again. Another Frenchman, to the left, fumbled with his musket's lock and Sharpe, not knowing if his captured musket was loaded, pulled the trigger and felt not the slightest surprise as it fired to rip a bloody hole in the man's throat.

That made a gap. A French sergeant, wise in war, saw Sharpe and lunged, but Sharpe was faster and his bayonet caught the man's arm, ripped down to bone, and a Marine, at Sharpe's shoulder, drove his blade into the sergeant's groin.

The fort could be lost for all Sharpe knew. He only understood that these bloodslick stones must be fought for and that the Marines were fighting like men possessed, overbearing the enemy with a ferocity and confidence that put terror into the French who had to fight them. And terror was the first and chief weapon of war. It was terror that brought this murderous rage beneath the dragon-slayer's banner that was wind-lifted above the fight.

A scream, prolonged, rising to a shout that would have chilled the horsemen of the devil, sounded beyond the enemy.

Sharpe knew that sound. 'Patrick!'

Harper, the courtyard cleansed of the enemy, climbed the ramp that twitched with the wounded thrown down by the cannon. He led a charge of bayonets to the ramparts and the French, assailed on three sides, began to give.

Frenchmen, come to the ladders' tops with fear, saw that their fear was justified. They forced their way back down, shouting to the men who waited behind that the enemy was imminent. One ladder, its rungs green, broke to tumble six men on to the sand.

Riflemen, sent by Frederickson on to the western rampart, cleared the water bastion and, leaning in its cannon embrasures, enfiladed the ladders. Captain Palmer led more Marines from the north.

'Charge!' Sharpe yelled it unnecessarily, for the victory was clear. The Marines had fought half the length of a rampart and now they carried their blades the rest of the way and the French, who had seen the redcoats snatch victory from defeat, took to the ladders or jumped into the ditch.

Harper had a lunge of his bayonet-tipped rifle deflected into an enemy's thigh so kept the rifle swinging so that the brass-bound butt smashed the man's jaw. He kicked him aside, ripped the blade into another man, and saw the rampart was empty of opponents. Marines were kneeling in embrasures to fire at the French conscripts. Captain Palmer, sword red with blood, was standing by the flagstaff that had somehow stood with its trophy of table-linen and uniform sleeves still flying.

'God save Ireland.' Harper, his huge chest heaving for breath, sat on a gunslide. His face, spattered with blood, looked up at Sharpe. 'Jesus God.'

'Close.' Sharpe, breathing like a blown horse, glanced back to the gate, but no trouble threatened there. He looked at the strange musket in his hand and tossed it down. 'God.' The French were fleeing north through the dunes. 'Hold your fire! Hold your fire!'

A Rifleman threaded the dead bodies, stepping in blood, to bring Sharpe his sword.

'Thank you.' Sharpe took it. He wanted to smile, but his face seemed frozen in the grimace of fighting.

The fort had held. Blood trickled thick in the rampart's gutters.

Briquet's men, defeated, ran.

The larger attack, beaten to bloody ruin at the gate, was a shambles in retreat. If that attack had lasted five minutes longer, just five minutes, then the fort would have fallen. Sharpe knew that. He shuddered to think of it, then stared at the bloody, edge-nicked blade of his sword. 'Jesus.'

Then the howitzer shells began to fall again.

CHAPTER 17

A man wept and could not be consoled. His right leg was gone at the thigh, taken by a howitzer shell. He wanted his mother, but he would die instead. The other wounded men, shivering in the foul tunnel that led to the makeshift surgery, wished he would stop his blathering. A Marine corporal, his shoulder mangled by a bayonet, read St John's gospel aloud and men wished that he too would be silent.

The Marines who had volunteered as surgeons wore clothes that were soaked in blood. They cut, tied and sawed, helped by lightly wounded men who held the badly wounded down while legs or arms were crudely butchered off and arteries tied and raw flesh cauterized with fire because they did not know if all the blood vessels were safely blocked.

The French wounded, under the angry rain of howitzer shells, were carried to the gate, across the crude bridge of fascines, and left on the roadway among their dead colleagues. Ten Marines, protected by ten Riflemen, moved among the carnage beyond the gate and collected enemy ammunition. The French artillery colonel, seeing his own wounded countrymen brought outside the fort, wanted to cease fire, but Calvet snarled at the gunners to continue. The twelve-pounders, loaded with heavy canister, tried to flick the ammunition collectors away, but the Marines dodged among the bodies and hurled the enemy pouches back to the archway. Only when they had retreated did General Calvet order his guns to cease their fire so that Frenchmen, armed with white flags, could go forward and rescue the injured.

Within the fort a dozen unwounded French prisoners were

herded down to the liquor store to join Captain Mayeron. Twenty dead Frenchmen were inside the ramparts. One of them, lying in the embers of the burned buildings, suddenly flipped in the air as the ammunition in his pouch exploded. There was a smell of roast meat to mingle with the stench of blood and powder. Men who saw the sudden jerk and flip of the body laughed because, they said, it was just like a frog. It was better to laugh than to weep.

'I'm sorry, sir,' Palmer said again.

Sharpe shook his head. 'We got rid of them.'

'I should have been watching.' Palmer was determined to expose his blame.

'Yes, you should.' Sharpe had used a bucket of well-water to clean his sword. Marines and Riflemen pissed into weapons, blocked the muzzles, and sloshed the urine around to scour the powder deposits from the barrels.

No one spoke much. Most men, their weapons cleaned, just sat by the embrasures and stared into empty air. Buckets of drinking water were carried to the walls while smoke drifted from the smouldering fires in the courtyard. The fort was a place of ruin, blood, smoke, ash, and exhaustion, as if the defenders had suffered a defeat instead of winning a victory.

'If they'd got on to the northern wall,' Sharpe said to Palmer, 'we'd be surrendering our swords by now. You did well to stop them.' Sharpe rammed his sword home. He could not remember a fight so bitter or so close, not even at Badajoz. There the horror had been the cannons on the walls, not the infantrymen behind them. 'And your Marines,' Sharpe said, 'fought magnificently.'

'Thank you, sir.' Palmer nodded at Sharpe's chest. 'That must have hurt.'

Sharpe looked down. The small holstered whistle, mounted on his leather crossbelt, was dented flat in its centre. He remembered the bang of the French musket and knew that had the ball been aimed a fraction either way it would have pierced his heart. The fight was a blur now, but later the individual moments would come to his half-waking dreams as nightmares. The memory of the moment when the French had driven him to the ground, the memory of the bullet thumping his chest, the sheer fear of that first glimpse of blue-uniformed men on his walls; those were the incidents that made a man shudder with delayed terror. Sharpe never recalled the moments of triumph after a battle, only those moments of near defeat.

Harper, a scrap of dirty paper in one hand, climbed the stone ramp. 'Seventeen dead, sir. Including Lieutenant Fytch.'

Sharpe grimaced. 'I thought he'd live.'

'Difficult with a bullet in your bellows.'

'Yes.' Poor Fytch, who was so very proud, Sharpe remembered, of his pistol. 'Wounded?'

'At least thirty are bad, sir.' Harper's voice was bleak.

A howitzer shell landed in the courtyard, bounced, and exploded. The shells seemed like small things after the fight. If the French had any sense, Sharpe thought, they would assault now. They should have men clawing and screaming at the walls, but perhaps the French were as shaken as he was.

Rifleman Taylor came up from the courtyard and spat tobacco juice over the ramparts. He jerked a thumb towards Harper's cannon. 'It's buggered.'

'Buggered?' Sharpe asked.

'Snapped a capsquare.' The field-gun's left trunnion had leaped out of its socket and broken the metal strap that should have held it in place. Doubtless Bampfylde's fire had weakened the capsquare and now the twelve-pounder was as good as useless. Sharpe looked at Harper. 'See what you can do, Patrick.'

'I can give wine to the lads?' Harper suggested bleakly.

'Do that.' Sharpe walked around the ramparts. French dead, stripped of their equipment, were being heaved on to the sand by the channel. If any of his men had shown the energy Sharpe would have ordered shallow graves dug, but even their own dead lay unburied. Two Marines, their faces still masked with powder, wearily hauled an abandoned French ladder through an embrasure and carried it down to the gate where it would be added to the new barricade.

Sharpe threaded the south-west citadel, wondering how he had ever come through it at the full charge. The French gunners, advised that the wounded had been cleared from the fort's apron, opened fire again. The jets of flame stabbed from the watermill and the twelve-pound shots crashed into the wall to fray the defenders' already shredded nerves. Sharpe found Frederickson. 'Thank you, William.'

'For doing my duty?' Sweat had trickled through the powder on Frederickson's face to make odd brown rivulets on his sun-baked skin.

'I'm leaving you in command,' Sharpe said, 'while I go to see the wounded.'

'I'd have that attended to.' Frederickson gestured at Sharpe's left thigh where the blood started by a French bayonet had crusted on to the overalls.

'It doesn't hurt.' Sharpe raised his voice so that every man about the gate could hear him. 'Well done!' Two Marines, carrying a body, grinned at him. The body, Sharpe saw, was young Moore, the boy from Devon, who had been shot in the forehead and who must have died instantly.

Sharpe felt a thickening in his throat and the prick of tears at his eyes, but he swore instead. Moore was luckier than the wounded who, in the foul stone gallery, waited for the surgeon's butchery. Sharpe went to give small, bleak comfort to men who were beyond consolation and whose future was nothing but pain and poverty.

The shells still fell, the blood stank, and Sharpe's men waited for the next assault.

The remnants of Captain Briquet's force returned to the village. Their faces were bleak, exhausted and bloodied. A wounded man, using his musket as a crutch, collapsed on the sand. A drummer boy, who had survived the attack on the main gate and who was not yet twelve years old, wept because his father, a sergeant, had died with Captain Briquet on the fort's western wall. The survivors of Briquet's force told stories of blades and blood, of faces screaming hatred, of a Rifleman swinging an axe, of a cannon blasting men into bloody scraps on the ramp, of soldiers gouging and cutting and dying.

Surgeons used sea-water to wash lime from the eyes of defeated men. No man had been blinded; for reflex had made attackers close their stinging eyes and stumble away from the white cloud, but the use of the quicklime infuriated General Calvet. 'They're savages! Savages! Worse than the Russians!'

The senior French officers were gathered in the hovel that was Calvet's command post. They stared at the map, avoiding each other's eyes, and were glad when Calvet, seeking a target for his anger, chose Pierre Ducos.

'Tell me,' Calvet said to Ducos, 'exactly why men died today?'

'They died,' Ducos was quite unmoved by the general's fury, 'for a victory that France needs.'

'Victory over what?' Calvet asked scathingly. 'A huddle of goddamn refugees who use quicklime?' He stared belligerently at Ducos. 'We agree their plans for a landing are foiled, so why don't I let this Sharpe moulder behind his walls?' No one in the room thought it odd that a general should seek permission from a major, not when the major was Pierre Ducos with his odd power over the Emperor's affections.

'Because,' Ducos said, 'if Sharpe escapes, he will take evidence with him that would betray the Comte de Maquerre.'

'Then warn de Maquerre!' Calvet snapped. 'Why should men die here for lack of a letter?' Ducos did not reply, implying that Calvet trespassed on forbidden territory. The general banged a big, splayed hand on the map in a gesture of irritated frustration. 'We should be down south, thumping

Wellington, not pissing about with a bloody major! I'll leave a Battalion here to pen the bugger in, then we can go south where we're needed.'

Pierre Ducos smiled thinly. The general spoke good military sense, but Pierre Ducos wanted Richard Sharpe in his power, and thus Ducos now played his final, winning card. 'Can you suggest, General, the manner in which I explain to the Emperor how a British major, with less than two hundred men, defeated the great Calvet?'

Those icy words stung. For a moment it seemed as if Ducos had said too much, but then Calvet gave a shrug of surrender. 'I hope you're right, Ducos. I hope the goddamns aren't pouring men ashore at the Adour while we're pissing about.' He growled with impotent menace, then slapped a hand on the map. 'So if it must be done,' Calvet said, 'then how do we prise this bastard out from his walls? I need a breach!'

'You can have one, sir.' To everyone's surprise it was Commandant Lassan, returned safely from the failed northern attack, who spoke, and who now told Calvet that he had written no less than twelve times in the last eight years to the Minister of Marine, responsible for the coastal forts, complaining that the Teste de Buch's main gateway was in danger of collapse. The stones had shifted so much that the gate pintles were a full inch out of true, and cracks had appeared in the guardroom walls. The Ministry, after the fashion of government departments, had done nothing. 'The whole gateway can be collapsed,' Lassan said.

General Calvet believed him. He ordered the twelve-pounders to concentrate their fire on the archway; artillery fire to make an avalanche of stone that would spill into the ditch and provide a slope up which attackers could scramble. 'That's where our main attack goes in the morning.' Calvet took a lump of charcoal and scrawled a thick arrow on the fortress plan. The arrow pointed at the gateway. 'I shall lead that attack,' Calvet growled, 'while you,' he gestured at an infantry colonel, 'will make a demonstration here.' He scored another arrow that aimed itself at the northern wall. 'That'll split their defenders.' Calvet stared at his broad arrow and imagined the archway tumbling its stones into the ditch to make a bridge; he saw his men flooding over that barricade and taking their bayonets to this so-called 'élite' of Riflemen and Marines. 'We'll parade the prisoners through Bordeaux to show what happens to scum who think they can defy France.'

'I insist,' Ducos said, 'that Major Sharpe is handed over to my department.'

'You can have the bastard.' Calvet looked back at the map and, with a sudden gesture, extended the larger arrow straight into the courtyard. 'Tell the men that the enemy is low on ammunition. Tell them we killed half the bastards today, tell them there's women and wine inside. Tell them there's a medal each for the first ten men inside.' Calvet looked at his scribbled arrow and remembered the sheer volume of fire that the goddamns had poured into his column. He remembered men screaming, clawing at their eyes, and he remembered the trails of blood across the fort's esplanade.

His men would remember just as clearly, and defeated men would be nervous about a renewed attack. Calvet needed something else, some new factor to change the second assault, and, with sudden energy, he scribbled marks in the sand-dunes by the channel. 'If we put two twelves there,' he asked the artillery colonel, 'they can rake the breach till the last minute?'

The artillery colonel was already doubtful of his guns' ability to bring down an archway in just a few hours. Even huge siege guns, twice the size of his twelve-pounders, could take weeks to shatter a well-built rampart, and now Calvet wanted to take two of the guns away from the breaching battery. 'And even if I moved two guns, sir, how do we protect the crews from the Riflemen?' Calvet wanted the two guns placed within two hundred yards of the ramparts.

Calvet grunted an acknowledgement. The closest howitzer fired, thumping the hovel with a punch of sound and air, and the beat of the great gun's firing jarred a scrap of reed from the thatched roof. It fell on to Calvet's map, landing on the channel. 'If I had a ship there,' Calvet mused aloud, 'it would win the day. But I don't have a ship, so your two gun-crews will have to take their dead and keep firing.' He stared belligerently at the artilleryman.

'But you can have a ship.' Ducos spoke softly from his place beside the fire.

Calvet swung round to face the small major. 'A ship?'

'There is an American,' Ducos said, 'and he has a ship.'

'Then fetch him!' Calvet crossed out his new gun positions and drew the outline of a ship around the fleck of straw. 'Fetch him, Ducos! And tell our ally he has to fight! Fetch him!'

Killick, summoned from Gujan, leaned over the General's map table. He saw that Calvet wanted the southern wall bombarded. A ship, moored off the fort's south-western angle, could fire till the very final second of an assault, long after the twelve-pounders in the mill would have been forced into silence for fear of hitting their own attacking column. The *Thuella*'s gunfire, coming at right-angles to the line of attack and aimed at the breach, would force the defenders away from that vulnerable point. Such a floating battery, Killick saw, would be a guarantee of victory to demoralized men. The American nodded. 'It could be done.'

'At dawn?' Calvet asked.

Killick drew on his cigar. 'It could be done, but not by me. I have taken an oath not to fight against the British.' There was silence, except for the sudden percussion of an howitzer that shook more dust free from the roof. Killick shrugged. 'I'm sorry, gentlemen.'

'An oath?' Ducos' voice was sharp with scorn.

'An oath,' Killick repeated. 'Major Sharpe spared my life in return for that oath,' the American grinned, 'and as the

273

promise wasn't made to a lady, it has to be honoured.'

Killick's levity stung Ducos. 'One does not keep oaths to savages. You, of all people, should know that.'

'Is that why you didn't send me the copper sheeting?' Killick stared with dislike at Ducos. 'Don't lecture me, Major, about keeping promises.'

The copper sheeting had never come, but the schooner had been patched with coffin-elm and smeared with pitch. The job had been done faster than Cornelius Killick had dared hope.

The topmasts had been swayed up on tackles and lashed into place. Tangled shrouds had been sorted, cleated, and winched home. The *Thuella*, that had given the appearance of a dead and burning ship, lived again.

That very morning, as Frenchmen died in a fort's gateway, anchors had been laid in the Gujan channel and, at high tide, the windlasses had hauled the empty hull off the mud. The *Thuella* had slipped into the water. In just a few seconds, an ungainly and grounded hulk had become a slender craft shivering to the touch of wind and waves. Her figurehead had been bolted into place. Meat and water and flour and bread and wine and biscuit and onions and more wine were taken aboard. The carpenter had sounded the bilges and, though some water was leaking through the repaired hull, he had declared the pumps could take care of the seepage.

'So, yes,' Killick now said, 'the *Thuella* can be moored in the channel tomorrow morning, General, but it can't fire a shot. I've taken an oath.'

Calvet, eager to harness the *Thuella*'s firepower, smiled. 'Major Sharpe forfeited all honour, Captain Killick, when he chose to use quicklime against my troops. You may therefore consider yourself released from any undertakings of honour made with him.'

Killick, who had already expressed profound disgust at the use of quicklime, now shook his head. 'I think I'm the best judge of my own honour, General.'

'You are a civilian,' Pierre Ducos, despite his small size,

was endowed with a voice of unusual authority, 'and by your own account, Mr Killick, you have trafficked with the enemy. I presume you do not wish to undergo a long period of questioning at the hands of French authorities?' Killick said nothing. The other French officers, even Calvet, were made uneasy by the threat, while Ducos, sensing that he had an advantage over the tall, handsome American, smiled. 'If Mr Killick does not offer some satisfactory explanation of his actions on French soil then I will use my authority to seek such an explanation.'

'My explanation . . .' Killick began.

Ducos interrupted him. 'Your explanations are best given with grapeshot at dawn. Do I have your oath, Mr Killick, that you will be there? Or must I investigate you?'

The American's quick temper flared. 'I was captured, you little bastard, because I volunteered to defend your bloody fort.'

'And you lost not a man killed,' Ducos said chillingly, 'and you were released within hours. I think those circumstances deserve investigation.'

Killick looked to Calvet, but saw that the French general was powerless to countermand the thin, bespectacled major. The American shrugged. 'I cannot be there at dawn.'

'Then I will order your arrest,' Ducos said.

'I can't be there at dawn, you bastard,' Killick growled, 'because the tide won't serve. I've got twenty miles of shallow water to negotiate. Unless you can threaten God into a premature high-tide?' He stared defiance at Ducos, then looked at the map. 'One hour after dawn. No sooner.'

'But one hour after dawn,' Ducos was relentless in victory, 'you will be moored off the fortress and bombarding the walls with grapeshot?' He had seen a flicker of hope on Killick's face, and knew the American was thinking that, once on board his ship, Pierre Ducos would be powerless to impose his will. 'I want your promise, Mr Killick, your oath.' Ducos had seized a piece of paper and, using the general's charcoal, scrawled big letters that formed a confession that Killick had unlawfully entered into a treaty with the enemy, and a promise that, as recompense, the *Thuella* would bombard the fortress until surrender or victory ended the morning's engagement. He thrust the paper forward. 'Well?'

Killick knew that if he did not sign Ducos would use his authority to detain him. Liam Docherty would not sail without Killick and the *Thuella* would stay in the Bassin, a hostage to Ducos' whim. In the embarrassed silence the American took the charcoal and scrawled his name. 'One hour after dawn.'

Ducos, triumphant, witnessed the piece of paper. 'You had better make your preparations, Mr Killick. Should you be tempted to break this oath, I promise you that your name will be known throughout America as that of a man who abandoned his allies and ran away from a fight. It is not pleasant, Mr Killick, to have one's name remembered for ever in the lists of traitors. First Benedict Arnold, then Cornelius Killick?' For a second the look on Killick's face persuaded Ducos that he had said too much, then the American nodded meekly.

Outside the hovel, Killick swore. The guns thumped from their pits and the first heavy rain, drumming from the north, began to fall. That rain, the American knew, was likely to last through the night, making rifles or muskets difficult to fire. The French now had the advantage of rain, so why did they need his ship?

'What will you do?' Henri Lassan asked.

'Christ knows.' Killick threw the remains of his cigar into the mud where it was snatched up by a sentry. The American stared at the low profile of the fort that gouted smoke with each burst of an howitzer shell. 'Is it worse to betray an enemy or an ally, Henri?'

Henri Lassan, who hated what Ducos had done, shrugged helplessly. 'I don't know.'

'I suppose I'll have to fire high,' Killick said, 'and hope Major Sharpe will forgive me.' He paused, wondering what carnage was being done inside the cauldron of the fort's walls where the smoke pulsed from the relentless shells. 'The bastard's my enemy, Henri, but I can't help liking the bugger.'

'I fear that if Major Ducos had his way,' Lassan said, 'Major Sharpe will be dead by this time tomorrow.'

'So I suppose it doesn't matter what I do.' The American gazed at the embattled fortress. 'You believe in prayer, my friend, perhaps you'd better pray for my soul.'

'I already pray for it,' Lassan said.

'Because my honour,' Killick said softly, 'is bargained away. Goodbye, my friend! Till the dawn.'

So the French had two allies; rain and an American, and their victory was thus made certain.

An hour before midnight the archway shuddered as the facing stones fell into the flooded ditch. Every shot thereafter worked more damage on the gateway, gouging out the rubble-filling and tipping the rampart's pavement above the arch. Frederickson, carrying a hooded lantern, climbed the gate's internal staircase to examine the extent of the destruction. He came out disgusted. 'It's going to fall. Sur-bedded work.'

'Surbedded?' Sharpe asked.

'Stone laid against the grain.' Frederickson paused as another roundshot thudded into the archway. 'The stone's cut vertically from the quarry and laid horizontally. It lets the water in. That gate's a shoddy piece of building. They should be ashamed of it.'

But if the French could not build, they could shoot. Even in the rain-curtained darkness the French gunners were hitting their target and Sharpe suspected that dark-lanterns must have been placed on the esplanade as aiming marks. Once in a while the French fired a light ball; a metal, cloth-wrapped cage filled with saltpetre, powder, sulphur, resin and linseed oil. The balls burned fiercely, hissing in the rain, showing the gunners what damage they had inflicted. That damage was more than sufficient to make Sharpe pull his sentries away from the ramparts by the arch, thus abandoning the gateway to the enemy's artillery.

Yet the rain did greater damage than the guns that night. At midnight, when Sharpe was going around the ramparts, a Marine sergeant found him. 'Captain Frederickson says can you come, sir?'

Frederickson was in the scorched cavern of the fort's second magazine, which had been the least damaged by Bampfylde's explosion. A lantern cast a dull, flickering glow on the blackened rear wall and on the pathetic hoard of powder and made-up cartridges that were Sharpe's final reserve of ammunition. 'I'm sorry, sir,' Frederickson said.

Sharpe swore. Water had seeped through the granite blocks of the magazine's arched ceiling and soaked the powder so that the barrels were now filled with a dark grey, porridge-like sludge, while the home-made cartridges had come apart in a soggy mess of paper, lead, and wet powder. The captured French cartridges were also heavy with water and Sharpe swore again; swore foully, uselessly, and savagely.

Frederickson fingered the wall over the barrels. 'The explosion must have loosened the masonry.'

'It was dry when we came,' Sharpe said. 'I checked!'

'Rain takes time to seep through, sir,' Frederickson said.

Six Marines carried the powder to the stone gallery where the cooking fires burned. There the powder could be spread out and some of it would be dry by morning, but Sharpe knew that this disaster meant the end of his defiance.

It was his own fault. He should have covered the powder with a tarpaulin, but he had not thought. There was so much he should have done. He should have foreseen that the enemy had mortars, he should have warned Palmer about the stone dam, he should have made a bigger sortie on the first night, he should have brought Harper's cannons on to the wall where they would have been safer from the shells. He should have had water ready to fight the fires, he should, perhaps, never have fought at all.

Sharpe sat in the cave of the magazine and a wave of despair hit him. 'We used over half our good ammunition?'

'Well over half.' Frederickson was as unhappy as Sharpe. He sat opposite, knees drawn up, and the lantern threw the shadows of the two riflemen high on the arch of the magazine's ceiling. 'We might as well bring the wounded in here now. They'll be more comfortable.'

'Yes.' But neither man moved. 'There's some French ammunition in the ready magazines, isn't there?' Sharpe asked.

'Only fifty cartridges in each.'

Sharpe picked up a shard of stone and scratched a square on the magazine floor. He marked the position of the gate on the southern side. 'The question,' he spoke slowly, 'is whether they're fooling us with the gate and plan to attack somewhere else, or not?'

'They'll come for the gate,' Frederickson said.

'I think so.' Sharpe scratched marks over the gate. 'We'll put everyone there. Just leave Minver with a handful of men to guard the other walls.'

Sharpe clung to the pathetic hope that a British brig, nosing up the enemy coast with the impunity that Nelson's victories had given to the Navy, might see his strange flag. A brig, moored in the channel, could fire hell and destruction into an attacking French column. Yet in this weather, with this fitful, veering wind and the blotting, seething rain that bounced four inches high off the shattered cobbles of the yard, Sharpe knew no brig would come. 'Your fellow might have reached our lines by now.' He was clutching at straws, and he knew it.

'If he survived,' Frederickson said grimly. 'And if anyone will take him seriously. And even then the Army will have to go on its knees to the Navy and beg them to risk one little boat.'

'Bugger Bampfylde,' Sharpe said. 'I hope he gets the pox.'

279

'Amen.'

A twelve-pounder ball crashed into the gate and there was a pause, a cracking sound like a bone breaking, then the grumbling, tumbling, roaring slide as tons of masonry collapsed inwards and downwards. The two officers stared at each other, imagining the stones thumping and sliding into the wet ditch, then settling in a shambolic mound as the dust, started from old mortar, was soaked by the rain.

'They have a breach,' Frederickson said in a voice which, by its very insouciance, betrayed apprehension.

Sharpe did not answer. If his men could hold off one more attack, just one, then it would buy time. Time for a ship to find them, time for French fears to settle in. Perhaps, if Calvet was repulsed again, the general would leave the fort alone, content to screen it with a half battalion of men. The rumble of the subsiding stones faded in the hissing rain.

'A week ago,' there was amusement in Sharpe's voice, 'men were hoping that Bordeaux would rise. We would be heroes, William, ending the war with a grand gesture.'

'Someone told lies,' Frederickson said lightly.

'Everyone lied. Wellington let those buggers believe in a landing so the French would be fooled. The Comte de Maquerre was a traitor all along.' Sharpe shrugged as though nothing much mattered any more. 'The Comte de bloody Maquerre. They call him Maquereau. He's well-named, isn't he? Bloody pimp.'

Frederickson smiled at Sharpe's rare display of knowledge.

'But it's really Ducos,' Sharpe said. Hogan, in his fever, he said both Ducos' and Maquerre's names, and this whole deception, that had stranded Sharpe's men so far from any help, stank of Ducos.

'Ducos?'

'He's just a bastard who I'll kill one day.' Sharpe said it in a very matter-of-fact voice, then grimaced because he knew that if this siege was truly Ducos' work, then the

Frenchman was very close to victory. 'It'll be bloody work tomorrow, William.'

'Very.'

'Do the men have the fight in them?'

Frederickson paused. Harper's huge voice shouted in the yard, bringing order to the men who had gone to see the collapsed gatehouse. 'The Rifles do,' Frederickson said. 'Most of mine are Germans and they'll never surrender. The Spanish hate the goddamn crapauds and just want to kill more of them. I think the Marines will fight to show you they're as good as the Rifles.'

Sharpe gave a half smile, half grimace. 'We can hold one attack, William. But after that?'

'Yes.' Frederickson knew exactly how bad things were. And this damned rain, he thought, would not help.

After one attack, Sharpe knew, he must think of the unthinkable. Of surrender. Pride demanded that they defended the breach at least one time, but French anger might not allow a surrender after that one defence. Sharpe had seen men, their blood-lust goaded beyond endurance, put a captured fortress to the sack. Frenchmen, beyond sense, would hunt with sharpened bayonets through the stone corridors to take revenge on the defenders. The butchery would be vile, but pride was still pride and they would fight at least one more time. Sharpe tried to imagine what Wellington might do, he tried to think back over all the sieges he had fought to see if there was something left undone that he could do, he tried to think of some clever move to unsettle the enemy. He thought of nothing useful. 'I'll bet their general's telling the poor buggers that we've got a hundred women in here,' Sharpe laughed.

Frederickson grinned. 'He'll give every man a half pint of wine, tell them they can rape every woman inside, then point them at the breach. It never fails. You should have seen us at San Sebastian.'

'I missed that.' Sharpe had been in England when the British had captured San Sebastian.

Frederickson smiled. 'It wasn't pretty.'

An howitzer shell exploded in the courtyard. 'You'd think the buggers would run out of ammunition,' Sharpe said. It was oddly pleasant to sit here, sharing a friendship's intimacy, knowing that nothing could now be done to diminish the slaughter that would come in the dawn. The French twelve-pounders still fired, even though the breach was formed, but now they sprayed the fallen stones with canister to prevent working parties from steepening the face up which their troops would swarm in the morning.

'If they capture us,' Frederickson said, 'perhaps they'll send us to Paris on our way to Verdun. I'd like to see Paris.'

The words reminded Sharpe of Jane's wish to see the French capital when the war ended. He thought of his wife dead, of her body taken for a hasty burial. Damn Cornelius Killick, he thought, for taking away his hope.

Frederickson unexpectedly broke into song. '*Ein schifflein sah ich fahren.*'

Sharpe recognized the tune that was popular among the Germans who fought in Wellington's Army. 'Meaning?'

Frederickson gave a rueful smile. '"I saw a small ship sailing." Pray for a frigate to come in the morning, sir. Think of its broadside raking the Frog camp.'

Sharpe shook his head. 'I don't think God listens to soldiers.'

'He loves them,' Frederickson said. 'We're the fools of the Lord, the last honest men, creation's scapegoats.'

Sharpe smiled. In the morning, he thought, they would give this General Calvet a fight to remember, and afterwards, when it was over, but that did not bear thinking about. Then, suddenly, he stared at his friend. '*Ein schiff?*' Sharpe asked, 'what was it again?'

'*Ein schifflein sah ich fahren,*' Frederickson said slowly. 'I saw a small ship sailing.'

'God damn it!' Sharpe's helplessness suddenly vanished with the burgeoning of an idea as bright as a shell's explosion. 'I'm a fool!' He faced defeat for want of a ship, and a ship existed. Sharpe scrambled to his feet and shouted into the yard for a rope to be fetched. 'You're to stay here, William. Prepare for an assault on the gate, you understand?'

'And you?'

'I'm going out. I'll be back by dawn.'

'Out? Where?'

But Sharpe had gone to the ramparts. A rope was fetched so he could climb down to the sand where the French corpses still lay, and so that, in a wet night, he could make a devil's pact that might bring deliverance to the fools of the Lord.

CHAPTER 18

In the morning the rain fell in a sustained cloudburst. It hammered and seethed and bounced on the fort and ran from the ramparts to slop in bucketfuls on to the puddled courtyard. It seemed impossible for rain to be so savage, yet it persisted. It drummed on men's shakoes, it flooded into the galleries carved into the ramparts, and its noise made even the firing of the twelve-pounders seem dull. It was like the rains before the great flood; a deluge.

It doused the cooking fires of the French and flooded the hovels where Calvet's men had tried to sleep. It turned the powder in musket pans to gritty mud. The fire-rate of the artillery was slowed because each serge bag of powder had to be protected from the rain and each vent had to be covered until the last second before the portfire was touched. The artillery colonel cursed that the damned British had burned out the mill's roof with their sortie, and cursed again because his howitzers had to give up the unequal struggle when their pits filled with yellow-coloured floodwater.

'Bacon for breakfast!' Calvet spoke with delighted anticipation.

His cooks, working under a roof, fried bacon for the general. The smell tormented those poor souls who huddled against hovel walls and cursed the rain, the mud, the goddamns, and the war.

The cavalry, who had vainly cast south for Sharpe's force, had been sent north in the dawn. A cavalry sergeant, his cloak plastered wet to his horse's rump, splashed back with news that, because the wind was so small this morning, the

Thuella was being towed down the Arcachon channel by two longboats.

'Bugger the wind,' Calvet said, 'and bugger the rain.' He stumped through mud to the sand-dunes and stared north. Far off, drab, black, and with wet sails dropping from her yards, the big schooner was just visible. 'We won't attack,' Calvet growled, 'till the damn thing's in place.'

'Perhaps,' Favier ventured cautiously, 'Captain Killick's guns won't fire in this weather?'

'Don't be a damned fool. If anyone can make guns fire in the wet it has to be a sailor, doesn't it?' Calvet took out his glass, wiped the lenses, and stared at the fortress. The gate was a heap of rubble, a mound of wet stone, a causeway to victory. He went back to his bacon with confidence that this morning's business would not take long. The British rifles would be useless in this rain and their lime would be turned into whitewash.

Calvet looked at his orderly who was putting an edge on to his sword. 'Make sure the point's wicked!'

'Yes, sir.'

'Won't be a day for the edge, Favier.' Calvet knew that wet uniforms resisted a sword cut much better than dry. 'It'll be a day for stabbing. In and out, Favier, in and out!' Calvet, feeling far better for his breakfast, glanced at the door where Ducos had suddenly appeared. 'You look damp, Ducos, and I ate your bacon.'

Ducos did not care that the general goaded him. Today he would capture Richard Sharpe and it would be a consolation to Pierre Ducos amidst the tragedies that beset France. 'There's a wind stirring.'

'Splendid.'

'The schooner should be anchored soon.'

'God bless our allies,' Calvet said. 'It might have taken them twenty damned years to join the war, but better late than never.' He went to the doorway and saw that the *Thuella* had indeed used the freshening wind to hasten her progress. A splash of water showed as the forward anchor was let go. 'I think,' Calvet said as the schooner's gunports opened, 'that we are at last ready.' He called for his horse and, from its saddle, saw his wet, dispirited troops forming into their attack column. 'We shall give our gallant allies twenty minutes of target practice,' Calvet said, 'then advance.'

Ducos was staring at the *Thuella*. 'If Killick opens fire at all,' he said. The schooner lay silent in the channel. Her wet sails were being furled on to the yards, but otherwise there was no sign of movement on the sleek vessel. 'He's not going to fire!' Ducos said savagely.

'Give him time.' Calvet also watched the *Thuella* and imagined the rain seething on the wooden decks.

'He's broken his word,' Ducos said bitterly, then, quite suddenly, the schooner's battle ensign broke open and flames stabbed across the water, smoke billowed above the channel, and the *Thuella*'s broadside opened the final attack on the Teste de Buch.

Cornelius Killick's qualms about honour had evidently been settled, and the American had opened fire.

The American grapeshot whistled over Sharpe's head. A few balls struck the flag of St George, but the rest went high above the fortress. Sharpe sat beneath the wet flag, his back against the ramparts. He was weary to the very heart of his bones. He had returned to the fort a half hour before sunrise, narrowly evading French cavalry, and now, after yet another night's lack of sleep, he faced a French attack.

'Are the Frogs moving?' he shouted to Frederickson who waited beside the breach.

'No, sir.'

Sharpe's wounded men, bloodied bandages soaking in the rain, lay on the western rampart. Marines, faces pale in the wan, wet light, crouched behind granite as a second American broadside spat overhead. Sharpe, huddling low, nodded to Harper. 'Now.'

The huge Irishman used his sword bayonet to cut the wet ropes which bound the flagpole to the merlon. He sawed, cursing the tough sisal, but one by one the strands parted and, just after Killick's third broadside, the pole toppled. The flag of St George, its white tablecloth stained red by dye from the sleeves which had formed the cross, fell.

'Cease firing!' Sharpe heard Killick's voice distinct over the water. 'Stop muzzles!'

Sharpe stood. The American captain, wearing a blue jacket in honour of this day, was already climbing down to one of the *Thuella*'s two longboats. The American crew, grinning by their guns, stared at the fortress.

Which Richard Sharpe had just surrendered.

General Calvet also stared at the fort. The smoke from the American broadsides drifted in the small wind, obscuring the view, but Calvet was sure the British had struck their colours.

'Do I keep firing, sir?' The artillery colonel, uniform soaked by rain, splashed through puddles towards the general's horse.

'They're not showing a white flag,' Pierre Ducos said, 'so keep firing.'

'Wait!' Calvet snapped open his glass. He saw figures on the ramparts, but could not tell what happened. 'Colonel Favier!'

'Sir?'

'Go forward with a flag of truce,' Calvet ordered, 'and find out what the bastards are doing. No, wait!' At last Calvet could see something that made sense. Men had come to the southern wall which faced the French and there they shook out a great cloth to hang down the wet, battered ramparts. The cloth signified that the fortress of Teste de Buch was no longer held by the British, but had been surrendered to the United States of America. 'God damn,'

Calvet said as he stared at the Stars and Stripes, 'God bloody hell and damn.'

Cornelius Killick, standing beside Sharpe on the southern ramparts, stared at the great French column that waited beside the village. 'If they choose to fight, Major, you know I can't fire on them.'

'I agree it would be difficult for you.' Sharpe opened his glass and stared at the French until the rain bleared the outer lens. He snapped the tubes shut. 'Do I have your permission, Captain Killick, to put my wounded on board?'

'You have my permission,' Killick spoke solemnly, as if to invest this agreed charade with dignity. 'You also have my permission to keep your sword that you failed to offer me.'

'Thank you.' Sharpe grinned, then turned to the western ramparts. 'Captain Palmer! You may begin the evacuation! Wounded and baggage first!' All the packs of Sharpe's small garrison were heaped next to the wounded men, for he was determined to leave the French nothing.

Sharpe's men, sensing that their ordeal was over, relaxed. They knew that Major Sharpe had gone into the night, and the rumour had spread that he had talked to the Americans and the Americans had agreed to take them away. The American Colours, bright on the fort's outer face, testified to that deliverance. 'It's all because we didn't hang the buggers,' a Marine sergeant opined. 'We scratched their backsides, now they scratch ours.'

Rifleman Hernandez, watching the French column, wondered aloud whether he would now be going to America and, if so, whether there were Frenchmen there waiting to be killed. William Frederickson assured him they were not bound for the United States. Frederickson was staring at the French and saw three horsemen suddenly spur forward. He cupped his hands towards Sharpe. 'Sir! Crapauds coming!'

Sharpe did not want the three enemy officers to come too close to the fort, so he ran, jumped from the broken ramparts, and sprawled in an ungainly, bruising fall on the jagged summit of the breach. He clambered down the outer stones, then leaped the gap on to the roadway. Frederickson and Killick followed more slowly.

Sharpe waited in the narrow cutting that led through the glacis. The road was thick with musket balls that had already half settled into the wet, sandy surface. He held up a hand as the horsemen came close.

Favier was the leading horseman. Behind Favier was a general, cloak open to show the braid on his jacket, and behind the general was Ducos. Sharpe, warned by Killick that he might see his old enemy, stared with loathing, but he had nothing to say to Ducos. He spoke instead to Colonel Favier. 'Good morning, Colonel.'

'What's the meaning of that?' Favier pointed to the American flag.

'It means,' Sharpe spoke loud enough for Ducos to hear, 'that we have surrendered ourselves to the armed forces of the United States and put ourselves under the protection of her President and Congress.' Killick had given him the words last night, and Sharpe saw the flicker of anger that they provoked in Pierre Ducos.

There was silence. Frederickson and Killick joined Sharpe, then the general demanded a translation that Favier provided. Rain dripped from bridles and sword scabbards.

Favier looked back at Sharpe. 'As allies of America we will take responsibility for Captain Killick's prisoners.' He doffed his hat to Killick. 'We congratulate you, Captain.'

'My pleasure,' Killick said. 'And my prisoners. I'm taking them aboard.'

Again there was a pause for the exchange to be translated and, when Favier looked back, his face was angry. 'This is the soil of France. If British troops surrender on this soil then those troops become prisoners of the French government.'

Sharpe dug his heel into the wet, sandy road. 'This is British soil, Favier, captured by my men, held by my men against your best efforts, and now surrendered to the United States. Doubtless you can negotiate with those States for its return.'

'I think the United States would agree to return it.' Killick, amused by the pomposities of the moment, smiled.

There was a fall of dislodged stone from the breach and all six men, their attention drawn by the noise, saw the huge figure of Patrick Harper, head bare, standing on the breach's summit. Over his right shoulder, like a dreadful threat, lay the French engineer's axe that Sharpe had used the day before. Favier looked back to Killick. 'It seems you do not disarm your prisoners, Mr Killick?'

'Captain Killick,' Killick corrected Favier. 'You have to understand, Colonel, that Major Sharpe has sworn a solemn oath not to take up arms against the United States of America. Therefore I had no need to remove his weapons, nor those of his men.'

'And France?' Ducos spoke for the first time.

'France?' Killick inquired innocently.

'It would be normal, Captain Killick, to demand that a captured prisoner should not take up arms against the allies of your country. Or had you forgotten that your country and mine are bound by solemn treaty?'

Killick shrugged. 'I suppose that in the flush of my victory, Major, I forgot that clause.'

'Then impose it now.'

Killick looked at Sharpe, the movement of his head spilling water from the peaks of his bicorne hat. 'Well, Major?'

'The terms of the surrender,' Sharpe said, 'cannot be changed.'

Calvet was demanding a translation. Favier and Ducos jostled each other's words in their eagerness to reveal the perfidy of this surrender.

'They're all Anglo-Saxons,' Ducos said bitterly.

Calvet asked a question in French, was answered by

Killick in that language, and Frederickson smiled. 'He asked,' he said to Sharpe, 'whether Killick's taking us to America. Killick said that was where the *Thuella* was sailing.'

'And doubtless,' Ducos had edged his horse closer so he could stare down at Sharpe, 'you have relieved Captain Killick of his sworn oath not to fight against the British?'

'Yes,' Sharpe said, 'I have.' That was the devil's pact, made in the seething rainstorm of last night. Sharpe had promised that neither he nor his garrison would fight against the United States, and in return Sharpe had relieved Killick of his own irksome oath. The price was this surrender that would make the escape of Sharpe's men possible.

Ducos sneered at Sharpe. 'And you think a privateer captain honours his promises?'

'I honoured the promise I made you,' Killick said. 'I fired till the enemy surrendered.'

'You have no standing in this matter!' Ducos snapped the words. 'You are not a military officer, Mr Killick; you are a pirate.'

Killick opened his mouth to reply, but Ducos scornfully wheeled his horse away. He spoke to the general, chopping the air with his thin, gloved hand to accentuate his words.

'I don't think they're impressed,' Frederickson said softly.

'I don't give a damn,' Sharpe growled. The boats must already be taking the wounded to the *Thuella*, and the Marines would be following. The longer the French argued, the more men would be saved.

Favier looked down sadly at Sharpe. 'This is unworthy, Major.'

'No more so, Colonel, than your own feeble effort to make me march to Bordeaux as a Major General.'

Favier shrugged. 'That was a *ruse de guerre*, a legitimate manouevre.'

'Just as it is legitimate for me to surrender to whom I wish.'

'To fight again?' Favier smiled. 'I think not. This is cynical expediency, Major, not honour.'

General Calvet was feeling cheated. His men had died in the struggle for this effort and no cheap surrender would deny them their victory. He looked at Sharpe and asked a question.

'He wants to know,' Frederickson said, 'whether you truly rose from the ranks.'

'Yes,' Sharpe said.

Calvet smiled and spoke again. 'He says it will be a pity to kill you,' Frederickson said.

Sharpe shrugged as reply, and Calvet spoke harsh, curt words to Favier, who, in turn, interpreted for Sharpe. 'The general informs you, Major Sharpe, that we do not accept your arrangements. You have one minute to surrender to us.' Favier looked to Killick. 'And we advise you to remove your ship from the vicinity of this fortress. If you interfere now, Mr Killick, you may be sure that the strongest representations will be made to your government. Good day to you.' He wheeled his horse to follow Calvet and Ducos back across the esplanade.

'Bugger me,' Killick said. 'Are they going to fight?'

'Yes,' Sharpe said, 'they are.'

The Marines were clambering up the side of the *Thuella*, leaving the Riflemen alone in the fortress. It would be close, damned close. 'Take your flag, Captain,' Sharpe said to Killick.

The American was watching the French column reform. 'There's hundreds of the bastards.'

'Only two thousand.' Sharpe was scraping with a stone at a nick on the fore-edge of his sword.

'I wish . . .' Killick began instinctively.

'You can't,' Sharpe said. 'This is our fight. And if we don't make it, sail without us. Lieutenant Minver!'

'Sir?'

'Your men next! Get them down to the water. Regimental Sergeant Major!'

Harper was inside the fortress at the foot of the breach. 'Sir?'

'Block it!'

Harper waited with a squad of men beside a *cheval-de-frise* made from a scorched beam to which had been lashed and nailed fifty captured French bayonets. The blades jutted at all angles to make a savage barricade that Harper, with six Riflemen, now struggled to carry to the breach's crest. As they did, so the renewed fire of the twelve-pounders struck the breach's outer face. A chip of stone whistled over Harper's head, but he heaved at his end of the beam, bellowed at the Riflemen to push, and the great spiked bulwark was slammed into place.

Sharpe was on the west wall. Minver's men were climbing down ladders to the sand, while the first of Killick's longboats was pushing away from the *Thuella*. Sharpe guessed it would take ten minutes to board Minver's company safely, and another five before the longboats would return for the last of the Teste de Buch's defenders. The tide in the channel swept far too strongly to risk swimming to the safety of the schooner, so Sharpe must fight until the boats could carry all his men away. Killick, carrying his American flag to safety, paused by Sharpe and stared at the French horde. 'Do I wish you luck, Major?'

'No.'

Killick seemed torn by his desire to stay and witness what promised to be a rare fight, and his need to hasten the longboats in the rain-flecked channel. 'I'll have a bottle of brandy waiting in my cabin, Major.'

'I'll look forward to it.' Sharpe was unable to express his emotions, instead, awkwardly, he thanked the American for keeping their pact.

Killick shrugged. 'Why thank me? Hell, I get a chance to fight you bastards again!'

'But your government. They'll make trouble because you helped me?'

'As long as I make money,' Killick said, 'the American

government won't give a damn.' The French drums began their sound, then, just as suddenly, stopped. The American stared at the column. 'Two thousand of them, and fifty of you?'

'That's about it.'

Killick laughed, and his voice was suddenly warm. 'Hell, Major, I'm glad I'm not one of those poor bastards. I'll have the brandy waiting, just make sure you come and drink it.' He nodded, then walked towards his boats.

Sharpe walked to the broken end of the rampart above the breach where half of Frederickson's company was stationed. The other half, with Frederickson himself, was in the courtyard.

Harper was still on the breach, jamming captured bayonets among the stones. The rain still crashed down, washing mortar and dust away from the breach and spreading dirty yellow floodwater out of the ditch.

The French drums, made soggy by rain, sounded again from the south. A Rifleman licked cracked lips. The rain, grey and depressing, blurred the massed French bayonets above which, glinting gold, Sharpe saw an enemy standard. Such, he thought, was the vision of death in the morning. The French were coming.

Commandant Henri Lassan would march, at his own request, in the front rank of the column. He had written to his mother, apologizing to her that he had lost the fortress and telling her that she could nevertheless be proud of her son. He had sent her his rosary and asked that the shining, much-fingered beads be laid to rest in the family's chapel.

'They're boarding the schooner,' Favier reported to Calvet. The northern attack had been abandoned and everything would be thrown into this one, final storm. Favier thought that was a mistake. The northern attack could have driven itself between the fortress and the water, blocking the garrison's escape, but Calvet was not worried.

'The cavalry can play on the beach. Send them an order.' Calvet dismounted, then drew his sword that had once impaled two Cossacks together like chickens on a spit. The general shrugged off his cloak so that his men could see the gold braid on his jacket, then walked to the column's head and raised his stubby, muscular arms. 'Children! Children!' The drummers, hushed by officers, rested their sticks.

Calvet's voice reached to the very last rank of the column. 'They're colder than you are! They're wetter than you are! They're more frightened than you are! And you're French! In the name of the Emperor! In the name of France! Follow!'

The drummers hauled leather rings up ropes to tighten wet skins then, as the cheer caught like fire in the ranks, the sticks started their tattoo again. Like a monster, lurching and shuddering, driven by the heartbeat of the drumsticks and bright with bayonets and given courage by a brave general, the column marched forward.

One of the German Riflemen, his left arm bandaged, played a flute. The tune came thin through the pouring rain to fill Sharpe with melancholy. He had always wanted to play the flute, but had never learned. There was small comfort in such thoughts so he dismissed them, wondering instead whether the boats had reached the shore to pick up Minver's men, but he could not see from beside the breach, nor could he spare the time to go and look.

The French column, swaying left and right as it marched in step, was halfway to the fortress. Sharpe's men knew not to fire, but Sharpe guessed half of the rain-sodden rifles would not fire at all when the time came. The rain dripped down his sleeves, soaked his overalls, and squelched in his boots. Goddamned bloody treacherous mucky rain.

Harper, Frederickson, and a dozen Riflemen were crouching high on the breach, just behind the *cheval-de-frise*. Frederickson watched Sharpe, who shook his head. Not yet, not yet. The German flautist carefully wrapped his instrument in wash-leather, tucked it into his jacket, and picked up his rifle that had layers of sacking wrapped round the lock.

The French twelve-pounder guns had ceased firing. The gunners, knowing that this was no weather for Riflemen, had come outside the mill's sheltering walls to watch the assault.

The rain glittered like polished blades. It seethed down vertically. Water flowed in great swathes off the battlements to flood the inner ditch. A bolt of lightning, sudden and scaring, cracked to the east.

The French were a hundred yards away. They shouted their 'Vive l'Empereur' in the drumbeat's pause, but the great shout was drowned by the hammering, silver rain that bounced in fine spray from the scorched and battered stones of the fort.

Sharpe turned. The west wall was ready. He could do no more there. That was his refuge, the place where he must hold the French just long enough to get his men down to the boats. He turned back to see the French skirmishers, red shoulder-wings darkened by rain, running clumsily up the glacis slope. He wondered if Calvet had sent men to the north who might cut between the west wall and the water and so bar the Riflemens' escape.

The French were nervous now. Some would be hoping that the rain had destroyed every rifle charge, but the veterans would know that even in this rain some guns would spark. They began to hurry, eager to get this first shock over. The skirmishers were spreading on the glacis and the first muskets banged smoke from the lip.

'Charge! Charge!' Calvet roared the words like a challenge as he led his 'grumblers', his veterans, through the gap in the glacis.

They charged. The column lost its order now. Some men, the timorous, sheltered in the outer ditch and pretended to fire upwards, but most, the brave, swarmed along the road towards the chaos of stone that was their shattered bridge to revenge.

Sharpe looked at Frederickson. 'Now!' Frederickson's men, ripping rags from locks, stood to fire directly over the breach's summit, while from the ramparts every man who could fire a weapon knelt or stood. 'Fire!'

Perhaps half the guns fired, while on the other weapons the leather-gripped flints sparked on to damp powder. Sharpe's rifle kicked back, then he was shouting at the men who guarded the broken edge of the battlement.

The lead torn from the church roof and not needed for bullets had been piled on the ramparts with cobblestones, dead howitzer shells, and broken masonry. It was all hurled down at the attackers. The French muskets were as useless as the defenders' rifles. One carefully protected charge of dry powder might spark, but once that was gone it was hopeless to think of reloading in this rain.

Riflemen stood and hurled missiles and the attack faltered. There were dead at the breach's foot, put there by Frederickson's volley, but then the living, roared on by Calvet, surged over the bodies. A lead sheet sliced into a man's skull and a howitzer shell bounced on the stones.

'On! On!' Calvet was alive. He did not know how many had died, but he felt the old joy of battle and his huge voice plucked men up the ramp of stones. He swung his sword at the *cheval-de-frise* and staggered sideways as a cobblestone hit his skull. 'The Emperor! The Emperor!'

A tide of men scrambled on the breach. An officer, armed with an expensive percussion cap pistol that was proof against the rain, fired upwards and a Rifleman toppled from the ramparts and was torn apart by bayonets.

'Push!' Calvet was shoving the *cheval-de-frise* forward, forcing a gap. A howitzer shell, thrown from the ramparts, hit his left arm, stunning it, but he could see a space at the end of the spiked beam and he jumped for it. His sword-arm was still good and he pointed the way as he breasted the breach's summit. 'Charge!'

The flood of men, pushed from behind and desperate to escape the rain of missiles from above, flowed over the breach.

Harper watched them. He saw the general, saw the gaudy golden braid and plucked the rag away from the seven-barrelled gun's lock. He pulled the trigger and three Frenchmen were hurled backwards on the inner face of the breach. Calvet, who had been leading the dead men, survived.

'Fire!' Frederickson, given the blunderbusses, bellowed the order and three of the six guns belched their stone scraps at the enemy.

A Frenchman was impaled on one of the bayonets jammed between stones and, despite his desperate screams, was trampled further on to the blade by his comrades. Other men, sobbing and struggling, had been forced on to the *cheval-de-frise* that now lay canted on the breach's inner face. Yet most men survived to leap down on to the courtyard's cobbles.

'Back! Back!' Frederickson's men were not there to contest the breach, but to guard the ramp. They went backwards, appalled by the scrabbling tide of men who surged into the fortress.

Sharpe, seeing that the breach was lost, blew a two-fingered whistle. 'Back! Back!' His men ran down the ramparts.

At the foot of the stone ramp, facing the collapsed gateway, was the single cannon. Its capsquare was broken, but the barrel was charged with the last of the garrison's dry powder and rammed with metal scraps, stone fragments, and rusty nails. A trail of powder had been trickled into its vent, then covered with a patch of oilcloth.

Harper stood by the cannon. Beside it, sheltered in a hole beneath the stone ramp, was a torch made of twisted straw, rags and pitch. He plucked it out and whirled it through the air so that the flames were fanned into a sudden, rain-sizzling blaze.

'Now!' Frederickson, halfway up the ramp with his men, shouted the order.

Harper plucked the oilcloth free and jammed the burning concoction of dripping pitch and straw on to the venthole. He saw the powder spark and threw himself sideways.

The cannon fired.

It recoiled viciously and the barrel, ramming with all the force of the dirty powder inside it, tore itself off the carriage, but not before the charge, spreading like duckshot, emptied itself into the courtyard.

The stones and metal scraps flayed into the French. A shower of blood momentarily rivalled the rain, then the barrel clanged down on to the carriage's right wheel, snapping spokes as if they were matchwood, and Harper was scrambling up the ramp and shouting for his axe.

Men screamed in the yard. Men had been blinded, eviscerated, torn ragged. Calvet had instinctively thrown himself flat and now listened to the horror about him. 'Charge!' He scrambled up. 'Charge!'

He could see how few defenders were left to face him, but at least they were Riflemen, the British élite, and he would capture these last few as a token of his victory. 'Charge!'

Men, made courageous by the paucity of the defenders and roused to gallantry by the general's voice, obeyed. From among the wounded and the dead, from the clinging smoke of the cannon, a pelting, yelling mass of men emerged. Calvet led them.

'Now!' Frederickson had the last seven lime-barrels at the head of the ramp. Sergeant Rossner threw one, it bounced, split open, then, spewing powder that was turned to instant whitewash by the rain, slammed into the first rank of Frenchmen. A man screamed as the barrel pinned him against the broken gun-carriage and as limewash flayed at his eyes.

Frederickson looked behind him. Sharpe's men, using the dry cover of the citadel where captured French ammunition had been stored, were holding the southern wall. Minver's men, with agonizing slowness, were being rowed towards the *Thuella*.

A second lime barrel thumped down the slope, then a third. More Frenchmen were scrambling on to the walls to attack the citadels, but the men in those small fortresses had the last dry charges and they forced the attackers into the cover of the embrasures.

'Now!' A fourth barrel bounced and struck a man full in the chest.

A pistol fired from the courtyard and Rossner grunted as the bullet hit his arm.

'Go!' Frederickson pushed him towards the sea. 'Go!'

More Frenchmen were coming, clawing at the ramp, fighting past the smashed gun carriage, over the broken barrel strakes, and across the bodies of their own wounded. The foot of the ramp was a grotesque mixture of whitewash and blood like a painter's accident.

'Now!' The fifth barrel went, then the sixth.

Sharpe had come to the head of the ramp. He could see Minver's men scrambling up the *Thuella*'s side, but the French could not be held for long. Some were trying to climb the inner wall to the ramparts, using debris from the burned offices as scaling ladders, and Sharpe ran back to stop them. He drove his sword down once, twice, and a man screamed as the blade raked his face.

'Now!' The last barrel was thrown by Harper. It did not bounce, but flew full tilt to smash into a fresh charge of men. The *Thuella*'s boats had still not started their return journey.

'Swords!' Frederickson shouted the order.

The French, exhilarated by their victory in the breach and seeing that no more barrels could plunge into their ranks, charged. A single rank of Riflemen, sword-bayonets in place, awaited them.

Then Harper broke the line.

With a shout that filled the whole courtyard with its echo, Patrick Harper charged down the stone slope. He carried the great, bright-bladed axe, and in his veins there was the keening of a thousand Irish warriors. He was shouting in his Gaelic now, daring the French to have at him, and the leading Frenchmen dared not.

Harper was six feet four, a giant, and had muscles like a mainmast's cables. He did not attack cautiously, feeling for his enemy's weakness, but screamed his challenge at the full run. The axe took two men with its first blow then Harper turned the blade as though it weighed less than a sword, brought it back, blade dripping blood, while his voice, chanting its ancient language, drove the Frenchmen backwards.

A French captain, eager for glory and knowing that the ramp must be taken, lunged, and the axe-blade slit his belly open to the rain. Harper screamed triumph, defying the French, daring them to come to challenge his blade. He stopped a few feet from the bottom of the ramp, victorious, and the rain dripped pink from the broad-bladed axe that he held in his right hand. He laughed at the French.

'Sergeant!' Sharpe bellowed. 'Patrick!'

The longboats, at last, were pushing back to the shore.

'Patrick!' Sharpe cupped his hands. 'Come back!'

Harper shouldered the axe. He turned, disdaining to run, and walked slowly up the stone ramp to where Frederickson waited. He turned there and stared down into the courtyard. The officer with the percussion pistol, its barrel charged with powder from a dry horn, slipped a percussion cap over the gun's nipple, but Calvet, who recognized bravery when he saw it, shook his head. That Rifleman, Calvet thought, should be in the Imperial Guard.

'Citadels!' Sharpe's shout was sudden in the odd silence that followed Harper's lone attack. 'Retreat! Retreat!'

The Riflemen who had guarded the extremities of the west wall scrambled from their strongholds and ran to the ladders.

Calvet, seeing it, knew his enemy was finished. 'Charge!'

'Back! Back! Back!' Sharpe pushed his men away. Now the French could have the fort, but now came the worst moment, the difficult moment, the end of Sharpe's battle and the race for the boats.

The Riflemen had no time to queue at the ladders, instead they jumped from the walls and fell headlong in the sand. Sharpe waited, standing in one of the embrasures with his sword drawn. Harper came to his side but Sharpe snarled at him to go.

The French charged over the bodies of the dead. They wanted revenge, but found an empty rampart. Empty but for the one officer, sword drawn, whose face was like death. That face checked them for a few seconds, enough to let Sharpe's men scramble towards the sea's edge.

Then Sharpe turned and jumped.

The landing knocked all the breath from him. He pitched forward, rifle falling from his shoulder, and his face hit the wet sand.

A hand grabbed his collar and hauled him up. Harper's voice shouted, 'Run!'

Sharpe's mouth was filled with gritty sand. He spat. He stumbled on the body of one of the Frenchmen dumped on this strip of sand the day before, sprawled, then ran again. His shako was gone. Frenchmen were standing on the ramparts above while to his right, from the north, the cavalry appeared.

The two longboats, oars rising and falling with painful slowness, inched towards the small breaking waves of the channel's beach. The first Riflemen were in the water, wading towards the boats, reaching for them.

Cornelius Killick, in the leading boat, bellowed an order and Sharpe saw the oars back, saw the clumsy boats swing, and he knew that Killick was turning the craft so that the wider sterns would face the shore.

'Form line!' Frederickson was shouting.

Sharpe swerved towards the shout, pawing sand from his

eyes. Thirty Riflemen were bumping into a crude line at the very edge of the sea. Sharpe and Harper joined it.

'Front rank kneel! Present!' Frederickson, as if on a battlefield, faced the cavalry with two ranks that bristled with blades. The leading horseman, an officer, leaned from his saddle to swing his sabre, but the light blade clanged along the sword bayonets like a child's stick dragged on iron palings.

'Back! Back!' Sharpe shouted it.

The small line marched backwards, step by step, into the sea. Waves drove at their calves, their thighs, and the shock of the cold water reached for their groins.

Horsemen spurred into the sea. The horses, frightened by the blades and waves, reared.

'Come on, you bastards!' Killick shouted. 'Swim!'

'Break ranks!' Sharpe shouted it. 'Go!' He stayed as rearguard. His rifle encumbered him and he let it drop into the water.

A horseman swung a sabre at Sharpe and the Rifleman's long sword, used with both Sharpe's hands, broke the man's forearm. The Frenchman hissed with pain, dropped his sabre, then his horse jerked back towards dry land. Another horseman was twisting his sabre's point in a Rifleman's neck. There was blood, splashes, and more yellow-teethed horses plunging into the foam. Harper, still holding the axe, swung it at the horseman who sheered clumsily away while the body of a Rifleman was tugged by the tide. Harper dragged the body towards the boats, not knowing that the man was already dead.

The infantry had jumped from the ramparts and shouted at the cavalry to make way. Sharpe, teeth snarling, dared them to come. He taunted them. He stepped towards them, wanting one of them to try, just one.

'Sir!' a voice shouted from behind. 'Sir!'

Sharpe stepped backwards and, seeing it, the French attacked.

A sergeant led them. He was old in war, toughened by

years of campaigning, and he knew the Englishman would lunge.

Sharpe lunged. The Frenchman jerked his musket aside, parrying, and bellowed his victory as he thrust forward.

He was still shouting as Sharpe's sword, which had been twisted over the bayonet's stab, punctured his belly. Sharpe turned the blade, pushing, and the blood spewed into the breaking foam as the blade seemed to be swallowed by the big belly. Sharpe stepped back, jerked the sword, and the blade came free in a welter of new blood.

'Sir!'

He went backwards. Another horseman drove into the water and Sharpe swung his blade at the horse's head, it reared, then a man came from his other side, an officer in a darker uniform, and Sharpe turned, parried a clumsy thrust, and drew his sword back for the killing thrust.

'Not him! Not him!' Killick shouted it.

Sharpe checked his thrust.

Lassan, knowing that he would not die on this day of rain and savagery, lowered his sword into the water. 'Go.'

Sharpe went. He turned and plunged further into the sea. The longboats were already pulling away. Men clung to the transom of the nearest boat while other men, safely in the craft, reached hands and rifles towards him.

A pistol bullet spat in a plume beside Sharpe's face. He was up to his chest now, half wading and half swimming, and he reached with his left hand, lunged, and caught an outstretched rifle barrel.

'Pull!' Killick shouted. 'Pull!'

A last cavalryman charged into the sea, but an oarblade, slapped down on to the water, frightened the horse. The French, their muskets made useless by rain, could only watch.

Sharpe clung to the rifle with his left hand. The weapon's foresight dug into his palm. The sword in his right hand was dragging him down, as was the heavy scabbard. He kicked with his feet, water slopped into his mouth and he gagged.

'Pull! Pull! Pull!' Killick's voice roared over the clanking of the *Thuella*'s windlass that dragged the anchor clear of the channel's silt. The sails were dropping into the small wind and the *Thuella* was stirring in the water.

The boats bumped on the ship's side and men pushed the Riflemen towards the deck. Someone took Sharpe's collar and hauled him dripping and heavy into the longboat. 'Up!'

A ladder was built into the ship's side. Sharpe, unsteady in the rocking longboat, thrust his sword into his scabbard that squirted water as the blade went home. He reached for the ladder, climbed, then American hands hauled him on to the *Thuella*'s deck. He had swallowed sea-water and, with a sudden spasm, he vomited it on to the scrubbed deck. He gasped for breath, vomited more, then lay, chest heaving, in the scuppers.

He heard cheers, German and Spanish and British cheers, even American cheers, and Sharpe twisted, looked through a gunport, and saw the coastline already sliding past. French gunners were wrestling the twelve-pounders through wet sand, but too late and to no avail. The longboats were being towed at ropes' ends, the *Thuella*'s wet sails were filling with a new, easterly breeze, and the French were left behind, impotent.

They had escaped.

EPILOGUE

Cavalry was nervous on wet fields. French horsemen would summon courage, ride a few yards forward, then swerve away from a threatened British volley. Unseen artillery, firing at unseen targets, punched the drizzling air, while infantry, shivering in the February cold, waited for orders.

Sharpe's force, pushing four handcarts loaded with wounded, came to the skirmish from the north. A squadron of French cavalry saw them, wheeled right, then drew curved sabres for the charge.

'Two ranks! Fix swords!' Sharpe sensed the enemy would not press the charge home, but he went through the dutiful motions and the enemy officer, seeing the waiting bayonets, and not knowing that there was not a single loaded musket or rifle in the twin ranks, dutifully withdrew. The battle, if battle it was, seemed too scattered and tentative for a cavalry charge that might leave the horsemen exposed to a sudden counter-attack. Besides, Sharpe could see that the French were dreadfully outnumbered, outnumbered as heavily as he had been at the Teste de Buch. The enemy, scarce more than a heavy picquet line, was everywhere being pushed back before a burgeoning number of British and Portuguese troops.

A mile ahead there was a sudden, rushing sound like a huge wave breaking on a beach and Sharpe saw a rocket rise into the air and plummet towards the east. It had been over a year since he had seen the Rocket Artillery and he supposed it was as inaccurate as ever. Yet somehow the odd sight made him feel at home. 'Remember those?' he asked Frederickson.

Sweet William, who had been with Sharpe when the rockets were first used against the astonished French, nodded. 'Indeed I do.'

A mounted infantry captain, red coat bright, galloped up the track towards Sharpe. His voice, as he curbed his spirited horse, was peremptory with a staff officer's vicarious authority. 'Who the devil are you? What are you doing here?'

'My name is Sharpe, my rank is Major, and you call me "sir".'

The captain stared with incredulity, first at Sharpe, then at the dirty, draggled mixture of Riflemen and Marines who stared dully towards the rocket's smoking trail. 'Sharpe?' The captain seemed to have lost his voice. 'But you're . . .' he checked. 'You've come from the north, sir?'

'Yes.' It seemed too difficult to explain it all; to explain how an American privateer captain had agreed to rescue a garrison and to land that garrison as close as he dared to the British lines. To explain how the *Thuella* had flogged her way south through a wet night, and how Riflemen and Marines had thumped the schooner's pump-handles till their muscles burned in the cold, or how Sharpe, his turn at the pumps over, had drunk brandy with an American enemy in a small cabin and promised, that when this damn fool war was done, to drink even more in a place called Marblehead. Or to explain how, in the rain-misted dawn, Cornelius Killick had landed Sharpe's men north of the Adour estuary.

'I wish I could take you further,' the American had said.

'You can't.' A strange sail had been spotted to the south, merely a scrap of ghostly white above a blurred horizon, but the sail meant danger to the *Thuella* and so Killick had turned for the shore.

Now Sharpe, marching south, had met British troops north of the river which could only mean that Elphinstone had built his bridge. 'Who are you?' Sharpe asked the staff captain.

'First Division, sir.'

Sharpe nodded towards another racing plume of rocket smoke. 'The Adour?'

'Yes, sir.'

They were safe. There would be surgeons for the wounded and a precious bridge across the river; a bridge leading south to St Jean de Luz and to Jane.

The bridge was there. The miraculous bridge, the bridge that only a clever man could build, a bridge to outflank the French Army, a bridge of boats.

The bridge was made from *chasse-marées*. A whole fleet of the luggers was moored side-by-side in the wide river mouth and, stretching from deck to deck and supported by vast cables, was a wide roadway of planks. Over the bridge marched red-coated Companies, Company after Company, an Army outflanking an enemy and going further into France. The Divisional headquarters, the staff officer said, was still south of the river.

Sharpe took his men to the northern bank where a surgeon had erected a tent and waited for customers. 'Best if you wait here,' Sharpe said to Frederickson.

'Yes, sir.'

Sharpe looked at his Marines and Riflemen, at Harper and Minver and Rossner and Palmer and all the men who had fought as no men should be asked to fight. 'I'll come back for you,' he said lamely.

Sharpe left them. He walked against the tide of the invading Division, edging his way across the plank bridge that rose and fell with the small waves of the estuary. It was for this bridge that his men had taken the Teste de Buch. They had drawn the enemy to the wrong place so that the bridge could be built undisturbed.

The bridge was nearly a quarter-mile in length and had to resist the massive rise and fall of ocean tides. Seamen, under naval officers, manned windlasses that governed the anchors of the moored boats. The windlasses balanced the long bridge against the currents of river and ocean and against the vast, surging tide that swept into the Adour.

The bridge, guarded by a fleet of brigs, was a miracle of engineering.

And the man who had built it waited on the southern sea-wall where a vast capstan, built into a cage of wooden beams, could compensate the roadway's cables against the estuary's tidefall. Colonel Elphinstone, standing on the capstan's platform, watched the dirty, blood- and powder-stained Rifleman approach. The expression on Elphinstone's face was one of sheer disbelief that slowly turned to pleasure. 'He said you were captured!'

The small rain stung Sharpe's face as he looked up to the colonel. 'Who, sir?'

'Bampfylde.' Elphinstone's eyes took in the blood on Sharpe's thigh and head. 'You escaped!'

'We all did, sir. Every last goddamn man that Bampfylde abandoned. Except for the dead, of course. There were twenty-seven dead, sir.' Sharpe paused, remembering that more had died since his last count. Two of the wounded had died on the *Thuella* and had been slid into a grey sea. And Sharpe supposed that the American Rifleman, Taylor, must be numbered with the dead, even though he lived and was even now sailing westwards.

'Maybe thirty, sir. But the French sent a brigade against us, and we fought the bastards to a standstill, sir.' Sharpe heard the anger in his own voice and knew that this honest man did not deserve it. 'I'm sorry, sir. I need a horse.'

'You need a rest.' Elphinstone, with surprising agility for a heavy, middle-aged man, swung himself down the cage of beams. 'A brigade, you say?'

'A demi-brigade,' Sharpe said. 'But with artillery.'

'Good God Almighty.'

Sharpe turned to watch a Battalion of Portuguese infantry scramble down the sea-wall towards the rope-held planks. 'I see Bampfylde brought you the *chasse-marées*. The bastard did something right.'

'He says he took the fort!' Elphinstone said. 'He said you went inland and were defeated.'

'Then he's a poxed, lying bastard. We took the fort. Then we went inland, beat the Frogs by the river, and came back to find the fort abandoned. We beat them there, too.'

'Not too loud, Sharpe,' Elphinstone said, ''ware right flank.'

Sharpe twisted round. Yards down the river bank was a party of some two dozen officers, both Army and Navy, who had come to see this prodigy; a floating bridge that crossed an estuary. With them were ladies who had been invited to witness the far smoke of battle. Gleaming carriages were parked on a marshy road two hundred yards to the rear. 'Is that Bampfylde?'

'Gently now, Sharpe!' Elphinstone said.

'Bugger Bampfylde.' Sharpe was streaked with mud, spattered with dried blood, salt-stained, and scorched with powder burns. He walked along the sea-wall's narrow path towards the spectators who clustered about two tripod-mounted telescopes. A spatter of applause and admiration sounded as another rocket arched towards the grey clouds.

Two naval lieutenants blocked Sharpe's progress. One of them, seeing the soldier's tattered, dirty state, suggested that Sharpe make a detour. 'Go down there.' The naval officer pointed to the swampy mud inland of the wall.

'Get out of my way. Move!' The sudden command startled all of the spectators. A woman dropped her umbrella and gave a small scream at Sharpe's bloody, dirty appearance, but Captain Horace Bampfylde, explaining at length how he had captured a fortress and brought these *chasse-marées* south to help out the Army, fell into a terrified silence.

'You poxed bastard,' Sharpe said. 'You coward!'

'Sir!' An Army officer touched Sharpe's arm in remonstrance, but Sharpe rounded on the man, who stepped back in sudden fear from the savage face.

Sharpe looked back to Bampfylde. 'You ran away.'

'That is not . . .'

'Just as you did not take the fortress, you bastard, I did. And then I held it, you bastard, I held it against a goddamned brigade of crapaud troops. We beat them, Bampfylde. We fought them and beat them. I lost some of your Marines, Bampfylde, because you don't fight a demi-brigade without losing men, but we won!' There was an embarrassed silence among the elegantly dressed party. A cold wind stirred the water to Sharpe's right, then a dull cough of artillery thumped its noise across the river. 'Do you hear me, Bampfylde?'

The naval officer said nothing, and there was nothing but terror on his fleshy young face. The other officers, appalled by Sharpe's face and by the anger in his voice, stood as if frozen.

'Over two thousand men, you bastard, and less than two hundred of us. We fought them till we had no bullets left, then we fought with steel, Bampfylde. And we won!' Sharpe took another step towards the naval captain who, terrified, stepped backwards.

'He told me . . .' Bampfylde began, but could not go on.

'Who told you what?'

Bampfylde's eyes went past Sharpe and the Rifleman turned to see the Comte de Maquerre, a girl on his arm, standing with Colonel Wigram. The Comte looked at Sharpe as though he saw a revenant come from the tomb. Sharpe, who had not expected to find the Comte, stared with equal disbelief.

Then, to both minds, came the shared knowledge of treachery and the Comte de Maquerre panicked. He ran.

The Comte ran towards the bridge that led to the north bank of the Adour where a handful of French troops retreated from the First Division. There should have been more French troops there, Calvet's troops, enough troops to turn the river into blood, but de Maquerre had been fooled by the story of a landing and so Calvet's troops had been frittered away at Arcachon. The Comte de Maquerre had unwittingly served Wellington well, but he was a traitor and so he ran.

Sharpe ran after him.

Colonel Wigram raised a hand as if to call for prudent decorum in front of ladies, but Sharpe pushed the man down the sea-wall and into the mud.

De Maquerre leaped down the sloping wall, miraculously kept his footing on the slippery river's edge, and climbed on to the bridge.

'Stop him!' Sharpe bellowed it.

Portuguese infantrymen crossing the bridge saw a tall, distinguished officer in British uniform being chased by a dirty, tattered wretch. They made way for the Comte.

Sharpe banged his wounded thigh as he clambered on to the roadway. Blood ran warm on his thigh as he snarled at men to make way. 'Stop him!'

A jittery horse, made nervous by the strange road across which it was being led blindfolded, checked de Maquerre's panicked flight. It swerved its rump into the Frenchman's path and the Comte was forced to leap for the safety of one of the moored *chasse-marées*. He turned as he landed on the deck, saw he could run no further, and drew his sword.

Sharpe jumped forward from the planks on to the boat's deck and drew his own sword.

The Comte de Maquerre, seeing the filth and blood of battle on Sharpe, sensed that the fight was lost before it began. He lowered his slim blade. 'I surrender, Major.'

'They hang spies,' Sharpe said, 'you bastard.'

De Maquerre glanced towards the water and Sharpe knew the man was contemplating a leap into the cold grey tide, but then a voice drew the Frenchman's attention back to the bridge.

'Sharpe!' It was the petulant voice of the mud-smeared Colonel Wigram who, with Elphinstone, was forcing his way past the Portuguese troops on the crowded roadway.

The Comte de Maquerre looked at Wigram and gestured towards Sharpe. 'He's mad!'

'Major!' Wigram stepped down to the *chasse-marée*'s deck. 'There are things you don't understand, Major!'

'He's a traitor. A spy.'

Wigram stayed by the cable-taut roadway. 'He was supposed to tell the French we planned a landing! Don't you see that?'

Sharpe stared at the tall, thin Frenchman. 'He works for a man called Pierre Ducos. Oh, you fooled him, Wigram, I understand that, but this bastard tried to trap me.'

De Maquerre, sensing survival in Wigram's alliance, gestured again at Sharpe. 'He's mad, Wigram, mad!'

'I'm mad enough,' Sharpe said, 'to hate hanging men.'

The Comte de Maquerre could step no further back. His retreat was blocked by two naval ratings who crouched nervously beside the anchor's winch. The Frenchman watched Sharpe's sword, then Sharpe's eyes. The boat shivered as Elphinstone leaped on to the deck from the roadway, and the movement seemed to prompt de Maquerre into a burst of pleading French directed at Wigram.

'In English, you bastard!' Sharpe stepped a pace closer to the frightened de Maquerre. 'Tell him who Ducos is! Tell him who Favier is! Tell him how you offered to make me a Major General in your Royalist Army!'

'*Monsieur!*' de Maquerre, faced with the Rifleman, could only plead.

'Sharpe!' Colonel Wigram made his voice very sensible and calm. 'There will have to be a formal inquiry before a properly constituted tribunal . . .'

'. . . and what will they do? Hang him?'

'If found guilty, yes.' Wigram sounded uncertain.

'But I don't like hanging men!' Sharpe said each word slowly and deliberately. 'I've discovered a weakness in myself, and I regret it, but I can't bear seeing men hanged!'

'Quite understandable.' Wigram, convinced he was dealing with a madman, spoke soothingly.

The Comte de Maquerre, sensing a reprieve in Sharpe's words, tried a very nervous smile. 'You don't understand, *monsieur*.'

'I understand you're a bastard,' Sharpe said, 'and a spy, but you won't hang for it. But this is for the men you killed,

313

you pimp!' The sword lunged as Sharpe shouted the final word. The blade, pitted with the rust of water and blood, twisted as Sharpe thrust it, twisted as it took de Maquerre in the upper belly, still twisted as the blood sprayed two feet into the air, and still was twisted so that the body's flesh would not stick to the steel as the Frenchman, blood drenching his white breeches, fell into the river that Calvet should have defended.

The sound of Sharpe's voice faded over the water. The two sailors gaped and one of them, spattered by blood, turned to retch into the scuppers.

'That wasn't wise,' Colonel Elphinstone pushed past an appalled Wigram who watched as the body of a spy, surrounded by diluting blood, floated towards the sea.

'He was a traitor,' Sharpe said, 'and he killed my men.' The tiredness was washing through him. He wanted to sit down, but he supposed he should explain. Somehow it was too difficult. 'Hogan knew,' he said, remembering his friend's fevered words. 'Michael Hogan?' He looked for understanding into Elphinstone's honest face.

Elphinstone nodded. 'It was Hogan's idea to let the French think we planned an invasion.'

'But Wigram sent de Maquerre, didn't you?' Sharpe stared at the grey-faced colonel who said nothing. 'Hogan would never have sent that pimp to risk our lives!'

'Hogan was ill,' Wigram spoke defensively.

'Then wait till he's well,' Sharpe glowered at the staff officer, 'then call him before your properly constituted tribunal.'

'That can't be done.' Colonel Elphinstone spoke gently. 'Hogan died.'

For a second the news made no sense. 'Dead?'

'The fever. May he rest in peace.'

'Oh, God.' Tears came to Sharpe's eyes and, so that neither Elphinstone nor Wigram should see them, the Rifleman turned away. Hogan, his particular friend, with whom he had so often talked of the pleasures to come when peace brought an end to killing, was dead of the fever. Sharpe watched de Maquerre's body turning on the tide, and his grief for a friend turned into a fresh pulse of anger. 'That should have been Bampfylde!' Sharpe pointed at the corpse and turned to Elphinstone. 'He ran away!'

The grimness of Sharpe's face made Colonel Wigram scramble back to the plank bridge, but Elphinstone simply reached for Sharpe's sword and dried the wet, bloodied blade on a corner of his jacket. He handed the sword back. 'You did well, Major.' He tried to imagine a handful of men facing a half brigade, and could not. 'You need to rest.'

Sharpe nodded. 'Can you get me a horse, sir?' He asked it in a voice that suggested nothing had happened, that no blood trickled on the rain-slick deck.

'A horse? I'm sure we can.' Elphinstone saw in Sharpe the weariness of a soldier pushed to the edge of reason. The colonel was an engineer, knowledgeable of the stresses that could shatter stone or wood or iron, and now he saw the same fracturing tension in Sharpe. 'Of course!' Elphinstone made his own voice redolent of normality, 'you're eager to see your wife! I had the honour of dining with her two nights ago.'

Sharpe stared at the colonel. 'You dined with her?'

'My dear Sharpe, it was entirely proper! At Lady Hope's! There was a ragout and some very fine beef.'

Sharpe forgot de Maquerre, forgot the bridge, and forgot the ragged skirmishes that flared and died across the river. He even forgot Hogan. 'And Jane's well?'

Elphinstone shrugged. 'Shouldn't she be? Ah, she did mention a cold, but that was soon gone. A winter's sniff, nothing more. She was distressed for Hogan, naturally.'

Sharpe gaped incredulously at the colonel. 'No fever?'

'Your wife? Good Lord, no!' Elphinstone sounded astonished that Sharpe should even ask. 'She wouldn't credit you were defeated, of course.'

'Oh, God.' Sharpe sat on the *chasse-marée*'s gunwale and, because he could not help it, more tears came to his eyes and ran cold on his cheeks. No fever. He had let Killick live because of Jane's fever, and he would not contemplate surrender to Calvet because of her fever, and it had only been a cold, a winter's sniff. Sharpe did not know whether to laugh or cry.

A gun banged over the river and a rocket wobbled into the sky to plunge uselessly into the river's mud. A French cavalry trumpet sounded the retreat, but Sharpe did not care. He wept. He wept because a friend had died, and he wept with joy because Jane lived. He wept because at last it was over; a battle that should never have been fought, but a battle that, through stubbornness, pride, and an American enemy's promise, had come to both this victory on a river's edge and to this vast relief. It was over; Sharpe's siege.

HISTORICAL NOTE

There was a fort at the Teste de Buch, though no such action as Sharpe's siege took place there. Yet the freedom enjoyed by the British to make coastal raids had been firmly established by Nelson's victories, and many such raids did take place. They were made possible, of course, thanks to the Royal Navy's mastery of the seas.

The Royal Navy had reached its apogee of popularity with Nelson (a fact that aroused envy in the Army, which was cordially disliked by most British people), but it was a popularity not shared by most of the Royal Navy's own seamen who endured vile conditions, low pay and, unless they were fortunate in their ship's captain, frequent and brutal physical punishment. One of the easiest escapes from such a regime was to an American ship where the men were assured of instant citizenship. Their fear of the punishment that awaited them, should they be recaptured, helped make such deserters into superb fighters. Cornelius Killick would doubtless have numbered such men in his crew.

That an American should rescue Sharpe is not so fanciful. Colquhoun Grant, whose real-life adventures have previously contributed to Sharpe's career, was rescued while a fugitive prisoner in Nantes by an American ship's captain who ignored the fact that Grant was his country's enemy. Blood and language, it seems, were often thicker than formal alliances. That, however, would not have prevented an American privateer's crew from being strung from the yard-arm by the Royal Navy, especially as the Navy had been piqued by American successes afloat.

Those successes had been gained in the War of 1812, a quite pointless conflict between Britain and America. Afloat, the Americans inflicted a stinging series of defeats on the Royal Navy, only to lose the final frigate battle, while ashore the course of the war was similar, but reversed; with Britain easily defeating the American attempts to invade Canada, capturing and burning Washington, but then losing the final battle at New Orleans. The causes of the conflict had been resolved before war was declared, and its final battle was fought after the peace had been signed. Sharpe is indeed fortunate to be denied any part of the nonsense by Cornelius Killick.

The *chasse-marées* existed, and were hired for the purpose of making the bridge over the Adour. The French made no effective resistance to that bridge, and the action on the northern bank was distinguished chiefly by the employment of the erratic Rocket Artillery (fully described in *Sharpe's Enemy*) in one of its rare appearances on Wellington's battlefields.

Wellington went no further north on the Biscay coast; instead he turned eastwards and marched on Toulouse. Throughout the campaign his men were met with the white cockade and there was no resistance movement in France like that which bedevilled Napoleon's armies in occupied Spain.

One reason for that French quiescence, apart from French weariness with Napoleon's wars, was Wellington's sensible treatment of the French population. Any criminal act against the French was punishable by summary execution though, like Sharpe, many officers found it hard to hang their own men. The Provosts, the military policemen, were less squeamish. Every item of food had to be purchased, and that endeared the British Army to a population accustomed to their own Army's habit of legalized theft. That the food was paid for in counterfeit coin did not matter, for Wellington's forgeries contained the proper amount of silver and were indistinguishable from the product of the Paris mint.

The British Army, richly blessed with gaol-birds, had no trouble in finding expert coiners in its ranks.

So, even though the merchants of Bordeaux, made poor by British blockade, are eager for the war's end, and even though the French population is giving a guarded welcome to men whose discipline is so much greater than Napoleon's troops, the war is still not over. The Emperor is at large and many die-hards in France believe that his genius can yet snatch glory from disaster. The last defences are often the toughest to take, so Sharpe and Harper must march again.

AUTHOR NOTE

For reasons that I can never quite understand, this is my favourite novel in the Sharpe series, though I shall ever regret giving the pusillanimous naval captain the name Bampfylde. I have no idea where the name came from, but long after the book was finished I discovered there was a Bampfylde family that had contributed many notable officers to the Royal Navy and I had, therefore, unconsciously maligned them, for which, belatedly, I apologise.

Bampfylde must have come from the subconscious, or else the telephone directory, which is a regular source of surnames, but Captain William Frederickson, who shares Sharpe's tribulations in this novel, was named for quite another reason. I was married by the Reverend William Frederickson who, being a conscientious man, decided he ought to read one of my novels before the ceremony. 'Sharpe,' he told me diffidently, 'is a very violent man.' Now I like the Reverend William very much, and I do not think he will be offended if I say that he is a very non-violent man; indeed, as befits a minister of the church, he is the soul of gentleness and kindness, but his mild comment provoked me into creating a character who would be even more violent than Sharpe, a character who would be called, of course, William Frederickson.

The action in the novel is entirely made up; there was no engagement in the Bassin d'Arcachon, but very similar actions punctuated the whole war and I was eager for Sharpe to take part in one of those combined operations. The navy excelled at these raids which were especially common on the French-held Mediterranean coast and on the eastern seaboard of the United States which, in 1812, declared war on Britain. These American actions are not much remembered, but they created an immense war-weariness in the communities that suffered from them. Thus, to take a typical example from 1814, the year in which the events of the novel take place, British marines and soldiers rowed six miles up the Essex River in Connecticut and destroyed the town of Potapaug (now Essex) and all its commercial shipping. Later that year the same kind of operation, though on a much larger scale, was responsible for the capture and destruction of Washington itself. Among the many buildings that were burned was the president's mansion. The lower walls were of stone, so they survived, but when the mansion was rebuilt those walls were painted white to hide the scorch marks and it has been known as the White House ever since. The navy could make these raids because, after Nelson's great victory at Trafalgar in 1805, there was no force to oppose them other than the nascent US Navy and a scatter of privateers like Cornelius Killick who preyed on British merchant shipping worldwide.

The background to the novel is the invasion of France. It must have seemed incredible to those soldiers who had been present at the beginning of the Peninsular War that they were now carrying the war into the French homeland, but so they were. The long road was ending, though it yet had a few surprises to spring.

AZINCOURT

THE LAST KINGDOM
THE PALE HORSEMAN
THE LORDS OF THE NORTH
SWORD SONG

The GRAIL QUEST series
HARLEQUIN
VAGABOND
HERETIC

STONEHENGE: A NOVEL OF 2000 BC

The STARBUCK Chronicles
REBEL
COPPERHEAD
BATTLE FLAG
THE BLOODY GROUND

The WARLORD Chronicles
THE WINTER KING
THE ENEMY OF GOD
EXCALIBUR

GALLOWS THIEF

By Bernard Cornwell and Susannah Kells
A CROWNING MERCY
FALLEN ANGELS